**Praise for the works
of Evelyn Richardson**

"Deftly incorporates historical details and superbly nuanced characters . . . quietly compelling, beautifully written, and wonderfully satisfying."　　　*—Booklist*

"A diverting read that will appeal to fans who like their Regencies intelligent, multilayered, and with more depth than the average romp."　　　*—Library Journal*

"Appealing . . . will charm readers with its atmospheric setting and full-bodied characters." *—Publishers Weekly*

"Each new work is a precious gem, Ms. Richardson creates unforgettable characters and a haunting ambience that make the subsequent joyous resolution an even greater treasure for readers."　　　*—Romantic Times*

The Education of Lady Frances

and

Miss Cresswell's London Triumph

Evelyn Richardson

A SIGNET BOOK

SIGNET
Published by New American Library, a division of
Penguin Group (USA) Inc., 375 Hudson Street,
New York, New York 10014, USA
Penguin Group (Canada), 90 Eglinton Avenue East, Suite 700, Toronto,
Ontario M4P 2Y3, Canada (a division of Pearson Penguin Canada Inc.)
Penguin Books Ltd., 80 Strand, London WC2R 0RL, England
Penguin Ireland, 25 St. Stephen's Green, Dublin 2,
Ireland (a division of Penguin Books Ltd.)
Penguin Group (Australia), 250 Camberwell Road, Camberwell, Victoria 3124,
Australia (a division of Pearson Australia Group Pty. Ltd.)
Penguin Books India Pvt. Ltd., 11 Community Centre, Panchsheel Park,
New Delhi - 110 017, India
Penguin Group (NZ), cnr Airborne and Rosedale Roads, Albany,
Auckland 1310, New Zealand (a division of Pearson New Zealand Ltd.)
Penguin Books (South Africa) (Pty.) Ltd., 24 Sturdee Avenue,
Rosebank, Johannesburg 2196, South Africa

Penguin Books Ltd., Registered Offices:
80 Strand, London WC2R 0RL, England

Published by Signet, an imprint of New American Library, a division of Penguin Group (USA) Inc. *The Education of Lady Frances* and *Miss Cresswell's London Triumph* were previously published in separate Signet editions.

First Signet Printing (Double Edition), February 2006
10 9 8 7 6 5 4 3 2 1

PUBLISHER'S NOTE
These are work of fiction. Names, characters, places, and incidents either are the product of the author's imagination or are used fictitiously, and any resemblance to actual persons, living or dead, business establishments, events, or locales is entirely coincidental.

The publisher does not have any control over and does not assume any responsibility for author or third-party Web sites or their content.

The Education of
Lady Frances

To my parents,
Hugh and Madeleine Johnson

1

Lady Frances frowned in concentration as she searched once again for the error that was keeping the accounts from balancing. She sighed and looked out the window hoping to clear her mind. That was a mistake. A second glance proved the figures no more comprehensible than they had been before. The sight of fields beginning to sprout after the last few warm wet days, and the fringe of green buds on the tree by the mellowed brick of the garden wall, made her long to be out-of-doors, smelling the newly washed hedgerows and feeling the warm sun on her face. "Botheration!" she exclaimed, and shut the ledger with a decisive snap. This interrupted the sound sleep of the terrier at her feet. He woke with a start and looked up expectantly, as did his more lethargic companion, a large, battered tabby cat who opened an inquiring eye. "Come on, Wellington," she called. "I've had enough for one day. Let's get some fresh air." Unfortunately, as they headed for the door, they were stopped in mid-escape by the sound of hooves on the gravel drive. Wellington sat down with a snort of disgust as a very agitated young lady burst into the entrance, brushing aside Higgins, the butler, in her haste to pour out her problems to Frances.

"Oh, Frances," she wailed, "my uncle has returned from Vienna and positively orders me and Cousin Honoria up to London. He insists that I come out this Season! You know Ned would be miserable there, and we can't possibly leave him here. Besides, I don't want to be a lady of fashion, simper all day long, and think of nothing but shopping and changing clothes. I want to be like you, free to enjoy the country and my books and not have to pretend to care about doughty dowagers and their eager, eligible prospects." Here she paused for breath while Higgins took her hat and gloves.

Kitty Mainwaring was a diminutive girl with large brown eyes, tumbled brown curls, and a pert nose. The impish features were overcast with worry, but otherwise it was a face that should have made its owner look forward to being the toast of the Season rather than an unwilling participant.

"Do come in, Kitty. Higgins will bring some tea directly and we can consider this further. In the meantime, come into the library. There's a fire to take off the chill, but the windows afford us a view of spring." Kitty allowed herself to be ensconced in a chair with a cup of tea and then waited patiently as Lady Frances settled herself. "Now, then, I quite agree with you that balls, flirting, and endless shopping make an empty life, but hundreds of people seem to enjoy that sort of life above any other, and it can be amusing for a while." Lady Frances tactfully refrained from mentioning the misery of standing alone at Almack's for lack of partners who would discuss something beyond the set of their coats and their hopes for favorite race-horses. Nor did she speak of her grateful return to her own books and country pursuits when the death of her father and his unusual will placed her at twenty in charge of the entire estate as well as the nine-year-old twins, Cassandra and Frederick. "Besides, my dear, you're far too lively and pretty to live alone the rest of your days. And you certainly have no prospects around here to share your life."

Kitty frowned. "But you aren't alone. You ride whenever you wish, wherever you wish. You read and write your children's books." She lowered her voice in alluding to this activity, which was a carefully guarded secret. "And you're constantly avoiding Lady Featherstone and her daughters because they're always discussing the latest fashionable *on-dits*."

"Yes, but I am older and more serious than you are. I don't necessarily avoid marriage, but I have found that anyone serious enough to talk of something other than fashion usually wishes to prose on about himself and his estate. I wouldn't mind sharing my life with someone interesting, but I have never met such a person. I am sure that with your looks and address you'll attract a swarm of young eligibles, and surely one among the crowd would suit." Lady Frances spoke as though she were an antidote, when in fact it had been a combination of intelligence and natural reserve rather than lack of countenance that had kept her in the less-crowded ends of London ballrooms. Eager partners initially attracted by her classical features and elegant figure were rendered uneasy by the glint of humor they saw creep into her expressive hazel eyes if they spent more than one dance describing the difficulties developing a cravat style that was intricate enough to be distinctive without being so elaborate as to be laughable. This humorous look was instantly interpreted as criticism by uneasy young aspirants to fashion, and it was not appreciated in the least. Lady Frances had not been successful with the members of her own sex either. Though brunettes were all the rage, her straight nose, tawny hair, delicate complexion, and generous inheritance made her enough of a threat to her marriage-mad companions that they were only too delighted to label her as "blue" because she actually listened to the plays and concerts she attended and refused to ridicule Lady Lucinda D'Arcourt, who, in spite of being an earl's daughter, and a wealthy one at that, was a shocking quiz and insisted on wearing the most outmoded frocks and huge bonnets. Nor would she discuss the latest escapades of Lady Caro Lamb, maintaining that she was sorry for the creature despite her shocking behavior and dampened muslins. But as the Season wore on and novelty wore off, Lady Frances had found herself left more and more to her own devices. It was with a queer sort of relief that she learned of her father's death and his unusual wish that she look after the estate and her family. His loss was severe in a family as close and loving as the Cresswells, but all of the children knew that Lord Cresswell had never been happy after their mother's death ten years before.

Lord and Lady Cresswell had been unusual in their devotion to each other. Both scholars of considerable standing, they had spent the early years of their marriage traveling around Greece and the classical world, working on their own translations of the more obscure Greek poets, and even venturing into Egypt until driven home by Napoleon and his designs on the world. It was their example of close friendship, love, and shared intellectual passion that provided Frances with a model of marriage that was both inspiring and, given her limited choice, discouraging. Having explored the temples of Greece and Rome as a child, and having received an education as good as if not better than that of most of her male counterparts, she soon found herself bored and slightly disgusted with the local gentry.

Kitty broke in on these unfortunate recollections. "Perhaps you are right. It would be fun to see the Tower and all the other London sights. And how delightful it would be simply to go to Hatchard's to procure the latest books! I suppose I am mostly put off by the suddenness of it and the peremptory tone of his letter. You know how I still miss Mama and Papa and the good times Ned and I had with them. They were always so affectionate and gay that the idea of having anyone as a guardian in their place, especially Lord Mainwaring, is daunting. I am sure he is haughty and cold. Why, he never visited us when they were alive, and he barely even acknowledged our existence until they were killed. I have heard that he's terribly fashionable. And, you must admit, the idea of leaving dear old Camberly to lead a terribly stiff and *à la mode* life in some imposing town house is more frightening than exciting." With this, Kitty produced a heavy sheet of crested stationery and handed it to Frances for her perusal. "My dear niece, Lady Streatham has agreed to chaperone your come-out. I shall send my groom and the post chaise for you in three week's time. Mainwaring."

"It does not sound as welcoming as it might, but remember that Lord Mainwaring is a busy man and probably considers his providing you with a Season generous rather than threatening. You mustn't attribute his previous disinterest to coldness. After all, he has spent the last year attached to Castlereagh in Vienna, and several before that attending to the business interests in the colonies left him by his uncle. So you see, my dear, even were he devoted to you and Ned, he would not have been much at Camberly.'' Examining the bold black script and the forcefulness of the scrawled "Mainwaring," Frances privately agreed that its writer was probably as arrogant as Kitty feared.

All further reflection and conversation were halted by the eruption of a whirlwind as the large and battered tomcat dashed across the room and leapt into the safety of a nearby chair. He was closely followed by Wellington and two rather disheveled eleven-year-olds. Wellington came to a screeching halt in front of the chair, while the cat, surveying him from the safety of his perch, switched his tail tantalizingly and made a swipe with a chubby paw. ''Arf, arf!'' was the encouraging reply as the dog, followed by his feline companion, raced to the other side of the room, narrowly missing the tea table. ''Cassie, do grab Nelson before he overturns the cake stand. It's all very well for them to chase each other, but must they always do it at teatime? Freddie, pick up Wellington and put him by the fire. However did all of you get so muddy and wet? And say hello to Kitty, both of you.'' The twins, with mops of curly blond hair and rosy cheeks now lightly smeared with mud, were barely distinguishable except for dress. Both grinned and did as they were bidden.

''Well, you see, we heard Wellington barking, so we followed and discovered that Nelson was stuck in a tree. You know that with only one eye he can see well enough to climb up but not well enough to get back down, silly thing. Freddie tried to climb up to get him, but he wasn't tall enough to reach the first branch so I had to stand on his shoulders. I slipped the first time,'' added Cassie matter-of-factly, pointing to a grass stain on the front of her frock and her muddy footprints on the shoulders of her brother's jacket.

''Oh.'' Frances accepted the explanation with aplomb, wondering aloud to no one in particular, ''When will Nelson learn to extricate himself from his scrapes on his own? If Wellington hadn't pulled him out of the pond when those nasty village boys threw him in, we never would have had him in the first place. It's not as though he were a fine specimen of the feline species, are you, Nelson?'' Nelson smiled apologetically as he rubbed against the hand that rubbed just the right spots.

Freddie spoke in their pet's defense. "But he's such fun for Wellington because he knows just how to chase him and play hide-and-seek."

"Arf, arf,'' agreed Wellington wholeheartedly.

Frances rang for Higgins to bring more tea and cakes, the earlier supply having completely disappeared the minute the twins entered the room. London and Lord Mainwaring were forgotten as the children related the latest tale of the hole in Farmer Stubbs's fence, which had allowed the sow and her piglets into the lane and nearly caused the wreck of the squire's gig. "You should have seen it, Frances,'' said Freddie through a mouthful of cake. "The squire came round the corner into the lane at a slapping pace and almost ran over the runt. Wellington saved the day, though, because he herded them all to one side. What a Trojan!''

"Arf, arf!''

"And then Cassie nipped in and grabbed the runt just as the wheel came by.''

"So I see,'' Frances remarked, surveying the splashes on Cassie's pinafore.

Unable to refrain from adding her bit to the tale, Cassie burst in, "Squire Tilden was so angry. You should have seen him! His face was all red and he was shouting and calling Farmer Stubbs a good-for-nothing. And he is too, because he said it would have been better for the runt to be killed. Can you credit such meanness? The runt couldn't help it that it was the smallest of the litter. So I took the dear little thing because it was squeaking so and I gave it to John Coachman because I didn't think you would want it in the house in spite of its being quite clean and pink with the sweetest ears and curly tail you've ever seen. Can we keep him, dearest Fanny, please?''

Fully aware of her younger sister's passion for animals of any type, Frances recognized that she was in for a long battle. She grimaced, but nodded, adding, "Off with you now. You must run get cleaned up and then we'll review your history lesson from this morning.''

"What a good sister you are! No wonder they love you," Kitty observed.

"Well, you know, having such a pet is the best way to teach any number of valuable lessons in responsibility, estate management, even natural history, if you will. And you know how much I value my own excellent education, which was all the work of both Father and Mother. I feel, if nothing else, that I owe it to them to share it with the twins." The touch of sadness which had crept into her voice was quickly banished as she gave herself a mental shake, ringing for Higgins and adding briskly, "But you mustn't be leaving your own brother to a lonely tea. Here's Higgins with your hat and gloves. Off with you now. I shall ride over tomorrow after I've thought it over, and see if I can devise some way to help you turn Mainwaring's orders to your best advantage."

"Oh, thank you ever so much, Frances. I do hate to burden you when you have so much to attend to, but Cousin Honoria, though she lends propriety, is too flighty to contribute much else, and I have had no one to advise me how to go on since dear Papa and Mama . . ." Here Kitty's voice was suspended by tears.

"It's no trouble at all, and I am happy to help," Frances assured her, but refrained from commenting that advice from her was probably far more sensible than any Kitty would have gotten from two such hopelessly romantic and indulgent parents as the late Lord and Lady Mainwaring had been.

2

At that moment the perpetrator of Kitty's dilemma sat staring into the library fire at a forbidding mansion in Grosvenor Square. A man of action who ordinarily avoided the social demands of life in the *ton*, the new Marquess of Camberly would have preferred to remain in his smaller, less-imposing establishment in Mount Street, but on succeeding to the title he had recognized the foolishness of maintaining two London residences. Reluctantly he and Kilson, his valet, butler, and general factotum, had left the freedom of their former abode for the formality of Mainwaring House.

Lord Mainwaring frowned down at the letter just delivered to him. "Blast, there's nothing for it but to go down to Hampshire and straighten this out! Thank you, Kilson." The flickering firelight revealed a dark, rather harsh-featured countenance rendered even more harsh by its owner's present expression. At thirty-five, Lord Julian Mainwaring, the new Marquess of Camberly, was a man more accustomed to the excitement of politics and the administration of business interests inherited from his uncle, a nabob of immense wealth and influence in the empire's financial circles, than he was to the more pedestrian concerns of estate management. These he had

happily left to his brother, never dreaming that he would
suddenly become responsible for the lands as well as the children
of one who was only a few years older than he. Because of his
far-flung financial concerns, constant attention to international
politics had been a necessity and Mainwaring had rapidly
become a man whose advice was often sought on the economic
consequences of certain aspects of British foreign policy. It was
for this expertise that he had been asked to join Castlereagh in
Vienna. To a man of action, Castlereagh's policies had seemed
hopelessly timid and tentative. Julian Mainwaring was more
inclined to favor the economic sentiments of Castlereagh's
opponent Canning, though when closely questioned by his
intimates, he was known to criticize the insular nature of
Canning's foreign-statesmanship. To an independent thinker
such as Mainwaring, political loyalties and party theory were
less important than the practical economic questions posed by
the issues raised at the Congress. For this reason he had
consented to go to Vienna. There he had found his element in
the dealing and intriguing, where the incredible collection of
heads of state, ministers, and hangers-on of every description
made it easy to communicate with a variety of states,
principalities, and nations, all of whom were committed to the
creation of a new Europe. He had found this sense of making
history an exciting and heady atmosphere, and it was with
extreme reluctance that he had returned to England at the notice
of his brother and sister-in-law's deaths in a tragic coaching
accident. The scenes of glittering soirees and heated conferences
faded as he turned back to the humdrum problems of country
estates: tenants' complaints, cottages to be repaired, fences to
be mended, fields to be drained.

It was Kilson's second "Ahem," preceded by a conspicuous
opening of the library door, that broke his train of thought.
"Lord Charlton to see you, sir . . . beg your pardon, milord."
Kilson was having difficulty adjusting to the new formalities
of his situation. He had preferred the free-and-easy life traveling
in the colonies and on the Continent, but realizing that the new
responsibilities and settled existence were even more onerous
to his master, he did his best to see they both remained aware
of and accustomed themselves to the changes.

"Send him in and bring a bottle of port. I've a feeling I'll need it."

"Julian, my boy, good to see you home!" The elderly statesman greeted him heartily as he came to warm his hands in front of the fire.

"Thank you. I wish I could share your sentiments, but I find it damnably dull to be here." There was a distinctly sardonic note in Mainwaring's voice.

"Well, yes," Lord Charlton agreed. "I expect anything would be sadly flat after rubbing shoulders with potentates and intriguers from every corner of Europe, but you know as well as I do that foreign policy begins at home. And at the moment we need you rather desperately right here, old boy."

"Oh?" Mainwaring tried unsuccessfully to keep the interest out of his voice.

"Rather. You know that sentimental idealist Alexander has dreamed up this romantic twaddle of the Holy Alliance—the most ridiculous piece of tripe you can imagine! It will simply mean that he will be even more free to meddle in European affairs and pontificate to his heart's content. We must keep Prinny from agreeing to such a thing. You are as familiar as anyone with his theatrical bent, and sometimes Alexander's playacting as 'Savior of Europe' can be rather more attractive to him than is good for England. Prinny is inclined to dismiss all of us as a bunch of power-hungry politicians, but perhaps he'll listen to you, since your friendship has more to do with aesthetics than politics."

"I'll try, George," the marquess sighed. "But just because Prinny consults my knowledge of Oriental architecture and admires some of the pieces I've collected here and there doesn't mean he'll pay the slightest attention to anything else I might say. He may have revolutionized artistic vision in this country, but politically the man is a complete fool. I only put up with him because he at least can offer an amusing conversation on something more stimulating than crop rotation. I'll put it to the touch, though."

"Thank you, my boy. We'll be very grateful for anything you can do. Now I must go. I promised I'd attend this affair at Sally Jersey's with my wife. Can't think why women like these things. Can't stand them myself, but we're puffing off Caroline this Season and Maria wants to be sure that Sally gives her a voucher for Almack's—ridiculous place.''

''My sentiments exactly,'' the marquess said sympathetically. ''At least there will be two sane people there. You'll be someone I can look for. I must get rid of my niece as well this Season. Got my cousin, Lady Streatham, you know, to do the real work dragging her around, but no doubt I shall be dragooned into appearing at some of the most important of these functions.''

It was in a much cheerier frame of mind that Mainwaring returned to the fire. In fact, he felt invigorated enough later to look in at his club, where he was welcomed both for his own attributes as a talented pugilist and noted judge of horseflesh and for the news he brought from the Continent. This reception further inspired him to stroll to a certain house in Mount Street.

There he was certain of his welcome. ''Julian, my dear, how charming to see you,'' exclaimed the opulent brunette rising seductively from an exceedingly becoming pink couch. ''It's been so long,'' she complained with a pout of full red lips and a sigh that called attention to beautifully rounded shoulders and bosom.

''I know it has been a tediously long time.'' He bent his dark head to kiss a perfumed hand, continuing the caress up to a dimpled wrist and elbow. ''But must we now waste our time dwelling on how long it's been?''

The beauty smiled a slow, confident smile. ''Ah, you think to make me forget how you've neglected me.'' She sighed voluptuously, leaning back against the satin pillows.

His gaze dwelt on her appreciatively. ''No, I came here to make *me* forget.''

''Trifler! I must demand some forfeit for such shabby treatment.''

''Naturally, your generous nature will keep you from such rash behavior,'' he murmured, kissing the nape of her neck, forcing her to abandon any further attempts at reprimanding him.

Unlike many of his cronies, Julian Mainwaring considered it a waste of time and money to pursue the numerous opera dancers and barks of frailty who constantly sought to attract his attention. The petty jealousies and competition for favor that were a necessary part of such a scene held no allure. He preferred the more mature charms of a sensible woman of his world. Lady Vanessa Welford was the perfect partner. Married at a very early age to a doddering peer who combined the advantages of immense wealth and an early demise, she had no intention of ending the freedom of her widowhood in another confining marriage. She juggled her many liaisons with such discretion that it was only the highest sticklers of the *ton* who could find the least objection of her. She had enjoyed her freedom immensely until she had met Julian at the Duchess of Marlborough's ball some months ago. Accustomed to manipulating her many and varied lovers without becoming emotionally involved in the least, she recognized, after being guided masterfully around the dance floor, that the new Marquess of Camberly was accustomed to dominating every situation—financial, political, or amorous. Gazing seductively into his dark blue eyes framed by fierce black brows and high cheekbones, she read a great deal of appreciation for her charming appearance but nothing of the blind adoration she was accustomed to inspiring. Intrigued, she had invited him to call the next day, and again found him completely charming and completely disinclined to become involved. Having thus set out in a spirit of pique to capture his attentions, Vanessa found that she rather than he was becoming captivated. An experienced woman of the world, she knew better than to make demands of him. She found his lovemaking, detached and infrequent though it was, more and more necessary to her existence. In fact, he was becoming an obsession with her—so much so that she had of late decided, against all her principles, to become Lady Mainwaring and had embarked on a discreet but intensive campaign to accomplish this.

For his part, Julian enjoyed the attentions of a clever, beautiful woman who exhibited an insatiable appetite and a thorough knowledge of the art of dalliance, but never having felt the need for female companionship or a family, he had not the least intention of going beyond a purely physical relationship. In fact, it was with rather a sense of relief that he left her house in the early-morning hours. After the cloying intimacy of her perfumed satin boudoir he found the prospect of a drive to Hampshire and a few days in the country a refreshing and welcome change.

3

U naware of the impending arrival of her "villainous guardian," as Kitty with her love of the romantic was wont to call him, Kitty and Lady Frances were strolling together in the conservatory at Cresswell, hatching a scheme to render the former's visit to London as unintimidating as possible. Lady Frances had conceived the notion that some of the worry might be taken out of the approaching ordeal if Kitty had a friend such as Lady Frances there with her. "But you loathe London and the Season and all that entails," Kitty protested.

"That was many years ago, when I was young and had entirely different expectations and aspirations. I might just enjoy it. For, you know, it would be a very good thing if I were to visit my publisher right now. I have done something slightly different in this latest book and I would wish to consult with him before I go further. Besides, Cassie and Frederick have never been to London. I am sure they would find it extremely diverting, as well as full of new opportunities for further mischief. I also confess to a great desire to see the marbles Lord Elgin brought back from Greece. He was a great friend of Father's and Mother's, you know. We met him in Athens, and such a wonderful time we all had," she said with a slight catch in her voice.

"Oh, that would be wonderful above all things," her companion said with enthusiasm. "Ned could come too, and we could have a fine time. With Lady Streatham to take me about, we shan't need Cousin Honoria, who is the greatest bore imaginable. And she will be happy because she can go visit that insipid niece in Bath whose perfections she is forever throwing up in my face when she considers I've been the least bit gay or impertinent."

"That's settled, then. I shall direct Higgins to have the staff open the house in Brook Street. It will be terrific work, I am sure, as no one has used it this age. But it should be ready within the month and it will certainly take me that long to convince Aunt Harriet to leave the country. We shall probably have to take all those orchids with us," sighed Frances, looking with dismay at the large and varied collection around her.

Ordinarily she loved the conservatory, which was her aunt's chief interest in life. She often came there to sit in its peaceful tropical atmosphere to think or to soothe her nerves after a long day poring over accounts or dealing with tenants. But at the moment she could only view the exotic blooms as an encumbrance. She dearly loved her aunt, whose acerbic wit and down-to-earth attitude had bucked her up after her unhappy time in London, but her eccentricities did complicate the Cresswells' existence. It was Aunt Harriet who had convinced Frances that there were many other ways for a woman to enjoy herself and feel successful beyond making a brilliant marriage or winning a name for herself as a diamond of the first water. Lady Frances had certainly had her own mother as an example of a happy, successful woman, but then Lady Cresswell had been married to someone who encouraged her interest in scholarly pursuits. Such companionship in marriage was unusual, if not highly unlikely, judging from the scandalous *on-dits* Lady Frances had heard in London. Harriet Cresswell had been born with the same scholarly inclinations as her brother, except that her passion was horticulture rather than history. While Lord Frederick Cresswell and his family were traipsing around the classical world, she had remained at Cresswell Manor enjoying free rein with its gardens and constructing an elaborate conservatory to house her growing collection of orchids. Ever since she had encountered Captain James Cook at a friend's dinner party forty years ago, she had become passionately interested in tropical plants, especially orchids. She had managed, via a mysterious network of naval and seafaring connections, to convince captains of various vessels to seek out and bring back any samples of exotic flora they could find. Undoubtedly her generous remuneration of the least of these efforts encouraged the captains' loyalty and ensured the regularity of these botanical delivery services. By now the household and surrounding countryside had become accustomed to the sight of some swarthy seaman uncomfortably astride a horse riding up the drive carefully clutching an oddly shaped package from which emerged some strange-looking greenery covered with brilliant blossoms.

When Lord and Lady Cresswell had returned from their travels, Aunt Harriet had made some halfhearted offers to remove to a house in Bath, but having put so much into the gardens and conservatory, she was quite relieved when no one paid the slightest attention to her. So she remained a fixture at Cresswell, largely ignoring the children and the world in general. She did take an interest in her eldest niece, especially after Frances returned from the Season disappointed in what the *ton* had to offer and as little interested in becoming a society matron as Aunt Harriet had been.

It was Aunt Harriet who, listening to the imaginative way in which Frances taught Cassie and Frederick their history lessons, had convinced Frances to write down these lessons and send them off to her father's publisher in London. And it was Aunt Harriet who shared in Frances' surprise and delight when Mr. Murray had written back that he was honored to print "these extremely edifying histories for young readers" and had requested more. By degrees, Aunt Harriet had proved to Frances that a lack of success in London by no means presaged an equal lack of success in the country. She encouraged her niece to read anything and everything, from politics and agriculture to literary and artistic reviews. Slowly the sound opinions and good judgment Lady Frances developed were appreciated and made her sought-after by local gentry and tenants alike. She still retained her natural reserve. Only her family and the Mainwarings were aware of her fun-loving side, her wonderful sense of humor and extravagant imagination that invented mythical beasts and hair-rising adventures for hours on end. This same sense of humor allowed her to be amused rather than discommoded by her aunt's eccentric ways, her habit of putting any visitor out of countenance either by cutting him dead or, if the slightest interest were evinced, by subjecting him immediately to an extended horticultural tour of Cresswell. Frances knew how much the prospect of cramped quarters, poor air, uneven sunlight, London society, and the parting with the Cresswell rose beds would upset her aunt. But she also knew that the *ton*, which was not only censorious but remarkably well-informed, would soon discover and comment on her behavior if she were to set up an establishment with only Freddie and Cassie as companions. She may have considered herself well on her way to being a respectable spinster at the advanced age of twenty-two, but the scandalmongers would be more than happy to gossip unless she had a more respectable chaperone than a pair of mischievous eleven-year-olds. There was no help for it but to drag Aunt Harriet along with them to Brook Street. Though, she mused, the constant attention required to check the insatiable curiosity and incessant antics of the twins makes them far more effective chaperones than an aunt who would continue to putter with her plants while thieves carried off the silver and ravishers abducted her niece.

Pushing these thoughts aside, she resolved to tackle her aunt by offering her the baggage coach and the services of James, the footman, for the plants a week before the rest of them were to travel, in addition to the enticement of having the front bedroom and dressing room as well as the morning room—all very sunny—at her complete disposal. Having settled that to her satisfaction, she bade Kitty good-bye and rewarded herself with the prospect of a long ride in the soft afternoon sunshine.

Half an hour later, having donned a new riding habit just arrived from the dressmaker and having ascertained from a quick glance in the mirror that the severe cut and jaunty hat were as becoming as she remembered, she strolled out to the stables to be greeted by her favorite mount. Ajax was eager to be released and could barely wait for her to be tossed into the saddle and be off. A handsome Arab, he seemed too strong a mount for a lady, but Frances was a skilled horsewoman and took great delight in the challenge of handling such an animal. The wind whipped the cobwebs from her mind, while the sight of the countryside with its delicate touches of green and the smell of fresh earth made her begin to regret her decision to exchange it for the crowds and the pavements of London. For some time she galloped along, letting Ajax choose the way across the fields, jumping hedgerows and slowing down to canter through the woods, both of them relishing the exhilaration of freedom. But soon thoughts of a myriad of tasks she had left undone intruded and she knew she should return to them. Regretfully she took one last jump and headed home to finish the accounts waiting for her on her desk.

Her good intentions were not to be fulfilled, however, for upon her return she was forestalled by Higgins, who informed her that a gentleman awaited her in the library. Alerted by the somewhat anxious expression on his normally wooden countenance, Frances questioned him further. "It's the new Marquess of Camberly, milady." Then adding in a confidential tone, "And he looks to be in not the best of tempers." Thus forewarned, Lady Frances removed her hat, smoothed a few unruly wisps of hair, and shook out the skirts of her riding habit. Then, fortifying herself with a deep breath and assuming as much dignity as possible after such an invigorating ride, she entered the library.

If he had not been a great deal too angry to care, Lord Julian Mainwaring would have described his first impression of Lady Frances Cresswell as charming rather than beautiful or dignified—an excellent figure, hazel eyes sparkling, and cheeks flushed after a ride. Her graceful entrance and melodious, "Good afternoon, my lord," added to the impression and further exacerbated Mainwaring's temper.

He had been intensely annoyed several days prior to this encounter to receive notice of an action led by the local magistrate against the agent at Camberly, which had forced him to abandon several interesting political projects in London and post down to Hampshire. He had been even further annoyed to discover that the action had been precipitated by the complaint of a Lady Frances Cresswell. If there were anything Julian Mainwaring loathed more than interference in his affairs, it was interference from an officious busybody spinster who had nothing better to occupy her time than causing trouble for everyone else. Years of dealings with a host of aunts and cousins bent on running his life had perfected his technique of discouraging such meddling. An aloof, coldly polite demeanor dampened the curiosity and helpful suggestions of even the most inveterate of busybodies. He had been perfectly confident that the use of this weapon, an icily polite setdown, would solve his problems with Lady Frances as effectively as it had with the others. The shock of encountering someone who was not only a mere slip of a girl instead of a withered-up spinster, but also a girl who did not conceal an annoyingly understanding humorous twinkle in her fine eyes and revealed a charming smile completely deprived him of his usual resources. Accustomed to dominating every situation, he felt himself at a loss in dealing with this one. Frustration merely added fuel to his anger with the situation and with his hostess.

Frances, waiting for his reply, had ample time to study her opponent. The fierce set on an arrogant jaw, the tightening of well-shaped lips, and the lowering of black brows over intensely blue eyes did nothing to dispel her original reading of his character from his letter. He was a man accustomed to command, arrogant and impatient of other people. The gracious manner and smile that good breeding forced her to adopt disappeared immediately and she faced him warily, determined not to be dominated.

"It has come to my ears, madam, that you have had the effrontery to complain to the magistrate about the conduct of my agent." If she had been bent on resisting him before, she needn't have worried. Her determination, which had sprung from her natural resistance to anyone overbearing, was now fueled by anger. An excellent estate manager herself, she had long been annoyed by the irresponsible behavior of Camberly's shiftless Synthe. Fair-mindedly she had to admit to herself that it was none of her business that the estate was poorly managed, but waste and disrepair upset her whenever and wherever she saw them. In some ways she had been affected. Common fences that had fallen down allowed Camberly livestock into the well-ordered fields of Cresswell's tenants. After all her complaints had been totally ignored, she had repaired the fences herself, but her annoyance had remained. She had been almost glad when her youngest housemaid's tale of woe had revealed Snythe to be a villain as well as negligent. Frances had surprised Sally in tears one morning, and after much cajoling had discovered that he had been forcing most unwelcome attentions on her. When she had rejected him he had threatened to turn her father, one of Camberly's oldest tenants, off the land. Her father's tenancy had been guaranteed by the late Lord Mainwaring's will, but Snythe had enlisted the aid of a disreputable solicitor from the nearest town and had managed to convince Mr. Clemson that it was in his power to remove him from the farm. Sally had been at her wits' end. Much as she loathed the slimy Snythe, she loved her family and knew the miseries of the certain poverty that threatened them should they be turned off. Having heard the entire story, Frances had bidden her dry her eyes and had ridden straight to Sir Lucius Taylor, the local magistrate. Bluff and honest, Sir Lucius had been Frances' adviser in all estate matters since her father's death. He had been glad of the opportunity to bring Snythe to account, something he had been longing to do even longer than Frances.

Thus it was with some asperity that Frances replied, "Yes, my lord, and you may be sure it should have been done long before this, for that man has been running the estate into the ground this age."

His expression became truly alarming. "How dare you interfere in my affairs, madam!"

"I assure you, I restrained myself with difficulty from entering your affairs long before this. It always grieves me to see an estate mismanaged, but I refrained from any action, feeling confident that surely someone would recognize Snythe for the scoundrel he is. Obviously I was guilty of misplaced optimism. It was only after his neglect destroyed some of our seedlings and he threatened my housemaid and her family with ruin that I took any steps at all."

If Lord Mainwaring had been annoyed before, he was furious now—furious because he had not had the time to follow up on his original suspicions of Snythe and come down to investigate, and furious because he had been put in the wrong by a girl little more than half his age. "And I suppose, my girl, that it never occurred to you that the most honorable and expedient way to handle this matter would have been to complain to me," he retorted contemptuously.

Lady Frances flushed. Though privately she acknowledged the justice of his remark and its good sense, she was not about to give in to such high-handed behavior. "I had no reason, sir, given your total disregard for Camberly and its people, to believe that you would pay any attention to a communication from a . . . a 'girl,' " she replied, her eyes kindling at his slighting form of address. "And now, seeing how arrogant you really are, I am surprised you should have paid the least attention to my complaints."

"I had to attend to my own and my brother's affairs in London before I could consider Camberly," he answered, further exasperated at having to defend himself to her. He continued, "As to the rest of the people at Camberly, who are also no concern of yours, I have arranged to bring out my niece this Season under my cousin's aegis, and I will thank you to stop interfering there."

"Interfering? I?" gasped Frances, angry beyond all decorum at this unexpected attack.

"Whom else must I thank for putting such prudish and blue-stocking notions into her head that she writes to me that she does not want to be 'sold to the highest bidder on the Marriage Mart,' as she phrases it? Where else must I look to find the example that makes living in the country, following 'simple, educational pursuits,' seem so attractive? Living in the country and managing an estate may be very well for one such as you, but you know that someone such as Kitty, who has the most naive outlook on life and possesses such romantic propensities, is not the type to enjoy it for long. Better by far that she come to London and learn the untaxing role of a young woman in society so that someone stronger and more sensible than she can take care of her."

Privately Lady Frances was in total agreement, but it would

never do to let this overbearing person know that. "Yes, and suppose no such paragon appears—then what will she fall back on?" was her swift rejoinder.

A cynical smile touched the corners of his lips. "Never fear. What young buck could resist the trusting simplicity of those big brown eyes?"

Before she could stop herself, Frances commented tartly, "Well, obviously men such as you could." Heretofore she had maintained her dignity in spite of being in such a rage, but as these words escaped her lips she realized how rapidly she had descended from a rational condemnation of Lord Mainwaring's business to peurile comments on his personal affairs. Guiltily conscious of this, she put a hand to her mouth and in a remorseful tone added, "Oh, I *do* beg your pardon."

This rapid change from the furious, contemptuous mistress of Cresswell to someone who suddenly looked like a school-room miss caught in an illegal escapade completely threw Mainwaring. Unwilling amusement crept into his eyes as he agreed, "Yes, but I am not the marrying kind anyway, you know."

That left Frances without a thing to say, but rescue was at hand as Higgins entered bearing a decanter of port, which he offered to his lordship. This interruption brought Mainwaring to his senses, and though he thanked Higgins, he declined, saying that he must be off to Camberly, where he was expected for tea. With that and a curt "Good day, ma'am," he strode off, leaving Lady Frances to smile gratefully at her butler.

"That was excellently done, Higgins. I do thank you."

"I thought perhaps his lordship was in need of some restorative," he replied, his impassive countenance belied by twinkling eyes.

It wasn't until he was halfway back to Camberly that Julian realized that though he'd received an explanation, he had certainly not received anything that remotely resembled the apology he had ridden over to demand. "In fact, it was *she* who seemed to think *I* was in the wrong," he muttered bitterly to himself. "Any man would have apologized openly, honestly, shaken hands, and been done with it." His eyes kindled. "In fact, no man would have interfered in such a damned officious manner without coming to me in the first place." Thoroughly irritated by the thought that a mere girl had dared to tell him how to go on, he refused to admit that he had been in complete agreement with her over the original problem. He urged his horse to a gallop. "Damned foolishness! Imagine leaving the management of an estate to a woman—and a girl at that!"

4

During Lord Mainwaring's short tour of inspection at Camberly, it was rapidly borne in upon him that young and female though she might be, Lady Frances Cresswell commanded the respect of the surrounding countryside. He could see for himself her well-drained, well-tilled fields, her neatly maintained cottages, and the excellent quality of her livestock. Sir Lucius confirmed this as they enjoyed their port together following an elaborate repast at his comfortable manor. "At first I couldn't believe that Cresswell would do such a damn-fool thing. Even if he did spend most of his time with his moldly old books, he was a mighty clever fellow. But Frances not only has a good head on her shoulders, she seems to know how to handle her people. Of course, she's got an excellent man in Dawson, her steward, but he tells me she knows all the accounts inside and out and can hold her own in any conversation with a farmer. I hear that she's always having the latest agricultural tracts sent from London. She has a quiet way with her that seems to reassure people and inspire trust. And it isn't easy having care of those twins, either. A rarer bunch of scapegraces I've never been privileged to see. Fine rider too." He waxed eloquent: "Never seen a better seat or lighter

28

hands." From such a purely old-fashioned country gentleman as Sir Lucius Taylor, this was high praise indeed. Mainwaring departed in a thoughtful mood. He respected the older man's judgment but not to the point of describing Lady Frances Cresswell as someone with a "quiet way" about her.

Of course, in his niece Kitty's eyes she could do no wrong. At any other time he would have been amused at her naively enthusiastic description of such a paragon, but it did not suit him to be forever hearing the praises of someone who had had the impertinence to interfere in his vastly complicated affairs. And then to imply that he wasn't succeeding very well at them was outside of enough. In fact Lord Mainwaring was beginning to find the companionship of Kitty, charming though she was, slightly tedious. Even in his salad days he had never had much use for the awkward enthusiasms or, worse, the false sophistication of young misses, and had done his best to avoid them at all costs, choosing instead the more amusing company of older women whose married status did not threaten his bachelor existence. Liaisons with them gave him freedom to choose charming flirtations or relations of a more intimate nature. In both cases each party was perfectly aware of the rules. In fact, young people of any age bored him. He could not understand his cousin Lady Streatham's extraordinary interest in her own offspring, let alone those of her friends. Having led a solitary life himself, abandoned largely to the care of nurses and tutors, he could see no earthly reason for parents to spend any more time and thought than was absolutely necessary on creatures who had no intelligent conversation to recommend them and who were more likely than not to make a mess of the drawing room. All in all, he was quite ready to leave the restrictions of marriage and families to his friends, while he retained the freedom to choose his own amusements.

It was not long before Lord Mainwaring was eager to leave Camberly and return to the more scintillating companionship offered in the metropolis. He had had his fill of dinner conversations that seemed to consist chiefly of a discussion of the varied and mysterious ailments that threatened Cousin Honoria and the manifold accomplishments of Kitty's idol, Lady Frances. Since these consisted of the decidedly dull ability to

tutor her brother and sister, manage an estate, and write books,
he was less than charmed. If there were a class of women who
bored Lord Mainwaring even more than simpering misses, it
was the bluestockings, whom he stigmatized as women forced
to affect eccentricities because they were too tedious or
unattractive to command attention in any other manner. It was
fairly easy to avoid the languishing eyes of hopeful young ladies
and the blandishments of their matchmaking mamas. A man as
wealthy and distinguished as Lord Mainwaring learned this skill
from the moment he entered the *ton*. Far more annoying,
because less obvious, were the tactics of these women whose
only aim in life seemed to be to meddle in others' affairs and
to advise them on how to conduct themselves with more
propriety, more social conscience, more virtue, more seriousness of purpose, and always—as in the case of his bevy of
aunts—to marry and produce heirs.

It was thus with relief that at the end of the week he bid good-
bye to his niece, gave final instructions for her journey to
London, climbed into his curricle, and set his powerful grays
on the road to London.

Lord Mainwaring was not the only one relieved that his visit
had come to an end. Kitty, having endured his rather critical
company for several days, felt her confidence at handling the
rigors of a Season fast slipping away. It was not that her uncle
had actually voiced any actual disapproval of her dress or
behavior, but his entire bearing and conversation betrayed such
exacting standards that she despaired of ever living up to
them.

She could see that at the very least her conversation was
uninteresting to Lord Mainwaring, and at the worst, it annoyed
him. Several awkward dinners had left her desperately wishing
that her parents' rather liberal interpretation of Monsieur
Rousseau's maxims had not encouraged them in a blithe neglect
of formal education. Rather, they had allowed their children
to educate themselves, following natural inclination at the
expense of a discipline which would have forced them to attend
to the newspapers and books likely to cultivate not only their
minds but also, more important, their conversation. Instead of
following such a program, as she knew Lady Frances had, Kitty

had familiarized herself with every dramatic episode, every improbable plot in the latest novels from the circulating library. However, her natural optimism, one thing that had been fostered in the indulgent atmosphere of Camberly, soon reasserted itself. The arrival of a letter from Lady Streatham, cautioning her not to purchase any of her wardrobe until they could consult the modistes in London, assuaged any lingering doubts she had about the forthcoming Season. So it was that before she had seriously begun it, Kitty abandoned the rigorous reading program she had devised for herself in favor of poring over the latest *Belle Assemblée*.

Lady Frances, lacking a guardian who ruthlessly ordered her affairs, had spent the better part of her week cajoling and effecting compromises among various members of her household. Cassie and Frederick had raised a loud wail of protest at the prospect of removing to town. "We won't have any places to explore, and we'll have to be clean all the time, with nothing to do but listen to a lot of dull conversations," complained Freddie.

"And there won't be any trees to climb at all," Cassie chimed in with disgust, only to break out again as a new, more terrible thought struck her. "We won't have our ponies to ride, or Wellington or Nelson to play with."

"Of course I would never leave our friends behind," Frances defended herself indignantly. "Do you think for one moment that I want to give up riding Ajax? John Coachman and some of the stableboys will take all the horses to London before we go, and then will return to drive all of us to London, including Wellington and Nelson. You don't seriously think I'd leave those two mischief-makers here, do you? They would have the place all to pieces in no time, I daresay." She continued wistfully, "It won't be as exciting to ride in the park for any of us, but we shall certainly ride. Who knows, you may make some new friends there. Of course we shall be sure to visit the Tower and Astley's Amphitheater. And no one visits London without tasting the ices at Gunter's. Perhaps, if we're lucky, there will be a balloon ascension." By the time she had finished describing some of the delights to be enjoyed in the metropolis, the twins were reconciled.

"And," Frederick assured his twin, "if we're *that* busy, we can't have time for too many lessons!"

Aunt Harriet was rather more difficult to convince. "Never heard of such a stupid notion! Leave Cresswell when the gardens will be coming to their peak? You are all about in the head, my dear. And you know that the aphids on the roses were so terrible last year that I must be particularly vigilant this spring." A cunning look came into her eyes. "You know that once people hear you are in town you'll be invited to balls, routs, and every type of frivolous amusement those fashionable fools can devise. Surely Kitty will insist that you accompany her to Almack's, at least the first time."

"Yes, but I shan't mind this time, now that I won't be disappointing the family if I don't snare some unfortunate for a husband. Having discovered I am not the romantic or marrying sort, I won't be the least bit upset if no one pays much attention to me. In fact, the less attention I attract, the better time I shall have. I don't believe a man I would enjoy marrying exists, so I shan't be hoping to meet him as I once might have done. Besides, I shall amuse myself observing the idiocy from the safety of the chaperones' corner. You see, you can't worry about me on that score. I thought we could have a few select dinner parties and invite Sir John Perth, now that he has returned from India. Perhaps he will have discovered some new horticultural wonder you know nothing about. Besides, he's a great friend of Sir Humphrey Repton and would perhaps agree to bring him along. Papa knew Sir Humphrey, but not well enough that I could invite him to dinner."

If Frances had counted on sparking some interest with the name of the botanist and noted landscaper, she was only partially successful.

"That's as may be." Aunt Harriet eyed her suspiciously. "But what about my orchids, miss? You know I can't leave them with Swithin. He thinks they're too outlandish." Her aunt dismissed the head gardener, her chief crony at Cresswell, with scorn.

"No, I had thought to take them with us. James will take them to the baggage coach when John takes the horses. You may have the front bedroom, which, in addition to being very sunny, has a dressing rom. If that's not sufficient, there is the breakfast parlor for the rest of your horticultural darlings." A wicked little smile accompanied this generous offer. "And surely you would like to visit Kew again?" her niece quizzed her.

"Very well, miss. I only hope you are not sorry you went to all this trouble for a silly chit like Kitty." She continued, nodding sagely at Frances' raised brows, "You're going about things in your usual style, putting yourself to a great deal of trouble on someone else's behalf without the least thought for the inconvenience to yourself. Kitty's a very sweet girl, but even you will allow that she's rather flighty. Any number of eligible young men will do for her, and she won't need your help or support in finding them. I had certainly better come to London to protect you from your own generous impulses." With that Parthian shot she swept out, leaving Frances in her wake, prey to conflicting feelings of amusement, exasperation, and gratitude.

It only remained for Frances to organize the twins and herself and leave instructions with the rest of the staff for the closing of Cresswell and preparation of the London house for their occupancy. This monumental task was far easier for her than convincing the people she loved to leave a place to which they all were so strongly attached. She truly did need to meet with her publisher, and though it was unconscious on her part, she did long for the mental stimulation of the metropolis with its plays, operas, exhibitions, and bookstores. It would never have occurred to her to think her life dull. Between the duties of the estate and the education and rearing of her younger brother and sister, she never had a quiet moment, but she did miss the interesting discussions she had enjoyed so much with her father. There was no one in the immediate area who understood her intellectual interests, much less shared them with her. Sir Lucius and his wife, though jovial and as kind as could be, didn't seem to feel the need to know or think about anything beyond the immediate concerns of farming and family, and looked with some suspicion at anyone who did. They had both adored her father, but whenever they had been with him, there had been something in their attitude that suggested apprehension that might at any minute burst into wild philosophical speech rather like a madman.

The following week found Kitty and a protesting Ned ensconced in Mainwaring's impressive mansion in Grosvenor Square, while Cassie, Frederick, Frances, Aunt Harriet, Wellington, Nelson, and the orchids were beginning to settle in close by in an elegant but less-imposing house in Brook Street. Within a few hours of arrival the household had reverted to normal. Cassie, summoned by Wellington to rescue Nelson from a precarious position in a tree, had torn her new pinafore. Freddie had discovered that the mews of London had far more horses and stableboys to befriend than the combined stables of Camberly and Cresswell. Higgins had taken the cook to task for selecting a scullery maid who was obviously in an interesting condition, turned the wench off, and procured a neat and willing young person much more suited to a genteel household. And Aunt Harriet, having bullied James, the youngest footman, was tenderly placing her orchids in the most advantageous positions, commiserating with them all the while on the miseries of a coach trip to London. Seeing that everyone and everything was in order, Frances, mindful of her most pressing reason for visiting the metropolis, dashed off a note to Kitty informing her of their safe arrival.

5

The note was delivered as that young damsel was trying on a bewitching confection just arrived from a very expensive milliner. Its high crown and broad brim trimmed with delicate plumes set her delicate features off to perfection and contrived to make her look both innocent and enticing. The bright red—*ponceau*, the modiste had called it—ribbons matched the trim and ruching on her striped walking dress, complimenting her large brown eyes, delicately rounded chin, rosebud mouth, dimples, and dusky curls. All in all, it was a very satisfying transformation from her serviceable brown merino. London would be thoroughly delightful, she thought, if she had a properly appreciative audience. The Cresswells were not the ideal audience for an attractive young girl, but they were an audience. And at present, they were the only ones she knew in town, so she decided to afford them the first taste of her newly fashionable appearance by taking a cup of tea with them and sharing news of the *ton* gleaned from her few previous days in the metropolis.

Just as she had ordered that odiously superior Kilson to procure a chair—she was too much in awe of her uncle to dare to ask for the use of his many conveyances—the knocker sounded and Lady Streatham was ushered in. Elizabeth, Lady

Streatham, cousin to Lord Mainwaring and the only relative
he had not labeled a "dead bore," had been a reigning belle
in her day. A merry rather than beautiful face, vivacious nature,
and abundant energy had won the hearts of scores of eligible
young men. To everyone's surprise, given her fun-loving nature,
she had chosen the quietest and shyest of them all, Lord
Streatham, and retired happily to his country seat to raise a
promising young family. In answer to her friends' protests
against such a seemingly unequal match, she had maintained
that for her to marry someone as lively as she was would be
to court disaster. For sanity's sake she had chosen someone she
could dominate. Her closest friends, seeing the warmth in her
eyes whenever she was with her husband, recognized that,
unlike most of her contemporaries, she had married for love
to someone who could give her a constant supply of admiration,
support, and emotional security. These same friends, while they
missed her gaiety and humor, realized that these lovable traits
now found an outlet with her four equally fun-loving and
energetic boys. In fact, the joy she derived from being mother
to a lively family far outweighed the gaiety of London. It had
been years since she had spared a thought for all that she was
missing, buried in the country until her youngest had begun to
spend more time with his tutor than he did with her. Just as
she realized with a slight shock that she was middle-aged and
had not attended for years anything more formal than a country
assembly, she had received Mainwaring's missive begging her
to chaperone his niece. With some trepidation she had broached
the subject to her husband. "I do think I ought to help him out,
as I am the only female in the family with whom he is on
speaking terms. Don't you agree, John?"

Her husband looked at her fondly, marveling that in spite of
her years and children she didn't look much older than she did
when he married her. "Of course, my dear, it's time we used
the London house ourselves. We all could do with a little town
bronze. I have some affairs to attend to in the city." He
continued, with an understanding twinkle, "Elegant as you
always are, I am sure you are years behind the London fashions.
My riding boots are in tatters. Come to think of it, we could
all stand to replenish our wardrobes as well."

Lady Streatham, knowing how much her husband loved the country and how difficult the social whirl was for someone of his shy nature, fully appreciated his sacrifice and the generous spirit which prompted it. Tears stung her eyes as she flung her arms around his neck. "Oh, John!"

"There, there, my dear, no need to get in a pother about it," said her husband, returning her embrace and smiling down into misty eyes. "I've selfishly kept you to the boys and myself all these years. It's time your friends enjoyed your company again."

"You're so good, my dear friend," she replied. "But won't you dislike it excessively?" she questioned anxiously.

"Not when I've got the gaiest member of the *ton* to watch out for me." Her husband smiled. "Now, no more. It's settled," he added, silencing her with a kiss that was unexpectedly passionate in such a reserved man. So it was that the entire Streatham household was removed without a great deal of fuss to their house in Bruton Street, not too far away from Mainwaring House. And Lady Streatham lost no time in becoming acquainted with her charge for the Season.

She had already met Kilson, who allowed the faintest of smiles to cross his countenance as he opened the door to her. Pulling off delicately shaded lavender gloves, she greeted her protégée. "I see you're on your way out, and looking vastly charming too, if I may say so."

"Yes," responded Kitty, highly gratified by such notice, "I've just received word that Lady Frances has arrived in town, and I do so want to see her. Won't you come too? I need your support because I know she means to avoid most of the social functions and I think it would do her good to attend them. She says she refuses to burden any hostess with someone for whom partners must be pressed into service, but I hardly see how that could be. I think she's very elegant and certainly easy to talk to. But she says people don't want elegance and conversation. She keeps telling me that she is not at all the type that is admired, but I think that her opinion is a result of her one and only Season, when she was taken about by Lady Bingley, who is excessively silly herself and moves in such fashionably empty-headed circles that Frances was bound to feel awkward and out-of-place. Do come and help me convince her at least to start off the Season by accompanying us to Lady Richardson's ball.''

Lady Streatham had not spent a week escorting Kitty to every fashionable establishment in London without having heard about Kitty's unusual neighbor, and her curiosity was aroused. Her own lively family and a devoted elder brother had given her enough confidence to enjoy her come-out and to view making the acquaintance of hordes of unfamiliar people as an exciting opportunity for discovery, but she knew she had been unusually lucky in her family and friends. Too well she could imagine the loneliness of a girl whose parents' tastes had kept them apart from the fashionable world and deprived her of the security of recognizing familiar faces among the *ton* crushes. The fact that the distant relative who had chaperoned her scarcely shared a single thought with Frances would merely have added to her sense of being completely out-of-place. ''I agree. We must see what we can do to change her mind. Come along. My carriage is just outside,'' offered Lady Streatham, drawing on her recently discarded gloves.

''We must be back by three o'clock, because Lord Mainwaring is taking me to tea at his grandmother's,'' warned Kitty in a tone tinged with misgiving at this prospect.

By the time they arrived at Brook Street Frances had succeeded in persuading Cassie into a fresh pinafore and lured Freddie away from the stables with promises that he could take a large lump of sugar to his pony after lessons. She intensely disliked playing the martinet, but knew the children would feel more comfortable and the household would run more smoothly if a routine were immediately established. Consequently it was a well-behaved, well-scrubbed schoolroom scene that welcomed Kitty and Lady Streatham as they entered the drawing room. This model of decorum instantly disintegrated as Cassie jumped up to greet Kitty, upsetting the globe in the process. Lady Streatham, whose maternal reflexes were never far from the surface, caught and righted it dexterously while extending her other hand to Frances, saying with her infectious smile, ''I am so glad to meet you. I apologize for coming uninvited, but Kitty persuaded me that it would not bother you. She was desperate that I should meet all the Cresswells. Besides, having rusticated for so long, I feel in need of support from another sensible woman if I'm to help Kitty sort out admirers. From what I hear, you're just the ally I need.''

She couldn't have chosen a more advantageous method of attack. What Frances would not do for herself, she would do for someone else most willingly. Appealed to in this way, she could only laugh as she rose to greet her visitors, removing the somnolent Nelson from her lap as she did so. Having deposited him in an equally comfortable spot, she extended a welcoming hand to her visitor. "I shall do my best to help you, ma'am. But with my experience, or lack of it, I am more likely to scare off suitors than to introduce Kitty to them.''

Looking into the frank hazel eyes fringed with thick lashes, the delicate features lighted now by a warm, generous smile, Lady Streatham agreed with her charge that Frances' one and only Season must have been badly mismanaged. Surveying the scene further as Frances directed Cassie and Frederick to make their bows to their guests and pushed Wellington from a perch on the sofa—illegally snatched in all the confusion—she reflected on what a great pity it was that someone who commanded love and respect as naturally as Frances did should so quickly resign herself to spinsterhood. No sooner had she decided this than she began to plan a strategy to avert such a tragedy. I shall force Mainwaring to help me, she resolved. To lend Kitty countenance, he will just have to overcome his dislike of the place and escort us to Almack's and to several balls as well. He detests partnering the young girls and their rapacious mamas so much that he should be only too glad to dance with someone as sensible as Frances. He'll get intelligent conversation and protection from matchmaking females at the same time. At this point she remembered hearing Kitty repeat Frances' account of the rather disastrous first encounter between the two. Never daunted, she set out to remedy this immediately by asking if one of the Cresswells' footmen could deliver a note to Lord Mainwaring requesting that his lordship call for Kitty at the Cresswells' on his way to his grandmother's. "For it's much more convenient and will give us more time together. How did we not think of it before?'' she wondered aloud. Once Mainwaring was at Brook Street, she felt fully confident of her powers to cajole him into meeting Frances and renewing their acquaintance on a better footing.

Her schemes were interrupted by a distinct tug at her skirts. She looked down to discover Wellington and Frederick looking at her hopefully. "Excuse me, Lady Streatham," broke in Freddie, "but Kitty says you have a boy about my age. Is he here in London with you? I should like ever so much to meet him if he is." He lowered his voice confidentially. "The thing is that I want someone to play with my soldiers with me. I have the dandiest collection! Cassie's a great gun. She can run and climb trees as well as I can, but she hasn't the knack for playing at soldiers. Frances knows ever so much about battles and history and such, but I don't really think she likes the thought of bloodshed. So if your son were here . . ." He trailed off rather wistfully.

Lady Streatham's infinite experience with small boys prompted her to respond with just the right note. "How delightful! I should think Nigel would like to above all things. He has a set of his own, so you two could have a whole campaign instead of one paltry battle. I'll discuss it with him when I return home this evening." Her eyes twinkled in a conspiratorial way that had won the hearts of countless children through the years.

"Oh, famous!" breathed Freddie, hardly daring to hope for such luck.

"Woof!" agreed Wellington with enthusiasm. The two dashed over to Frances, breaking into Kitty's excited recital of all the advantages to be found in London.

"You must come to Hatchard's with me straightaway," she was saying when Freddie burst in.

"Fanny, I say, Fanny. Lady Streatham has a son who is about my age and he has his own soldiers and she thinks he might like to visit and play with me and she's going to speak to him about it directly!"

"That sounds like great good fun," approved his sister. Catching sight of Cassie's forlorn face out of the corner of her eye, she added, "While you and Nigel are together it would be an excellent time for Kitty and me to take Cassie and Ned with us for ices at Gunter's."

The woebegone look vanished instantly from Cassie's, to descend on her twin's. "But, Fanny . . ." he wailed.

"Now, Freddie, you can't do two things at once, you know, so you must choose." With only the briefest of hesitation he selected the more bellicose amusement, as she had known he would.

"Besides," she teased him, "I couldn't bear the strain of taking both you and Cassie there at the same time, when either one of you alone is a walking disaster. Together, I shudder to think!" The twins grinned good-naturedly, but neither one could let such a remark pass without a spirited defense. These rather vociferous protests were cut short by the entrance of one of the footmen bringing tea and cakes. Neither Lady Streatham nor Kitty, looking forward to the forthcoming tea at the dowager Marchioness of Camberly's, was able to do more than nibble daintily, for which Cassie and Freddie, not to mention their furry friends, were abundantly grateful.

"Kitty tells me that you brought not only your entire household and stables, but your conservatory as well," Lady Streatham commented with some awe. Looking at the twins, she felt that she would be unequal to anything greater than shepherding those two lively charges. Her esteem for Frances rose mightily when she saw how surprised she was that anyone should consider it an effort.

"Oh, yes." Frances laughed. "We have brought all the comforts of a country home, and then some."

Here, Freddie, who had barely finished his cake in time to enter the conversation, burst in eagerly, "Lady Streatham, does your son ride and does he have his own pony?" Assured on both counts, and having arranged to meet Nigel in the park very soon, he was satisfied, and the ladies were left to compare notes on the various unpleasantnesses encountered in removing to town for the season.

This agreeable conversation was interrupted by the entrance of Higgins. "My Lord Mainwaring," he announced, wondering as he did so whether milady and milord would wind up having another set-to. Certainly milord had looked rather forbidding as he strode up the steps, the wind whipping the folds of his many-caped driving coat.

He had, however, underestimated Lady Elizabeth, who, deftly stepping over Nelson and Wellington's teatime tussle, extended both hands to Lord Mainwaring. "Thank you for coming to collect Kitty here. It has saved me taking her back to Mainwaring House, and I'm late for Nigel's tea as it is." Then, plunging on with her irresistible smile, she added, "I know you've met Lady Frances before, but you two haven't been properly introduced. I daresay if you had, each one of you would have been much more civil to the other and wouldn't be looking daggers at each other right now." At this direct attack the two principals, who were both ramrod-stiff and eyeing each other warily, looked slightly sheepish.

Appreciating the humor in the situation, and recognizing a master stroke when she saw one, Lady Frances extended her hand, saying in her frank way, "How do you do, my lord?" No proof against the lurking amusement in her eyes, Lord Mainwaring thawed slightly to extend his own.

"There," Lady Streatham chined in gaily. "Now, if we're all to survive this Season and bring Kitty out in proper style, perhaps we'd best put country matters out of our minds." She looked meaningfully from Kitty to the two who had established an uneasy truce.

Frederick, who had been gazing with rapture out of the window at something in the street below, could bear it no longer. Pointing at Mainwaring's elegant equipage, he asked, "I say, sir, are those grays yours? What an absolutely bang-up pair! They look to be very sweet goers. You must drive to an inch if you can hold them. Do you, sir? How are their mouths? They look as though they'd respond to the lightest of hands. They must go like the very wind when you spring 'em!"

The forthright speech and blatant admiration of a scrubby schoolboy were something totally beyond Lord Mainwaring's vast experience. He discovered, too late, that he was no proof against them. "Yes, they are mine. Would you care to have a look at them?"

Frances noted with surprise that he spoke as casually as though her brother were one of his driving cronies. She had not thought to discover such sensitivity in one who had previously shown himself to be unpleasantly blunt—to put it mildly. Mainwaring had certainly won her brother's undying loyalty.

"Shouldn't I just!" exclaimed Freddie as he dashed downstairs, leaving Mainwaring and the others to collect themselves.

"We mustn't keep Grandmother or the horses waiting. Good to see you in town at last, Elizabeth. Since you've commandeered me for Lady Richardson's ball, I hope you'll drag Streatham along with you so there will be at least two men of sense there to support each other." With that and a "Good day" to Lady Frances, he followed Freddie's tumultuous descent in a more leisurely manner and handed his niece up into the curricle. His lips twitched slightly at the sight of Frederick earnestly debating the grays' good points with his tiger, who, seeing his master, bade a speedy good-bye to the boy and leapt up behind.

Lady Elizabeth stayed long enough to invite Frances to dinner with them before the ball, thus ensuring her presence. She forestalled the protest she knew was coming. "My dear, you simply cannot forgo all social intercourse while you are here, you know. You must come because I shall be very busy with Kitty, and someone must keep an eye on Streatham and Mainwaring. Both of them loathe these things so, and they are being so good in attending them for Kitty's sake. But if you aren't there, Streatham is bound to fall asleep in a corner and Julian will be besieged by matchmaking mamas or, worse, their daughters. Such chivalry should not be so poorly repaid. I know you found these scenes a dead bore before, but how could it have been otherwise with Lady Bingley and her set? Why, they have more feathers on top of their heads than they do inside them."

Lady Frances laughed outright at this, but Lady Streatham could see that she had been struck by the truth of the remark and its interpretation of the cause of her previous disenchantment with the fashionable life of the *ton*.

6

Though ill health had forced the dowager Marchioness of Camberly to relinquish her former role as one of society's leading patronesses, it had not deprived her of an active interest in or reliable information on all of its comings and goings. Julian Mainwaring, who possessed a spirit and intelligence to match her own, had always been her favorite among her children and grandchildren. It had always seemed unfair that he and not the soft and sentimental John was the second son, when Julian had all the natural attributes befitting the master of Camberly. She had been delighted when his uncle, recognizing these abilities, had made him heir to his vast interests at home and abroad, though it had saddened her that fulfillment of these responsibilities made it impossible for him to visit her very often. However, whenever he was in England, he made it a point to come see her before seeing anyone else. She enjoyed his rather caustic wit, which recognized and ridiculed pretension as quickly as she did, and she greatly relied on his interpretations of social and political events for knowledge of the true state of affairs in the world, where she was no longer able to observe and judge for herself. The one point on which the two of them were not in complete agreement was matrimony.

Lord Mainwaring categorically refused to see any value in an institution that forced people of dissimilar interests and propensities to endure each other's presence under the same roof. To his grandmother's acid suggestion that there was such a thing as love, he had replied that she might be right, but as that usually didn't last very long anyway, surely it was unwise to hasten its demise by marrying, when it could be enjoyed perfectly well and perhaps longer outside of marriage. She knew she would sound uncharacteristically sentimental to him if she were to suggest that the passion to which he referred and true love—a combination of that passion and mutual respect—were two very different phenomena. So she had held her tongue, hoping against hope that he would discover his error and find someone to share his life and interests just as she had. So far he had closed his eyes to the type of female who might be expected to be both companion and lover, concentrating instead on the entangling and purely passionate liaisons with expensive and experienced matrons of the *ton*. She hoped his succession to the title and the obvious necessity of introducing his niece to society would force him to abandon these and look around for a suitable partner. Though he might not choose matrimony, Julian had enough respect for history and his family name to recognize his duty in providing an heir. In order to discover his sentiments on that subject, and to give herself the chance to exert at the outset what little influence she had, the dowager Marchioness had invited him and Kitty to tea immediately upon their arrival in town.

They entered the ornately decorated drawing room to find her well-wrapped in a variety of richly embroidered shawls, ensconced on a sofa before a roaring blaze. "So, Julian," she barked as she extended her hand for him to kiss. "It's about time you took a position in society instead of skulking on the sidelines with the excuse you were too busy or gallivanting all over the world. And this is Kitty. Come here, child, and let me have a look at you. Very pretty. Not quite so lovely as your mother, but you'll do. And very well-behaved too," she observed as Kitty shyly curtsied to her. "You should have no trouble at all firing her off, Mainwaring. I congratulate you on having charge of a charming ward." Then, turning to Kitty, who was trying to keep her awe of this alarming old woman from showing, she continued, "How do you like town life?" Kitty responded shyly that she liked it very well but had not been about a great deal yet. "You will do, my dear, you will do. And soon you'll be in such a whirl you'll not have a moment to yourself."

Further observations were cut off by the entrance of her aged butler staggering under an enormous tea tray, which, in addition to a hugely ornate tea service, contained incredible quantities of sweetmeats. It was fortunate for Kitty, who possessed a healthy appetite, that there was an abundant supply, as she was totally ignored while the dowager pumped her grandson for the most recent political news as well as the most scandalous *on-dits*. These he recounted with such skill that she was soon laughing merrily and contributing her own share of satiric comments. Never being one to wrap things up in clean linen, she soon broached her main reason for inviting them, demanding in her abrupt fashion, "Have you given Lady Welford her congé yet?" The amusement vanished from Lord Mainwaring's eyes. "Don't poker up at me, my boy. Do you take me for a flat? We both know it's all very well to live the gay bachelor existence, but as head of the family you now have responsibilities that go beyond managing the estate. You need a marchioness and an heir. Dancing attendance on someone like Vanessa Welford, who is no better than she should be and greedy to boot, won't do." Correctly interpreting Julian's raised eyebrows and quick glance at a round-eyed Kitty, she snorted, "Don't worry about Kitty. It's time she learned a thing or two. I have no patience with these niminy-piminy modern gels and their overnice scruples. Far better that she go into the world with her eyes open than to cry them out later when she discovers her husband has 'another interest.' "

Seeing that the old lady was becoming agitated, Julian took a beringed hand in his firm clasp, remarking, "Just so, ma'am, but we'll discuss this some other time. You must save your strength to rake me over the coals another day."

The dowager gave him a sharp suspicious look but the genuine concern she read in his eyes demonstrated that his remark had

truly resulted from solicitude rather than evasion of a sore point.
Sighing, she agreed that she was just the slightest bit tired, but
only the slightest, and rang for Biddle to show them out, murmuring, "Do please come often, Kitty, to share your latest
adventures and conquests with me."

Mainwaring laughed. "As to that, Grandmother, you will
know all about her conquests even before Kitty does, probably."

"Off with you, you wicked boy!" The dowager was inordinately pleased with his assessment of her incredible network
of social reporters.

Kitty was unusually silent on the ride home, digesting this
latest piece of information about her guardian. Less in awe of
him than she had been at first, she no longer annoyed him with
numerous nervous attempts to engage him in conversation, but
behaved more naturally—to the relief of both of them. They
rubbed along as well as might be expected of a worldly thirty-
five-year-old man and a sheltered schoolgirl of seventeen. Try
as she would, she could not picture her reserved and haughty
Uncle Julian in the passionate embraces of some ripe beauty.
The vision of him as a lover just did not coincide with all that
she had heretofore seen of him conferring in his library with
distinguished-looking peers, discussing voyages and the status
of his colonial enterprises with captains recently returned, or
pursuing the purely gentlemanly pursuits at Brooks's, Gentleman
Jackson's, Manton's, and Tattersall's. Kitty resolved to pay
more attention in the future, hoping to elicit some interesting
details from her new abigail, Alice.

This recent addition to the household was only too happy to
regale her country-bred mistress with interesting tidbits about
the ornaments of London society. It was to this lively damsel,
more than to Lady Streatham, that Kitty owed her growing
knowledge of what was "done" and what was "not done" in
the *ton*. Those belowstairs had an even more rigid code of
conduct for those they served than did their masters. For it was
better to be a mere housemaid in a house of the first stare of
respectability than to be abigail to someone of more dubious
reputation, such as Lady Welford. Alice hoped to ensure her
own position by keeping her mistress on the most narrowly

virtuous path. The best way to do that was to keep her informed of the pitfalls along the way and to warn her of the disastrous mistakes that less-well-informed maidens had made.

When Kitty approached her, she was more than willing to talk about her employer's formidable reputation as successful wooer of some of society's most dazzling women. Kitty listened openmouthed as Alice, not a little proud that her master was so dashing, added one name after another to the list of his conquests. "But, Alice," she gasped, "those ladies are all married!"

Her preceptress nodded. "Aye, so they are, my lady. Them's the sort that gets married as quick as possible to some bloke who is as dull as he is rich so they can live like they really wants to and choose their own lovers."

The description of the standard marriage of convenience was all news to Kitty, whose parents had been unfashionably and madly infatuated with each other, and she remained a little confused. Still unable to envision her forbidding guardian in the role of ardent lover, she asked incredulously, "But is he in love with all these ladies at once, then, or one after the other?"

Alice snorted. "Good Lord, no! He's just—ahem—'attracted' by their beauty, if you understand my meanin', miss. He's a reg'lar conoosewer and won't be seen with nothin' but the best, most fashionable ladies. You won't catch his lordship with anyone who isn't what you call a reg'lar diamond. But, Lord, he ain't even that good friends with them. They don't understand all the complicated political things he's into and they don't want to bother their pretty little heads trying. They're happy just so long's he keeps givin' them jewels and takin' them to the opera and suchlike, for they be right proud to have caught him and they want all their friends to see them with him."

Kitty admitted to herself that she had seriously underestimated the variety and magnitude of her uncle's abilities. She knew that to succeed with women in these days of social refinement, any man must possess a good deal of address. She could not picture the Uncle Julian who corrected her conversation, and who was more likely to point out what was wrong with her appearance than compliment her on it, whispering gallant nothings into some lady of fashion's ear. Alice assured her that, contrary to appearance, her seemingly taciturn uncle was famed for his expertise in the art of dalliance when he wished to put forth the effort. Kitty could hardly wait to share her discovery with Lady Frances and to discover whether she were any more conversant with the *à la mode* way of marriage. If she were, it would certainly go a long way toward explaining her distaste for the London season with its universally acccepted goal of the advantageous match. Mulling all this over, she gave herself up to Alice's deft ministrations in preparation for dinner.

7

The marquess, feeling that he had done his duty and endured enough female company for at least a week—certainly for the day—strolled to Brooks's after dinner in search of convivial company. Luck was his. He encountered the Honorable Bertie Montgomery, exquisitely garbed in delicately shaded pantaloons and a coat that had taken the best of his own and his valet's efforts, as well as an inordinate amount of skill, to smooth onto his slender form without a wrinkle. The Honorable Bertie had been a close friend of Julian's since their days together at Eton and then Oxford. It was a friendship that continued to puzzle many who failed to see that the constantly cheerful Bertie provided a relaxing companionship for his more serious friend, while Julian's intelligence and adventurous nature flattered the sociable Bertie and provided him with a glimpse of exciting worlds without involving him in them.

"Hallo, Julian," he greeted him, his amiable face lighting with pleasure. "Hear you've become an ape leader this Season. Don't do it, my boy. M'mother was in a rare tweak all last year trying to pop off Susan."

Julian tried vainly to conjure up a vision of this damsel, but having been abroad much of the time, gave up.

Sensing his difficulty, Bertie came immediately to his friend's rescue. "A nice little thing, Susan, but a bit on the mousy side. You wouldn't remember her."

Looking at his friend's open but undistinguished countenance, Julian could readily believe this.

"Get your niece betrothed quickly," continued Bertie. "Mother found someone for Susan directly, and we were much more comfortable after that."

Julian smiled, "I shall keep your advice in mind, but I shall have very little to do with it. Lady Streatham is taking Kitty under her wing." The marquess handed his cape to the servant at the door and ordered a bottle of port from another who rushed up to attend to their wishes. "I shall leave everything in her capable hands and lend my presence only when absolutely necessary. I would be exceedingly grateful to you, Bertie, if you would come support me tomorrow at the first fulfillment of my guardian duties at Lady Richardson's ball." Lord Mainwaring rarely asked anything of anybody, but this time the look he directed toward his friend was definitely beseeching.

"Certainly, Julian, but Lady Richardson's ball is the opening event of the Season. Everyone will be there. It should not be so onerous a duty as all that."

The sardonic curl of the marquess's lips and the arrogant lifting of heavy dark brows were eloquent testimony to this gentleman's expectations of such an evening.

"Oh, don't be so damned high in the instep, Julian! Such an evening can be quite entertaining. And not everyone there will be on the catch for you. I tell you what, my boy, it would do you a great deal of good to encounter some woman, any woman, who is not after you for herself or her daughter."

A distinctly cynical look settled on his friend's handsome features. "It may surprise you, Bertie, to hear that I have met such a female, but I don't find prudes any more attractive than I do the most rapacious mama or her daughter."

"Whoever was it?" Bertie questioned, agog to discover the identity of one female who had not fallen victim to Mainwaring's fortune, social position, attractive harsh-featured countenance, or reputation as a perpetual bachelor.

"It was Lady Frances Cresswell," was the unwilling reply.

"Fanny, a prude?" Bertie gasped. "Upon my word, she must have been more shattered by her father's death than I thought."

"You know Lady Cresswell?" Julian asked, wondering at the same time if he had been entirely fair in labeling the lady in question a prude. After all, it was only on the basis of Kitty's description of her learning and his own single experience of estate matters that he had decided she must be a bluestocking. In his experience, most bluestockings were shocking prudes, among many other equally unattractive things. But the more he thought about it, the more he realized that he had been rather hasty in assigning her this trait. No prude would have spent a minute unchaperoned in the company of any man, let alone a man of his reputation, in the library or any other room. Lady Frances had spent fully half an hour alone with him trying to put him in his place, without showing the least sign of discomfort. It was true that she objected to Snythe on moral grounds, but her opinion of the slimy agent was no more censorious than his own. A true prude would have dropped her eyes, blushed, and meekly given in to any of his wishes instead of standing her ground, cheeks flushed, and eyes looking directly and angrily into his own. Not only had she not been meek, she had gotten the better of their encounter. No, he admitted ruefully to himself, whatever Lady Frances was, she was not a prude.

Bertie had been watching the variety of expressions flitting across his friend's face with interest. He would have given a great deal to be able to read them accurately, but, being the good friend he was, contained his curiosity, merely volunteering, "I knew her father."

Julian's patent disbelief in the friendship between one of London's most dedicated dandies and a scholarly recluse forced Bertie to defend himself. "Dash it all, Julian, you needn't look at me as though I'm a half-wit. If you knew the least bit about these things, you'd know that it takes more than a tailor to make someone an arbiter of fashion. It takes exquisite taste, my boy, and exquisite taste demands long and careful cultivation. I first met Cresswell in Greece when I was on the Grand Tour and he and Elgin were convincing the Greeks to sell them bits of the Parthenon. He knew a devilish lot about Grecian art and

had some very interesting aesthetic ideas of his own besides.
He took me home to see some of the objets he'd collected on
his travels. We became quite friendly and I visited him and his
family fairly often while I was there. Frances was only a child
at the time, but mature beyond her years, and she used to join
us and listen to our discussions.''

Harking back to his visit to Cresswell Manor, Mainwaring
couldn't remember anything distinctly, but cudgeling his brains,
he did dimly recall an impression of lightness and elegance
which had given a clue to the artistic interests and eclectic tastes
of Lord Creswell.

Bertie continued, ''When they returned, I visited them down
at Cresswell. Not long after, Lady Cresswell died and Frances
took over the care of the twins. At times she seemed little older
than they were, ready to engage in any romp from tree-climbing
to punting on the lake. Well, at any rate, she certainly didn't
seem as though she were eleven years older. Lord, I remember
one night when she dressed up as the headless horseman reputed
to haunt the district. She had us all quaking in our boots, what
with her bloodcurdling yell.'' He chuckled heartily at the
memory. ''No, Frances never cared two pins about what anyone
else would think.''

Julian, who had found it difficult to picture Lady Frances
Cresswell as anything but self-possessed, certainly had no
difficulty agreeing with his friend on this last point, but confined
himself to remarking, ''Well, you'll have a chance to judge for
yourself. She's to be one of my cousin's party at the
Richardsons' ball. It is one thing to partner Kitty, simpering
miss that she may be. After all, she is my niece, but I draw
the line at Frances Cresswell. She and I have nothing to say
to each other, and if I know Elizabeth, she'll consider me at
least as responsible for amusing Kitty's friend as I am for
squiring Kitty herself. Be a good fellow, Bertie, and do the pretty
for me with Lady Frances.'' Lord Julian Mainwaring rarely felt
the need to ask a favor of his fellowmen, but there was a
distinctly cajoling note in his voice.

''Always happy to oblige a friend, Julian, always happy to
oblige,'' Bertie agreed good-naturedly, relieving his friend of

the unpleasant task, which had intruded on his thoughts at the most inauspicious moments. That settled, they could turn their minds to the contemplation of an excellent bottle of port and several games of whist before going in search of more enlivening entertainment onstage and off at the opera.

8

L ord Mainwaring was not the only person looking forward with some misgiving to the Richardsons' gala. Kitty, though highly excited at the thought of her first ball, was beset by all the ordinary fears of a young lady making her first entrance into the adult world of fashion. Would she know how to go on? She had been able to dance delightfully with Ned and her dancing master, but performing complicated steps with one's brother in one's own empty drawing room was a good deal different from executing them with a total stranger in a crowded ballroom under hundreds of critical eyes. Would she be pretty enough to attract the attention of anyone at all? Fortunately her brown eyes and shining brown curls were in vogue, brunettes being all the rage at the moment. What would she ever say to everyone? She was confiding this rapidly increasing list of worries to Lady Frances as the two awaited the arrival of the dressmaker at the Cresswells'. This was the final fitting for both of them before the ball, and Kitty had begged to be allowed to try on her gown at Lady Frances' in order to have the benefit of her opinion as well as general moral support. Naturally she wore the requisite white of one making her come-out, but with rose trimmings designed to bring out the enchanting color in her cheeks and emphasize the rich color of her eyes. Lady Frances, by her choice of dove-gray silk, claimed her position as a woman midway between maiden and dowager. She had been kept from further declaring her ineligible status—with a delicate lace cap—by the vehement protestations of both Kitty and the dressmaker.

"Madam is far too young for such a thing. A cap is only for someone who no longer has any possible claim to youth—not one as young and elegant as Madam. It would be a crime to cover up Madam's lovely golden hair with such a thing!" The seamstress was scandalized that anyone would welcome the advent of maturity.

Kitty, far less tactful, added, "Frances, if you wear that dreadful thing, no one will ask you to dance." When Frances finally made it clear that such had been exactly her intention, she was reminded in no uncertain terms of her promise to Lady Streatham to take care of Lord Streatham and Lord Mainwaring. This recollection, coupled with memories of other balls and other partners, caused her serious doubts about the wisdom of coming to London at all. Then she remembered Lady Streatham's merry face, her strictures concerning Lady Bingley and her cronies, and comforted herself with the thought that perhaps things would be different now that she was several years older, virtually her own mistress, and acquainted with more people than she had been before. At any rate, having stood up to something as threatening as Lord Mainwaring in a rage, she couldn't let the mere idea of dancing with him and other supercilious partners put her in a quake. This was a salutary recollection, as it brought to mind her first encounter with him. He had called her a bluestocking, and the remark, unjust though it was, still rankled. All thoughts of the matronly cap were banished and she resolved to get out the famous Cresswell set of baroque pearls to add to her éclat.

This settled, Frances decided to reward herself with a trip to Hatchard's to purchase *Waverly*, which had not been available in the country. Kitty was also fond of Scott despite her propensity for more frothy romances, and she was easily persuaded to accompany her. They set off in the carriage with Wellington. The little dog seized every opportunity for a ride, though he was still leery of the great amount of traffic in the city and much preferred sitting on the box next to John to dodging among the wheels of the throng of vehicles, avoiding the heavy hooves of cart horses or the wickedly quick ones of the highly strung prime bits of blood belonging to the Corinthians. From his perch he could sniff the gratifying variety of city smells and survey the scene with detachment while still attracting the attention of admiring ladies in passing carriages, who never failed to exclaim over his engaging countenance. All in all, he was in a fair way to preferring London to the country.

The tempting array of books catering to every taste and fancy banished all thoughts of the ball that evening from the minds of Kitty and Frances as they browsed happily among elegant gilt volumes. So engrossed was Frances that she failed to notice an exquisitely garbed elderly gentleman next to her, poring over a book of engravings of scenes from classical antiquity. As she stepped back to get a better view of the shelves above her, she bumped into him, rousing him from his absorption. "I do beg your pardon, sir." As she paused to frame a further apology, recognition dawned. "It's Monsieur le Comte de Vaudron, isn't it?" she hazarded, hoping that her memory served her as well as it usually did.

The gentleman regarded her quizzically for a minute before an answering smile broke. "*Cèst ma chère Fanny!*" he exclaimed, kissing her hand with Gallic fervor."

"How delightful to see you! But what are you doing in London, sir? I had thought you were still in Greece. Thank the merciful heavens you did not return to France as you were planning to when we last saw you." The questions and concern in Frances' face betrayed a warmth and fondness not usually present in her manner to those outside the immediate family.

The count laughed gaily. "Always the curious one, eh, my Fanny? I am staying with Lord Elgin. Originally I helped him to transport his precious marbles here from the Parthenon, but I have remained here to add my influential friends' pleas to his in order to make your so-stuffy government purchase them for England. Of course, it is very difficult. You English, the Cresswells and Elgins excepted, are not a cultured race. These treasures will be wasted on such a nation of shopkeepers, but at least they will be safe from barbarians and vandals. Not that I do not appreciate this nation of shopkeepers. After all, so far they have saved all Europe from *ce monstre* Napoleon—definitely a man of genius, but genius run mad with power. And I personally have cause to be grateful to these shopkeepers. Long ago I recognized that my own countrymen, whatever their talents in the more refined aspects of life, have no head for finance or politics, so I brought my money to your English bankers and businessmen, whose acumen now permits me to live like a human being—"

Frances interrupted this elaborate explanation to ask, "But what of your estates, your lovely château? Were they all destroyed in that revolutionary madness?"

"Ah, my child, who knows? News is so difficult to come by, and so unreliable. Whether they exist or not is a matter of indifference to me because they were no longer mine." Seeing Frances' look of horror, he hastened to reassure her. "I saw what that stupid Louis and the rest of his crowd were doing to the country. As you know, I never felt comfortable with the life of the so-called *ancien régime*. That is one of the reasons I left France—that and my wish to study the classical cultures. I left the management of the estate to my nephew Claude. He was a greedy young man and I knew he could be counted on to keep it productive. Soon I realized that he was beginning to consider my lands his own, so I merely formalized it by exchanging them for the family treasures he possessed. He cared nothing for historic tapestries, paintings, jewelry, furniture, but I loved them. He thought he had gotten himself a bargain, poor boy, but I have no doubt it's all gone, and he with it. The way he treated his peasants, I am certain he would have been one of the first to be consumed in the rage of the Revolution. Still, I do not wish such a horrible fate on anyone. Claude was not a particularly cruel man, just unenlightened and rather self-centered, as so many of those people were." He sighed and turned to her. "But, Fanny, tell me of yourself." A look of sadness crossed his face. "I was so very sorry to hear about your poor papa, but he and your mother were so very close, such a well-matched team of students, that I am certain, in spite of you wonderful children, his life must have been lonely after she died. He was a brilliant and amiable scholar, and so was she—perhaps the dearest friends I ever had." He fell silent. "And how do you and Cassie and Freddie go on? You are all still my mischievous little devils, *non*?"

Frances answered as best she could, filling in the two years since her father's death. The appearance of Kitty followed by a heavily laden footman recalled her to her surroundings. Presenting Kitty, she bid the *comte* adieu, begging him to call on them in Brook Street at his earliest convenience. She wondered if he would be at Lady Richardson's ball, and hoped that she would have another friendly face and intelligent conversation to look forward to.

Frances did not like to ask, but the irrepressible Kitty suffered no such qualms. Extending a small white hand and dimpling up at him with her most enchanting smile, she inquired, "Do you go to Lady Richardson's tonight? I am looking forward to it ever so much, as it's to be my first one." The *comte* assured both of them that he would not miss it for the world, and begged a dance from each of them.

"If your card becomes crowded, Mademoiselle Kitty, *naturellement* you will cross out my name and leave me to the dowagers, but if you become weary of inarticulate adoration, overblown compliments, or infatuated young bucks, I am at your service." His eyes twinkled. "Now, let me escort you to your carriage."

As Lady Frances mounted the steps back at Brook Street, she met Bertie Montgomery on the steps, exquisitely attired in a plum-colored coat, jonquil waistcoat, and fawn pantaloons, bearing a delicately shaded nosegay. "Bertie, how lovely to see you!" She smiled, realizing for the second time that day that she knew more people in London than she had imagined.

"Hallo, Fanny," he replied, presenting his offering. Her surprise and delight were ample reward for a harrowing afternoon. Bertie had spent the better part of his day trying to deduce what color gown Frances was likely to wear to the ball that evening. Fortunately, he was on excellent terms with Lady Streatham, he hastened to call at Bruton Street, where she was most happy to furnish him with the name of the modiste whose creation was to grace Lady Frances at Lady Richardson's that night. An even quicker visit to Bond Street established the color of her gown and allowed him to select an exquisite combination designed to enhance without overpowering her toilette.

It was more regard for an old playmate than obedience to Mainwaring's wishes that had then sent him posthaste to Brook Street to present it and enroll himself among her partners for the ball. Bertie had no idea how or why Lord Mainwaring had arrived at the conclusion that Lady Frances Cresswell was a prude, but he was determined that such a misguided opinion should not be allowed to take hold in his friend's head, much less spread elsewhere. In fact, by helping both Frances and Mainwaring, he was giving himself the pleasure of dancing with a partner whose grace could be counted on to put his own considerable skill in the best light. Moreoever, he could rely on her not to flirt with him or try to interest him in some pudding-faced daughter. It was an admirable situation. He could enjoy himself while indulging in the luxury of feeling exceedingly virtuous.

As Bertie sauntered off down Brook Street, having presented his posy and made his request, Lady Frances realized that she was well and truly committed to this ball. Even before crossing the threshold, she had no fewer than three partners. With the exception of Lord Mainwaring, they were all calculated to inspire confidence in even the most anxious of females. It came as a slight shock to discover that she was actually looking forward to the evening.

9

An elegant dinner at Lord and Lady Streatham's was a prelude to the ball. Arriving slightly later than she had planned after gratifying Cassie's and Freddie's request to see her in her finery, Lady Frances found the others already assembled. In addition to the family there were a few close friends of the Streathams', but she was acquainted with most of the company. Lady Streatham had tactfully placed Frances next to her husband, knowing that two such serious landlords could find much to discuss concerning the problems and particularities of their respective estates. Though Lord Streatham did not particularly enjoy London society, preferring the more relaxed atmosphere of country entertaining, he was a genial host and excellent conversationalist who welcomed the opportunity to discuss something other than the latest scandal of Byron's or the fashion in bonnets. Sensing a kindred spirit, Lady Frances relaxed and allowed herself to be drawn into a completely unfashionable discussion of the proposed Corn Laws and their undoubted disastrous effects on the farmers. It was thus that Lord Mainwaring, glancing around the table, had leisure to study Frances when she was most at her ease. Bertie Montgomery's revelations concerning her had surprised him and sparked his interest—not that he found her in the least attractive, but he prided himself on his ability to assess people accurately at his first meeting, and it piqued him not a little to be told he was wrong. Grudgingly he admitted to himself that her animated face and graceful gestures were not those of a prude, nor was her attire. The dove-gray silk, ornamented only by a flounce at the hem, was a perfect foil for the magnificent baroque pearls that had been the pride of Cresswell women for generations. Her hair, though simply done, shone a rich gold, which, coupled with her honey coloring and dark brows, made her appear less insipid than most blonds of the pink-and-white variety. The pearls and the silk gave a luster to her skin and made her eyes under their thick dark lashes more intensely hazel. The tasteful simplicity of her costume gave her an air of quiet elegance which, if not at the height of fashion, was not that of a prude.

However, snatches of her conversation confirmed his opinion of her as a bluestocking. He smiled with inward satisfaction as he caught the latest, ". . . the poor harvest I expect this year will drive up the price of corn and make the lot of the small farmer more difficult unless something is done to stop the Corn Laws, which make it impossible to buy cheap foreign corn, or eliminate the burden of taxes . . ."

His dislike of blue women did not stop him from voicing his total disagreement. "And how do you propose, ma'am, to finance the debt which we have incurred during this costly campaign against France, if you eliminate the tax? Besides, the Corn Laws were proposed to help your poor farmer."

Startled by the entrance of another party into her *tête-à-tête*, and stung by the condescension in Lord Mainwaring's tone, Frances raised an eyebrow and responded coolly, "I am referring to the small farmer, sir. Of course I'm not such a nodcock as to think we can completely do away with taxation. I meant merely that it must be redistributed to release the poor farmer who is suffering from the added burden of expensive grain. You don't seriously consider that it is the small farmer, who must devote much of his land to pasturage, that benefits from these Corn Laws, do you?"

Thus challenged, Mainwaring forgot that he would be wasting

his well-considered arguments on a mere slip of a girl and replied with some heat, "No, but I am more concerned with our fledgling industries—our gunmakers and steelworkers. Your farmers still have a market for their produce, but what will the gunsmith or foundry worker do with the decline in his market? Or would you tax him instead of the farmer?"

"Of course not!" Frances could not keep her annoyance at being viewed as a naive girl out of her voice. "But I would rearrange taxation so that those who can pay it are taxed. The American colonies spoke out against such an arbitrary and ill-conceived system, and so ought we."

"So we have a Jacobin in our midst!" he taunted.

"No, sir, you do not. I am not against a system of taxation. I merely ask for one that has been well-thought-out, not one that has been rushed through Parliament in response to the interests of a small group of people. But I do admire the Americans for one thing, and that is their originality in devising an entirely new political system based on soundly reasoned principles. It takes creativity and great courage to do so. However much we, and perhaps they too, may regret the separation between us, one must give them credit for it."

At this point Lord Streatham deemed it prudent to intervene. "Come now, both of you give over. You both talk a good deal of sense, but this is not the place to do so. You must empty your heads so that you can mind your steps later in the ballroom and render your conversation light enough to allay the suspicions of even the most fashionable members of the *ton*. It wouldn't do to *think* at a ball, you know," he added, shaking his head and quizzing them both. "I can see, Frances, that you must dance first with me so that I can get you off your high horse and to the weather, Kitty's chances of success this Season, or something equally likely to make you sound benignly insipid." Frances laughed, and recognizing the justice of his remark, accepted his offer with pleasure.

Lady Richardson's ball had already been dubbed a "dreadful squeeze" by the time Kitty, Frances, and the Streathams ascended the wide marble staircase to the brightly lighted ballroom above. For an instant Frances felt a knot in the pit of her stomach as the music, elegant dresses, sparkling jewels, and hundreds of chandeliers brought back memories of another Season, but this vanished as Lord Streatham, who, guessing her disquiet, patted her arm as he led her and his wife into the throng. Not allowing her to chance to do more than glance at the beautifully dressed women, masses of candles, and banks of flowers, he swept her onto the floor into a set that was just forming. Though neither he nor Frances was enamored of the social scene, Lord Streatham and she were both graceful enough that they enjoyed the exercise of dancing, and Frances, who loved music as well, soon forget herself completely as she gave herself up to the pleasure of executing the steps in time to it. Thus she appeared at her best—graceful and unself-conscious— to those dowagers and dandies who were scrutinizing every face new to the London scene. Not being a "diamond of the first water," nor decked out in the first stare of fashion, she did not attract a great deal of attention, but that which she did attract was approving.

Frances hardly had a moment to look around for Kitty before Bertie Montgomery came to claim his dance. Having ascertained from Lady Streatham that Frances waltzed, and having assured himself from her performance that she would do him credit as a partner, he resolved to demonstrate to anyone interested in observing that Lady Frances Cresswell showed to advantage in the ballroom. While he guided her expertly around it, he kept up a running commentary on the famous and infamous members of the *ton* to be seen there that evening. Did she see the elegant gentleman in the corner haughtily surveying the scene through a gold quizzing glass? That was Lord Petersham, tea connoisseur of the most exquisite sensibility and possessor of a different snuffbox for every day of the year. Mr. "Poodle" Byng, minus his omnipresent canine companion, thank heaven, was to be seen in the alcove chatting with Lord Alvanley. Now, Alvanley had his own peculiarity, being so fond of cold apricot tarts that he ordered a fresh one prepared daily and set on his side table so that he could indulge his fancy whenever it came upon him.

Frances had heard outrageous tales of extravagance, but, from her rational perspective, had put them down to the natural wish on the part of the local gentry to depict London as the scene of every absurdity and folly. Truly, it seemed they were not far wrong. The amusement in her eyes deepened as every whirl of the waltz faced them toward yet another person who had tried to win the fickle interest of society by carrying some personal fetish to an extreme. "And you, Bertie, I can see you are on the best of terms with all of them. What are you noted for?"

"Nothing at all," he replied airily.

"Well, I think it must be for your nicety in dress, for you do look quite fine, you know."

Bertie turned quite pink with pleasure and said he supposed he might be known as a fellow who possessed the happy knack of choosing and keeping a good valet and tailor.

"As well as possessing exquisite manners and a warm heart," she added, smiling.

He again flushed vividly but said simply, "I would do anything for a true friend of mine."

When the waltz ended, he restored to her to Lady Streatham and went in search of refreshment for both of them after their exertions. "Enjoying yourself, my dear?" Lady Elizabeth queried, noting with pleasure the flush in Frances' cheeks and a distinct sparkle in her eyes. Frances, however, merely nodded while her companion continued. "Mainwaring asked me to secure your next waltz with him if he were not here to claim it when you finished with Bertie." She glanced toward the end of the ballroom, where his lordship was escorting Lady Jersey to a gay-looking group of people.

"Oh, no!" Her ladyship looked surprised at Frances' vehemence. Then Frances explained candidly, "I don't think that's advisable in the least. He and I always seem to be dagger-drawing."

Lady Elizabeth dismissed this unworthy thought. "That's as may be, but his reputation as a severe critic of the female sex is well-known, and it will do you no end of good socially to be seen as his partner for the waltz." Bowing to unanswerably superior social wisdom, Lady Frances acquiesced.

The truth of the matter was that earlier Lady Elizabeth had seen Mainwaring propping his broad shoulders against a wall as he eyed the assembled throng sardonically. He had just finished telling himself that, having done his duty and danced with Kitty, he was free to go in search of diversion more to his taste, when Lady Streatham strolled by. He was fond of his cousin, so he had invited her to stand up with him. "How the devil did you get Streatham to accompany you to London?"

"Brute force," she confided ruefully. "And he possesses naturally fatherly instincts which have been roused both on Kitty's and on Frances' behalf."

"Frances!" his lordship echoed in astonishment.

"Yes." Lady Elizabeth explained: "She had a most dreadful time of it with that silly Lady Bingley. And who would not have been bored to distraction by that set? So she has come to think of herself as a misfit. Well not a misfit exactly, but certainly as someone who doesn't quite belong. It was only her great fondness for Kitty that brought her. I'm sure she would be happier by far in the country."

Suspecting what was coming, Lord Mainwaring glanced to where Lady Frances was expertly performing the quadrille with the Comte de Vaudron, and remarked that the lady in question did not seem to be having any difficulty that evening.

"But, Julian, you could do her such a world of good just by waltzing with her. You know how everyone will ape your every move—though why they should is more than I can understand." He grinned appreciatively. "And if it is seen you consider her a partner worthy of your notice, she will truly take."

"Oh, very well, Lizzie," he responded, no proof against the pleading in her eyes. "But I see Sally Jersey waving to me, and you know that one ignores 'Silence' at one's peril." He strolled off in response to a coyly beckoning finger.

"My dear Julian, how perfectly delightful to see you in England again, but whatever are you doing here, my friend? This is hardly your usual fare."

"True, alas, Sally," he agreed.

"Come." She laid a jeweled hand on his shoulder. "Dance with me and relieve this insufferable tedium."

"Bored, are you, Sally?" He manuevered her expertly around a panting red-faced gentleman and his equally red-faced partner.

She smiled mischievously at him. "Not anymore, Julian, not anymore." The mischief disappeared and the sparkle in her eyes became more pronounced as she asked, "What of Vanessa Welford? Are you still dancing attendance on her?" Her partner's dark eyebrows snapped together but she continued throatily, a wealth of meaning in her voice, "You can do much better than that, Julian, you know."

"Ah, but, Sally, do I want to?" The words were spoken softly, but there was no mistaking the tone. Completely silenced, she allowed him to return her to her friends, where she once again became the center of a laughing group.

Julian had no wish to become one of Sally Jersey's *gallants*, and highly resented her calm assumption of her absolute power over all men. The idea of dancing with someone who did not like the world where Lady Jersey and her sort were queened was becoming more attractive to him by the minute as he sauntered toward the spot where Frances and Bertie were chatting gaily. "Hallo, Bertie, do you mind if I deprive you of your companion?"

"Not in the slightest, old fellow," Bertie responded punctiliously, but the quizzing look in his eye was not lost on Julian. Mainwaring turned to his companion. "Lady Frances, may I make amends for my earlier conduct this evening by asking you to stand up for a waltz with me?" he invited. She raised her eyebrows at his calm assumption that a waltz with him was such a handsome means of rectifying his earlier attitude toward her, but she thanked him prettily enough and allowed him to lead her to the floor.

He was an excellent dancer, moving with the agility of a natural athlete. The strength in the arm circling her waist, the masterful guiding of her steps, made this an entirely different experience from her friendly *tête-à-tête* with Bertie. She found it slightly disturbing, but told herself that it was doing her no end of good socially. Another glide and she admitted to herself that it was not only good for her reputation to waltz with Lord Mainwaring but also a delightful sensation. After several minutes of silence the marquess decided he had seen all of the top of Lady Frances' golden head he wanted to see. He had been slightly piqued at her unenthusiastic acceptance of an invitation that would have cast any other woman in the room into transports. "Am I forgiven for annoying you?" he asked, looking quizzically down at her.

Frances, who had been completely absorbed in the music and

the motion, came to with a slight start. "Oh, certainly, sir. But naturally you could not expect anything but an argument when you disagreed with a 'bluestocking.' " This was spoken blandly enough, but there was a wicked twinkle in her eyes.

Looking at her more intently after what appeared to be a deliberately provocative remark, the marquess realized with a slight shock that she was laughing at him! No, he decided, she was laughing at both of them, and inviting him to laugh with her. This was a rather novel sensation for Lord Mainwaring. Ladies young and old, proper and improper, had smiled at him, simpered at him, looked at him with soulful intensity, but none of them had ever regarded him purely with amusement. He found it irresistible and smiled his own very attractive smile in return.

At least Frances thought it was attractive. It brought warmth to the dark blue eyes which were apt to look hard. The whiteness of his teeth gleamed in a face tanned by years in the tropics.

Rising to her bait, he could not resist teasing her in turn. "I had not thought that someone of your serious tastes would frequent such frivolous scenes as this."

Frances, accustomed to the constant teasing of Cassie and Freddie, was not in the least disconcerted. "Judging from the surprised and delighted look on the faces of our hostess and several other ladies, I assume you don't frequent them much yourself."

An appreciative gleam shone in Julian's eyes. "Touché, Lady Frances." The marquess's enjoyment of this bantering was not lost on the assembled company, and his partner was subjected to careful scrutiny, some of it jealous, some of it intrigued, depending on the sex of the particular observer.

Intrigued himself, Julian continued, "And how do you like London? I gather it has been some time since you have been here."

Ignoring the last part of the question, she replied rather archly, "I keep myself tolerably amused, for there are diversions to be found here that appeal to even the most serious of minds, sir. Why, just tomorrow I have planned an extremely edifying tour of the Tower and an evening at Astley's Amphitheater."

"Astley'sAmphitheater!" He was astounded.

"Cassie and Frederick," she confided. "I'm afraid I've been accompanying Kitty about so much that except for giving them lessons, I have neglected them sadly."

"Lessons? You don't mean *you* teach them," he demanded incredulously.

"And why ever not? I know far more Greek, Latin, and history than the local curate, and I am a *much* more amusing teacher," she added defiantly.

His smile flashed again. "No, don't get on your high ropes again, my girl. I merely meant that a London Season is considered more than sufficient occupation for any young girl, much less handling an estate, much less instructing two energetic youngsters."

"I'm not just *any* girl, Lord Mainwaring." A corner of her mouth quivered in a half-smile as she added, "Nor am I young."

"Now, that's doing it much too brown, my child. I'm more awake on all suits you know, and you look like a green girl to me."

She retorted, "Well, I'm not. I've been attending to the management of the estate since a few years after Mama died so Papa could continue with his work."

Lord Mainwaring looked down at the girl—for she really was little more than a girl—dancing with him and began to wonder just how many other surprising talents she had. Considering the weight of the responsibilities she bore, he thought that her whimsically uttered words were far truer than she appeared to think them. She certainly was not "just any girl," but what that did make her, he wasn't quite sure. She appeared to possess the intellectual confidence of a much older, more worldly woman, but if Lady Streatham was to be believed, her apprehension of the challenges of the Season and life in the *ton* was that of any unfledged young woman. That being true, he supposed he owed her the sanction of his social support. He could not say exactly why he felt the urge to assist Lady Frances, except that as someone who had complicated affairs of his own to deal with, he sympathized and felt compelled to help smooth over as many difficulties as he could.

Neither Lord Mainwaring nor Lady Frances had been looking forward to Lady Richardson's ball, but as they rolled home in their separate carriages, each one was occupied by more pleasant thoughts of the evening than either one had anticipated.

10

It would be too much to say that Frances was besieged by admirers after her appearance at the ball, but she did have several callers. The first was the Comte de Vaudron, whose exquisite manners were put to a severe test the minute Higgins ushered him into the drawing room. Here he encountered Aunt Harriet, whose stiff "How de do" and basilisk stare were hardly encouraging. Fortunately his quick eye and Gallic genius for conversation connected the collection of orchids blooming in the window with this dry, spare little woman, and through a combination of adroit questioning and some happy reminiscences on the horticultural wonders of Greece, the Mediterranean, and his French possessions in the Caribbean, he soon had her happily discussing the various soils of these locales and the exacting climatic requirements of her own blooms.

It was thus that Lady Frances, descending from a morning session of lessons in the nursery, was astonished to discover the two of them together in the window bending over one of Aunt Harriet's particular favorites. So intent were they in their discussion that they did not hear her enter, and were both quite startled to find her regarding them amusedly when they turned around to resume their seats.

"Ah, *chérie*, the belle of the ball," began the *comte*, bowing over her hand.

"Don't be absurd," Frances reproved, but she looked pleased all the same.

Aunt Harriet's attention was fairly caught. "Frances, the belle of a ball?" She gave her niece a sharp look.

"No, Aunt Harriet, though I did have a better time than I expected."

"*Mais non*, Fanny, how can you say that you were not a belle when outside of Kitty, Lady Streatham, and Lady Jersey, you were the only one with whom Lord Mainwaring danced the entire evening? He enjoyed himself too."

"Oh, Monsieur le Comte," interrupted Frances.

He held up a graceful hand. " 'Uncle Maurice,' please, but Fannie, *ma chère*, you may not pay attention to what the *ton* thinks or says, but me, I know that it is no small triumph to partner Lord Julian Mainwaring and to amuse him while doing so."

She sighed. "You may be correct, but that doesn't concern me. What does concern me is that I have spent so much of my time attending to dress and balls and my own affairs that I have neglected Cassie and Frederick dreadfully. So I have promised to take them on a surfeit of excursions this week. We're on our way to the Tower directly, I'm afraid. Would you care to join us, Uncle Maurice?" Frances invited him.

"*Mais, certainement*," he accepted, rising to greet the twins as they burst into the room.

"Cassie! Freddie!" Frances brought the two of them to a screeching halt. "This is Uncle Maurice, a dear friend of Mother and Father's. He has agreed to accompany us to the Tower."

The twins did not appear to be entirely gratified by this change in plans, but the *comte* speedily dispelled their doubts. "*Mes enfants*, please tell me if you do not wish me to join your outing, but I hope you will let me come because I do confess a wish to see the room where those two poor princes were so foully murdered." This very natural interest convinced them that Uncle Maurice was a "right one," and they enthusiastically added their invitations to their sister's. There was a brief scurrying for bonnets and coats while the carriage was brought round to the door.

As they rolled along toward the Tower, with Wellington in his usual position on the box, Freddie turned to the *comte*. "Uncle Maurice, sir?"

"*Mais oui, mon ami.*"

"You *are* French, are you not?"

"*Assurément.*"

"And you are a count, aren't you?"

"That, *mon ami*, depends on who is ruling France. Soemtimes I am Monsieur le Comte and sometimes plain *citoyen*, but I find 'Uncle' a far more honorable and amusing title than all of these."

"But what I mean, sir is: did you see anyone guillotined, or did you barely escape with your life?" Freddie asked in a hopeful tone.

The comte shook his head apologetically. "*Non*, Freddie, I regret to inform you that I was in Greece with your mother and father when the Bastille fell, and I have been traveling or in Great Britain the rest of the time, so I missed everything, even the Terror. I am afraid to say that my life has been extremely dull."

Fortunately for the comte's reputation, Lady Frances interrupted. "That's not at all true. Tell them about the time when you were captured by Greek bandits."

The twins' eyes widened expectantly. "Oh, please tell us, do," they breathed.

"Let us save that for another day. Here we are at the Tower, and one can't have too much blood and adventure in one day, you know—bad for the digestion." The twins looked doubtful; both were possessed of stomachs that would have done a goat proud, and both had an insatiable appetite for exactly such stories of gore and daring, but it wouldn't do to press their new friend too much.

The myriad of attractions to be explored at the historic spot put an end to all further discussion. Cassie and Frederick gazed at the yeoman warders in their Tudor uniforms, listened to the croaking of the sinister ravens on the green, and pictured all those who had laid their heads on the block there: Anne Boleyn,

Sir Thomas More, Sir Walter Raleigh, Lady Jane Grey. They followed an ancient woman who unlocked the vaults containing the crown jewels. Cassie was particularly captivated by the great golden orb reputed to contain, according to her elder sister, a piece of the true cross. Freddie, on the other hand, scoffed at the pile of useless jewels, preferring the golden spurs worn at coronations. They emerged from the gloom to peep at the lions in the Tower menagerie, but gave them scant attention in their haste to see the highlight of the visit—the room where the two little princes had been imprisoned before their mysterious and unfortunate end. They listened in fascinated horror as Frances recounted the tragic tale with all its grisly overtones. She was an excellent storyteller and her small listeners were spellbound. Even the *comte* was captivated. It would have been difficult to improve on the delights of the day, but when the *comte* treated them all to ices at Gunter's, their cups were filled to the brim. "I say, Fanny, London *is* a great place. Why've we never been here before?" Cassie asked. Freddie, his mouth too full of ice to say anything, nodded his head in fervent agreement.

The only member of the party not entirely satisfied with the day was Wellington. His winning expression and engaging manner, which never failed to win him friends and admirers wherever he went, had not done the least bit of good with the grim-faced yeoman at the Tower. "The Tower bain't be no place for dogs. Hit's han 'istoric monooment and that bain't no place for dogs," he stated stubbornly. Wag his tail and smile though he would, Wellington could not get him to abandon this unreasonable position, so he waited rather glumly with John Coachman on his box, regretting that he would not be able to brag to Nelson about seeing such a bloody spot. Fortunately John was a friend, and his companionship lessened the indignity and boredom of it all to some extent.

They arrived back at Brook Street to discover that Bertie had called but had promised to return. He was ushered in not much later, to find Aunt Harriet tending her orchids and Frances writing instructions to be delivered by John to the housekeeper back at Cresswell. Bidding him a barely civil "Good-Day," Aunt Harriet made a swift exit, leaving him to gaze after her in a slightly bemused manner. "Lucky thing you ain't countin' on her to introduce you to the *ton*," he observed.

"You are right, of course, but she never meddles, you know. And if I need to display the respectable nature of our establishment, she is always available to stare down the impertinent."

Bertie was in total agreement there. He had come to say that thinking she might like to hear Catalani sing, he had procured a box and wondered if she would join him, Lady Streatham, and Kitty the next evening at the opera. Guessing that he had no real love for this type of amusement, she was touched by his generosity. "Bertie, it is too kind of you! I am assured you can't like to hear one of those 'dashed females screeching in Italian.' " Bertie looked slightly conscious at this perspicacious observation, but remained silent. She continued, "I hope that you may be well-rewarded for your magnanimity and that the prettiest opera dancers will be onstage later in the evening."

"Fanny!" He was scandalized. "You *mustn't* say such things!"

"I know, Bertie, but you're like a brother to me."

He replied with some heat, "But dash it, Fan, a gently bred female ain't even supposed to *know* such things." He continued, fixing her with a minatory stare, "And if she does, she certainly ain't supposed to let on—not to *anyone*!"

"I suppose you are right, Bertie," she sighed. "But it would make so much more sense if gently bred ladies paid more attention to these opera dancers. If they did, their husbands wouldn't need the dancers in the first place."

This piece of logic completely overset her companion. "I am not at all sure I dare escort you tomorrow," he sputtered.

"No, Bertie," she said soothingly, "I was just thinking aloud, and I promise not to do it again. I shall behave with the most rigid propriety, truly I shall."

"Well, don't think aloud. Better yet, don't think at all," he cautioned.

She laughed and held out her hand. "What a good friend you are. And I thank you kindly for arranging such a treat for us all."

Frances enjoyed Catalani's singing immensely the next

evening, though privately she wished the prima donna had demonstrated a little less histrionic and a little more dramatic talent. Catalani shared her attraction as a curiosity, at least for Kitty and Lady Frances, with someone else. Kitty had been begging Bertie to point out all the notables, a task for which he was admirably suited. He was happy to oblige, but seemed deliberately to ignore one astoundingly beautiful dark-haired woman in the box opposite. She was ablaze with diamonds and scantily attired in a dress of vivid green satin which clung to every curve of her voluptuous figure. This she displayed to the delight of several gentlemen crowded around as she reclined seductively in her chair. "But, Bertie, who is that?" Kitty demanded, nodding behind her fan in the woman's direction.

"Don't look!" Bertie almost upset his own chair in his frantic attempt to distract her. Kitty was taken aback at such a reaction from the ordinarily phlegmatic Bertie. "Take no notice of her, Kitty. That's Lady Vanessa Welford."

She was puzzled. "But if she's a lady, why shouldn't I notice her?"

Bertie ran his fingers rather desperately under his elegantly tied cravat, which suddenly seemed to be strangling him. "Well, she's a lady, but not much of a *lady*, if you see what I mean," he hazarded hopefully.

The familiar sound of the name which had been nagging her memory suddenly jogged it back to tea at the dowager Marchioness of Mainwaring's. "Oh," she exclaimed as she leaned forward to get a better view. "That's Uncle Julian's mistress."

Bertie was now certain that his valet had, in a fit of murderous rage at the number of cravats ruined that evening, tied this one too tightly on purpose to strangle him. It definitely seemed as though he had to gasp for breath, but at last he did manage to force out a good "Ssh!"

Though Kitty's remark had seemed to thunder in his ears, it had in fact gone no further than Lady Frances', but she was eager to discover just what type of woman did attract a man reputed to have such exacting standards for feminine attractiveness. Undoubtedly Lady Welford was magnificent. Her raven hair contrasted with seductive ivory shoulders and a tempting red mouth, but Frances took exception to her self-satisfied expression and guessed that she would not improve upon acquaintance, at least not acquaintance with another female. She told herself that it was far better to be appreciated for oneself and the less-tangible personal attractions of intelligence and character than to be admired for purely physical attributes. She had certainly educated herself on this premise, paying more attention to developing her mind and her values rather than a sense for fashion or the other feminine arts of attraction and dalliance. However, for one brief moment as she observed the magnetic woman across from her, so secure in her beauty, so confident of her power to win love and admiration, she questioned the wisdom of her choice. No matter that she told herself that a few years would prove her attractions to be the more durable ones. For once she would have preferred to have men love her beauty to distraction and women envy it to the same degree than to be respected for good sense. But such treacherous thoughts were gone in an instant as she again gave herself over to the pleasure of Catalani's rich voice and the fineness of the music.

11

B ertie Montgomery was not the only one who took it upon himself to introduce Lady Frances to some of London's fashionable haunts. In keeping with his impulsively formed resolve to smooth her social path, Lord Mainwaring decided that a drive with him in Hyde Park would be just the thing to set her feet firmly on this path. His lordship was a man of decision. Having settled upon a course of action, he executed it immediately, and the next day saw him knocking on the Cresswell's door while his magnificent grays stamped impatiently. Higgins ushered him in at a slightly inauspicious moment as Aunt Harriet, in a black humor at the inexplicable dropping of blossoms from a particular favorite, came bustling out of the drawing room without the least looking where she was going and collided solidly with him. "Oh, *do* get out of the way, you beast." It was a minute before Mainwaring, somewhat taken aback by this abrupt address, realized that as the collision and remark were simultaneous, she could not be referring to him. He looked down to see the culprit—Nelson—brushing affectionately against her skirts. "Oh!" Aunt Harriet recovered herself and directed a quelling stare at his lordship.

"And who are you, sirrah, to come barging in like a great looby?"

Mainwaring took her measure instantly and replied meekly, "Mainwaring, at your service, ma'am. I do apologize. I had not realized you were quitting the room. I shall be more careful in the future." Though he had introduced himself, Mainwaring had not the slightest idea of the identity of the tartar whose gaze had lost some of its ferocity at this graceful speech.

He was rescued by Lady Frances, who appeared just then in the doorway. Seeing her aunt and guest eyeing each other warily, she hastened to introduce them, mentioning to Aunt Harriet as she did so the great number of out-of-the-way places Lord Mainwaring had visited. Her aunt, never one to miss an opportunity to learn about or procure more specimens to add to her collection, looked speculatively at him, but before she could ask any useful questions, Lady Frances forestalled her. "How nice to see you, Lord Mainwaring. I hope I haven't kept you. Higgins tells me you came in your curricle. I hope your horses have not been kept waiting too long."

"No, ma'am, thank you. I drove here hoping I could convince you to come for a drive in the park."

Lady Frances may not have agreed with the *ton*'s unquestioning adulation of Lord Mainwaring, but she recognized an honor when it was offered, and was gratified. Regretfully she answered, "It is too kind in you and I would love it of all things, but I promised Cassie, Freddie, and Ned that I would take them to see Lord Elgin's marbles. It is the most unfortunate thing, and I do truly appreciate your offer."

"Don't refine upon it too much. Perhaps you will like to another day." Mainwaring's words were gracious enough, but there was a hard light in his eyes and he looked to be a little put out. In point of fact, he was. People of any sort, especially young females, rarely received his invitations with anything but excessive gratitude. The fact that he usually scorned such gratitude did nothing to lessen his pique at Frances for refusing him, and refusing him in favor of a parcel of brats at that!

Correctly interpreting these signs, Lady Frances experienced a tingle of satisfaction at having pierced his arrogance. She swiftly banished this ignoble thought, asking instead, "Would you like to go with us?"

Cassie and Frederick, who had now appeared and had seen from the expedition to the Tower that grown-ups could enhance an expedition, chimed in, "Oh, please do come along, sir."

Julian couldn't remember when his mere presence, regardless of social position or fortune, had been of material importance to anyone. He was oddly touched by the genuine invitation he could read in three pairs of eyes. Before he knew what he was about, he was not only accepting a place in a schoolroom outing but also offering Freddie a ride next to him in his curricle, with a promise of the return trip to Cassie. His second surprise came when he realized that, in a reversal of the usual way of things, he was highly gratified at the approval he saw in Lady Frances' eyes. It was certainly all very odd.

During the ride to Lord Elgin's mansion in Park Lane, he had ample opportunity to become acquainted with the loquacious Freddie. The conversation centered chiefly around the various points and capabilities of the "prime bits of blood" drawing the carriage, but in the course of the discussion Mainwaring learned a great deal about the Cresswell household. Freddie artlessly confided that Lady Frances, though an excellent horsewoman, usually left the selection of her horseflesh to her groom, which Freddie thought was a great deal too bad. "I know she has a superior eye for a horse, and I've asked her times out of mind why she doesn't choose her own. After all, I could help her. But she says that horse fairs and Tattersall's are no place for a lady. Can you believe such sad stuff? Fanny doesn't say that running Cresswell or teaching in the schoolroom is no place for a lady, so I don't understand such a paltry attitude in this case."

By describing some of the ugly customers who turned up at the fairs, and the purely masculine nature of the clientele at Tattersall's, the marquess was able to restore Lady Frances' credibility with her younger brother. "After all, Freddie, choosing a good horse is a tricky business. In addition to being able to recognize a thoroughbred from ear to hoof, it requires a good deal of discussion about the price. There is not much time for social niceties and polite conversation in this sort of business, so it is best that men who are less likely to be offended by plain dealing take care of the entire business. Don't you agree?''

Freddie listened intently to this description of the male world. The idea of purely masculine society appealed mightily to him. Cassie and Fanny were great guns. They never fussed if one tore one's clothes or got them dirty. In fact, Cassie was as likely to do this as Freddie. But they couldn't share all his interests the way brothers would, he confided. This rather wistful comment brought back a fleeting memory of the marquess' own childhood and the scrapes and adventures he had shared with his brother. He felt the wish to see that Freddie was given an opportunity to enjoy male companionship. The thought developed no further than that because they had arrived at the building Lord Elgin had built next to his residence to house the marbles he had brought back from Greece.

The twins had not been at all sure they would find these "old statues and stuff," as Freddie scoffingly referred to them, nearly so interesting as the Tower, but they knew that their sister had been there with their parents when Lord Elgin first began to send them home, and that she was longing to see them. So they had gone with as good grace as possible in two eleven-year-olds dragged along to look at antiquities, and were agreeably surprised. Once again Frances' talent for narration held them enthralled as she identified various figures on the friezes and described the battles and contests among the various gods and goddesses, who turned out to be no less bloodthirsty and conniving than the monarchs who had given such an infamous history to the Tower. Freddie was extremely taken with the war horses that charged with such strength and fury, while Cassie marveled that the delicately streaming draperies were carved out of marble and not the gauze they resembled. Even though she had been quite young, Frances was able to remember and describe the magnificent temples that Pericles had had built on the ruins of Persian buildings high on the Acropolis. She told of the magnificent columned porch of the Parthenon and explained where various pieces they were now observing would have been. Her pictures of life in Periclean Athens were so vivid and the recreation of the mythology so gripping that even

Mainwaring, hearing snatches of her monologue from the other end of the room, moved slowly toward the little group to catch more. He was naturally familiar with most of what she was saying, but he was caught by the colorful language and animated delivery and found himself thinking rather wryly that it was a pity such histrionic talent would never appear onstage.

The door at one end of the room opened to admit none other than the Comte de Vaudron. He was welcomed joyfully by the twins. "I thought it would not be long before you paid them a visit," he remarked to Frances, including the entire collection with a graceful sweep of his hand. In answer to the questions with which Cassie and Frederick were besieging him, he continued, "One at a time, *mes enfants*. I am here because I originally helped Lord Elgin rescue these works of art, and now I am helping him to convince your government to buy them from him so that everyone will have a chance to admire them." He led them off to look at some of his particular favorites, telling them as he did so about the careful crating and shipping of these priceless pieces and the difficulties in transporting them from Greece to London. The details of this saga were almost as interesting as Frances' stories, and the twins listened eagerly.

Meanwhile, Mainwaring had joined Frances as she examined the flowing draperies that had so captivated Cassie. "I agree with you," he said, correctly interpreting her expression. "It is a pity the grace and simplicity of such artists should have been ignored for so long."

"Yes, and their beautiful sense of architectural proportion, and the lightness of their interiors as well," she added. Then, as she realized that he had voiced her own thoughts, she asked, "But however did you know what I was feeling?"

He replied with some amusement at her astonishment at what was merely a shrewd observation: "I could have guessed, knowing who your father was, that you would have shared this admiration for the culture. But having observed the elegance and simplicity of your own taste, I know it to be so."

"But how, after such a brief acquaintance, can you know what my tastes are?" she pursued.

His amusement deepened. "My dear child, the design of the

library at Cresswell, the Adam decorations in Brook Street, and the uncomplicated lines of your style of dress all show you to be an appreciator of classical simplicity. Besides, you are not a fussy person. Anyone who has spent the least amount of time with you would know that."

She was surprised that a man reputed to pay so little attention to his fellowmen should be so perceptive, but remarked, "I see you are determined to make me a bluestocking, sir, and would have me making an intellectual feat out of something as mundane as decorating my house and my person."

He answered with unwonted seriousness, "No, not in the slightest. It is the very consistency of it all that proves you are not a bluestocking. Bluestockings try to stun the world with their erudition, and they usually pay a good deal of attention to the current tastes of the *ton* when selecting an area in which to excel. You, on the other hand, have shaped your own tastes after your own reading and learning, else they wouldn't all contribute to what is more a style of living than an aesthetic preference."

Frances was gratified and not a little touched by this sympathetic reading of her character. She remained thoughtfully silent for some time until the children and the count rejoined them. Remedying her earlier omission, she introduced Julian to the count, who recognized him with pleasure. "Ah, Julian Mainwaring, I hear great things of you from my friend Charlton. I am delighted to know you, *monsieur*." Mainwaring, disclaiming any real political or diplomatic expertise, discovered that the *comte*'s was more than the conventional flattery. "I agree with your opinions, my boy. The world may say that history is shaped by battles and the valor of its leaders, but I believe more and more it will become a question of economics. It is the businessman and not the generals who will shape history from now on. The countinghouses and the Exchange will be the true battlefields, and England will need men such as you, who are experienced in these things, to lead her." This approbation was not lost on Lady Frances, and she wondered if she had not been a little foolish in taking on such an opponent at the Streathams' dinner.

They bade good-bye to the *comte* and headed home, this time with Cassie sitting proudly next to the marquess. She was less voluble than her brother, but by no means less enterprising, and by the time they reached Brook Street, had managed—Mainwaring was still not sure exactly how—to extract an invitation to Astley's Amphitheater. She had barely been lifted down from her perch before she was sharing this delightful prospect with her brother and sister.

Lady Frances was well aware of her small sister's cozening ways and strongly suspected that the marquess, clever though he was, had been skillfully maneuvered into this position. She sent the children inside, then turned to him, extending her hand. "Thank you, sir, for joining us. It was very kind in you, but you mustn't let Cassie inveigle you into what would be very poor entertainment for you."

The marquess had just been wondering about this himself, but her words put him on his mettle. "By no means. It has been an age since I went. I enjoy good showmanship and beautiful horseflesh as much as anyone. I don't pretend to know a great deal about children, so I do hope you will accompany us. Actually, I suppose Cassie and Freddie would be happy to enlighten me if I didn't know how to go on, but I don't feel I have quite your talent for making an outing memorable."

She smiled ruefully. "All you have to do is invite them. It is I, their sister, who must resort to stratagems to keep them amused and in line." All the same, she found herself looking forward to the entertainment as much as Cassie and Freddie.

12

The marquess was as good as his word, but having considered the claims of Ned and Nigel, decided it would be extremely impolitic of him to exclude them merely because Cassie had had the originality and temerity to instigate this amusement. Until now, he had paid scant attention to Ned, who was as quiet and studious as Kitty was gay, and he felt a trifle guilty for having overlooked the lad. This seemed an excellent opportunity to become better acquainted. Nigel, he knew, was a lively, friendly boy who could be counted on to enjoy anything and anyone. Besides, Mainwaring did owe Lady Streatham a debt of gratitude for taking the burden of Kitty's Season off his hands. So it was quite a large party that was ensconced several evenings later in a box at Astley's Royal Amphitheater. The mere spectacle of the theater itself, with its huge chandelier illuminating the largest stage in London, was enough to take the children's breath away. Even the irrepressible Frederick could not find words sufficient to the occasion. He gazed in awed silence as Philip Astley, resplendent on his white charger, led the circus parade. The children's eyes grew rounder and rounder as wonder succeeded wonder. It seemed impossible to believe that a horse could dance a hornpipe. That he could improve upon this exhibition by lifting a kettle from the fire to make a pot of tea was beyond all belief. They held their breaths as John Astley rode round and round the arena on two horses before dancing on their backs. There were conjurers and trapeze artists, but nothing could outshine the horses and the magnificent equestrian feats of the Astleys themselves.

Glancing at Frances, Lord Mainwaring could see she was enjoying it as much as the others. He found her unconscious enthusiasm refreshing after the boredom so assiduously cultivated by most Londoners. He still could not refrain from inquiring, "Are you enjoying yourself?"

She turned to him, her face alight with pleasure, and exclaimed, "Oh, ever so much! I came with Mother and Father when we returned to England twelve years ago, and I have been wanting so to come back ever since. But the twins were born and Mother died the next year so I have not until now had the chance. But it is just as wonderful as I remembered it!"

Mainwaring reflected that if her mother had died so soon after and that if even a few of the anecdotes concerning Lord Cresswell's legendary absentmindedness were true, she must have had very little time in her life for amusements of any kind. The thought of this, coupled with the very real pleasure he derived from witnessing her simple enjoyment, made him resolve to provide her with an amusing time in addition to smoothing her path socially. It had been a long time since he had been with people who were simply having a wonderful time, unconscious of everyone else around and wholly involved with what was happening onstage. Even Ned, ordinarily so quiet and reserved, was exclaiming pointing as excitedly as everyone else. The natural ebullience of Nigel and Freddie appeared to have done the lad some good.

"I can't wait to get home to practice. I bet I could stand on Prince's back like that . . . with a bit of practice, of course," Freddie boasted.

"With practice, of course," Nigel jeered. "You know you couldn't do it the way Mr. Astley does, without holding the reins."

"I'm sure I—" began Freddie.

Frances interrupted him. "Well, it isn't as easy as it looks, I can tell you. I had John Coachman balancing me on top of my pony for hours on end after I first came here, but to no avail. I did well enough when he let go, until the pony moved, and then I slid off his back as if it had been greased. I landed with a crash, tore my dress, covered myself with dirt, was stiff and disgraced for weeks." The children were highly diverted at the idea of the immaculate Lady Frances covered with dirt.

But Freddie was not to be put off. "Thank you for your advice, Fanny, but you *are* a girl, you know," he said with lofty superiority, "and girls aren't as expert with horseflesh as men are." The marquess recognized echoes, though improved upon by the speaker, of his own conversation with the boy, and smiled to himself. He had no doubt at all that such an opinion would find little favor with Frances.

He was entirely correct in his suspicions. "Freddie, you insufferable prig!" Both Cassie and Frances rounded on him. "You know that both of us ride as well as you do."

"And," Cassie continued triumphantly, "Fanny can drive horses and a phaeton and you've only tried the pony cart once around the park at Cresswell."

Freddie deemed it wise to withdraw from such an unequal contest and retired to the background with an air of injured dignity.

At this moment Frances became aware of their host, who was sitting back, arms crossed over his chest, regarding the scene with a great deal of amusement. "I do beg your pardon. I can't think how I came to be so ill-bred."

"I can," he replied, smiling. "Deliberate provocation." He turned to Freddie. "Next time, my boy, you should be more subtle in your attack and take on your opponents only one at a time."

Freddie grinned shamefacedly. "I'm sorry, sir, to act so childish." He threw a challenging look in his elder sister's direction.

"Not at all," replied his lordship. "It was a salutary lesson. I can see that I should have had sisters. With such treatment, a fellow could never come by a high enough opinion of himself to become 'arrogant.' '' He quizzed Frances wickedly as he made his last remark. Try as she would, she could not keep a becoming blush from suffusing her face. Whether this was a result of having her insulting reference to him thrown back in her face or her sudden realization that the marquess had a singularly attractive smile, Frances was not at all certain.

The schoolroom party labeled it a highly successful time, and the marquess was pleased to see that Nigel and Freddie were questioning Ned as to his collection of tin soldiers and that Frances looked relaxed and free of the slightly wary look she had worn at Lady Richardson's ball.

13

After spending so much time among the schoolroom set, Lord Mainwaring looked forward to a respite from such fatiguing company in the welcoming and flattering arms of Lady Vanessa Welford. She was far too clever to let her true feelings show, but she had been vexed by his absence. She knew that he had his niece to escort to Lady Richardson's ball, to which Lady Welford had not been invited. She schemed a great deal to maintain her air of respectability, and it was a source of constant irritation to her that some hostesses still refused to include her on their guest lists. Unfortunately, it was just those ladies who held the most influential positions in society. Though she had not been at the ball, Vanessa knew very well that Mainwaring had danced with his niece, Lady Sally Jersey, Lady Elizabeth Streatham, and Lady Frances Creswell. His niece and cousin were an obvious duty. Sally Jersey would equally obviously be unavoidable, and Lady Welford knew Mainwaring to be immune to that flirtatious lady's charms. But Lady Frances Cresswell was not so obvious. This roused her curiosity, and because she was attracted to Lord Mainwaring, her jealousy. It was not actually jealousy, but it was considerably stronger than mere curiosity. Had she been a less-fashionable creature, one whose existence extended beyond the ballroom, opera, theater, and Bond Street modistes, she might have been even more curious about his latest expeditions to Lord Elgin's or Astley's Amphitheater. It was fortunate for her peace of mind that she was not, that she did not move in such circles, or that she was not acquainted with anyone who did, or she might have been more alarmed than she was.

Lady Welford and Mainwaring were in his carriage en route to see Kean at Drury Lane when she began to question him subtly about the ball. She had heard it was a sad crush. Did Kitty enjoy herself? Was she a success? Had he even been able to dance with her amongst all the younger men aspiring to her hand? Had the rest of the company been very dull and respectable? They must have been if he had been forced to dance with Sally Jersey and some hitherto unknown young lady whose name escaped her.

"Lady Frances Cresswell, perhaps," he hazarded with a dangerous glint in his eye. Lord Mainwaring did not relish anyone taking a proprietary interest in his affairs.

"Yes, that was it." She nodded, the diamonds at her throat sparkling in the light of a passing streetlamp. "I have not ever heard her name. Who is she, Julian?"

His reply reassured her. "She is a neighbor of Kitty and Ned's who was kind enough to come to London during Kitty's first Season, as she knew Kitty to be a little apprehensive."

"Oh, she is quite a bit older, then?" Lady Welford's sources had implied that the lady in question was young, but someone who was this much a mistress of her affairs and who lent support to a young girl must be a spinster of some years.

Lord Mainwaring could have undeceived her, but he did not relish the tone of the conversation. "I had not thought to ask the lady her age," he answered blightingly.

"Oh, Julian, do not be angry," she pleaded, tracing the strong line of his jaw with a caressing finger. "I was only thinking of you. I know how you detest all those women who constantly throw out lures to you, whether they are the girls or their mamas."

The marquess was not so easily hoodwinked and he did not believe her for an instant, but in the interests of a peaceful evening he appeared mollified as he caught her hand and kissed it lingeringly. "Your solicitude overwhelms me, Vanessa, my dear," he murmured, gazing intently at her.

Vanessa, responding to the attraction of those dark blue eyes, failed to detect the undertone of sarcasm in his voice. She sighed contentedly and leaned back luxuriously against the squabs, revealing, as she did so, rounded white shoulders and a daring décolletage.

Kean was performing his much-celebrated *Richard III*, but Mainwaring, who considered him a shade on the melodramatic side, though admittedly an inspired actor, had come to the theater for other purposes than watching the famous man rave and roll his eyes. He was certain that he would encounter Lord Charlton there, and he felt that the delicacy of the business for which Charlton had approached him required the discretion of a seemingly chance encounter. His surmise was correct and he came upon Charlton in the gallery. They exchanged a few desultory remarks on Kean, the general public's opinion of his intensely original interpretation of Shakespeare, and their own slightly more critical views before Julian remarked casually, "Speaking of dramatic and theatrical natures, I saw Prinny the other day."

"Oh? And how is he? I haven't seen him this age." The other man's tone was equally casual, but there was a wealth of unspoken questions in his eyes.

"He's fine as fivepence. And he is slowly abandoning the idea of a purely Chinese theme for his Pavilion for an Indian motif, and wanted to consult me on decorations and architecture. You know the plan Repton submitted to him years ago was in the Indian style, but he hadn't the money at the time. Now he seems to think he has, and has urged Nash to make his alterations in that style. What a damned extravagance! But his pioneering use of cast-iron construction is something I would like to encourage, considering the plight that industry will be facing without the war and demand for artillery. We naturally turned from Indian art to India, to the world in general, and affairs in Europe in particular. He seems to be losing all his enthusiasm for Alexander as the world's enthusiasm for the Tzar grows. Poor Prinny, he doesn't like others to be more popular than he—as though that would be difficult. At any rate, as well as being a notable diplomat—or meddler, however you see it—Alexander is much more slender and fair than Prinny. He is also an absolute monarch and Prinny is inclined to be jealous of all that power. He seemed to welcome the chance to throw a dash of cold water on the flames of Alexander's enthusiasm for his much-vaunted Holy Alliance.''

Lord Charlton voiced his approval. ''Very good, my boy, and I do thank you. I know it must have been a crashing bore to listen to those never-ending plans of his.''

''No trouble at all, George. Besides, one must give him credit, you know. Prinny is really quite an amusing and artistic fellow. It's a great deal too bad he happens to be a prince as well.''

Having concluded this satisfactory interchange, they proceeded to their respective boxes. It was with some difficulty that the marquess entered his, owing to the number of admirers crowded around Vanessa. Lady Welford might have lost her heart to her latest flirt, but she had certainly not lost her craving for masculine attention. She laughed and flirted, flashing her magnificent dark eyes, which seemed to promise anything and everything to whomever her glance lighted on. Her more rational self also dictated that it would be a politic thing to encourage other *cicisbeos*, despite her interest in the marquess. Seeing her constantly surrounded by males would make him proud to have won a prize so desirable to others, and it would keep him from becoming sure of her affections. When that happened, men were all too often known to ignore their mistresses as thoroughly as they ignored their wives. It would do Mainwaring good to be forced to compete with other men for her attention. And last, if by some incredible chance he did leave her, she didn't want to be caught without anyone to pay her court. It thus behooved her to cultivate as many admirers as possible. Hearing the door to the box open, she turned to see Mainwaring. Extending a swanlike white arm to him, she cooed invitingly, ''Do come back and sit down, my lord.'' She pulled a chair for him close to her, creating a sense of intimacy, as though they were the only occupants of the theater. She looked so lovely with diamonds sparkling at her smooth white

neck and in her dark hair, her brows arched delicately over eyes
alight with the flattery she'd been receiving, and a faint flush
suffusing her beautifully sculptured neck and arms. Julian
wondered at himself that he remained so unmoved by all this
beauty, that he could mentally note and catalog all these features
without feeling the least desire for her. He supposed he had been
thinking too much about his conversation with Lord Charlton
and all its political ramifications. He dismissed his lack of feeling
as only natural in someone who had switched in an instant from
playing a vital role in world politics to being reduced to flirting
in a box at a play. He watched the rest of the act in thoughtful
silence while his charming companion continued to laugh and
chat with her eager swains.

As he escorted her in his carriage back to Mount Street, the
marquess reflected rather cynically on the flatness of the
evening. With the exception of the encounter with Charlton,
it had been like so many other evenings: dressing to be seen
and admired; selecting a place to be seen and admired; and then
being seen and admired, as though there were nothing more
to life. Unconsciously he compared this evening to the one at
Astley's and the pleasure every person in the party derived from
the skill and daring of the performers. Everyone had been in
high spirits that owed nothing to a selfish craving for attention,
but to a zest for living and enjoying each other. That last thought
caught him up short. I'm not only becoming cynical but also
entering my dotage, he admonished himself.

Vanessa had ordered an intimate supper in her boudoir.
Certainly she had done everything to create a romantic
atmosphere: peach satin draperies and upholstery coupled with
the warm glow of a few strategically placed candles enhanced
the warmth of her skin, lent her dark eyes an air of mystery,
and hid any possible wrinkles. The food was exquisite, the wine
a perfect complement to the dinner and the evening. Her conversation, consisting chiefly of the latest *on-dits*, was both amusing
and provocative. But somehow, the very skillfulness of her
creation robbed it of all romance for Mainwaring. The perfect
setting was more a credit to her skill as a woman of the world
than to her heart and its supposed passion for him. Or, if passion

did exist, he reflected cynically, it was more for the money and position he represented than for his personal or mental attractions. The evening was anesthetic to his senses. He did not even bother to protest when she draped her soft arms enticingly around his neck, though he did not feel in the mood for lovemaking. I think too much, he told himself. Deliberately emptying his mind of all possible thought or observation, he gave himself up to her skillful seduction.

Sometime later he slipped out of her house and into the fresh night air. He was glad he had sent his carriage home as he sauntered along savoring the coolness of the breeze that ruffled the leaves on the trees in Berkeley Square and cleared his head. The entire evening had all been so predictable, so . . . so very . . . "flat"—that was the word. Even the passion had been practiced rather than experienced. How can I feel so thoroughly jaded at thirty-five? he wondered. It must be time for a change of scene, a change of climate. As soon as Kitty has had her Season and I have found a man to look after Camberly properly, I shall get away. It's been some time since anyone has visited the plantations in Jamaica. I ought to take a look at them for myself. Somewhat cheered by this, he entered Mainwaring House, where Kilson was waiting for him. The sight of that old ally's battered face with its reminders of the adventures they had shared further improved his temper, and he was able to fall into a deep sleep untroubled by additional disquieting reflections.

14

I n contrast to the marquess, Lady Frances was finding London progressively exciting. Lady Streatham had most graciously taken her around with Kitty and introduced her to a variety of fashionable and intellectual delights she had not before encountered in the capital. If someone had told her before she left the country that she would spend an entire morning shopping in Harding, Howell, and Company's Grand Fashionable Magazine, she would have laughed at the absurdity of it. Yet she heartily enjoyed wandering from one department to another admiring the taste of the fittings and the glass partitions that separated them. When it came time to go, she was astonished at how quickly the time had passed while she strolled around looking at everything from furs, fans, silks, and laces to jewelry, clocks, perfumes, and toiletries. Always slightly inclined to scorn fashion and the hours people spent at modistes' and milliners', she was surprised to discover the artistic satisfaction to be found looking at beautiful silks and damasks, exquisite laces and gaily colored ribbons, not to mention the challenge in envisioning how to display them to their best advantage. She realized that to many, the pursuit of fashion was a form of aesthetic pleasure which, in addition to exercising their artistic and creative sensibilities, brought the additional reward of being regarded with envy and admiration by those around them. She purchased a handsome shawl of Norwich silk and some ribbons to brighten up a bonnet that had somehow always lacked the style she liked. Kitty found a beautiful corsage of silk flowers to add some color to the delicate pastel hues of the requisite attire of a young unmarried woman this Season. Lady Elizabeth discovered some magnificent beading at an excellent price, so all three ladies voted the excursion exceedingly satisfactory.

Lady Frances' more formal artistic tastes were stimulated and gratified when she was invited to join Lady Elizabeth on an excursion to the Royal Academy's exhibition at Somerset House. "I simply must go so that I shall be able to tell people that I have seen it," Lady Elizabeth declared. "Besides, Lawrence's portrait of my dear friend Georgiana Beaumont is being shown, along with his portrait of the Prince Regent, so you see it is imperative that I at least take a peep. Critics insist that Lawrence's portrait of Prinny is 'the finest portrait of the heir apparent that has yet been painted,' but I am not the least interested in paintings and have no artistic tastes whatsoever to help me understand or criticize them. Music, I enjoy and understand, but painting, especially portraiture, does not speak to me. Mainwaring says that you have an excellent eye, and Bertie praises your aesthetic sense excessively, so I do hope you'll come with me and tell me what to think or say, should someone ask me."

Frances could not help feeling gratified at both the wording and the invitation, though she suspected Lady Elizabeth of improving on Mainwaring's and Bertie's admiration of her aesthetic sensibilities. Still, it was very flattering to have them remarked on at all. "I shall do my best, ma'am," she replied. "But don't depend too much on me to articulate what is thought to be the most fashionable opinion. I do not in general admire Lawrence, and certainly do not agree with so many nowadays who consider him the equal of Gainsborough and Reynolds. Lawrence encourages social pretensions, painting the flashy exteriors of his patrons—the way they wish to be seen—instead of trying to reveal the personality underneath. Still, with those two great portraitists gone, he is the best of those that remain. I confess I am more interested in Turner.''

"Turner!" exclaimed Lady Streatham. Though she knew little about this unusual artist, she was nevertheless surprised that he should appeal to Lady Frances Cresswell. "I shouldn't think you would care for his work in the slightest. I remember seeing *Snowstorm* at the exhibition some years ago. It was all sky and violence, far too emotional for someone of your quiet elegance, I should think.''

Lady Frances was oddly upset by this remark. Did she appear so cool and unfeeling, then? She knew her natural reserve was interpreted at best as dignity and at worst as shyness. But perhaps it was also interpreted as indifference. Could it be true that Mainwaring's description of her as a prude—a remark she had interpreted as one made solely to provoke her—was in fact the articulation of general opinion?

Lady Elizabeth, noticing an unwontedly thoughtful expression creep into Frances' eyes, wondered what in her remark could have prompted such serious reflection. She promptly strove to banish this during the drive to Somerset House by chatting gaily of Freddie's and Nigel's latest antics. "I hear from Nigel that Mainwaring took the schoolroom party to Astley's. How did you ever accomplish that? If he even notices the existence of children, which is highly unusual, he ordinarily doesn't pay the least attention to them.''

The serious look vanished instantly, and Lady Frances laughed. "It was not my doing. Cassie was riding in his curricle on the return from seeing Lord Elgin's marbles, and I believe she merely asked him. Lord Mainwaring never had the slightest chance. Once Cassie has set her mind to a thing, she will brook no refusal.''

It was Lady Elizabeth's turn to look thoughtful. If she had been surprised to hear of the marquess's party at Astley's, she was astounded to learn of his expedition to view the marbles. He must be interested in Frances in some way to allow himself to be saddled with such lively children twice in one week. She had pushed him to waltz with Frances simply to ensure her acceptance in the *ton* and subsequent enjoyment of the Season.

Now she wondered if she might not have unwittingly done more than that. Julian rarely put himself out except for a few select relatives and friends. For those few, he would do anything in his power, or beyond it, to secure their happiness, but he had a hearty dislike of obligations to anyone else, and was brutal in squelching expectations before they arose. She immediately resolved to visit the dowager with this piece of information, and perhaps the two of them could puzzle it out. That lady had a way of selecting the most reliable gossipmongers and expertly separating mere conjecture from fact so that she unerringly arrived at the truth of the matter. Lady Elizabeth very much wanted to test out her speculations on that reliable sounding board.

Somerset House was a sad crush, so they had very little opportunity to study anything at great length. The portrait of Georgiana was seen and admired, though Frances thought privately that it could have been any face atop the magnificent gown and jewels, so little did the painting reveal of the sitter's character. However, she kept this particular opinion to herself. She did not hesitate to voice her annoyance that most of the paintings with true artistic merit had been "skied" high above the portraits that would capture the attention and commissions of the fashionable viewers, so that it was only with great difficulty that one could see them. "The way to recognize a person with true aesthetic sense," she confided to Lady Elizabeth as they left, "is to identify those with severe eyestrain and a crick in their necks." Still, she had enjoyed herself very much and was glad to have a sensible companion to view them with her.

Such had been her entertainment in London that Lady Frances began to feel quite guilty for having ignored her responsibilities. It seemed an age since she had given any serious thought to the affairs at Cresswell, and she had not even executed the business for which ostensibly she had come to London in the first place. She kept meaning to send a note around to Mr. Murray, once her father's publisher and now hers, but somehow each succeeding day brought with it a new amusement of some kind. One day she and Lady Streatham had taken the children to a balloon ascension at Vauxhall Gardens. Then, remembering her promise to Aunt Harriet, she arranged for a picnic party, consisting of the same group, at Kew Gardens, as well as another trip to the hothouses of the Botanic Society. These excursions were followed by a trip to Sadler's Wells, where the famous Grimaldi amazed them with his acrobatic feats, the absurd expressions on his mobile face, and his skill in juggling a seemingly incredible number of objects. Last, there was a visit to the British Museum to see two helmets. One had been dug up from the ground where the Battle of Cannae had been fought in 216 B.C. The other was completely covered with feathers and had been brought back from the South Seas by Captain Cook. Cassie was interested in these curiosities, but her twin was entranced. Freddie could talk of nothing else for days, and immediately discarded the prospect of a promising career at Astley's in favor of exploring the world with Cook. Even Cassie's "He's been dead these past thirty-six years, you gudgeon!" could not dampen his enthusiasm, and he resolved to consult Lord Mainwaring on a captain who could be considered a suitable successor to the immortal Cook.

In addition to these various expeditions, Frances spent a great deal of time conferring with Kitty and Lady Streatham about the ball to be given for Kitty at Mainwaring House. In reality, there was little conferring to be done. Lady Frances simply provided an appreciative audience as Kitty, alive with enthusiasm, rapturously described the masses of flowers ordered to transform the ballroom into a fairy garden; debated the rival merits of lobster patties, jellied eel, iced champagne and ratafia, *gâteaux*, and marrons glacés; and boasted of the quantitites of red carpet that had been ordered and the enormous troop of linkboys pressed into service for the gala occasion. "Truly, Frances, I believe it will be the most elegant event of the Season," breathed Kitty. "At first I didn't care for Mainwaring House in the least. It was so formal and grand that it seemed cold after dear old Camberly, but I do admit it is a most impressive edifice, and the ballroom is magnificent. Lady Elizabeth and Kilson seem to know just how to go on, and Lord Mainwaring"—Kitty still could not feel comfortable referring to anyone as imposing as the marquess as "Uncle Julian"— "is sparing no expense."

Lady Frances had attended enough balls to feel that one was very much like another, differing only in scale of grandeur and expense, but she was happy to see Kitty so excited and pleased.

It was thus some time before she was able to visit Mr. Murray at his establishment in Albemarle Street. His enthusiasm for her new idea of a history written with more emphasis on biography and a livelier narrative style, which would lend vitality to important episodes instead of turning them into a dry series of dates and names to be memorized, was most encouraging. He advanced several suggestions of his own, which caught her imagination and made her eager to try them out on her own. "It is a revolutionary approach, Lady Frances, but it just might appeal," he remarked thoughtfully.

"Oh, I feel certain it would, Mr. Murray. I would never dream of suggesting it if I had not found this storytelling method to be most effective with Cassie and Freddie. They are both bright enough but would far prefer to be out-of-doors in search of adventure instead of trapped in a schoolroom. And, being only their sister, I find it more difficult than an ordinary tutor would to capture and hold their attention. I must say that I have met with remarkable success," she admitted candidly.

"Very well, then, continue with your project. I look forward to seeing the final product," he encouraged her as he escorted her to her carriage.

That task accomplished, Lady Frances felt exonerated from her guilty feelings of frivolity and at liberty to give herself up to the pleasures of the metropolis without further interference from an overactive conscience.

15

The marquess, having recovered from a bout of cynicism precipitated by the shallowness of the evening with his mistress, decided that a further restorative would be the encouragement of someone who was worthy of society's notice. If he had stopped to consider, he would have been amazed at how far he had come in so short a time from condemning the lady in question as a prude and a bluestocking to wishing to introduce her to the *ton* as someone worthy of its admiration. With this plan in mind, he drove around to Brook Street one afternoon to hold Lady Frances to the promise he had extacted from her on their visit to the Lord Elgin's marbles. Arriving at Brook Street, he discovered Freddie and Nigel intent upon cricket and witnessed the narrow escape of the drawing-room window from a misdirected hit. Assuring himself that he was merely looking after Frances' peace of mind, the marquess strolled over to where the two boys were arguing over the most effective method of improving one's aim. The truth of the matter was that Mainwaring was more interested in sharing his own cricketing skill than in the continued serenity of Frances. "A capital hit, Freddie, but rather glaringly abroad," he remarked, sauntering up.

"Oh, sir, how famous that you should come along just now! Could you settle a question, do you think?" Freddie inquired, outlining the basis of their disagreement.

"By all means, but here, give me the bat. It is easier to demonstrate than explain. You must grip it more this way and pay closer attention to the ball, marking with your eye exactly the direction you wish to send it—thus." The bat connected with a resounding thwack, sending the ball precisely to the spot indicated. If he had been concerned at all over the possible deterioration of his prowess on the cricket field, the marquess's notion was swiftly dispelled by the blatant admiration in the boys' eyes.

"Thank you ever so much! You are very good, sir, aren't you?" Freddie said, looking worshipfully up at him. Mainwaring was not a little touched by the lad's appreciation, and wondered at this unusual rush of feeling himself. I *know* I'm approaching my dotage, he concluded as he nodded to Higgins and allowed himself to be ushered into the drawing room, where a most unusual sight assailed his disbelieving eyes. Lady Frances was precariously balanced on a footstool by the window, engaged in earnest conversation with . . . a tree! For one dumbfounded moment Lord Mainwaring thought Frances had succumbed to her aunt's horticultural passion, until Nelson appeared inching his way cautiously along a branch, meowing pitifully.

Nelson had been blissfully sunning himself on the steps when the nasty overfed pug from the adjoining house had stumbled out for his morning shuffle. Being a city dog of impeccable pedigree, he had been highly insulted at the sight of a moth-eaten cat who had the colossal nerve to sit in the sun in this exclusive neighborhood. He had voiced his disapproval immediately and vociferously. Nelson was more startled than frightened by the vehement yipping, but he had not stopped to consider this as he scrambled up the nearest available tree. When he reached the first branch, he stopped to look down and was immediately disgusted with himself for having fled from a canine that would have made a mere mouthful for Wellington. In fact, the pug was so fat he wouldn't have been able to move fast enough to pose any real threat to Nelson. Staring at the ground that was beginning to sway under his horrified gaze, the cat bitterly regretted his flight. Before he was completely overcome with vertigo, something grabbed his tail and he leapt up scratching and spitting, his fear of heights forgotten. The thing that had caught at his tail withdrew, and then, to his intense relief, he heard the comforting tones of Lady Frances reassuring him, and he inched carefully toward her.

Mainwaring strode across the room to help lady Frances and her burden off their perch. His eyes, brimming with amusement, laughed down into hers. She smiled mischievously up at him. "No doubt you thought my wits had gone begging when you came in, but Nelson has one bad eye, which makes him very upset at heights. He already scratched James, the footman, so I was summoned to reassure him."

"I understand perfectly, ma'am," he assured her gravely, but his lips twitched suspiciously. "After this heroic rescue, are you in fit condition to go for a drive in the park with me?"

She laughed. "What a poor creature you think me. I should like it of all things," she thanked him. "But I must fetch my bonnet and pelisse. I shan't be a moment."

Julian, well-versed in the ways of women, was surprised when it was just a moment later that she reappeared in her white satin pelisse, tying the bow of a matching twilled sarcenet hat.

It was a fine day and Frances was content after a morning of tending to estate business and the rescue of Nelson to sit and watch the passing scene as the marquess skillfully maneuvered his powerful grays through the traffic on the streets. In fact, there was no less traffic when they arrived in the park, but it was traffic of a more modish kind than the carts and mail coaches they had been forced to dodge en route. It was the fashionable hour of five o'clock and the park was crowded with beautiful thoroughbreds and elegant ladies taking the air in carriages of every hue and description, attended by gorgeously liveried footmen and coachmen. They saw the "diamonds" of the day: Lady Cowper, the Duchess of Argyll, and Lady Louisa, holding court among the gentlemen who clustered thick about them. The Marquess of Anglesea, accompanied by his lovely daughters, all superbly mounted, trotted sedately by. Lady Frances even caught a glimpse of the Prince Regent and Sir Benjamin Bloomfield. All in all, it was an animated and colorful scene that she surveyed, deciding as she did so that the fresh air and magnificent horses made this fashionable promenade infinitely preferable to the ballroom.

Having negotiated the streets and worn off some of the restiveness of his horses, the marquess was at leisure to study his companion, who was looking quite lovely in the new white pelisse, which accentuated the delicate flesh on her cheeks and the opalescent clearness of her complexion. The startched lace collarette and plume of feathers on her bonnet framed her face charmingly and enhanced the delicately molded features. However, her face wore a slightly abstracted expression that puzzled him. When she did not reply to his question as to whether or not she planned to attend Lady Harrowby's Venetian breakfast, which Kitty was anticipating with enthusiasm, he became concerned. "Lady Frances . . ." he began.

She started, and turned to him with an apologetic look in her expressive eyes. "I do beg your pardon, Lord Mainwaring. I was not attending."

"I am well aware of that," he responded dryly. "What serious concern was exercising your thoughts so thoroughly?"

A conscious look spread over her face as she admitted rather shamefacedly that she had been deliberating over a letter she had received that morning from Dawson, down at Cresswell. "You see," she confided, wrinkling her brow thoughtfully, "Squire Tilden is selling his prize bull and approached Dawson about it." She saw amusement creep into his eyes, and one corner of his mouth twitched, but having given herself away, she contiued determinedly. "Our bull is very old. I am surprised he made it through the winter. We must think about procuring a new one. Squire Tilden's is certainly a fine specimen, but I am sure he comes very dear, and I do not anticipate a good harvest this year, so I wonder if it is wise to purchase it." Turning to him, she added contritely, "I don't know why you are so kind as to take me driving with you. Well, I mean, I do know why you do it. You do it because you are helping me become more fashionable and more sought-after in the *ton*, but

I don't know what motivates you to do that. Whatever does, I am excessively grateful for it, but I don't like you to put yourself out from such a hopeless case. I am ever so sorry to be prosing on about country matters, but you *did* ask.''

He interrupted this tangled speech. ''My dear girl, don't refine upon it. Where else would I encounter a lady who would discuss prize bulls with me?'' This won a chuckle and almost erased the wrinkle between her brows. Seeing that it remained to some degree, he became more serious. ''Besides, I am glad you mentioned it. If the price of the bull turns out to be a burden to Cresswell, you may sell him to me. Camberly does not have one and my income is from such a variety of sources that a poor harvest will not affect it to the degree it does yours.''

She was silent for a moment, considering the proposition, trying to decide whether it was motivated by a true need or some unfathomable wish to help her. ''Very well, but I am convinced you are doing this to be kind, and I do not want to be given any special favors, for that will make it more difficult for me to judge the true consequences, and therefore the real wisdom of my decisions.'' He thought wryly that most of the women with whom he was acquainted cultivated favors to the top of their bent, and these favors were ordinarily in the form of jewelry or other extravagances. Here, on the other hand, was a woman who worried about being obliged to someone over livestock! Truly, he did not know as much about women, or this particular woman, as he had imagined. And somehow, her determined self-reliance made him wish more than ever to ease any burdens she might have. But he had driven her to the park with the express purpose of erasing such cares from her mind, not discussing them. Trying for a lighter tone, he pointed to a high-perch phaeton whose driver and canine companion closely resembled each other in their tightly curled locks and disdainful surveillance of the assemblage.

''That miserable dog needs a salutary dose of Wellington to wipe that supercilious sneer off his face. Why, Wellington could dispose of that fop of an animal in no time flat.'' Frances laughed. ''And he would certainly enjoy putting him in his place. He seems to have taken exception to every canine on Brook Street. With the mongrels, however, he has established fast friendships. The stable dog is his greatest crony, and the pug in the adjoining house was his bitterest enemy even before he scared Nelson up the tree. Ever since Wellington pulled Nelson from the pond, he has looked upon that cat as his personal responsibility, and he highly resents anyone or anything who upsets that miserable animal.''

They finished the drive in companionable silence—a new experience for both of them.

As he escorted her to the door, Mainwaring took Lady Frances' hand in his and smiled down at her. "I feel certain that you won't believe me when I tell you I enjoyed myself."

"No, I do not," she replied forthrightly. "I saw the shock on your face when I told you about the bull. It is not exactly the topic of a fashionable conversation. But you seem to be such a friend, and I cannot dissemble with my friends."

He looked at her intently, an unreadable expression in his dark blue eyes. "That is precisely why I enjoyed the drive."

She thanked him for the outing and the conversation. Then, as she entered the door Higgins had held patiently during this interchange, she remembered yet another debt of gratitude she owed him. "I saw you coaching Freddie today. I do so appreciate that. I truly do try to give him all that a father and mother could, but I am afraid I do have my limits. I did help him with his cricket, but with his batting only. I can only pitch, you see. I have no affinity for batting," she apologized.

A swift smile illuminated his features and warmed his eyes. "I can see that you are in need of some coaching as well, then. I shall be happy to oblige," he offered.

"Thank you again." She smiled shyly and, at last, to Higgins' intense relief, entered her elegant hallway.

16

Higgins brought tea, and for some time Lady Frances sat stroking a subdued Nelson and reflecting on the outing. She was at a loss to explain the marquess's attentiveness when she was neither a relative to whom duty owed such consideration, nor was she the sort of ripe beauty to whom his own personal tastes would attract him. It was a puzzle in which she suspected Lady Elizabeth Streatham played a major role. She recognized that that amiable and energetic lady felt herself honor-bound to give Lady Frances an enjoyable Season. Having observed at first hand that redoubtable female's forthright but effective methods, she felt reasonably certain that it was she who had coerced Mainwaring into partnering her at Lady Richardson's ball and inviting her to drive with him in the park. Both of these activities were implemented in the most public places of the *ton* and thus served to attract a maximum amount of fashionable attention, thereby ensuring the rapid establishment of a favorable social reputation. On the other hand, the two other times he had honored them with his company had had nothing to do with Lady Streatham. In each case, his escort had been demanded by her irrepressible brother and sister. Frances had no illusions about the difficulty of resisting the blandishments of either one of the cozening pair, but then, she was fond of the children. If Kitty's impression of Mainwaring was to be trusted, his lordship was not. Still, no one had asked him to help Freddie and Nigel with their cricket. Whatever his motives, he had provided her with no little enjoyment and a feeling of easiness, even pleasure, in his company. It was not surprising that a man as attractive as the marquess would have developed a charming manner, but it was more than charm that made her look upon him as a friend. After their unfortunate initial encounter, he had treated her as he would have treated any one of his friends, discussing politics and estate matters with her as if she were another man, instead of a young woman whose mind should have been filled with fashionable *on-dits* and social repartee. Beyond teasing her the tiniest bit, he never indicated by tone or gesture that he considered it unusual for her to have the interests she did. Heretofore she had encountered either criticism of a woman's participating in traditionally male preserves or condescension. Above all, he shared her sense of humor. Even those such as Sir Lucius Taylor, who did take her seriously, rarely saw the humorous aspects of life that she saw. She was grateful for Julian Mainwaring's attention, but she certainly expected no more of it now that he had danced with her and driven her in the park. Why, for most women in the *ton* that could have been considered the apex of existence.

Mainwaring's attitude not only perplexed Frances but also agreeably surprised two veteran Mainwaring watchers—the dowager Marchioness of Camberly and Lady Elizabeth Streatham—who discussed this interesting situation one day over tea. Though Lady Elizabeth had visited her at the dowager's "kind request," she recognized a command when it was given and knew that her role would be to share all her privileged information in return for the honor of drinking tea with her formidable relative and agreeing totally with that lady's interpretation of the information Lady Elizabeth divulged. In truth, Lady Elizabeth was longing to speak with the dowager, who, whatever she might lack in firsthand knowledge of the goings-on in the ballrooms, promenades, and drawing rooms of the *ton*, made up for it with a natural sharpness of perception and a wealth of experience that had refined this into a nearly infallible ability to predict the outcome of almost any social encounter.

Lady Streatham had barely untied the bow of her bonnet when, tapping her ubiquitous walking stick, her hostess demanded sharply, "Now, Elizabeth, what's all this I hear about Mainwaring and the Cresswell chit?"

"Well . . ." Lady Elizabeth stripped off pale lemon kid gloves. "He has danced with her at a ball where Sally Jersey and Kitty were his only other partners."

"That would have been Belinda Richardson's squeeze." The dowager nodded sagely. "Very well done of you, Elizabeth."

"But I did not force him by asking him to do so. You know Julian. That is the quickest way to make him do what you least wish him to."

The dowager nodded again. "But he enjoyed it, didn't he? He laughed with her and conversed with her later. It's a rare person, least of all a female, who makes Mainwaring smile as he apparently did."

Lady Elizabeth was not a little put out that the dowager, who had only her social spies to rely on, seemed to be so well-informed and so perfectly capable of arriving at her own conclusions without her guest's assistance. "I certainly can add nothing to what you have already discovered," she replied with some asperity.

"Now, Elizabeth, don't fly up into the boughs. I didn't ask you to tea to find out about the ball. Anyone could tell me about that and the drive in the park, but my observers do not ordinarily visit Lord Elgin's marbles, nor do they habituate Astley's Amphitheater. Now, what on earth possessed Mainwaring to go to either of those places, and with a pack of children besides? You know both Lady Frances and Mainwaring. What do you think? Is he caught at last? From all accounts, she isn't his type, but why ever else would he allow himself to be dragged along on nursery outings when he don't even like children? Do tell me, Elizabeth, what is Lady Frances Cresswell like?"

Mollified, Lady Elizabeth tried to express Frances' style as best she could, but found herself at a loss to put that young woman's unique charm into words. Concluding that physical description was the easiest, though the least informative for Lady

Frances in particular, she began. "Decidedly, she is extremely elegant. She has style, but because she is reserved and does not put herself forward, one doesn't recognize it immediately. She's of average height, with features that give a sense of character despite their delicacy. She is reserved, but not at all shy, meaning that she converses elegantly and easily without revealing anything about herself. Her hair is dark blond and her eyes, which are definitely her best feature, are large and hazel, but often take on the color she is wearing."

"Humph!" The dowager was unimpressed. "She don't sound like Mainwaring's style in the slightest. He has always chosen well-endowed women of the world—ripe' uns, every one of 'em."

Lady Elizabeth was miffed at this brusque dismissal of the portrait of her friend. "That's as may be, but I haven't heard that he ever wanted to marry one of them, or even to be seen very much with them."

"Aye, you have a point there," conceded the dowager. "But I have heard that she manages her own estate or some such nonsense. If she's Cresswell's daughter, I don't know as I would believe that. He had a lot in his brain box, but practicality wasn't his long suit. I can't picture any daughter of his being able to take care of herself, much less an entire estate and two lively twins besides."

"Not at all," her informant assured her. "Frances is the most unusual girl. Without one's precisely knowing how she does it, she contrives to get the children and the staff to do exactly as she wishes, with the minimum amount of fuss. She doesn't look to be the 'managing' sort of female at all, but she must be. I gather from Kitty that she did call Mainwaring to task about the agent at Camberly, and there was a rare set-to over that." Lady Elizabeth paused, contemplating the scene with relish. "I only wish I had been there," she commented regretfully. "To continue: when I forced him to call for Kitty at the Cresswells' and he could not avoid saying how-de-do to her, he looked as black as a thundercloud, but I made the two of them act like civilized human beings to one another."

"That I can well believe," her hostess remarked dryly. "Mainwaring was always strong-willed. What with his father dead and no one but that flighty mother around, there was never anyone to oppose his least little wish. Do him good to be sent the right-about now and then. I like a girl with backbone. How about her mind? Mainwaring may have mistresses that are beautiful dull-wits, but he won't tolerate that in his friends."

Lady Elizabeth lowered her voice confidentially. "You couldn't guess it for the world, because she is so charming, but Lady Frances is excessively well-educated. I believe her father taught her not only French and Italian but also Greek, Latin, and mathematics besides. At first, something Julian said made me think he considered her a bluestocking, but John says that didn't stop him from bluntly interrupting the quiet discussion he and Frances were sharing at the dinner party before Lady Richardson's ball. John reports that Julian monopolized her from then on, arguing about the economy, of all things! Julian, of course, because of his uncle's affairs, knows a great deal of such matters, but John says Frances is remarkably well-informed, and she gave as good as she got."

A speculative gleam appeared in the dowager's sharp black eyes as she absorbed this revealing bit of information. "You may have something there, Elizabeth. Julian has never really had a friend. That silly brother of his was certainly no match for him, and by the time he went to Eton he had developed a tough, self-reliant streak that made everyone a little uneasy with him. Of course there's Bertie, but how can one have a friendship with someone who reserves his most serious conversations for his tailor? Julian can be perfectly charming when he wishes, but he usually doesn't come across people who interest him enough to win his attention or his friendship. Maybe an intelligent woman who cannot be brushed off as nothing but an attractive appendage, a mere titillation of the senses, is precisely what he needs. It certainly is time he settled down. And now that he has inherited the title, he must do so and get himself an heir with all speed." Her eyes softened, and she continued almost as though to herself, "But above all, he needs a friend. He is the sort of man who prefers to go it alone, but even such a man as that needs one very special friend. For a man like that it takes a special woman. Once he has found her, though, he will never need anyone else. He will be to her what

Alistair was for me—everything: friend, lover, protector, critic, and admirer. And she will be very lucky indeed,'' the dowager concluded, looking reminiscently into the fire. For a moment she seemed to have forgotten Lady Streatham's existence, but the sound of a passing carriage recalled her and she looked up sharply. ''Bring the gel to visit me someday, Elizabeth. I want to meet her. And now I am tired and I must rest. Please ring for Minter and tell her I want another shawl and some pillows.''

Lady Elizabeth bade the old lady adieu and rode back to Bruton Street in a most thoughtful mood indeed. She agreed wholeheartedly with the dowager as far as it went, but the dowager had been solely concerned with the marquess. Much as she liked and admired Julian, Lady Elizabeth was now more interested in Lady Frances' happiness. The girl had moved her somehow. Perhaps it was because she herself was so happy with John and wondered how she could have lived had she not met and married him. Perhaps it was because she felt that she alone understood and appreciated Lady Frances' excellent qualities— knew and appreciated their fineness and uniqueness—even better than Lady Frances herself did. And, unlike anyone else, she had been able to see the kind and impulsively generous, loving nature beneath the reserved exterior. She wanted this loving nature to be awakened and made to flourish. It would take a special man to appeal to Frances' keen intelligence, her integrity, and her sense of humor, but such a man would be able to arouse the passion and enjoyment of life that Lady Elizabeth knew existed, even though it lay dormant, unaroused by the beefy squires and dissipated macaronis that seemed to populate Lady Frances' world. She needed someone who was man enough to enjoy and challenge her. Lady Elizabeth had decided long ago that Lord Julian Mainwaring was such a man. And having decided this, she was wasting no time in fostering the acquaintance—an acquaintance that she fully intended to develop into the first true love affair for either Lady Frances Cresswell or Lord Julian Mainwaring.

17

Blissfully unaware that her fate was being skillfully manipulated by two experts in the field of intrigue, Lady Frances went blithely about her business. Her second visit to her publisher was as gratifying as the first. He highly approved of several chapters she had given him and offered not the slightest criticism of style or content. This visit did, however, cause a slight deterioration in her developing friendship with the marquess and thus a slight setback to the Machiavellian plans of his female relatives.

Having bid a cordial good day to Mr. Murray, Lady Frances had just stepped out into Albemarle Street. As Aunt Harriet had taken the carriage to pick up two highly unusual rosebushes from a horticultural crony, Lady Frances had been forced to take a hackney to Albemarle Street. She had very properly been accompanied by James, but, not having been able to convince the hackney coachman to wait, he had been forced to go some ways off to procure one. It was thus that Mainwaring, driving back from a satisfying morning at the Royal Exchange, was astounded to see Lady Frances Cresswell alone and unattended in a neighborhood not at all the normal haunt of a fashionable lady. Mainwaring himself was not a rigid stickler for the niceties of *ton*-ish behavior. He certainly was not at all interested in the rigid propriety of most of society's grandes dames and had occasionally found it inconvenient in the extreme, but he thoroughly understood the minds of those who controlled social opinion. They *did* subscribe to such propriety and would have instantly condemned Lady Frances had they seen her. He could not have said why he cared so much that Frances not run the slightest risk of incurring their censure, but he did. He was not about to allow her to behave in a manner that would ruin her chances in the select society in which they both moved.

Consequently, his "Lady Frances, whatever are you doing alone in this vicinity!" which assailed that startled lady's ears was tinged with concern.

Recovering from her initial surprise, Lady Frances looked up to see him frowning down at her in a most discouraging manner. The frown and the tone of Mainwaring's voice were more indicative of his apprehension for her own good reputation than of disapproval, but Lady Frances, already guiltily aware of what the *ton* would think of an authoress, especially one who had the temerity to meet her publisher, heard only the severest censure in his tones. Annoyed that he should have discovered her in such a situation, and more annoyed that he seemed to think her answerable to him for her conduct, she put her chin up and greeted him defiantly. "Good day, my lord. And may I ask whatever are *you* doing here?"

Mainwaring, who had immediately realized the infelicity of his tone, tried for a gentler one in hopes of mollifying her antagonistic response. "It is not at all the thing, you know, for a young lady to be in this neighborhood and alone."

Well and truly roused by this piece of condescending solicitude, Lady Frances had to exercise the strictest control to keep her temper in check. How dare he tell her what to do! She would have resented such censure from anyone, but from someone she barely knew, who surveyed her with a superior air from his elegant curricle, it was intolerable. She did not acknowledge the more personal hurt she felt, that someone with whom she had trusted her friendship thought so little of her that he should immediately leap to such an unflattering conclusion instead of relying on her judgment. In spite of all her resolution, the anger quivered in her voice as she answered, "I am not such a greenhead, my lord, as to have come here unescorted, but my footman has gone in search of a hackney. I had business to conduct here, and surely you would not have a lady sully her drawing room with trade?"

The set of her jaw and the martial light in her eye would have told a less-perceptive man than Lord Mainwaring that he had deeply offended her. He was slightly taken aback at the intensity of her anger, which resulted more from her sense of betrayal than from her taking exception to his criticism. In an attempt to retrieve his position, he offered her a place in his curricle, but his calm assumption that this magnanimous gesture would instantly repair any damage done to her social standing merely served to antagonize her further, and she coldly declined.

Fortunately, before the situation could deteriorate further, James arrived with a carriage and helped his mistress as she regally climbed into it without so much as a backward glance at the now furious Mainwaring.

The marquess would have been hard pressed to say whether he was more furious with himself for badly managing the affair, or with Lady Frances for her prickly independence and her refusal to let anyone assist her in the least. His actions had been motivated by the best intentions, but somehow Lady Frances had contrived to make them appear an intolerable insult and he was just as hurt as she that she should have so little faith in his judgment or actions. These reflections did nothing to improve his temper during the drive to Mainwaring House. His face looked like a thundercloud as he descended, throwing the reins to his tiger, and strode into the hallway. Kilson, relieving his master of his many-caped driving coat, sagely refrained from making any remark. Privately he tried to recall when he had ever seen his lordship in such a taking, and decided that only a woman could have made him angry enough to wear such a black look. He knew that Mainwaring, having dealt with chicanery and insulting behavior in every corner of the world, was too experienced and too much in control of himself to be overset by any man. Kilson was well aware of his lordship's liaison with Vanessa Welford, but he could not believe that a woman who catered only to the more basic aspects of Mainwaring's nature could arouse such anger. Lady Welford was too predictable to have done such a thing. Clearly it was another female. And Kilson knew of no better source of information on that head than Kitty's Alice.

Upon being approached by the great Mr. Kilson himself, Alice was practically speechless with the honor, but in defense of her reputation as confidante, she rose nobly to the occasion and confided to her august interrogator that she suspicioned it was Miss Kitty's great friend Lady Frances Cresswell who had overset his lordship—that lady being the only one, besides the dowager and Lady Streatham, mentioned by Kitty in connection with his lordship. Kilson knew as well as, if not better than, the dowager his master's taste for voluptuous females. The news that a young lady whom he recalled as being a mere slip of a girl was taking up so much of his master's time gave Mainwaring's seasoned henchman pause for thought. If Mainwaring preferred ripe beauties, he also preferred those whose sophistication made dalliance with them a much more comfortable and predictable affair than it was with those who were young enough to retain romantic notions and thus make unreasonable demands. That his lordship was paying even the slightest attention to someone who was more elegant than alluring, was unmarried, and only twenty-two besides, meant that the situation was serious indeed. In all the years he had been with his lordship, Kilson could not remember his having enjoyed a woman for a companionship other than the type supplied by his mistresses. The single exception to this was the dowager, for whom he retained a deep, though well-concealed fondness and respect. Kilson completed his inspection of the wine cellar, where he'd gone to mull over this revelation in privacy. As he slowly mounted the stairs, he resolved to keep a much closer eye on things. Years of sharing every sort of uncomfortable lodging and adventure with Lord Mainwaring had given him a great fondness as well as a healthy respect for his master. He had often wished that Lord Mainwaring had had a brother or cousin who possessed the same curiosity, the same keen mind, the same willingness to take risks that so endeared his master to him and made him stand out among men the world over. No man should be as constantly alone as Lord Mainwaring was, not that he was without friends, but none of them ever seemed to be a true companion who could share the same view of the world he had. It had been Kilson's dearest wish that such a companion would appear. Until now, it had not occurred to him that such a companion might be female, but the more he considered it, the better such an idea seemed, and he began to devise ways in which he could learn more about this Lady Frances of whom Alice seemed so sure.

The object of these reflections, having failed to quell his ill humor by tossing off a glass of the best brandy and immersing himself in some complicated business correspondence, gave up and strode over to Gentleman Jackson's, hoping to work off his ill humor through physical exertion. There he was welcomed enthusiastically by the noted pugilist, who was often heard to remark that his lordship had excellent science and was certainly wasting his talents in diplomatic circles. The physical exertion and the reassuring male sporting atmosphere, whose simple codes offered a direct contrast to the complicated patterns of polite behavior imposed by the *ton*, restored his good humor in part. He decided to improve it further by dropping in at Brooks's. Apparently the exertion at Jackson's had not dissipated his ill humor as much as he had thought, for Bertie, encountering him on the steps, greeted him with an inquiring look. "Hallo, Julian. Whatever has put that murderous scowl on your face?"

"Hallo, Bertie," his lordship responded, not a little put out that he was still annoyed by such a trivial incident. As Bertie's inquiring look showed no signs of fading, Mainwaring sighed and confessed, "Very well, if you must know, it's that high-handed friend of yours. She's too independent for her own good."

Comprehension dawned in Bertie's eyes, but he agreed in a conciliatory tone, "Yes, she never would be led by anyone else. But whatever does that have to do with you?"

Mainwaring related with some acerbity the entire encounter. "Well, you do have a point, Julian. She undoubtedly was wrong, and not a little stupid in being there—especially unattended by more than her footman—but I don't blame her for being annoyed at your interference in her affairs. You should be the first to understand her resentment. You're too accustomed to running your own show, Julian. You forget that she might be as little inclined to take anyone's advice as you are." Bertie's look seemed to suggest he was recalling an incident when he had been foolhardy enough to do just that. Mainwaring grinned ruefully, acknowledging the accuracy as well as the justice of his friend's observation.

18

L ord Mainwaring was saved by his grandmother from having to debase himself with a call of apology to Lady Frances. Curious about the young woman who seemed to be occupying an unusual amount of her grandson's busy life, she took matters into her own hands and invited the elder daughter of her dear friend Lady Belinda Cresswell to tea. Taking a more active role in the matchmaking, she instructed Julian himself to drive the young lady. She had also invited Lady Streatham and Kitty, who, having spent the morning together running up bills on Bond Street, came separately in the Streathams' carriage.

It was an unusually fine day and Mainwaring took advantage of the opportunity to drive Lady Frances around the park before proceeding to the dowager's. For some time they rode in silence while Mainwaring tried to phrase an apology for his interference in her affairs that would convey his sympathy with her resentment at this interference while at the same time maintaining the correctness of his original censure of her conduct. Judging correctly that an abject apology might mollify Lady Frances temporarily, but would in the long run weaken her confidence in the strength of his character or judgment, he decided to forgo any apology in favor of offering assistance. Still, he hesitated, searching for just the words, asking himself at the same time why he should care in the least what he thought of her or she of him. "Lady Frances," he began tentatively, and then continued with more assurance, "I have some experience in the business world and would be more than happy to put that and any personal connections I might have at your service should you have any affairs you would wish settled."

Recognizing this offer for what it was—a very handsome and practical offer of assistance and an assumption of some of the responsibility for the unpleasantness of their last encounter—Lady Frances was both surprised and touched. She turned to him with a grateful smile, "Why, thank you, my lord. It is very kind of you." Mainwaring was unprepared for the relief he felt at her ready acceptance of his peace offering, and found himself thinking what very fine and expressive eyes she had.

Frances knew that her own bristly independence had been at least as much responsible for their contretemps as Mainwaring's interference, and she offered her own form of apology by admitting the true nature of her business. "Ordinarily I would accept your generous offer, because though I may be a green 'un, I am not fool enough to insist on doing myself what someone else can do better. But in this instance I am afraid I can't. You see"—a slightly conscious look crept over her face—"I was conferring with my publisher."

"Your publisher!" her companion echoed in thunderstruck tones. "No doubt we can expect to see ourselves pillored in print soon in *Society Unmasked*, by a Lady of Quality."

Lady Frances laughed, but she had recognized the suspicious look at the back of his eyes. "Oh, no, I am not *that* sort of female who preys on society in order to satisfy a craving for power or notoriety. This is, I am afraid to admit, a project that is far more in keeping with a 'bluestocking' than a 'lady of quality.'"

Julian cocked a quizzical eyebrow.

"You see," she continued, "I have always felt that people go about educating children in a way designed to set up their backs in the least amount of time possible. They stuff their brains full of dry, disassociated facts and expect them to repeat them in the same disembodied manner. Then they are astonished when children fail to do so. Yet children can remember and repeat a story quite easily, and the more adventurous the tale, the more readily they remember it. What is history, what are wars, kings, queens, scientific discoveries, but great adventures? I have written a history book in this style and taken it to Mr. Murray, who was my father's publisher. He had already published some of my tales for children, but nothing so ambitious as this, and he felt he needed to consult with me personally before doing so.'' Here Frances paused to draw breath and look anxiously at Mainwaring.

His face softened and he smiled at her enthusiasm. ''An excellent idea. If your book is half as enthralling as the two expeditions I was privileged to join, I predict an enormous success. You certainly have no competition.''

She turned pink with pleasure. ''I had thought that if the author were identified as 'F. Cresswell, child of the noted classical scholar Lord Charles Cresswell and product of this excellent educational scheme,' it might win further approval.''

The bland tone of this suggestion did not deceive his lordship, who caught the wicked gleam in her eye and smiled appreciatively. ''What a wily creature you are,'' he teased.

''Oh, no, my lord, merely practical,'' she assured him innocently.

''Eminently so, believe me.''

By this time they had arrived at the dowager's and the door was thrown open by her stately if aged butler. Lady Frances glanced apprehensively at her escort, but he smiled reassuringly and took her arm in a firm grasp to conduct her to the drawing room, where the dowager awaited them ensconced in an enormous chair by the fire and flanked by Kitty and Lady Streatham. ''Come in, my child, come in. Excuse the fire on such a lovely day, but my bones are so old they need all the warmth they can get. Come, let me get a good look at you, my dear. Don't be shy. I was so fond of your mother—liked her more than my own brats. You have the look of her, but not quite so pretty, I think. Belinda Carstairs was one of the most beautiful girls I've seen in many a season—a real diamond she was—and gay as she was lovely. I missed her sorely when she married your papa and went off to those outlandish places. But who could help being happy for her? You rarely find such love as theirs except in literature. Those two adored each other. Once they met, the rest of the world didn't exist.'' She sighed and patted a chair that Mainwaring had placed next to her. "Sit down and tell me about yourself. I hear you have charge of the estate now, as well as two rambunctious twins and that crazy Harriet Cresswell. She's a bright woman, Harriet, and she can be amusing, but tetchy—lord, she is tetchy, and always was.''

Frances, whose eyes were not a little misty at the mention of her beloved parents, smiled and sat down gratefully. "Yes, ma'am, I have managed Cresswell really ever since Mama died.''

The dowager interrupted, "Yes, I can imagine that Charles wasn't much good at it. He was a brilliant man, but he never could manage the practicalities of life. Belinda took care of those, in addition to sharing his intellectual passions. She was truly a remarkable woman. I hear you're not unlike her. But continue.''

The others, completely ignored, were left to their own devices. Lady Streatham and Kitty were quite happy to devour the abundant supply of cakes while gloating over their purchases from a successful morning on Bond Street. Mainwaring leaned against the mantel, content to listen to Frances' recital of family affairs. As her musical voice described her taking over the household at the age of twelve under the aegis of an elderly housekeeper, gradual assumption of duties connected with the estate, and finally, with the death of her father, undertaking the education of Cassie and Freddie, he began to appreciate more fully the enormity of the burdens she bore. Such responsibilities often proved too much for men of his own age, much less a girl of twenty-two. No doubt, he thought wryly, she would object strongly to being labeled a "girl,'' but that was in fact what she was. He had never been one to seek frivolous amusements for himself or encourage them in his friends, but he found himself longing to immerse her in a whirlwind of totally self-indulgent frivolity. She had probably done nothing solely for her own diversion since the age of twelve. As he examined her more closely, he could detect the marks these years had left.

She had a charming smile, but it was gracious rather than gay. Her large hazel eyes fringed with long dark lashes were her most attractive feature, but there was a gravity in their expressive depths that was never completely banished even when she was most amused. And always she exhibited a certain awareness of her surroundings that belied a consciousness of what the children were doing, of things that needed her attention. Thinking of her in a variety of past situations, he realized that despite an excellent sense of humor, she was more often serious than not, and she never completely forgot herself. This seriousness he found oddly touching, and at the same time attractive. Her honesty and her openness made him trust her in a way he had never trusted a woman, and very few men. Her simple acceptance of responsibility for herself and her family, her down-to-earth approach to problems, kindled admiration—an emotion that was unusual in someone as capable as the Marquess of Camberly. And here he felt himself at a loss. Because he understood the reality of her responsibilities, because she accepted her duties as a matter of fact and without complaint, he wanted very much to relieve her of them while at the same time he realized that the best expression his respect for her capabilities could take would be to trust her to be as adept at solving her problems as he would be. After all, using Bertie's logic, he would look upon any assistance offered him as indicative of a friend's lack of confidence in his abilities, even if it stemmed from a purely generous impulse to ease the burden of a fellowman. He sighed ruefully and confessed to himself that he was at a standstill and could only hope for some chance to smooth her path without seeming to interfere.

A sharp "Ahem, Mainwaring, are you even in the same country with us, or at any rate the same room?" broke his train of reflection.

He grinned sheepishly. "Ah, yes. Were you addressing me, ma'am?"

"I most certainly was, young man. Don't you know it is excessively rude not to pay attention to your elders? I was wondering if you planned to grace your own ball for Kitty."

He looked affronted. "But of course, ma'am. How can you think otherwise?"

"Well, knowing how independent you are, how little you care for social opinion, and how much you loathe such squeezes, I should be surprised if you did not contrive to be called away on some matter of urgent national business."

This forced an answering grin from her grandson. "I assure you, I know the duties of a guardian very well, and I am not such a ramshackle fellow as to run off on the big day. I have even made sure that she opens the ball with me, and now shall take advantage of the opportunity you have provided to secure the first waltz with Lady Frances." He turned to Frances with a quizzical gleam.

It was not for nothing, Lady Frances reflected a trifle bitterly, that Lord Mainwaring was in the diplomatic service. Even if she had wished to hesitate or refuse, she could not in such a public place and in front of someone who cared for him so dearly. It seemed that whether she wished to continue it or not, their misunderstanding was to be cleared up. With as good grace as she could muster when so obviously maneuvered into a situation that allowed no alternative, she smiled and thanked him.

"Lucky gel," the dowager, who had watched the scene with great interest, commented enviously and not without a trace of self-satisfaction. "Not only will he be the most handsome man there, he is an excellent dancer. After all, he had plenty of practice in Vienna, where, according to some, that was about the extent of the activity."

Julian's eyes twinkled wickedly. "If you weren't such a snob, Grandmama, forgoing all but the most rigidly select tea parties, I would ask you, but I know you detest these squeezes more than I." The twinkle became a speculative gleam as he saw her begin to consider his invitation seriously.

After a moment's hesitation she thumped her stick on the floor. "Dashed if I don't accept you."

Mainwaring bent over one frail beringed hand and said with real gratitude, "Thank you, Grandmama."

Here they were interrupted by Lady Streatham. "Do my ears deceive me? Did I actually hear you convince her to come?" Mainwaring nodded, "I must confess, you are the most complete hand, Julian." She turned to Kitty, exclaiming, "What

a triumph, my love! Now I know you are assured of success.''
Then, noticing how tired the dowager looked, ''We must be
going or my men will be sending out the Bow Street Runners.''

Lady Frances bade adieu to the dowager, promising to honor
her request and provide her with intelligent conversation at the
ball. Kitty curtsied and thanked her prettily, and the whole party
left the old lady to some very interesting reflections of her own.

The drive home for Lady Frances and her companion was
equally pleasant. Mainwaring retrieved his position by
apologizing for asking her to dance in such a public situation.
''It was rather high-handed, but you are so busy, I wasn't sure
of having another opportunity before the big event.''

''That's of no account, my lord,'' she replied, but he
recognized from the slight constraint in her answer that she truly
had felt manipulated.

''I am sorry,'' he continued. ''Tell me what I can do to show
that I truly do apologize.''

He had offered this more as a matter of form, and was rather
surprised when she tilted her head speculatively and began,
''Well, I . . .''

''Yes, go on,'' he encouraged, wondering what possible
request could cause her such difficulty.

She brought it out in a rush. ''I was just wondering if you
would mind very much telling me what it was like at the
Congress in Vienna.''

He burst out laughing. ''No, don't poker up, my child. It was
just that you looked so apprehensive, I made certain you were
going to make some impossibly difficult demand. No, I don't
have the slightest idea what I thought it was likely to be, but
I felt sure that I would be traveling at least to the West Indies
to accomplish it. No, of course I shouldn't mind in the least.
It's just that most people are barely aware that it is going on,
much less expose any interest or curiosity.'' He began giving
her a rather general account of the proceedings, but soon
recognized from her questions that he was dealing with a very
informed listener. As he warmed to his subject, he realized that
she was helping him clarify his thoughts on some points that
had remained muddy for him until now. In fact, so involved
was he in trying to capture the exact scene, the precise

atmosphere, every machination, and every insinuation, that he was unaware of the slackening pace of the horses until they came to a dead halt in the middle of the park. This brought him up short and he finished with a laugh. "So, you see, it really did not challenge my mental skills as much as my social ones."

Lady Frances wrinkled her brow thoughtfully. "Hmm, yes, I can see it must be a little bit like running an estate—with more important consequences, of course. One thinks one will spend one's time evaluating and putting into practice agricultural principles and deciding how to make the wisest use of financial resources, when, in fact, all one's energies seem to go toward soothing ruffled tempers, exhorting the lazy or the uninspired, and listening to a steady stream of complaints that have more to do with neighbors' stupidity or carelessness than with estate management." Her sigh was not lost on her companion.

"Exactly," he responded dryly. "It is amazing how human vanity continually reduces the most lofty and inspiring situations to triviality."

She twinkled up at him, "Well, then, the Prince de Ligne's comment, '*Le Congrès ne marche pas, il danse,*' was not too far wrong. And, Lady Mainwaring's prejudice aside, you have returned an excellent dancer."

"Why, thank you, ma'am," he replied meekly. "And if I thought you cared for that at all, I might be flattered."

"Well, I should think you would be pleased," she remarked candidly. "My opinion is not worth anything in particular as far as fashionable tastes go, but I do recognize grace and finesse, which are to be found in not only the social world. And since you, with your diplomatic duties, are constrained to be constantly in the most exclusive social circles, it is no small thing that you are so adroit. Even Princess Esterhazy and Madame de Lieven must be impressed. Right there you are assured of success in all that you attempt."

He knew from the wicked sparkle in her eyes and the smile hovering around one corner of her mouth that she was quizzing him, but in spite of that and despite the triviality of the accomplishment, Julian felt a warm rush of gratification at her approval. I am becoming positively infantile, he told himself severely. Women have been flattering me more lavishly for years, to no effect, and this chit makes me feel grateful for a teasing remark. He smiled at her. "Enough of such world-shaking events. We must concentrate on the more important present, and I must get you home before Cassie and Frederick have completely torn the house apart."

She agreed ruefully. "Yes, they are a precious pair, aren't they?"

The carriage drew up in front of her house, but he did not immediately alight, turning instead to say, "Thank you for the drive. And don't forget that I do mean to have that waltz, even if my methods annoyed you."

It seemed odd to her that he should thank her for the drive, especially since he said it in such a way that made it more than a mechanical social response. Some of this puzzlement must have shown on her face, because he explained, "It's rare to find someone who can understand and share in my concerns. In fact, some of your questions have directed my thoughts toward other possibilities."

The puzzled expression was replaced by one of astonishment at this, but she merely replied, "I suppose 'bluestockings' do have their uses."

"Off with you, baggage. Since you never seem to forget an insult to your precious pride, don't forget that waltz I forced out of you." He handed her down and escorted her to the door being held open by Higgins.

The look of long suffering on Higgins' face had not been merely the result of having to hold the door open while the marquess and his mistress chatted. He had more disturbing matters on his mind, but was at a loss how to begin. He could hardly remember a time when he'd seen such a glow on his mistress's face, and now it fell to him to banish it with the worry of yet another problem. He was rescued from his dilemma by the timely entrance of Aunt Harriet bearing a bowl of broth. While Farnces had been gone, Frederick, who had thought of nothing but Astley's for weeks—so much so that his tin soldiers gathered dust—had at long last prevailed on a stableboy to let him try standing bareback on his pony. For several weeks the lad, who stood in awe of John Coachman, had resisted, but eventually Freddie's blandishments, supplemented by hefty offerings of sweetmeats, had had their inevitable effect and he had been won over into agreeing to stand in the stableyard holding the rein of Prince while his scapegrace young master did his best to imitate the famous equestrians. Freddie had been doing quite well and had managed several circles upright when a large fly was his undoing. For several seconds after his head hit the paving he lay motionless, but before the stableboy could decide whether to run away or run for John, he came to, grinning sheepishly. "Here, give me a hand. I shall be right as rain in a moment." Gasping with relief, the lad leapt to help him up, but this was easier said than done. As Freddie slowly returned to a vertical position, he was overcome with faintness. His head buzzed uncomfortably and the world receded into a blur. At this crucial moment John came around the corner with one of the carriage horses he had been grooming. After one look at Freddie's white face, he turned fiercely on the unfortunate stable lad. "Oho, laddie, and what mischief have you been letting young Master Frederick get into?" The miserable boy stammered out the tale as best he could, but before he was half through, John had picked up Freddie and borne him into the house. Fortunately Cook and the housekeeper were women of sense and in no time at all had him in bed and, upon the advice of Aunt Harriet, had sent the stableboy posthaste to summon Dr. Baillie.

All this had occurred not twenty minutes after Lord Mainwaring had handed Lady Frances into his curricle. The staff and Aunt Harriet agreed unanimously that the afternoon treat so rare in Frances' life was not to be spoiled until absolutely necessary, and by the time she returned, Freddie had been examined by the good doctor and pronounced a lucky young devil who was fortunate to get off with a mild concussion and a number of scrapes and bruises. "And so I hope he's learned a good lesson, though I doubt it," sniffed Aunt Harriet, concluding her tale. Her undramatic recital of the afternoon's events had calmed Frances' worst fears, but failed to allay them completely. "Very well, come see him if you must, but he's quite safe now and the less fuss there is, the better, to my way of thinking. And any bother at all is more than the scamp deserves."

Frances, seeing her little brother propped up against the
pillows, pale but absorbed in the neglected tin soldiers, said
to herself that Aunt Harriet was probably completely in the right,
but another part of her, which had never fully recovered from
the loss of her mother and father, felt desperately afraid that
another one of her dearest companions was in danger. She
managed, at least outwardly, to stifle such fears and was able
to say in an admirably offhand way, "What a silly clunch you
are, Freddie. Don't you know the Astleys spend years practicing
with all sorts of special aids and tricks before they try such a
stunt?"

She had hit the right note. Frederick, prepared to resist and
resent an onslaught of sisterly tears of remonstrance as feminine
silliness, was stricken with guilt at the thought of the worry he
had caused by the stupidity of his escapade. But he managed
to smile in his usual winning way. "I am most dreadfully sorry,
Fanny. I was a regular chawbacon. I do promise not to do it
again . . . leastways not without more practice," he amended
truthfully.

"Yes," she agreed. "I should think your head will be too
dizzy for you to balance with much skill for a considerable
while. Wait until we return to the soft turf at Cresswell and
then John and I shall help you."

"You're a great gun, Fan," said her small brother appreciatively. This tribute and the subsequent wince of pain as he
shifted position went straight to her heart, and she left the room
in some haste. The careless attitude she had so carefully
maintained in front of Frederick evaporated as she closed the
door to the nursery and fled to her own dressing room to collapse
in a chair, drop her head into her hands, and think. No
constructive, rational thoughts came, and she stared out of the
window, fighting the conviction that she was naive and
optimistic in thinking it a mere schoolboy mishap.

A light tap on her door broke into these unwelcome thoughts,
and her maid came bearing an exquisite bouquet in a filigree
holder. There was nothing at all unusual about the inscription
on the card. In fact, there was rather less inscription than ladies
ordinarily received, but something about the forcefully scrawled
"Mainwaring" brought the faintest flush to her cheeks and left

her slightly breathless. "Ain't it lovely, though, miss," breathed Daisy.

"Yes, thank you," agreed her mistress as she savored their scent. And then, "Heavens! The ball! Daisy, you must ask Higgins to send a footman round to deliver a note to Lady Streatham." She hastily wrote a note, briefly recounting the mishap and begging off the evening's festivities.

It seemed no time at all before Cassie appeared to inform her breathlessly, "Lady Streatham is below, Fan, and she's been telling me all about the time Nigel fell off his horse going over a jump. He was unconscious half a day but was right as a trivet in no time. Is she come to tell you to go to the ball? I think you should go. It will be the most famous thing. Ned has been telling Freddie and me about the quantities of flowers and red carpet and how everyone has been cleaning chandeliers and polishing for weeks. He says the ballroom looks like a palace and there's going to be ever so much food—jellies and cakes and ices. You must go. I can take care of Freddie. All he has to do is sit quietly. We can play jackstraws, and if his head aches I can read to him. Just tell me what you would do. I know where the lavender water is and I remember just how you put it on my face when I had measles last summer. Please, Fan, let me take care of Freddie," she pleaded.

By this time they had reached the drawing room and Lady Streatham was able to add her voice to Cassie's. "Yes, Frances, I think that's an excellent idea. Cassie seems a sensible girl. I'm sure she could do very well. After all, you did quite passably when you were left in charge of twin babies. I believe you were not much older than Cassie is now." She shot a conspiratorial glance toward Cassie, who was looking eagerly at her sister. "Besides, this is such a momentous occasion that Kitty and I are in far more need of you than Freddie is." After a brief hesitation, Frances capitulated and was given a hug and glowing look by her younger sister, who dashed off to inform her patient.

"Truly," Lady Streatham continued after the little girl had left, "he needs no care—just confinement to his bed. He'll probably fret less at that if Cassie is there than if you are."

"I suppose you are right," sighed Frances. "But that still does not put me in the mood for a ball."

"You may certainly disregard that, because you know perfectly well you are never 'in the mood' for a ball," her friend teased.

Frances, forced to admit the accuracy of that observation, also recognized the necessity of her presence at the most critcal moment in her young neighbor's existence. "Very well," she said, and was rewarded with a quick, grateful hug from her ladyship, who declared that she must be on her way in order to keep Kilson from slitting his throat or someone else's. "He does very well organizing Mainwaring's affairs in some outlandish backwater, but he isn't up to London servants. Thank you again, my dear—see you this evening. You will see, everything will come about." And with a wave of her hand, Lady Streatham drove off.

Left alone, Frances wandered back into the drawing room and sat for the better part of an hour staring out of the windows and pulling absently at Wellington's ears. This, though highly gratifying to the little dog who lay on his back with a blissful smile on his lips, did nothing to relieve her mind. In her years as mistress of Cresswell, Frances had become accustomed to emergencies of every variety, from broken legs to pregnant maids, from sick horses to flooded fields. She had schooled herself to deal with them in a cool and rational manner. However, none of her family had been directly involved in these, and she had thus found it fairly easy to remain detached. Now it was a different matter altogether. Her intelligence told her there was nothing to fear. Little boys always had adventures that more often than not ended in disaster. Such unfortunate accidents were a requisite part of any young man's education. But her heart, which had suffered the great losses of a beloved father and mother, anticipated the worst in a manner that made a mockery of her rational approach of life's problems.

Before Lady Frances had been able to demoralize herself completely, she as interrupted in the middle of her visions of doom by Aunt Harriet. "Buck up, my girl. You really don't want to make a cake of yourself over this. If you weren't everlastingly letting your infernal sense of responsibility for the family's welfare cloud your senses, you would remember that you were no older than Frederick when you fell off your own pony. Not only were you dead to the world for an entire day, you broke your wrist as well.''

"You're right, of course." She smiled ruefully. "If Papa were alive, I would be telling him it was nothing a good solid rest wouldn't cure." Giving herself a little shake, Frances jumped up. "And I would be right! If I am not to be an antidote at Kitty's ball, I must get some fresh air and make sure that the dressmaker has done what I asked with the pink-and-white satin."

"That's my girl. Run along now and I shall endeavor to keep Cassie from completely wearing out her twin with her ministrations."

Wellington, who enjoyed a walk even more than having his ears stroked, leapt up determined to give his mistress an outing invigorating enough to restore her equanimity and make her positively glow with good health.

19

Wellington performed his duties so well that if Lady Frances, mounting the steps of Mainwaring House that evening, did not outshine all the accredited beauties, she certainly presented a picture of grace and elegance. The delicate pink in her gown enhanced her fine coloring and the sparkle of her mother's diamonds at her throat and in her ears was reflected in her eyes and brought out the warmth of her skin while lending sophistication to the simple line of her dress. Not even the most prejudiced observer would have singled her out among London's beauties as a diamond, but her assured and graceful manner was a refreshing contrast to those tricked out to absurdity in the highest kick of fashion.

If anyone were the cynosure of all eyes that evening, it was Kitty, standing at the head of the stairs with her uncle and the Streathams. The exquisitely simple white muslin, relieved only by cherry ribbons at the sleeves and hem, gave her the ethereal look of a fairy princess just awakened. Her wide brown eyes took in the glittering scene with shy fascination. A delicate flush just rising in her cheeks matched the ribbons in her hair and dress. Her toilette was completed by her mother's pearls, and a delicate nosegay made her truly radiant with youth and anticipation, becomingly timid, but eager to please and be pleased.

"Oh, Frances," she exclaimed breathlessly, "isn't it beautiful?" Her eyes clouded with sisterly sympathy. "Thank you ever so much for coming. I am so glad you were able to, and I do hope Freddie is doing better."

Frances answered with an assurance she was far from feeling. "Yes, a few days of rest and he should be quite the thing." She smiled fondly at her friend. "I am glad I came. You are looking fine as fivepence, Kitty. But I can see that I am not the only one to notice. I'd best let the rest of them meet you." Lady Frances moved along to give room to a hatchet-faced dowager leading a blushing son who could only gaze admiringly as he stammered his greetings.

Lady Streatham kissed Frances on the cheek while her husband pressed her hand and smiled at her warmly. "My dear, not only do you look lovely, but you appear as though you had nothing on your mind more serious than dancing—not that that is not serious business at a ball. Thank you again for coming."

Her husband added his reassurance. "You know Freddie should be sleeping now anyway, my dear. If you were at home, he'd only be begging you for stories instead of getting the rest he needs."

Frances smiled gratefully at him and found herself looking up into Mainwaring's tanned face, where she could read a wealth of understanding and approval in his dark blue eyes. "Now that you and Grandmama are here, our ranks are complete and we can rush to Kitty's defense as she takes the *ton* by storm." The sardonic tone was belied by the encouraging pressure of his fingers and the warmth of his lips as he bent over her hand. Inexplicably Frances felt more comforted and reassured by that simple gesture than she had by all the sage and carefully expressed advice offered by Aunt Harriet, Lady Streatham, and several others.

Before she had time to reflect upon this perverse state of affairs, she was accosted by Bertie. "Hallo, Frances!" he greeted her gaily. "I do hope you are saving the opening dance for me. Except for Kitty, of course, you are quite the finest lady here, and I shall be extremely puffed up if I'm allowed to do the pretty with you." He glanced quickly over his shoulder to ascertain whether he had spoken loudly enough for Kitty to hear, and was gratified to see her blush with pleasure. "Seriously, Fan," he continued in an undertone as he took her arm, "I'll be more than puffed up, I shall be spared a fate worse than death. That Dartington woman has been throwing her platter-faced daughter at me everywhere I turn."

"What, the duchess? But, Bertie, you ae to be congratulated! She will only take the most eligible *partis* for that girl. You are excessively fortunate. Willoughby has been trying to fix his interest for years." Frances tried desperately to keep a straight face, but Bertie's patent dismay was too much and she gave a gurgle of laughter.

"Dash it, Fanny," he complained in an injured tone, "it ain't funny."

"I know," she gasped. "But your face is. How good it is to see you! I can count on you to put things in the right perspective. Here I am worrying about a bump on Freddie's head when you stand in danger of being saddled with an antidote for the rest of your life."

"Give over, Fan. It ain't the least bit funny to be chased, and I mean *chased*, by that hag. My peace is entirely cut up. I can't walk down Bond Street or take a stroll in the park but what she's there. I shall have to get myself invited on one of your educational excursions just to save myself."

She smiled sympathetically. "You're too well-mannered for your own good. You need to give her a sharp set-down."

He nodded. "Several of them, I should think." He added gloomily, "But it takes such a devilish lot of work to think one up. Tell you what." He brightened. "You're good with words. You think of some during this set and I'll practice on you when there's a waltz." And, his equanimity restored, he led her gracefully through the opening quadrille.

To Lady Frances' utter astonishment, she was able to forget Freddie in the music and the steps of the dance. Bertie's diverting chatter was just what she needed at the moment. Knowing that his insouciance hid a very kind heart, she half-suspected that the story of Lady Dartington had been concocted on the spot to take her mind off more serious things.

When the set broke up, he led her over to the corner where Lady Streatham and the dowager marchioness were surveying the festivities with barely concealed satisfaction. "Haven't seen the place so crowded since you were puffed off, Elizabeth," the old lady chortled gleefully. "You and Mainwaring have done Kitty proud. Shouldn't wonder if this ain't one of the events of the Season." She nodded sagely and turned to a breathless Kitty, who was being restored to her chaperones by an eager young man.

"Oh, Frances, isn't it just like a fairy tale?" the girl asked when she had had a moment to catch her breath. Then, remembering that she was now a grown-up young lady, "But, of course, it is a sad crush, isn't it?"

"A terrible squeeze," Frances agreed, shaking her head gravely before quizzing her. "Are you enjoying it, then? I am so glad." Kitty barely had time for an enthusiastic nod before another swain appeared to lead her away.

Lady Streatham broke her own discussion with the dowager concerning Kitty's probable success, the possible choices she might have among the various eager young men, and a shrewd reckoning of their eligibility, to turn to Frances. "But are you enjoying yourself? Almost any young girl . . . well, any impressionable young girl," she amended, remembering the misery that had been Frances' first Season, "is bound to enjoy herself at her own ball if she is not an antidote and is elegantly dressed. It is the older, more critical, but still young ladies I worry about such as you." This was said with a meaningful look.

"Me?" Frances demanded in some surprise. "What can it signify, how I feel?"

"Really, Frances, for a bright girl, sometimes you are a muttonhead! Did it never occur to you to do something for the sheer pleasure of it? Must you do everything for a reason, and a reason that usually involves helping someone else?"

"Of course, but . . ." Frances was at a moment's loss as the truth of Lady Elizabeth's observation sank in. She shut her mouth with a snap.

"If you won't look after your own amusement, may I induce you to take care of mine?" a deep voice at her elbow interrupted some rather unpleasant revelations. She whirled around to meet the marquess's quizzical smile. "Come . . ." He held out a shapely hand. "Waltz with me. I have spent the entire evening thus far trying to get blushing young women to speak to me, pompous dowagers to be silent, blushing young men to speak to blushing young women, and no one has spoken two sensible words to *me* the entire evening." Lady Streatham had voiced her hope that Frances was having a good time. Her cousin was determined to carry this out. He had kept his eye on Frances' progress around the room, and seeing her free, had rather abruptly left a dashing young matron who had been casting languishing glances at him, to arrive in time to hear the end of Lady Elizabeth's remarks. He wholeheartedly agreed with her observations and thus ascribed the rush of warmth he felt when Lady Frances smiled at him to mere sympathy for one who bore too many responsibilities. If he had thought about it at all, he might have realized that this agreeable feeling could more accurately be ascribed to the way her hazel eyes widened with pleasure and seemed, along with an enchanting smile, to sparkle for him alone. But he did not stop to wonder any of these things, giving himself up instead to the pleasure of whirling around the floor with someone whose movements matched his to perfection.

His partner's feelings mirrored his as completely as her steps. It was true that she rarely did anything without a very good reason, but for the moment she was content to forget everything except the joy of gliding over the floor and the agreeable sensation of being expertly guided in the marquess's firm clasp.

For a time neither broke the spell, but the marquess, misinterpreting Frances' abstracted expression, demanded bluntly, "Are you still blue-deviled about that ridiculous brother of yours? Because you shouldn't be, you know."

She was startled out of her reverie, blushed, and admitted, "No, in truth, I wasn't."

He cocked an incredulous eyebrow.

"If you must know, I was thinking how much I was enjoying this dance." She looked impishly up at him. Decidedly it wasn't the standard answer for a society lady, but it was a gratifying one. Her eyes clouded. "I know I shouldn't worry about him, and ordinarily I wouldn't. After all, I did nearly the same thing myself once. It's just that I have lost two of the people I care most about in the world, and now, if the least little thing happens to any of the family, I fear the worst. It's silly to let a little thing like that overset one, I know . . .'' Her voice trailed off.

"My child, there's not the least need to excuse yourself."

"But I detest such missishness, and fear that at the same time I am turning into the protective type of female I heartily loathe."

"You need to inspire Freddie to teach Wellington equestrian tricks instead of essaying them himself. You know how that misbegotten mongrel adores horses and attention."

"He's not a mongrel!" Lady Frances rose instantly to her pet's defense. She smiled. "But he *is* virtually indestructible. How clever you are. But enough of my affairs. We must be the only ones in the entire room who aren't discussing this ball or Kitty's chances of becoming an incomparable. And speaking of incomparables, who is that Adonis partnering her now? He looks to be so besotted as to be in danger of suffocating."

Mainwaring glanced in his ward's direction. "My God, now we are in the basket!"

She was puzzled. "He seems perfectly unexceptionable to me."

"That, my dear, is Willoughby's eldest."

"What could be better—a title, an old name, and a fortune?"

"But he's barely dry behind the ears, and to make matters worse, he's a budding poet," he finished in accents of disgust.

"That's as may be, but I fail to understand your objections."

He snorted. "They're both babes in arms. He's as romantic as she is, and neither one of them has the least notion how to go on in the world."

"Well, of all the queer starts!" she gasped. "And why, pray tell, did you come to Cresswell if not to convince me that it was in Kitty's best interests to be married and off your hands as soon as possible?" A dangerous glint aappeared in the corner of her eye. "Doubtless you worked yourself up then for no other purpose than to brangle with me."

H had the grace to smile sheepishly. "Will you forgive me if I admit you were totally in the right of it? She is a dear girl, but she does want some town bronze and definitely a mature and sensible man for a husband."

She was mollified and impressed too by this handsome concession. Her mischievous smile as she magnanimously forgave him was so appealing that he decided there was a great deal to be said for humility.

The dance had long since ended, but the two of them, so engrossed in their conversation, might never have noticed it had not Bertie come up and said meaningfully, "I'm ready now, so you must dance this next with me, as you promised." Frances laughed gaily, nodded a smiling thank-you to Mainwaring, and whirled off, leaving his lordship slightly miffed at the easy way she quitted him to share secrets with his friend.

I must be in my dotage, he thought. A chit with an unbecoming habit of arriving at and voicing her own opinions is on intimate terms with the friend I asked to take charge of her. I should be congratulating myself on my own cleverness at ridding myself of her with such aplomb. And I *do* congratulate myself, he averred with total lack of conviction.

A sharp voice at his elbow observed, "I like that gel. She's got style and she's got sense—a looker, too."

"A little too much sense for her own good, but . . . she does have a certain something."

Unlike her grandson, the perspicacious old dowager marchioness had no difficulty in interpreting the cause of the slight frown creasing his brow. She chuckled gleefully and settled herself to await further developments. It was going to be a long time. Mainwaring had not the slightest inkling of how much Lady Frances meant to him. And, by the looks of it, the girl was no more aware of her feelings than he was. When and if they tumbled to their situation, the ensuing courtship would be even more interesting. The dowager hadn't enjoyed herself so much in years.

Meanwhile, on the dance floor Lady Frances finally broke in on her companion's thoughts. "Out with it, Bertie. The suspense is killing me. The look on your face tells me that you have devised A PLAN."

A smile of satisfaction spread across his features. "It's quite simple, really," he admitted modestly. "I shall just tell her I ain't the marrying kind, and if I were, her daughter ain't the kind I would want to marry." Frances eyed him skeptically. "Well, it's the truth, ain't it?" he muttered defensively.

"Oh, I'm not challenging your veracity, merely your optimism. I think you underestimate Lady Dartington's determination and her desperation. A woman of her kidney isn't put off by something as paltry as the truth. Let me see," she ruminated. "I shall tell her that Lady Streatham and I had had you in mind for her daughter until we began to wonder about your past."

"Past!" he exclaimed indignantly. "I haven't got a past!"

"That's exactly why we've been wondering about it."

Comprehension dawned. "I must say, Fan, that's devilish clever. Because the less you say, the worse she'll think it is, and that old beldame is quite gothic. Even my mother thinks she's hideously straitlaced, and the Mater's so rigid herself it don't bear thinking of." He maneuvered her deftly back to the corner where Lady Streatham and the dowager were holding forth.

These two ladies looked slightly conscious as Frances approached, but she was too busy trying to catch a glimpse of Kitty to notice. They had been amusing themselves the past half-hour counting the number of times Mainwaring's eyes had strayed to whatever part of the room happened to be graced by Frances and her partner at that moment. Naturally, Julian was the perfect host, moving easily among his guests, chatting with this dowager, helping along that young woman's reputation by stopping to talk with her, giving his opinions on the probable speed of Stapleton's new bays to a group of young bucks, but this behavior seemed curiously mechanical to those who knew him best. In fact, after his last waltz, he had seemed, for Mainwaring at least, unusually abstracted.

He approached now as he saw Frances joining them. She had laughed and chatted gaily enough all evening, but to him her face looked pale and slightly drawn. He smiled kindly at her. "Do me a favor and sit the next one out with me. I fear I am getting too old for this frantic frivolity."

"Doing it much to brown, my lord, for one who has just

returned from Vienna. I expect there might be some skills of yours that became rusty there, but dancing was not one of them.''

''No? Well, let's just say that I had enough of dancing and diplomacy to last a lifetime, and not nearly enough rational conversation. But do let me get you some refreshment.'' He disappeared into the supper room, his tall form towering above those around him. Unbidden, and certainly unexpected, the thought came to Frances that with his broad shoulders, severe dress, and air of command, he dwarfed almost everyone else in the room. She had never really paid much attention to what men looked like. She either liked or disliked them, but recognizing the attraction that a strong face, responsive dark blue eyes, and well-knit physique could hold was a novel sensation. Before she had time enough to explore and feel threatened by this sensation, the marquess had returned to ply her with a variety of delicacies and an absurd description of Kilson's struggles to adjust to the snobberies of London servants. She enjoyed it hugely, for he was a good storyteller, but some of the strain remained at the back of her eyes. He frowned slightly and offered to have someone call her carriage. ''You have done your duty here and I am persuaded you would feel much more the thing if you were to get some rest.'' She started to protest, but with so little conviction that he soon overrode her objections and summoned one of the footmen hovering at the side of the ballroom. ''I shall spirit you out so no one will know you have left. Besides, you have made your appearance, so if you are now missed, no one can fault you.'' She smiled gratefully and allowed him to lead her to her carriage.

Before handing her in, he adjured her to get a good rest. ''Are you still worried?'' She shook her head slightly. Not at all satisfied by such an equivocal response, he cupped her chin in his fingers and tilted it up. ''Now, look at me and tell me you promise not to fret yourself, especially since you know I shall call tomorrow to give that young would-be equestrian a severe talking-to.''

Frances looked into his dark blue eyes and read such a wealth of concern that she was too touched to reply. She nodded. ''That's my girl.'' He handed her into the carriage, but retained her hand in his strong clasp. "No more giving way to irrational fears. Promise me?"

She looked at him and for an instant as transfixed by the intensity of his gaze. "I promise." He squeezed her hand ever so gently before placing it in her lap, shutting the door and sending her on her way. She leaned back against the squabs. It had been quite a day. One that had forced her through a gamut of emotions: fear for Freddie, unexpected enjoyment of the ball, and now an odd feeling of some special bond, some private communication with Mainwaring. She didn't know what to make of it or of the attention he seemed to be paying her, and she wasn't at all certain how she felt about it. At the time, she had enjoyed the strength of his arms around her as they danced, sensing a special friendliness in the smile he seemed to reserve just for her, and had appreciated the attractive picture he presented as he moved among his guests. She hadn't thought much about it until he had held her hand and looked at her in such a way. Then she began to realize just how disturbingly attractive he really was to her. She felt slightly breathless and excited. Now it dawned on her that she had felt that way with him several times this evening. Whatever it is, it won't do, my girl, she admonished herself sternly. Men, particularly those of Lord Mainwaring's discriminating taste, aren't likely to feel anything for one such as you, much less heightened pulses. Best to forget it all. With this salutary thought, which somehow vanished as quickly as it came, she fell into a pleasant reverie that lasted until they arrived in Brook Street.

20

T rue to his word, Lord Mainwaring appeared in Brook Street at the unfashionably early hour of ten o'clock the next morning. He too had undergone some soul-searching the night before, and as he sauntered leisurely along, all his thoughts from the previous evening returned with a vengeance. Until the ball he had enjoyed Lady Frances' company for her quick grasp of a variety of subjects, her interested and intelligent comments, and her complete disregard for any of the flirtatious arts most women practiced assiduously on him. He admired her elegant taste and the quiet courage with which she shouldered enormous responsibilities, but he certainly had not felt anything more for her than admiration and a friendly wish to alleviate some of her responsibilities. Somehow, as they had been whirling around the floor, things had changed—so subtly that it had been some time before he was aware of the difference. She had felt so slight and graceful in his arms that her brief admission of her fears for her graceless brother tore at his heart. When she had tried to smile and quickly blink away the tears in her clear hazel eyes, he had wanted nothing more than to crush her in his arms and kiss the lips that would tremble in spite of her best efforts. He too had sensed that strong bond between them as he helped her into her carriage, and had tried ruthlessly to suppress these unwanted and most disquieting feelings. You're returning to your salad days, my boy. You've been away from the charms of London and London beauties so long that when one of them looks at you gratefully you are knocked into the middle of next week. She's only one of a dozen pretty faces—and not the prettiest of them either. But he knew he was wrong, that beauty had very little to do with it. Botheration! The more you try to define it, the worse case you become. It was almost with relief that he recognized Lady Jersey beckoning to him. That lively lady's naughty flirtation had soon banished all such unwelcome reflections.

Fortunately for his peace of mind, Lady Frances was not at home when he arrived. As a treat after her nursing of Freddie, she had taken Cassie to the Tower, as Cassie had been wishing to view the lions at greater length than they had the previous visit. Frances had come home the previous night to find the little girl reading to Freddie in a valiant effort to put her twin to sleep and keep herself awake. She had barely managed to keep from bursting with pride as she shushed her sister. "Be very quiet, Fan. I've just now managed to get him to sleep." She nodded importantly. "He was a little feverish, but I bathed his face with lavender water. I believe it is said a good night's sleep is the best thing for a fever." Frances had no trouble in identifying the source of this wisdom, having heard Aunt Harriet intone it repeatedly during her childhood illnesses.

So it was that Mainwaring had the patient all to himself when Higgins showed him into the nursery. Its occupant was sitting up in bed scowling at *Robinson Crusoe*. He glanced up fretfully when he heard Higgins cough, but on seeing his visitor, became instantly animated. "Sir, I did not expect to see you here!" he exclaimed in astonishment, but with such a look of unfeigned admiration that the marquess began to question his ability to measure up to the demigod status to which Freddie seemed determined to elevate him.

"Well, cawker, I came to see how you did. And since I think this, ahem, unfortunate incident is partly my fault, I've come to take your mind off any ill effects of your adventure and to keep your sister from feeling compelled to amuse you. I thought you might enjoy this. I found it rather well done." He handed the invalid the latest engravings of some "prime bits of blood" done in the manner of Stubbs.

"Oh, sir," Freddie breathed. "They're wonderful! They do look so real they seem to step right off the page, don't they?" Then, remembering his manners, he added shyly, "I do thank you. It's very kind of you to think of me."

"Not at all. As I say, I feel slightly responsible for putting the idea in your head. Besides, I know just how tedious recuperation can be. I once took a rather ugly gash one night in India from a dacoit who was trying to break into the shipping office. It wasn't all that bad, just across my arm, but it was deep, and out there you never know what complications will occur, what with their dreadful fevers and such. I knew that for my own good I should stay quiet, but I can tell you it was dull as dishwater lying there with nothing but my account books for amusement. However, I was right to do so, and I breezed right through it, unlike another poor fellow I knew. He cut his hand on a nail in a packing barrel he was unloading, contracted the most violent fever, and was gone within the day."

"Fanny said you had traveled, but I thought she meant around the Continent, you know, the Grand Tour and the Congress. She didn't tell me you'd been in India. Did you see any tigers? Were there lots of deadly snakes and spiders?" Freddie asked hopefully.

The marquess had purposely brought in his accident to amuse the boy, but he had underestimated the curiosity of an intelligent eleven-year-old starved for tales of masculine adventure. Before he knew it, he was regaling Freddie with one story after another, from Cape Town to Calcutta. It did him good in the rather stifling atmosphere of mid-Season social London to recall those free and easy days when his quick intelligence and athletic skills were more useful and more admired than his name and the size of his rent roll. And he truly enjoyed making Freddie's eyes shine with excitement as he drew exotic pictures of tiger hunts, ships battling monsoons, and hostile rajahs. Moreover, he was impressed with the thoughtfulness revealed by the boy's questions and felt a real sense of pride in being able to bring to him a world that was at once diverting and educational. He experienced a sense of usefulness that he had not felt in a long time. In fact, he couldn't remember when he had last sensed that he, as a person apart from all he stood for, was important to anyone. Having spent a rather lonely childhood as the second son of a father who concentrated all his affections and energies on his heir, Julian had never looked on children as anything but necessary encumbrances for other people concerned with carrying on family names and traditions. He was surprised how much he enjoyed Freddie's company. He was even more surprised, when Frances appeared, to discover that he had been there an hour and a half.

She had come dashing up the stairs in a most unladylike fashion to check on her little brother. When she saw him, arms encircling his knees, listening with rapt attention to a description of tracking a man-killing elephant, she screeched to a halt, but it was too late to keep from interrupting. "Fanny, look at this capital book Lord Mainwaring brought me! And he's been telling me the most bang-up things about India. They make the Greek bandits who attacked your trip to Delphi seem pretty tame, I can tell you."

She smiled at the marquess, shrugging apologetically. "I can see that my one claim to fame, my storytelling skill, has been completely cast in the shade. I can only warn you, my lord, that with fame comes responsibility, and you will now be hounded to death."

"Oh, Fan, come now, you know I don't *hound* you and I certainly wouldn't bother his lordship," protested her outraged sibling. "Besides," he added with his engaging grin, "I know how much store you grown-ups set by learning, and these stories are as good as a geography lesson any day."

"Freddie, my boy, you are incorrigible even when you are ill. I wish you'd gotten a stronger bump on the head. But, there, I only came up to check on you, not to give you a bear-garden jaw. I'll let Lord Mainwaring finish his tale."

As she closed the door behind her, Freddie whispered conspiratorially to his companion, "She's a great gun, and I do love her. She doesn't ever nag or worry. But sometimes it is nice to talk to a man. I mean, women don't have many adventures, do they, sir? Fan has set-tos with Snythe and frequently she has to give Farmer Stubbs a talking-to, but those aren't really exciting. About the most dangerous thing she ever did was to go tell a wicked-looking Gypsy king that his band couldn't camp on our lands because she didn't want them stealing the chickens. But you'd never find her doing anything as thrilling as hunting a tiger.''

Privately Mainwaring thought that Lady Frances Cresswell led a more hair-raising existence than most of his London acquaintances, but he realized the futility of explaining that to a bloodthirsty eleven-year-old. "Well, I do agree she is an excellent sister. You mustn't be too hard on her. After all, she isn't as old as I and she's been too busy looking after Cresswell and you two to get herself into as many ticklish spots as I have.''

Freddie was much struck by this novel view. He had never really stopped to consider that his sister might have wished to do something else besides managing the estate and bringing up him and Cassie. It suddenly occurred to him that teaching them Latin and geometry might be as dull and dry for her as it was for them. After all, they were only doing it for the first time and she was doing it for the second! Such drudgery didn't bear thinking of. Being a sympathetic lad, he was already concerned about the worry his accident might have caused her, but he had never stopped to think that the routine of daily existence at Cresswell might be as unadventurous for her as it was for him— more so because she wasn't constantly falling out of trees or tearing her clothes or getting caught trying to free the rabbits in Snythe's snares.

Mainwaring said good-bye to the patient, warning him that though his head might feel perfectly recovered to him in a horizontal position, any attempt to assume a vertical one would probably make him extremely unwell. Freddie grinned. "I may get into scrapes, but I'm not a complete bacon-brain, sir.''

"No," agreed his lordship. "But you certainly are an impudent scamp.''

The marquess stopped in the front parlor, where he found Frances sorting through a sheaf of bills and frowning over the price of feed. She rose, saying in her frank way, "How very kind of you to visit and to hit upon the very thing to keep him quiet.'' She would have gone on, but Mainwaring dismissed her thanks with a wave of his hand.

"I like Freddie. He's a bright lad and he has a great deal of spunk. Besides, if I hadn't taken you all to Astley's, he never would have gotten such a maggot in his brain in the first place.''

She interrupted, ''Well, that is complete nonsense, because you know any child even halfway interested in horses feels compelled to experiment just as he did. After all, I had a very similar escapade and I am sure you did too.''

He smiled rather bitterly, she thought. "No, in a vain attempt to win my father's approval, I was a model child.''

"Thus your excessively adventurous existence in subsequent years,'' she teased.

He grinned. "You must admit that these 'excessive adventures,' as you so skeptically call them, served their purpose today. I told Freddie such a hair-raising story about complications attending a seemingly simple accident that I promise you he won't stir from his bed for days.''

The quizzing look in her eyes disappeared, to be replaced by one of shy gratitude. "How very good you are to us, and just when you've had to take on such irksome new responsibilities of your own.''

He stood looking down at her, but his thoughts were elsewhere, and there was a rather fierce expression in his dark blue eyes. "My lord . . .'' She claimed his wandering attention.

His eyes softened. "Did you have no male relatives?''

Somewhat taken aback, she replied, "No, but we had no need of them.'' She raised her eyebrows, and a distinctly frosty note crept into her voice. "Are you again questioning my capabilities? I assure you I have more sense than Papa's nearest relatives, distant as they are, all rolled into one.''

"Gently, my child. I have no quarrel with your obvious capabilities. I was merely thinking of you and the time you are forced to lavish on others when you should be spending it on yourself.''

"And what would I do with that time? Do as everyone else would have me do and flit from one social event to another, flirting with all and sundry to catch myself either someone who spends his entire time and energy choosing and changing clothes or some beefy squire who does nothing but hunt and is a great deal worse than I at managing Cresswell?''

He took both her hands in a firm clasp. ''Don't fly into a pelter. I would, if I could, give you time to ride or to write without eternally having to stop and cope with some problem. I would wish you free from worrying about the twins' education so you could visit all the museums, attend all the lectures, and enjoy all the concerts and plays that you wish.''

She glanced at him in some surprise. He truly was thinking of her, and showing an understanding that no one had ever shown before. Such sympathy quite undid her, and tears pricked at her eyelids as she gazed down at her hands in his. He raised them to his lips, forcing her to look up at him. ''Don't wear yourself out, my girl. You take things so much to heart that *your* health is in far more danger than Freddie's.'' He pressed a warm kiss on each hand, gave her an encouraging smile, and was gone, leaving her in a daze.

Finally she shook her head and returned to her bills, but try as she would, she could not focus on the figures. She kept seeing, instead, the concern in his eyes, hearing the understanding in his voice, and feeling the pressure of his lips on her hands. She tried to recapture her equanimity by explaining away his concern: he is so accustomed to running everything, to being admired and flattered, that he can't bear the thought that he might be responsible for some mishap. All this attention is to keep you from thinking the same thing. Now that he's done his duty and called on you, he'll think no more about it. But try as she would to put it down to arrogance, she kept remembering his sympathetic reading of her life and interpretation of her dreams.

21

Contrary to Lady Frances' prediction, Lord Mainwaring continued to demonstrate his interest in the invalid and his family. Ostensibly, he came to see Freddie, maintaining that he didn't trust such an adventuresome spirit for a minute, but he managed to inject some enthusiasm into Cassie, who was at the same time concerned for her twin and ever so slightly jealous of all the attention he was receiving. As she later confided with great pride to her sister, "He came and asked Higgins if I were free to drive in the park, just as if I were a grown-up lady. And he has such a bang-up pair and drives so well that simply everyone was looking at us." Freddie took this in good part, though he would have willingly traded all his tin soldiers to Cassie for the honor of driving with his hero.

Even Aunt Harriet had a good word to say for him. "He brought some excellent cuttings that his gardener had sent, as well as some fine fruit from the hothouse at Camberly, and how he talked that uppity gardener out of them is more than I can tell."

Despite his attention to the other Cresswells, his real concern was for Frances, and he made sure that every day she got to the park for some fresh air and adult conversation. His earlier impressions were confirmed and he found her informed and interested in a wide variety of subjects. Their discussions ranged from Prinny's evolving designs for his Pavilion to the constant bickerings at the Congress of Vienna to crop rotation. Lady Frances was rediscovering the joys of intelligent companionship, a component of her life that had vanished with her father's death. How delightful it was to be able to share ideas and worries with someone who could understand them and offer a perspective different from her own. It was rare that she could talk with neighbors about anything more theoretical than breeding horses, and even then, they looked askance at any ideas more recent than the previous century. Here was someone who was ready to try new things, who had an inquiring mind that he stimulated by constant reading and travel. This adventurous outlook, as much as the information he had gathered from a vast array of experiences, excited her interest and her own curiosity, making her realize how much of her own personal development she had been neglecting for the past few years.

They had just considered in great depth the relative merits of a free, relatively informal exchange in international politics so beloved by Castlereagh. Having thrashed out the pros and cons to their mutual satisfaction, they were driving along in companionable silence, enjoying the fineness of the day, when the marquess suddenly turned to her, remarking, "Freddie tells me that you are always having some set-to or other with Snythe."

This was dangerous ground, and Frances considered for a moment before venturing mildly, "Well, he isn't the easiest person to rub along with."

"Meaning . . . ?" he prompted, raising one dark brow.

She saw that he was not going to let her escape with generalities, but remembering the great exception he had taken to her previous criticism, she trod warily. "He doesn't know how to get along very well with your tenants or mine."

"To be exact, he bullies those who stand most in need of his advice and makes unwelcome advances to their daughters, while behaving most obsequiously to the other, more respectable elements in the district."

"He is the most odious toad of a man it has ever been my misfortune to meet!" she responded, her eyes kindling at some unfortunate memories. Yet she was impressed at his accurate reading of the man's character and his grasp of the situation.

"And what would you have me do with such a man? Turning him over to local justice will merely serve to exacerbate the situation. He will become a more intolerable bully and a more groveling toad than ever."

She looked up in some surprise. His solicitation of her opinion, for which he had taken her to task a few months earlier, was unexpected. A man as accustomed to command and as sure of himself as Julian Mainwaring was not given to asking advice—especially from women who had only a particle of his experience and were much younger besides. She half-suspected him of mockery, but one surreptitious glance out of the corner of her eye assured her that he was serious.

In fact, she would have been even more astonished to learn that the man she had just labeled as self-assured was, at that moment, at a loss. He was trying to decide what it was about his companion that made him find her so charming. She was no more than pretty, and he was a man who could, and did, demand nothing less than overwhelming beauty in his mistresses. In spite of her air of quiet elegance, she was not at all fashionable, nor did she care to be. She had not the least notion how to carry on a flirtation. In fact, she was far more likely to ask him about improving her stock than she was to admire the cut of his coat, the truly legendary quality of his horseflesh, his rig, or his skill in managing both. No, she had none of the standard qualitites of the women he usually admired, but somehow she made him feel more appeciated for the qualities that were uniquely his than the most flattering of his mistresses. He liked the frank way she looked at him when talking to him. The questions she asked revealed how closely she listened to what he had to say and how much she respected his judgments. Only a very few of his closest and oldest friends recognized how carefully he considered before forming them. And none of them felt close enough to quiz him in quite the manner that she did. In a way, this teasing was complimentary because it showed that she believed him aware enough of her high opinion of him to recognize that her criticisms were purely ironic. It was an intimacy that no woman except his grandmother had shared with him. He found it endeared her to him and touched him at the same time. In spite of their early differences, she had come to value his opinion and to trust him as a friend. Oddly enough, he found this trust more gratifying than many greater honors he had achieved over the years.

Her thoughtful reply interrupted his speculations. "Yes, I know it is difficult, especially as he is someone who bitterly resents criticism and is so relentless in bearing a grudge. What if you were to send him to one of your establishments in India or the West Indies? You could allow him to think of it as an advancement, a chance to make his fortune, when in reality you would probably be throwing him among a group of people who are as conniving as he and would make short work of him. They certainly wouldn't allow him to bully them as the poor people around Camberly and Cresswell do."

Mainwaring was much struck by her perspicacity and the soundness of her suggestion. "A very good idea. You have an excellent sense of people. I wish it were you I could send to oversee my affairs."

"A fine mess I should make of them if I can't even keep an eleven-year-old from making a fool of himself." Nevertheless, she flushed with pleasure at this unexpected praise.

They found themselves in such charity with each other that they were both surprised and sorry at how swiftly the time passed. It seemed they had been gone no time at all when they completed their tour of the park and returned to Brook Street. In fact, they had been out the better part of two hours. Higgins was the only member of the household to note this, but its significance was not lost on him. "I can't recall when Miss Fanny took such pleasure in anyone's company, excepting her dear father's, of course," he confided to Cook. Though she had been in name, as well as fact, the head of Cresswell for some years now, and had been managing the household in a highly efficient and satisfactory manner, she was still "Miss Fanny" to her loyal servants.

Kilson and Higgins were not the only ones observing with interest the growing intimacy between Lady Frances Cresswell and Lord Julian Mainwaring, Marquess of Camberly. In the opulently decorated house in Mount Street, Lady Vanessa

Welford was beginning to be seriously annoyed at the turn of events. She was aware of precisely the amount of time her lover was spending in Brook Street, exactly the number of drives during which Lady Frances was his companion, not to mention the dances when she had been his partner, and she was not the least bit pleased. She would never have stooped to ordering her servants to spy on him for her, but Polly, her abigail, soon discovered that the number of dresses thrown her way because her ladyship "couldn't bear to be seen another time in that old rag" increased in proportion to the number of reports she brought of the marquess's doings. And a certain footman noticed that Miss Polly acted far more interested in him if he were able to tell her precisely where Lord Mainwaring's equipage had seen that day.

The friendship between Mainwaring and Frances had even come to the attention of some sharp-eyed members of the *ton*, who were not behindhand in putting this intriguing tidbit to the best possible use. Thus at Lady Billingsford's card party, the marquess's mistress was forced to appear conveniently hard of hearing when Lady Stavely confided to her bosom friend Edwina Hamilton in tinkling tones clearly audible throughout the room, "I do believe Mainwaring must be looking for a wife. He seems to have changed his preference for older, ahem, 'sophisticated' women to those who have a number of childbearing years left. Lady Frances Cresswell is a delightful girl. I would be happy to see her so well-settled, and it does seem as though he's trying to fix his interest there. My dear, he's her constant companion, they say."

Lady Welford, a determined smile pinned on her face, never stopped to consider that Lady Stavely's good opinion of the girl she would never have noticed two months ago had less to do with the delightfulness of Lady Frances than with the fact that until the advent of Lord Mainwaring, Lord Stavely had been Lady Welford's most devoted escort. Fuming inwardly, she managed to continue her hand, ignoring the knowing looks cast in her direction. She maintained her equanimity with aplomb, but took her leave as soon as it was possible to do so without occasioning further comment.

She spent a restless night pacing the floor, working on various ploys to heighten the marquess's dwindling interest. But no sooner had she conjured up one scheme than she discarded it as being too obvious or too desperate. Morning found her no closer to any plan of attack and a good deal more frustrated. Of course, the sleepless night had not improved her countenance, and it seemed to her, after nearly an hour spent contemplating her reflection in the mirror, that she had never looked more hag-ridden. Wrinkles and gray hairs, which had never dared show themselves before, now popped up all over. By the time her maid appeared with her morning chocolate, she was in a thoroughly bad humor, which she alleviated only slightly by giving the poor girl a regular tongue-lashing for having let it become lukewarm. The arrival of a new walking dress of a muslin so fine it made only the barest pretense of covering her limbs restored her humor somewhat, as did the arrival of a huge bouquet from a callow youth who had seen her at the opera the previous evening. She had no intention of allowing him to dangle after her, but the intensity of the infatuation was gratifying nevertheless.

Several hours later, a testimony to the art and artifice of her abigail and the expert hands of a wonderful new French hairdresser, she was at last able to face herself in the mirror again with satisfaction. The elegant visage looking back at her was encouraging enough to send her off to display her charms in the park. The flimsy walking dress, trimmed with deep flounces that made it cling even more, was further enhanced by a bonnet of straw-colored satin, matching parasol, green kid sandals, and a green sarcenet pelisse that she left open to reveal the full effect of the muslin dress. And she was able to console herself with the thought that though she lacked the youth of Lady Frances, she certainly was quite at the top of the mode, something which even the most enthusiastic of Frances' admirers could not say of that young lady.

Fortune, so noticeably absent the previous evening, was smiling on her today. She had not gone ten steps into the park when she encountered Mainwaring cutting through on his way to Mainwaring House. "Julian," she trilled, shrugging the

pelisse open further. "How delightful to run into you. I haven't
seen you this age."

The marquess did not look best pleased at this encounter.
"Hello, Vanessa, you're looking exquisite as usual," he greeted
her, edging in the direction of Grosvenor Square.

Not about to let such a golden opportunity escape her, Lady
Welford slipped her hand through his arm and leaned her ample
charms tantalizingly close. "Do walk with me a little way,"
she invited, gazing meltingly up at him and fluttering dark
lashes.

He was fairly caught, but managed to stifle his annoyance
with a semblance of good humor. "Very well, but I can't spend
too long, as I am taking tea with my grandmother."

Lady Welford knew very well what that old tartar thought
of her grandson's latest flirt, and she also knew that she
demanded punctuality. Sighing inwardly, she determined to
make the most of the little time she had. Try as she would to
win his lordship's attention with her most amusing stories and
her most scandalous *on-dits*, she could see that his thoughts
remained elsewhere. She eventually decided to abandon her
verbal attempts to attract his interest in favor of a more physical
approach. She had just draped herself more voluptuously along
his arm and tilted her gaze even more seductively up at him
when they rounded a bend and came face-to-face with Lady
Frances in charge of a schoolroom party.

Freddie had adhered so scrupulously to Mainwaring's
strictures that he had recovered rapidly and was soon
pronounced well enough to venture out-of-doors. Cassie, in-
spite of her drive with his lordship, had been frantic to get out
and enjoy the beautiful weather. Thus at the soonest possible
moment, Frances had taken them for a leisurely turn around
the park. In addition to the twins, she had invited Ned, who
was often left to his own devices while Kitty made her social
rounds. He provided a quieting influence on the twins' high
spirits that was especially useful at this stage in Freddie's
recuperation. Naturally, Wellington was not about to allow any
one of the Cresswells out without his valiant escort. Who knew
what horrible mongrels might be lurking in the bushes? And
even Nelson, his courage bolstered by the fineness of the day

and the size of the expedition, overcame his fear of London traffic enough to join them. Frances had her hands full trying to convince Wellington not to chase after Mr. Poodle Byng's carriage to challenge the right of his canine companion, that supercilious cur, to respect from all other dogs. Cassie, Freddie, and Ned were in whoops at the absurdity of Mr. Byng's turnout. Thus they were a sizable, miscellaneous, and noisy group that approached Lady Welford and the marquess.

Confronted with the source of her ill temper, who was, furthermore, at a distinct disadvantage, Lady Welford seized the opportunity to eliminate the recipient of so much of the marquess's time and attention. As Lord Mainwaring helplessly ground his teeth and made the unavoidable introductions, she smiled indulgently at the younger woman and remarked with ill-concealed condescension, "Small wonder we see so little of you in society, Lady Frances, when you have all these claims on your attention. Of course, with these responsibilities and your bluestocking propensities, it is no wonder you haven't the time to be fashionable."

For a moment Lady Frances was speechless at the unexpected intensity of the attack. She was simply astonished by the animosity she saw in the other woman's eyes, and totally at a loss to explain it. However, she was not about to be snubbed by one such as Lady Welford. Gazing limpidly up at her opponent, with the faintest of smiles she explained, "But you see, I would so much rather be *respectable* than fashionable." Her deceptively mild tone was not lost on anyone as she continued, "I've heard so much about you, Lady Welford. I am glad I had the opportunity to meet you, but Freddie has not been well. I am sure you will forgive us for hurrying him home. Come, children. Good day to you, Lord Mainwaring, Lady Welford." With that she turned her back on both of them and shepherded the group along in the opposite direction.

An unbecoming shade of red suffused Vanessa Welford's features. Eyes narrowed, she hissed furiously, "Why, that impudent little nobody! How dared she! How dreadfully ill-bred of her!"

"Quite the contrary, Vanessa," an icy voice interrupted. "She showed considerable restraint in the face of one of the most vulgar and uncalled-for setdowns it has ever been my dubious privilege to witness.'' If Lady Welford's eyes flashed, her companion's glittered like chips of ice. The set of his jaw and the line of his dark brows were truly alarming as he hurried her to the edge of the park. Catching the attention of a passing hackney, he hailed it and handed her in, instructing the coachman as he did so, ''Take Lady, ahem, *Madam* Welford wherever she wishes to go.'' With that, he handed the man a heavy purse, slammed the door, turned on his heel, and strode furiously back into the park, leaving Vanessa staring after him, prey to the most unpleasant reflections.

Despite his hasty pace, Lord Mainwaring could catch no sight of Frances as he headed angrily back through the park in the direction of Mainwaring House. The disagreeableness of Vanessa's reflections was nothing compared to the turmoil of emotions besieging the marquess. The foremost was anger—anger at himself for allowing her to entrap him as she had that morning, for not rescuing Frances from an unpleasant situation even before Vanessa's insulting remarks, for not retrieving the situation after those remarks. There was blind fury at Vanessa for reading more into his relationship with her than there was, for putting him in such an impossible situation, and for behaving with such gratuitous cruelty. Anger was his instant reaction, but it was followed by a stronger, more complicated sense of unhappiness. The impression that remained with him the longest and the most bitterly was the shock and betrayal he had read in Frances' eyes. It had been almost immediately replaced by the anger that produced her effective reply, but for a brief moment her eyes had revealed the hurt of a loyal pet whose master has turned on it without cause or warning. Julian was tortured with remorse for being the unwitting instrument of such pain, and he wished with all his heart that he could have taken her in his arms then and there and kissed it gently and reassuringly away. And last of all, he was cynically grateful to Vanessa for having shown him at the same time how little he cared for her and how much he valued the friendship and good opinion of Lady Frances Cresswell.

By the time he arrived back at Grosvenor Square, the anger had burnt itself out, leaving him subdued, but with a corroding sense of loss and disillusionment. Kilson was totally mystified. "I ain't never seen himself look like that before in all the years I have been with his lordship," he confided later to Alice as he tried to fathom the cause. He nodded sagely. "If you ask me, this bears some watching."

22

"But, Fanny," protested Cassie, struggling to keep pace with her sister's angry stride, "I thought this was supposed to be a *restful* outing."

"It was," Frances snapped, slackening her pace somewhat. The twins exchanged puzzled glances and hurried along, eager to reach the privacy of the schoolroom, where they could sort out this unusual show of temper.

After bidding a hasty good-bye to Ned, they raced upstairs. "What do you think, Freddie?" his sister demanded. "I just asked her a question and she snapped my head off."

He considered a moment. "I'm not sure, but I think it had to do with Lord Mainwaring's being a friend of that lady. P'raps Fanny thought if he was a friend of that lady's he wouldn't be her friend. And I must say, I don't blame her. I wouldn't like a special friend of mine to be friendly with someone like that. You want to watch out for people like her," he confided darkly. "She has mean eyes. I think she's a bad 'un. We'd better warn Fan to keep a weather eye out for her."

"She doesn't seem to like Fan much either, though I can't think why," observed Cassie. "I wish there were some way we could keep that lady away from his lordship. Maybe we could ask Neddie to keep an eye out, and if she shows up at Mainwaring House, he could discourage her,'' she added, warming to the plan.

"Nah,'' scoffed her twin. "Don't be a bacon-brain. Ladies don't call on gentlemen.''

"Much you know,'' she retorted. "Ladies that wear dresses like that do!''

This unexpectedly superior worldly knowledge awed Freddie into silence, but his busy brain was scheming ways to keep his friend the marquess out of the clutches of someone who was so clearly a bad 'un.

Meanwhile, Higgins had stopped Frances in the midst of her angry flight. "The Comte de Vaudron is in the front parlour, my lady.''

"Thank you, Higgins,'' she managed as she stomped uptairs in a most unladylike fashion. Actually, the *comte* was just the person she needed at this particular moment. A combination of the sophisticated man-of-the-world and paternal adviser to her and the twins, he would be able to offer her the exact amount of wisdom and sympathy that the situation warranted.

"*Ma chère Fanny*,'' he exclaimed, rising to bow gracefully over her hand. His quick glance apprehended the state of affairs and he drew her to the couch, inquiring gently, "*Mais, ma petite*, what has put you in such a pucker? A young lady moving in the highest circles in the *ton* should be *aux anges* instead of wearing a face like a thundercloud.''

The sympathetic look and calmly supportive manner almost overset her, and she wished with all her heart that she could climb into his lap and burst into tears, as she had so many years ago in Greece when her pet bird had flown away. "It is nothing, really, *monsieur*.'' She pushed aside a stray lock of hair, grimacing at her overwrought state.

" 'Uncle Maurice,' please. And I know you, Fanny. You are of such good sense that you do not fly into a pelter over nothing. Come, tell me about it.''

And as she had done so many times before, she found herself confiding in him. He sat silent during the entire recital, raising a speculative eyebrow here and there, but otherwise making no comment. When she had finished, he stared thoughtfully into space for some time, wondering exactly how conversant Frances was with his lordship's amorous affairs.

She broke in on his thoughts. "Am I that much of a quiz, then? Is that truly what they say of me?"

He snorted. "*They* don't say anything at all about you, my dear."

"But," she pursued, "am I so dowdy, then?"

"You are always *très elegante, ma chère,*" he replied slowly. Then, recognizing the seriousness of her concern, he added, "But *un peu sèvére, n'est-ce pas?*" He hastened to reassure her, "But, my child, with all you have to think about, how could you be anything else?"

"It isn't fair," she protested. "Why is it that women of lively intelligence and high values are labeled prudes, while someone such as Lady Welford, with only her beauty to recommend her, wins admiration and attention?"

The picture suddenly became abundantly clear to the *comte*, but he managed to phrase his answer in the same vague generalities used by Frances. "I can see that for all your intelligence, you are not very clever about people, *mon enfant*, and about *les hommes du monde* in particular. Everyone wants to enjoy himself. No one wishes to worry, to think seriously and question deeply. Thus they are attracted to those who make them enjoy life, make them forget any cares or responsibilities. Now, someone such as Lady Welford devotes all of her energies to making people, men in particular, do just that. She makes them forget anything except how beautiful she is and how important she makes them feel, and the pleasure she can bring them. Ah . . ." He held up an admonishing hand. "I know that you will say this is hypocritical, and you would be entirely correct. But there are other people who enjoy life in a less-cynical and manipulative manner. They delight in life, relishing everything from playing with their children, to attending concerts of ancient music, to giving balls and parties, to gardening, and they are loved and enjoyed wherever they are, whether or not they are beautiful or fashionable. Your Lady Streatham is such a one who has this *joie de vivre, non*? And there are others who cultivate this most supreme of all social talents. I know you scorn those who live in the lives of social butterflies, but you must look upon the *ton* in the civilized way we French do. To us, this social intercourse is an art to be cultivated, as much as proficiency at watercolors or the piano-forte. To dress oneself beautifully, to bring wit and intelligence to conversation, is to bring pleasure to other people. Just because one is a skilled conversationalist does not mean that one must confine one's conversation to superficialities. And selecting clothes that are exquisite or hair styles dressings that are appropriate, particularly to oneself, are as much expressions of one's personality and aesthetic philosophy as collecting Dutch masters or antiquities.'' He could see she was much struck, and pressed his point home. "And this is not self-indulgent or frivolous. Quite the contrary, it shows an awareness and a concern for the enjoyment of other people.''

Frances sat quietly, her brow wrinkled in thought. Unpleasant as it was to face, she admitted that she did allow herself to become immersed in the seriousness of her responsibilities, to the exclusion of enjoyment. To others she must seem dull and prudish. She raised troubled eyes. "And how would you have someone who knows nothing of this change?''

The count's eyes twinkled as he thought: I knew we should soon get around to this. But he kept these reflections to himself as he continued blandly, "I would first have that person go to a modiste of my acquaintance, who is exceptionally skilled at designing creations that are accurate reflections of the wearer's true personality. These modistes today, bah! They are clothes-mongers who pay no attention to the person they are dressing. They cover fat dowagers with ruchings and flounces. They over-whelm delicate ladies with bows and elaborate corsages. In short, they fit their patronesses to their fashions, instead of the way it should be. Once a woman is elegantly garbed in something that makes her feel beautiful, without changing her into a doll dressed up in what fashion dictates, then she is confident and relaxed enough to pay attention to others, to share her wit and conversation in a way that amuses.''

"Do you think your strategy would work for someone like me?'' Frances asked shyly.

With just the correct mixture of surprise and interest he reassured her. "You, *mon enfant*? But it would be the most delightful thing! And certain to prove the efficacy of my system." He held up an admonitory hand. "But even though you could be assured of success, I couldn't guarantee to make you into an incomparable or even a diamond . . . at least not overnight. Even *I* don't dictate society's whims to that extent. But you don't want that, do you?" He asked this with deceptive innocence, having a very good idea of exactly what she did want.

The sparkle reappeared in Lady Frances' eyes. "That would be capital, *monsieur*. Thank you ever so much."

"*Mon enfant*, we shall begin at once," he began with Gallic enthusiasm. "But, please, no more, '*monsieur*'—'Uncle Maurice,' as I once was for you."

Frances smiled. "*Eh, bien, mon oncle. En avant.*" If the energy and gaiety in her voice were a trifle forced, no one but an uncle, and one well-versed in the ways of the world at that, would have noticed this unnatural exuberance.

He gave a conspiratorial wink and replied, "We shall visit my friend immediately, as soon as you are ready."

Frances dashed upstairs to assure herself that Cassie and Freddie were at their lessons, which, hearing her on the stairs, they were perusing diligently when she entered the schoolroom. "I am just going out with the Comte de Vaudron. You can finish that chapter on Caesar without me, but I shall ask you to tell me all about it when I return."

The twins nodded and kept their expressions of earnest scholasticism until they heard the carriage roll away. "Now, where do you suppose Fan is going in such a hurry?" Freddie wondered.

"At least she no longer seems so angry," his twin volunteered. "I hope she won't remain angry, because she's not nearly as good a friend when she is. Remember the last time she got really mad, I mean, really, really mad at Snythe? Why, she even snapped at Wellington and Aunt Harriet," Cassie reminisced.

Meanwhile, Lady Frances and the Comte de Vaudron were en route to the establishment of the count's friend Madame Regnery. Modiste to many of France's most aristocratic families, Madame had discovered her name on the list of the enemies of new republic just in time to make a hairbreadth escape in a linen draper's cart. Since coming to England, she had worked long, arduous hours to establish herself. Forced to inhabit the smallest of shops on South Moulton Street, which, if not directly on fashionable Bond Street, was at least within hailing distance of this mecca of the *haut monde*, she had had a difficult time of it. Those of her former illustrious customers who had not succumbed to La Guillotine were in no circumstances to patronize her. The English, an unadventurous race altogether, lacked the imagination to try someone new. Moreover, they were naturally suspicious of a novelty that also happened to be French.

Thus, the sight of such an old and still solvent patron as the *comte* was a very welcome one indeed. Madame hastened to him, hands outstretched in greeting. "*Monsieur le Comte! Il y a longtemps, n'est-ce pas*? But," she broke into prettily accented English, "I can see your companion is English. What may I do for you today?"

"*Eh bien*, Henriette, you may do nothing less than effect a transformation," he replied, bending over one work-worn hand.

"A transformation? But of whom? Surely you don't mean of this young lady? But she is already so charming."

Here Frances broke in. "*Mais non, madame*. I do not wish to be merely '*charmante*.' That is what one says of someone neither pretty enough to be a diamond nor ugly enough to be an eccentric or an heiress. In short, it means one is mediocre or, at the very least, excessively dull. I no longer wish to be either."

The count interrupted this impassioned diatribe, the bulk of whose significance was slightly lost on Madame. "What Mademoiselle would like to be is fashionable, *à la mode*, in a style that is particularly her own."

Comprehension dawned. "Ah, I understand," Madame replied, wrinkling her brow speculatively. "It should not be so difficult. *Mademoiselle est d'une taille elegante.* She carries herself with style already. She does not need all those laces, flounces, ruchings, and ribbons with which these young ladies ornament and obscure themselves. Bah! Such stupidity! One looks very much like another, and they all resemble a milliner's window. Mademoiselle has intelligence, character, and, I think, a subtle charm which is enhanced by simple design, *n'est-ce pas*?" She cocked a birdlike head in Frances' direction.

"I believe so, *madame*. At any rate, that is always what I have preferred," Frances began timidly.

"*Eh bien*. Marthe, bring the gossamer silk at once," demanded the little lady. "We begin with a ball dress because that is where one makes the greatest impression on the most people."

The faithful Marthe appeared bearing a shimmering roll of material which sparkled gold and emerald according to the light. "Oh, how lovely!" breathed Frances involuntarily as she caught sight of it.

Madame wore a satisfied smile. "You are quite correct, *mademoiselle*. It is most unusual. *Un ami* . . . a dear friend gave it to me just before I left. It was something they had just begun to work on at Lyons when . . . when . . ." She broke off.

Frances held out her hand. "But surely something such as this is far too precious for you to waste on someone who has no claim to fame, fashion, or great beauty."

The seamstress smiled through the tears she could not hide. "Mademoiselle sadly underestimates herself. But in any event, I would much rather adorn a heart as warm as yours than the most-toasted incomparable in London."

The next hours were, for Frances, a blur of laces, satins, gauzes, plain and printed muslins, ruchings, and flounces, the chatter of French and deft fingers pushing, pulling, fitting, and sewing. She emerged somewhat dazed, her wardrobe increased by an exquisite ball gown from Madame's special material, a carriage dress with a white satin pelisse, a walking dress of jaconet muslin over a peach-colored slip, two morning dresses, and another evening dress of an unusual rose satin slip with silver spangled gauze over it giving a most ethereal look. "I cannot thank you enough, *madame*, for having created costumes that fit me and the type of person I am," began Frances. But Madame was not yet through. While Frances was bemused by the selection of trimmings to embellish her choices, Marthe had been sent to fetch Monsieur Ducros, hairdresser to many of the ladies of Versailles. Frances was not at all certain she wanted the transformation to extend quite so far. "But I don't think . . . that is, I like the simple style I have now. It is not fussy, and that, you know, is of paramount importance when one leads a country life," she objected.

"Mademoiselle does have beautiful hair," agreed Monsieur. "But," he added severely, "she does nothing to show off its true beauty. As to the care . . ." He shrugged with true Gallic expression. "Why, the time you spend brushing it now is twice the care this new style would require."

"Very well," sighed Frances. "Never let it be said that I didn't do my utmost to be worthy of one of Madame's creations."

It would not be entirely accurate to say that Lady Frances Cresswell emerged from Regnery's establishment transformed into a diamond of the first water and bearing no earthly resemblance to the serious young woman who had entered some few hours before. She remained Lady Frances, but it was a different Lady Frances—one whose curls caught the light, softened her face, and gave it a slightly mischievous look. She was elegant as ever, but, wearing a new bonnet and a walking dress Madame had happened to have at hand, she somehow looked lighter, more carefree. The dress of primrose sarcenet under matching jaconet muslin with puffs down the sleeves and trimming at the hem was more elaborate than her usual style and lent an interesting air of fragility and delicacy. The ruffled parasol completed her toilette. The *comte* walked round and round, examining every detail. At last he stood back, his face breaking into a smile of paternal pride and satisfaction at his own cleverness. "Ah, *madame,* you have not lost your genius. And you . . ." He included Ducros in an expansive gesture. "You are more talented than ever. Thank you. Now, come, my child, we must show the rest of the world that you are a woman of exterior, as well as interior, beauty and taste." He bowed and escorted Frances to the carriage.

Though no one stopped to stare as they made their way home, their reception on Brook Street was highly gratifying. The twins, who had become more curious the more they discovered that no one in that establishment had the slightest idea of their elder sister's whereabouts, had been watching for her return from the drawing-room window. Higgins had barely closed the door behind Lady Frances and the *comte* when they came clattering downstairs, closely followed by Wellington and Nelson. The cavalcade screeched to a halt at Frances' elegant parasol and lemon kid slippers. "Fan!" Cassie exclaimed. "You look . . . you look beautiful!"

"Slap up to the echo," her twin agreed heartily.

Frances didn't know whether to feel flattered or insulted at the disbelief in their voices.

They walked around her, Cassie remarking in puzzled tones, "But, Fan, whatever for? I thought you detested dressing up. And at any rate, we thought you were pretty before." Wellington sniffed the new parasol but gave over as soon as he had established that it was too new to have acquired any interesting scents. Nelson examined the flounces with equal curiosity.

Frances was touched by their loyalty, but said in a rallying tone, "Well, now that I've been so thoroughly inspected and met with your approval, will you let us come in?" She smiled and led the way into the morning room. "Monsieur le Comte has, in addition to asking that we call him Uncle Maurice, invited us on a very special outing." Immediately all eyes were riveted on him. "He has invited us and Aunt Harriet to go with him to the botanic gardens at Kew. We shall pack a lovely picnic and make a real expedition of it. I thought we would ask Kitty and Ned to go with us as well."

"May we take Wellington and Nelson?" begged Cassie, seconded by Freddie. "Yes, please, Fan, may we? It's been so long since either one of them has been in the true country. I think they're becoming a bit tired of all the London traffic." Freddie remembered his manners. "But, I say, sir, it sounds like a bang-up idea. Thank you."

"Yes, thank you ever so much," added Cassie as the twins dashed out the door to tell their aunt of the forthcoming treat. "Aunt Harriet, Aunt Harriet, Uncle Maurice has invited all of us, even Wellington and Nelson, to the gardens. Aunt Harriet, Aunt Harriet . . ."

Frances turned to the count. "Thank you for giving us all something to look forward to."

He bowed over her hand, his eyes twinkling. "I shall be watching future events with interest myself," he replied somewhat enigmatically.

23

The Comte de Vaudron had no intention of concluding his campaign with the mere transformation of Frances' appearance. He was too much a man of the world to let it ride without laying further plans. He knew that no man, no matter how well-versed in fashion and the ways of the *ton*, could effect a change in someone's social reputation as well as a woman could, so he made his way as quickly as possible to someone who had been making and breaking reputations for forty years—the dowager Marchioness of Camberly.

She was delighted to welcome a visitor who brought, along with news of the latest scandals, memories of a past in which she had lived close to the edge of scandal herself. "Maurice," she sighed as he bent over a beringed hand. "You look as distinguished as ever. How delightful to have you back in London."

He smiled. "I wish I could say how delightful it is to see you queening it over all of them in your old haunts, but you insist on remaining a recluse."

"Well, to tell you the truth," she responded in a conspiratorial whisper, "I find that I hear just as much of what is happening if I remain here entertaining a few select friends who visit me.

It's much less fatiguing than the eternal dressing and promenading, and it's far more entertaining because one sees only whomever one wishes.''

He smiled fondly. "But, my dear Marianne, it is so much more boring without you for those of us who continue to dress and promenade.''

"Be off with you, Maurice. You always were too charming for your own good." But the dowager looked pleased in spite of herself. Not being one to waste time with mere civilities, she inquired, "You know how glad I am to see you, but as you are not one of my regular callers, more shame on you, I surmise you have some special object in visiting me?''

"*Mais certainement*, Marianne, I do. Though you maintain you have left the *ton* for a more peaceful existence, I know that you retain as much influence as ever in that select little circle of reputation-making matrons.'' She raised an eyebrow but made no comment. He continued, "There is someone very dear to me, whose life would be a great deal happier were her path to be smoothed for her by someone such as you.''

The dowager did not look enchanted with the idea. She rarely put herself out for anyone. It ruined her image as a crotchety and demanding old town tabby. "And who might this person be?" she inquired somewhat coolly.

"Don't get on your high ropes with me, Marianne. She is someone worthy of your sponsorship in every way—beauty, intelligence, and a handsome fortune.'' The *comte* paused for effect before adding the clincher to his argument. "And, I believe, she has just had a most unpleasant encounter with that haughty grandson of yours.''

The dowager rose instantly to Julian's defense. "He's a good lad who's awake on every suit. If he's a bit high in the instep, it's because someone deserved it.''

"That's as may be," rejoined the *comte*, equally hot in the defense of his favorite. "But in this case it wasn't Lady Frances Cresswell, but Vanessa Welford who deserved to be made uncomfortable.''

The dowager's interest, piqued already, was fairly caught at the mention of these two names. "You always were a deep 'un, Maurice. You didn't come here just to get me to put a few good words about this gel in a few well-chosen ears. Now, cut line."

The count poured out the entire story of the encounter in the park and the subsequent trip to Madame Regnery. "But, Marianne, you know as well as I do that a fashionable appearance is only the start. One must be known to be all the crack, and that's where you come in. If you tell a few of those friends of yours that Lady Frances Cresswell is all the rage, she will be."

A look of amused comprehension appeared on the marchioness's face. It turned to satisfaction as the tale progressed. "It seems, Maurice, that you and I can be of the greatest help to each other." As the count looked totally blank, she explained, "I met my grandson in Bond Street this afternoon. He had just been sparring in Jackson's and seemed to have derived singularly little satisfaction from this exercise. In fact, he looked as blue-deviled as I can ever remember having seen him. He was perfectly polite to me, but his replies were completely at random—really quite unlike him. I've seen him furious at women times out of mind. I've known him to despise them, but I've never known him to be in such a rare taking as he was today. Mark my words, your Frances is having a most unusual effect on my grandson. And it's about time someone got beneath that well-controlled shell of his. I'll play your game, Maurice, and if I'm right, and she means as much to him as I think she does, we'll win more than social cachet for your Lady Fanny."

"Ah, Marianne, I knew you wouldn't disappoint me. Still the same sharp observer of human nature. What a pity we're too old to intrigue on our own behalves. We could teach this namby-pamby generation a thing or two."

She smiled mischievously up at him. "Too true. But be off with you now. If we're to pull this thing off, I must get to work at once."

Well pleased with himself, the count bade good-bye to the marchioness and sauntered over to White's to set the second half of his strategy in motion. He stopped to exchange greetings and news with several old friends in the card room, but his eyes strayed to another part of the room, where Bertie Montgomery was listening attentively to a furious debate over the rival merits of two newly discovered opera dancers. "Come now, Forsyth," admonished one buck. "She may have the figure of a Venus and legs beyond compare, but her face ain't much. It don't hold a candle to Aimée's."

"There you're fair and far out," argued Forsyth. "Aimée ain't pretty. She's too flashy by half. Mouth's too wide and her nose ain't nearly so pretty as Babette's."

"But her eyes, man," the enthusiast protested. "Have you ever seen such eyes? A man could drown in them."

The *comte* expertly detached Bertie from this group without his being aware of it and led him out of earshot. In no time he had this young man's entire attention and allegiance to his cause, through a time-honored method of flattery—the appeal of an older man-of-the-world, to someone much younger and less sophisticated, for aid and advice. The count mounted his attack with a gambit certain to succeed. "I come to you directly, *mon ami*, because a certain lady has named you as one of her oldest and dearest friends." Bertie gave a start of surprise and opened his mouth to blurt out some indiscreet remark. The count forestalled him. "But of course we both know the identity of the charming lady to whom I refer—the daughter of an admired friend. I had hoped . . ." Here the count, with his unerring sense for the proper dramatic touch, sighed gently. "I had hoped that, once in London, she would forget her duties and cares and give herself over to the delights of the Season. To some degree she has. Little by little she has begun to forget here familial responsibilities and certain other serious concerns of her own. I have seen her more often at balls, the opera, the theater, and have been satisfied. I started to relax my vigilance, but now something has occurred that might make her think that her original reading of the *ton* and all its amusements—as vain, silly, useless, harmful even—was the correct one." Bertie, who had been frowning earnestly as he followed the thread of the count's narrative, looked up in some alarm. "The Lady Vanessa Welford," was the count's somewhat cryptic response to the look of inquiry directed at him.

Mysterious as this reply was, it appeared to be enough for Bertie, who remarked with a conscious look, "Oh, ahh."

"Just so. I have done my best to counteract this unfortunate episode by immediately escorting my young friend to a clever modiste who, with her usual skill, has recreated my young friend's look. But in order for this new image to succeed, it must be carried off with assurance. And that is where you, as an arbiter of taste among the younger set, can help. All you need to do is observe several times, in such discussions as the one I interrupted, that Lady Blank seems to be all the rage. That should be sufficient for young bucks as impressionable as those.''

Bertie, who had turned quite pink with pleasure at the count's confidence in his influence, assured him earnestly that he would do his utmost.

Well-satisfied with his choice of conspirator, the count bade him adieu and hastened off for a well-deserved hour of relaxation poring over the latest arrivals at Hatchard's. He had not gone far before he caught sight of Lord Petersham. ''The very man,'' he chuckled slyly to himself. He was especially cordial in his greeting as he resolved to introduce this avid connoisseur to Lady Frances at the earliest possible moment. Her elegance of mind and manner, her excellent conversation, refined taste, and well-informed mind were certain to appeal to this rather eccentric peer who, depsite his eccentricities, was an acknowledged judge of beauty and style. The encounter was highly successful. Petersham looked forward to meeting someone who had lived and been brought up among the aesthetic dictates of classical antiquity. Well-pleased with his morning's work, the *comte* gave himself up to the pleasures of Hatchard's.

24

On the other hand, the objects of the *comte*'s machinations, Lady Frances Cresswell and Lord Julian Mainwaring, were having an encounter as disastrous as his had been successful. After passing a more sleepless night than he ever remembered having endured, the marquess resolved to call in Brook Street as early as it would be proper to do so. He had spent the last twelve hours trying out various speeches in his defense. As all of these sounded insufferably priggish, he threw out the lot and began phrasing apologies. But here too he was at a standstill. He could think of no combination of words that would convey his sympathy for the hurt Frances had suffered, his assurance that the opinions of Vanessa were completely without foundation or the concurrence of the *ton*, and a total disavowal of any interest in that manipulative woman, while still managing to retain Frances' respect. At last he tossed out all his carefully constructed phrases and resolved to be guided by the situation—an unheard-of attitude for a man known the length and breadth of the British Empire for his judicious and diplomatic conduct.

It was with some trepidation, a feeling he had not experienced since his days at Eton, that Julian knocked at Brook Street. Higgins greeted him with his usual dignity, while trying desperately to make his well-modulated "Good day, Lord Mainwaring" carry to the morning room. The butler need not have worried. Lady Frances, prey to her own unsatisfactory thoughts, had been pacing back and forth in front of the window and had witnessed the arrival of Mainwaring's curricle. With a desperate effort she stopped her perambulations and assumed a calm and dignified demeanor that was in total contrast to her feelings.

She presented a charming picture with her newly cropped curls catching the light that streamed in behind her. However, the marquess was too intent upon his mission to take in such a minor detail. In fact, in contrast to Lady Frances, he seemed singularly ill at ease. "Lady Frances," he began abruptly, "I wish to apologize for the epi . . . ah, encounter in the park." He cursed himself for this bald way of putting it. Her gaze remained calm and steady, giving him no clue to her thoughts and no help in organizing his own. He began again. "I am aware that my companion . . . I mean, that you may have suffered some discomfort from the . . . ah . . . for which I apologize." This was hardly better, and he bit his lip uncomfortably.

Fortunately, Frances' pride and social graces came to the rescue. "Think nothing of it, my lord. If I were someone who craved public acclaim, I might have been upset, but as you know, someone with my preferences cares perhaps too little for such things. Therefore, I was not the least concerned. It is kind of you to apologize, but I assure you I do not regard it in the least." Lady Frances congratulated herself on her delivery. It was all she could have hoped for—rational, detached, gracious. She only wished he would leave before her carefully constructed facade crumbled into a million pieces.

Mainwaring was left with nothing to do but murmur, "You are too kind," before bowing over her hand and departing. Once outside, however, the last shreds of his dignity disappeared. "Damn and blast! What a cowhanded fool you are, Mainwaring!" he cursed. No, he thought bitterly, it wasn't that I was so lacking in address, as that she was so completely mistress of hers. Why did she have to be so gracious and understanding? No, why did she have to be so damned cool, so completely unaffected? That last, he realized, was what tormented him.

Though he sympathized intensely with the hurt he was certain he had seen in her eyes yesterday, he had secretly been glad of it because it showed him that she cared for his friendship. Today she acted as though this disastrous encounter had changed nothing between them because there had been nothing there to be changed. Infinitely more uncomfortable though it would have been, he found himself wishing that she had raged at him for spending time with someone as useless as Vanessa Welford, for allowing his mistress to be seen with him in public, for not coming to her, Frances', defense. At least then he would have known where he stood. Now, as he was beginning to be aware of just how much their friendship meant to him, she gave him ample proof of how little it meant to her. With this gloomy conclusion he was forced to be satisfied for quite some time, because the moment he arrived at Grosvenor Square, Kilson put into his hand a letter from one of his captains requesting that he come down to Plymouth to inspect a new merchantman under construction there.

Frances' hard-won composure deserted her the instant the sound of the carriage wheels died away. She sank limply into a chair and bowed her head in her hands. Wellington, sensing his mistress's distress, swallowed his scruples—he scorned lapdogs with passionate intensity—and climbed into her lap, sighing sympathetically. Frances knew she had done the only thing she could have. Under the circumstances, she had carried off the interview magnificently. Why, then, did she feel so utterly wretched? Gone was the easy camaraderie, the trust between friends. But what could she have done to change all that? Nothing. The tears slipped through her fingers onto Wellington's rough coat. He sat looking curiously up at her. This was a behavior he had never witnessed before, and he was not at all sure what he should do about it. Finally he placed a paw gravely on her hand. She gathered him closely in her arms. Much as he scorned lapdogs, he felt this was not the time to stand on principle, and contented himself with licking the tears on her cheeks. She soon came to herself. "And why should *I* be miserable? *I* have not behaved badly. *I* have not put a friend in an awkward situation. Come, Wellington. We need some fresh air.'' Relieved to see that he had recalled her to her senses, Wellington barked his approval and frisked on ahead of her as she went to fetch a bonnet and pelisse.

25

While Frances was taking a brisk salutary turn around the park, the other party in the contretemps was bowling along at a spanking pace toward Plymouth in a rapidly decaying frame of mind. At any other time he would have welcomed the opportunity to inspect the ship, the chance to use his brain and swap stories of foreign ports with the captain and crew. During any other Season he would have been delighted to have an excuse to leave the stuffy ballrooms, smirking young ladies, and rapacious mamas, but now he damned it as an inconvenience of the highest order. He was determined to reestablish his friendship with Frances. Recognizing her as a woman of decision and character, he realized that it would take a great deal to regain her trust in him. A campaign of such magnitude required his constant presence in London, at the balls, operas, and plays Frances was likely to attend. It was this campaign and the strategy called for, rather than the upcoming business, that occupied his mind as he tooled along, mentally rehearsing one scene after another. If anyone had told him that he would have spent that much time analyzing a relationship with anyone, much less a woman who was only passably pretty, and a bluestocking as well, he would have questioned his sanity. However, he was in no state to reflect on this departure from his usual attitudes.

He arrived at Plymouth late one evening and spent the next day walking the decks of his unfinished ship with the captain, discussing the fittings, requirements of the cargo, and the disposition of the crew. But all the while he was conscious of the small corner of his mind that dwelt on Frances and the state of her mind. Becoming aware of the direction of his thoughts, he would dismiss them with an impatient gesture and try to concentrate more deeply than ever on the business at hand, but he was never entirely successful.

Later that night he sat gazing into the fire as he lingered over his port, ruminating over the entire state of affairs. The longer he dwelt on it, the more he cursed himself for a fool in expending such thought and energy on the matter. Mainwaring, you're all about in the head to waste another second's consideration on any of it, he told himself sternly. Besides, you never wanted a friendship to develop in the first place. You should count yourself lucky, old man, to be so well out of it. Satisfied with this conclusion, he set down his glass with a decisive gesture and prepared to go to bed. He had not risen from his chair before he was overcome with such a sense of loss and emptiness that he remained staring moodily into the flames, his dark brows drawn together in a deep frown. How long he stayed that way he didn't know, until the guttering candles recalled his attention and he cursed softly to himself: "You know what's wrong with you, Mainwaring? You've fallen in love like any callow youth." This realization, coming as it did after their recent disastrous encounter, only intensified his somber mood. He fell to thinking of Frances and all the little ways that were peculiarly hers— Frances comforting the terrified Nelson, Frances telling the children stories, Frances laughing at Grimaldi as hard as any child, or Frances looking up at him with that special teasing look of hers. He realized that the thought of life without any of that was no longer possible.

But how shall I ever set it right with her? he wondered. Ordinarily Julian Mainwaring was never at a loss for an answer. In point of fact, it was known in business and diplomatic circles that the stickier the situation, the more he enjoyed it. Nor did he ever doubt his ability to win a point in the end. Now, when so much was at stake, he found his usual confidence had vanished, leaving him with only a desperate desire to do the right thing. I mustn't fail. I can't fail! he told himself. And with that, he resolved to return to town at the earliest possible moment.

Frances, in the meantime, was allowing herself no such thoughts. On the contrary, she had thrown herself so vigorously into the social whirl that she was astounded at herself. In this endeavor she was aided and abetted by the Comte de Vaudron, who seemed to be everywhere at once.

He squired her to the opera, drove her to the park, and escorted her to a variety of routs and balls. And always he seemed to produce the most amusing companions. Following his lead, she found herself enjoying conversations that only a few months ago she would have been too shy to enter. Much to her surprise, they were not as trivial as she had imagined. Also, to her surprise, she discovered that people seemed to think she had something to say, even to find her amusing. If the shadow cast on her life by her disappointment in Mainwaring kept her from being happy, she was at least occupied and amused. And always at a distance there was the *comte* noticing and encouraging the change in her. With smug satisfaction he saw her respond to admiration and begin to sparkle and grow more witty.

He was congratulating himself as he stood one evening at the Mountjoys' ball watching Frances whirling around the floor with the totally captivated son and heir of the house. "You have done very well, my friend." It was so much his own thought that it took some minutes before he realized that the dowager Marchioness of Camberly had come quietly up behind him.

"Ah, from you, Marianne, that is high praise indeed."

She nodded at him, smiling slyly. "My grandson will have something to think about when he returns from Plymouth. He will have a run for his money." She nodded sagely. "Not a bad thing for either of them, I should think."

The marquess did in fact return the very next day, but in spite of an hour spent circling the park and religious attendance at a very dull ball indeed and an equally uninspiring opera, he did not lay eyes on Frances. After one particularly frustrating day spent sauntering with studied casualness along Bond Street and persuing more tomes at Hatchard's than he cared to remember, he repaired to Brooks's. His unpropitious mood was destined to be further impaired by the conversation he overheard as he entered the gaming room. "I quite agree with you, Wytham. She is all that is charming," drawled a well-known man-about-town. "But she's quite above my touch. Don't know her that well."

"Meaning that she knows you ain't too full in the cockloft," interposed his friend.

"I don't argue with you, Wythy. I'm the first one to admit that I ain't all that bobbish. Now, Alvanley here is just her sort. You ask him. He seems to be quite taken with her. Leastways, he spent the longest time at the Marlowes' rout discussing some dashed picture on his snuffbox."

"Sounds suspiciously like a regular bluestocking to me." Wytham dismissed the subject of their conversation with an airy wave of his hand.

"That's just it, she ain't at all," chimed in another young buck. "She's as easy to talk to as your own best friend. Don't put on all of those die-away airs. Don't expect you to bow and scrape and do the pretty all the time. I like her. I can tell you, it's a great relief to dance with a female who can laugh and who don't expect much. Besides, she's quite a taking thing too. Oh, she ain't exactly an incomparable, because she don't look like a dashed china doll, but for my money she's a lot prettier than all those peaches-and-cream misses everyone admires." A brief pause ensued as he conjured up an image of his favorite. "Tell you what. She's got the most beautiful eyes. They look right into you. Let you know what she's thinking too," he concluded enthusiastically.

"Good God," Wytham's sardonic voice broke in. "She must be a diamond if Langford likes her. Can't remember when he ever liked a female that wasn't a horse. Can it be he's going to become leg-shackled at last?"

"No." Langford sighed. "She's as friendly to me as she is to everyone else, but I don't stand a chance, with Alvanley and all those others who surround her all the time. And Wolvercote is so taken with her, he's ready to do battle with anyone who even looks at her. Tell you what, he's making a dashed cake of himself with his poetic airs and constant haunting of her house. Wonder she doesn't get demmed sick of it. But she's too kind to upset anyone, even someone who's as big a gudgeon as Wolvercote.''

Mainwaring turned to the Corinthian who had entered with him. "Who is this, Boxford? A female that isn't silly or a diamond but is all the rage? Only tell me the name of such a paragon.''

Lord Boxford looked at him with surprise. "Where have you been, old boy? You need catching up with the *ton*. *She* is Lady Frances Cresswell, Charles Cresswell's daughter. Apparently she had a Season several years ago, but when her father died she went back to Hampshire to manage the estate and hasn't come to town since. Now she's going about with the Comte de Vaudron, who stands as some sort of godfather to her. She isn't exactly a diamond, but she's got great elegance and style, and what's more, she's pleasant to be with. Doesn't put on any of the airs and graces that our usual incomparables seem to feel they must adopt.''

Lord Mainwaring had the oddest sensation in the pit of his stomach, as though someone had broken through his guard and tipped him a leveler. Lady Frances, an incomparable? *His* Lady Frances? But she wasn't the sort to appeal to bucks like these. It took a man of intelligence and perception—someone such as himself, for example—to appreciate her very special qualities.

This turn of events killed all his interest in Brooks's and he returned to Grosvenor Square to throw himself into a pile of correspondence that had accumulated during his absence. After two hours of intense concentration on some very delicate diplomatic issues, he was in no better state. His thoughts and feelings were still in a turmoil. There was nothing to do but possess himself of as much patience as he could muster until the Duchess of Devonshire's ball that evening. It was the event of the Season, and Frances was sure to be there.

In the meantime, his staff crept about quietly making their own observations and reaching their own conclusions. "He's in a bad way," Kilson commented to himself. "Never seen him as blue-deviled before, especially over any woman. Wonder if he knows it?'' Ordinarily Mainwaring's henchman had the highest respect for his master's intelligence, but lately it had seemed to him that Lord Mainwaring had been unaware of the simplest situation. Any fool could see that the mere mention of Lady Frances Cresswell caught his immediate and total attention. And one didn't have to spend much time in that lady's presence to know that she was the one for him. Why, he never talked to other women the way he talked to her, or cared to hear their thoughts on any subject. Why, the other day he had even asked whether or not she had used the latest seed drill. And, what's more, what she had thought about it. However, it was more than that. There was a certain warmth in his eyes whenever he looked at her or mentioned her that Kilson had never seen before. He only hoped that Lady Frances was of the same mind. Of course, he didn't know her very well, but he rather thought she was. But something must have happened to upset this nicely progressing state of affairs. Discreet inquiries among the coachmen and footmen had revealed nothing, and Kilson, at a loss to know what had occurred, was at an even greater loss as to how to remedy it. Like his master, he finally decided that all he could do was to await developments with as much patience as possible.

26

The Duchess of Devonshire's ball was predicted to be the most important event of the Season. No member of the *ton* worthy of that appellation would have even considered missing it. No more did Lady Frances, though she was certain it would prove to be a sad crush. Much to her astonishment, she had rather enjoyed her social transformation. At first she had been inclined to doubt the Comte de Vaudron's opinion that the more elegantly she was attired and the more fashionable she was, the more confident she would feel. In fact, he had been astoundingly accurate. Her locks, shorn of their heavier tresses, felt light and frivolous, encouraging her to toss her head, laugh, and smile in a manner totally foreign to her previous, more dignified self. She knew her toilette to be the height of elegance, and this, to her total amazement, actually did give her the absolute composure she had lacked before in the face of social scrutiny. Before, a stare, no matter how ill-bred, left her quaking in her boots, wondering if her dress were horribly dowdy, her toilette in disrepair, or her conversation lacking. Now she could attribute such stares to envy rather than to censure, and this envy, though she was loathe to admit it, gave a certain spice to social affairs. It was, of course, a lowering thought for one bred to disregard the superficialities and appreciate the finer points of people's characters, but that made it no less true. It was thus that she looked forward to the ball. Despite Lady Frances' protests, Madame Regnery had insisted on creating a ball gown for her out of the material carefully brought from Lyons. Because of the uniqueness of the silk, which shimmered between green and a rich gold, the dress was of the simplest design, cut low over the bosom and softly gathered above the waist. Its only ornamentations were several heavy rouleaux of the same material at the hem, which served to make it mold to the elegant lines of her figure, and a Medici collar of rich blond lace at the neck. It was true that silk was now less favored than muslin, but this was of a type that had never before graced the ballrooms of London—or Paris, for that matter. A magnificent parure of her mother's emeralds and a matching brooch in the corsage completed the ensemble, complimented the color of her eyes, and emphasized the creamy richness of her skin. Her hair, brushed into a riot of golden curls, shone with the same highlights as her gown.

"Oh, Frances, don't you look just like a princess!" Kitty exclaimed when she saw her. "No, much grander than that . . . a queen, I think," she amended.

Kitty was not alone in her opinion. Bertie, who came to escort her, was equally appreciative. "I say, Fanny, that's a bang-up rig. I am certainly lucky to be with you. You'll take the shine out of all of 'em. Did you get it from Fanchon?"

"What a complete hand you are, Bertie. You always know just the right thing to say, don't you?" Frances was gratified.

"Now Fan, you know that's a plumper. I ain't one of those poetic fellows who knows just how to put things."

"You can't flummery me," she interrupted sternly. "Whether or not you or anyone else acknowledges it, the most important words are those that come directly from a kind heart, which you have in abundant degree."

"I say, Fan," he stammered, pleased in spite of his evident embarrassment. "Now it's time for you to cut a dash with a larger audience. Are you ready for it?" he inquired as he escorted her to the carriage.

It was gratifying to Frances, slowly making her way up the

magnificent staircase, to see so many familiar faces. How different from her first Season, when everyone was not only strange to her, but critical as well. Now, though many of the familiar faces were no closer friends, they represented no threat to her equanimity. And much as she disliked admitting it to herself, she enjoyed causing a stir, however minor, when she entered. Heretofore Frances had looked upon vanity with distaste, but she allowed herself to indulge in it just briefly when Lords Alvanley and Boxford, closely followed by the Viscount Wytham, hastened over to secure dances and form a laughing coterie around her.

It was thus that Mainwaring first saw her in the glow from the chandelier directly overhead, laughing gaily at a sally of Alvanley's. Mainwaring's ordinarily bored expression deserted him and he stared at the warm, vital creature who caught the light with every graceful gesture.

Long hours spent staring into the fire had brought Julian to the conclusion that Lady Frances Cresswell was someone he cared enough about to consider spending the rest of his life with. She would make a fine wife. She was intelligent in a greater variety of areas than most men of his acquaintance. She faced life with courageousness and purpose. She had a quick wit that teased and delighted him, and the heavy responsibilities she had borne so competently and quietly endeared her to him. But tonight, for the first time, he saw her as a beautiful woman. It quite took his breath away. Never had her smile seemed so bewitching or—his jaw tightened at the thought—intimate. The slim perfection of her body and grace of movement were emphasized by the material of her gown, which clung to her and shimmered enticingly at the least motion. The brilliant parure called attention to the beautifully molded neck and shoulders, not to mention a décolletage that might even have been called daring. In the midst of all the pale fluttering gauzes she stood out like a gilded vital young goddess with a warm and vivid beauty that would have taken any man's breath away.

In a daze, Lord Mainwaring guided partners around the floor, nodding and commenting mechanically at the appropriate moments, but his eyes never left Frances as she whirled by with one partner after another. Just as he felt he could stand it no longer, that he simply must talk with her at whatever cost, he saw her disappear through a French window onto the terrace. Not far behind her followed the besotted young man Wolvercote, a great deal the worse for the effects of the punch. Barely staying to restore his partner to her party, Mainwaring strode off after the pair, his blue eyes smoldering dangerously in a face dark and threatening as a thundercloud.

If he had not been beside himself with rage and jealously, he might have appreciated the picture that met his furious gaze. Slim and ethereal, her dress shimmering in the moonlight, Frances leaned on the parapet surveying the garden below. Wolvercote, who, whatever his faults, was a picturesque and graceful youth, had just flung himself to his knees and caught her hand to his mouth in a passion of youthful ardor. But Mainwaring was in no mood for aesthetics, nor did he register the look of intense annoyance that crossed Frances' face as she tried to recapture her hand. All he saw was the woman he wanted, being ardently kissed by another man. By this time Wolvercote, intoxicated with his own boldness and the romantic atmosphere, had risen, grabbed Frances inexpertly in his arms, and was trying unsuccessfully to kiss her.

"Most affecting." Mainwaring's harsh voice shattered the idyllic scene.

"Lord Mainwaring!" Frances exclaimed, striving for a normal voice and wishing fervently that the earth would open up and swallow her. "I had not thought to see you here." There! She had achieved at least a semblance of conversational tone, though the thudding of her heart threatened to suffocate her.

"Obviously not," he responded grimly.

The contempt in his face goaded her as she realized the infelicity of her last remark. "I had *thought*," she continued with emphasis, "I had *thought* you were out of town on business and had not expected to see you for some time."

"And so made yourself the talk of the town in my absence."

Thoroughly roused, she flashed back. "*You* are certainly not my chaperone, my lord. And if I were looking for models of propriety, I certainly shouldn't look to you."

"Oh, wouldn't you? Let me tell you, my girl, I was on the town and conversant with all its rules and restrictions long before you were out of the schoolroom. And disappearing to an isolated terrace with besotted young men has never been acceptable behavior." Here he turned to the miserable Wolvercote, who had been standing, his mouth open, observing this astounding scene. "Get out of here, you puppy. And don't you go compromising Lady Frances again."

Wolvercote fled with relief, but Lady Frances, thoroughly enraged, drew herself to her full height and turned to Julian. Eyes flashing, she responded in a low passionate voice that she could barely keep from trembling with anger. "What right have you to interfere in my affairs or comment on my conduct?"

Mainwaring, as angry as she, lashed out, "The right of any sensible person who sees someone behaving like an idiot."

"And what concern is it of yours, my lord, whether or not I choose to behave like an idiot?" In fact, Frances did feel like a complete idiot. She had been as intensely aware of Lord Mainwaring all evening as he had been of her, and, upset at her own interests and attraction to someone so obviously a cad, she had sought the solace of the terrace, never dreaming that her escape would be noticed or that she would be followed. She had been as revolted as Mainwaring by young Wolvercote, but her censor's next words forced her to adopt a totally opposite position.

"I never thought to see you with such a foolish young jack-anapes."

Lady Frances thoroughly agreed, but would have died before admitting such a thing. "Wolvercote happens to be a serious young man who shares many of my tastes. We admire many of the same things, and *he*, at least, respects and admires me." She was thoroughly disgusted at the petulance of this last remark, which, in spite of its childishness, seemed to be the last straw for Mainwaring.

"If it's admiration you want . . ." he hissed, grasping her by the shoulders and pulling her roughly to him. His arms tightened painfully around her as his lips came down on hers fiercely, possessively, angrily demanding.

Caught off guard, Frances felt herself overwhelmed by the hardness of his body against hers, the insistence of his lips as they moved on hers, exploring, forcing her to respond. For a moment she gave herself up to the warm tide that was flooding her, spreading languorously up from her trembling knees to the pit of her stomach and her breast. For an instant she wanted to free her arms, pull him to her, and return the kiss as passionately as he. But at the back of her mind a cold little voice admonished. "He is doing this out of anger and disgust. He despises you. Get away. Run!" Marshalling her fading resistance, she pulled away, her eyes dark with passion, and in a voice throbbing with emotion demanded, "And I suppose *this* is proper conduct? You seem to forget I am not Lady Welford, sir." Then, in a swirl of green-gold, she turned on her heel and vanished into the garden.

Left alone in the darkness, Lord Mainwaring suffered a thousand conflicting emotions, chiefly anger—anger at Frances for having forced him to behave like the most callow of overheated young bucks, anger at himself for having given way so completely to his emotions. But also there was desire—desire for her as she stood facing him, her eyes alight with anger, her whole body vibrant with passion and fury. And he, who had flirted with scores of beautiful, sophisticated women in all the capitals or Europe, felt sick with longing for her, for the suppleness of her body beneath his hands, the warmth and softness of her lips against his. Surely, for a moment, she had responded, her lips clinging to his with equal fevor before she ran off into the night?

You're a cad and an utter fool, he derided himself bitterly. And now you have ruined whatever chance you ever had of getting her back. In his despair, he realized now exactly how much he did want her back, not just as a friend, but because he needed her, desired her, wanted her more than anything he had ever wanted before. With his painful discovery, he too strode off to find his carriage and the dubious solace of a bottle of brandy in his own empty library.

Lady Frances, hardly knowing where she was headed, except away from Lord Mainwaring, stumbled through the garden in the vague direction of her carriage. Just when she was beginning to despair of finding a way out and wondering how she could possibly face returning to the ballroom and the curious eyes of the assembled multitude, she discovered a small door in the

garden wall. Mercifully, it opened quietly and she found herself
on the cobblestones of the stableyard. Somehow she found John
Coachman, was helped tenderly into the carriage, and collapsed
thankfully against the squabs.

For a time she gave herself up to the motion of the vehicle,
happy to enjoy the peace and darkness alone. But on alighting
at Brook Street and entering her dressing room, she found that
she had escaped the crush and Lord Mainwaring only to find
herself prey to thoughts as unwelcome as any she had ever
experienced. Her anger at being criticized so unfairly and
handled so peremptorily, which had sustained her through the
scene with Mainwaring, had now evaporated, and she was left
with unsettling memories of the entire episode. Mainwaring had
been entirely correct in his hope that she had yielded briefly
to her feelings and returned his embrace. When he had first
pulled her to him, she had been too angry to do anything other
than resist, but as his lips pressed more insistently on hers,
forcing them apart, and his arms tightened around her, molding
her body against his, she became more and more aware of the
warm lethargic feeling stealing over her and subduing her
resistance. A quick glance stolen up at him revealed a strange
intensity in his gaze that she had never seen before—almost a
hunger—and for some reason she wanted desperately to deliver
herself up to this hunger and to forget herself in the hardness
of his body pressing on hers, the strength of his hand tilting
her head to his kiss. She hadn't known whether she was glad
or sorry for the small corner of her mind that had brought her
to herself, to the realization of Lord Mainwaring's probable
feelings for her at that moment. But, she sighed sadly as she
recalled it all in vivid detail, she wished she had been able to
wipe out everything, to delude herself into believing that he
wanted her, Frances Cresswell, for herself and not out of anger.
She wished desperately that she had been able to forget herself
in one moment of passion. And that's what it was, my girl, she
told herself severely. You did want him to desire you, to love
you the way he loves Lady Welford. It's not respect or friendship you crave. It's love. You want him to love you because
you love him that way.'' For a long time after reaching this
totally upsetting conclusion, she sat staring at her hollow-eyed

reflection in the mirror, her only thought: Now whatever am I to do?

Eventually her characteristic energy and independent spirit reasserted themselves. I must get out of here, away from him, away from London, away from everyone. And she feverishly began planning and packing for her immediate return to Cresswell. It was not her customary, organized preparation, but by the time dawn broke, she had a valise ready, and instructions for the servants completed. She felt slightly guilty, slipping off without saying good-bye to Aunt Harriet and the children, but she couldn't bear to stay in London a moment longer than absolutely necessary. Besides, her hasty departure was in keeping with the note she had left, implying some pressing business at Cresswell that required her immediate attention. Such haste and deception were so totally unlike her that she was not at all sure she would be able to fool Aunt Harriet or Higgins for a minute. But then, such emotions had never before entered her life. True, she had mourned her parents deeply and she had loathed and detested her first London Season, but she had never before doubted herself or the rightness of her own feelings. It was certainly lowering to reflect that a pair of dark blue eyes set in a harsh-featured face and a sardonic smile could affect her so powerfully. Inexplicable as it was, that seemed to be the case, and she was not at all happy about it.

For the remainder of the journey she allowed herself the luxury of recalling the times they had shared, the special smile that seemed to lurk in his eyes just for her when he knew she would understand some fine point. The care and gentleness with which he handed her into a carriage or entered into her particular worries over the children and Cresswell, and last, the brief moment when he had seemed to want her as much as she now admitted to wanting him. But upon arriving at Cresswell, she resolutely put all thoughts of Lord Julian Mainwaring out of her mind to immerse herself in a flurry of activity.

By day she kept up a backbreaking regimen of riding over the estate checking crops, fences, tenants' cottages, and listening to complaints, problems, or just neighborly chatter. In the evening she pored over accounts or studied the authors and texts she wished to share with Freddie and Cassie, until she was exhausted. Despite her best efforts, the occasional memory of some shared moment with Mainwaring or speculation as to his whereabouts or the state of his emotions would intrude. At that, she would shake her head briskly, call to Wellington, who, much to his delight and pride, had been the one being allowed to accompany her in her flight, and head off for a vigorous walk, whatever the weather or the hour.

By degrees, she soon recovered her equanimity, but it was a peace without much joy or expectation. Odd to think that the very same life, the same daily round of activities that had seemed so full before she went to London, could now seem so flat, so empty. But she knew from experience that time would restore much, if not all, of her former sense of herself.

In the meanwhile, those she had left behind were reacting in their own particular ways to her escape. As she had suspected, neither Higgins nor Aunt Harriet believed for a single moment her pretext of pressing business at Cresswell. Both knew her to be far too good a manager and far too judicious in her choice of stewards to be caught unawares by some crisis. Contrary to her expectations, they both, without knowing precisely the true circumstances, immediately divined the cause of her departure. "Drat all men," muttered Aunt Harriet, swiping viciously at a faded blossom. "Why must they be forever imposing themselves on women? They make 'em love 'em and then make 'em miserable. There's not a one of them worthy of a good woman, especially one like Frances. With all the ladybirds in London dying for him, why did that Mainwaring have to go and upset my precious girl? Why, I'll give that arrogant, interfering so-and-so a piece of my mind if I get half the chance."

Higgins was taking out his frustrations on his particular pride and joy—the family silver—and mumbling to himself. "Something certainly has overset Miss Frances. It isn't any emergency that has called her away." Buff, buff. "And she is running away. That's certain. I've never known her to run away from anyone or anything before, so it must be his lordship that has upset her so. She has never known anyone like him before. Top-of-the-trees, a real out-and-outer, he is." Buff, buff. "Or was," he amended darkly. "If he's done anything to cut up Miss Frances' peace, we shall certainly see what will have to be done." And setting down a sauceboat with an ominous thump, he marched off to set investigations in motion, beginning with Lady Frances' Daisy.

"Ooh, I don't know, sir. I didn't see her ladyship till this morning, but she didn't sleep a wink, that I'm sure. Her bed wasn't touched and she did a powerful amount of packing."

In the breakfast room, Frances' departure was being discussed with some dismay. "But, Aunt Harriet," wailed Cassie, "she couldn't have gone! She promised to take Ned and me on another trip to the Tower and then to Gunters.' "

Freddie's consternation was just as real, though premised on more complicated circumstances. With Frances went his only link to Lord Mainwaring, and he had dearly hoped that his lordship would remember his promise to take him, Nigel, and Ned to see a cricket match at the recently established Lord's.

"Well, Cassie, she has more important things to attend to than taking a pair of schoolchildren on outings and for ices," her aunt responded tartly, covering up her own concern over the situation by appearing more brusque than usual. All of these various household members had their suspicions—Frances being one of the most organized, least impulsive of mistresses, sisters, or nieces, as the case was. They were all alike, however, in that each one struggled with his or her doubts in silence, not daring or deigning to confide in anyone else.

Freddie alone of the assorted interested parties engaged in unraveling the MYSTERY. He had A PLAN. It had seemed to him that just as he had begun to recognize that Lord Mainwaring, though a real out-and-outer, was not at all toplofty where truly inspired young schoolboys were concerned, his lordship had become a noticeably less-frequent visitor in Brook Street. After nearly an hour spent scowling over a most boring passage that Fanny had assigned for translation, he began to see a PATTERN to the situation. It all dated back to that odd encounter in the park. It was after that that he had noticed his sister's unusual social gaiety. Really, she had almost completely ignored him and Cassie while she ran around buying clothes or going to parties. It must have been something to do with that episode that he didn't fully understand. For after that, Fanny, ordinarily so willing to discuss Lord Mainwaring's manifold accomplishments with him, had been positively put out every time he brought up the subject for conversation. Her usual response, "Really, Freddie, Lord Mainwaring is far too busy to be interested in any of us," made him think that perhaps she was mad at his lordship. In that case, he, Freddie, who was out of favor with Lady Frances more than anyone else and knew exactly how unpleasant that could be, felt it his duty to apprise his lordship of the situation and perhaps suggest some remedies.

It was with this laudable goal in mind that he set out, not exactly stealthily, but with a good deal less commotion than ordinarily accompanied his comings and goings, for his lordship's mansion in Grosvenor Square.

27

A s Lord Mainwaring's constant and sometimes only
companion in his travels, from huts in the West Indies to
palaces in Persia, from boats on the Nile to elephants in India,
Kilson had encountered and protected his lordship from many
strange people and many even odder requests, buy he had never
been more taken aback than when he opened the door to young
Master Frederick. Events have taken a most interesting turn,
he remarked to himself. Behind his impassive face, speculation
ran wild. Not even the flicker of an eyelid betrayed that anxious-
looking lads of eleven were not Lord Mainwaring's most
frequent visitors.

"Master Frederick Cresswell to see you, sir," he announced
impressively, ushering Freddie into the library.

Lord Mainwaring was no less astounded than his butler, but
detecting the unease that would flit momentarily across Freddie's
face despite his valiant efforts to hide it, he said in a tone that
implied these visits were a regular occurrence, "Hallo, Freddie.
What brings you to this part of town?"

With an effort, Freddie, who had been gazing in awe at an
imposing ancestor astride a horse over the mantelpiece, pulled
his thoughts together and said in as offhand a manner as he could

muster, "Well, sir, as we haven't seen you this age, I just thought I would pay you a call to see how you are doing."

Mainwaring was amused. "That is most kind of you. I am doing very well, thank you."

"I am glad of that, sir," his young guest responded politely while he sought desperately for some conversational gambit to introduce the subject occupying his mind. No such phrase came to him, so, in characteristic fashion, he blurted, "Well, you see, sir, you used to come to see us all the time, and now you don't. And, well, the last time we saw you it seemed as though Fanny was not best pleased with you." The quizzical lift of his host's eyebrow did nothing to encourage him, but he plunged bravely on. "Well, sir, you see, sir," he began unhappily, "it seemed to me as though you and she were as thick as thieves. I mean . . ." He blushed guiltily at his cant phrase. "You seemed to be such good friends. And then you weren't, and . . ." He looked fleetingly, pleadingly, at Lord Mainwaring's impassive countenance. "I thought you might like to be friends again, sir."

"Ah," said his lordship.

"So I thought if I explained to you what a right 'un Fan is and how she never holds a grudge or keeps harping on it after she's let you have it, I thought you might feel brave enough to go tell her you're sorry she got mad and you'd like to be friends with her again." He looked up appealingly, adding ingenuously, "And then you wouldn't feel at all odd about coming to call or taking Ned and me to a cricket match at Lord's, or whatever."

With a supreme effort Lord Mainwaring was able to keep his lips from twitching at this clincher to Freddie's argument, but for a moment his eyes twinkled with barely suppressed amusement. This was quickly replaced by the strained hollow look that had been worrying Kilson all week. He smiled and laid his hand on Freddie's shoulder, saying, "I appreciate your coming, old man, but it is more serious than that. It's not that I have made your sister angry. It's that I have given her a disgust of me and my life that could hardly be remedied with an apology. She's not mad at me. She simply does not like me." In this simply put speech to a boy who could not possibly understand all the bitter thoughts with which he had been torturing himself, Mainwaring revealed more of his feelings than he had ever let slip to another human being.

Freddie stood silent for a moment, his brow wrinkled in a fierce effort at concentration. "Well," he said in a burst of perspicacity that took even him by surprise, "I think she must not dislike you, because if she did dislike you, she wouldn't have been the least upset if you had done something very bad. And she *is* upset. I could just tell by the way she looked. When she's blue-deviled she likes to walk in the country. And she went to Cresswell because she's in the dismals, not because there's anything amiss there," he concluded triumphantly. "The staff there can take care of anything that comes up. She herself said that the day we left. So you see, sir . . ."

A slightly conscious look stole across Lord Mainwaring's features. "You may not be too far wrong, lad. We may just have to put your theory to the test."

"Oh, please do, sir," his youthful mentor begged. "I know I am not wrong. You could say you have come to visit Cassie and me. Promise to try, sir."

Mainwaring seemed to consider the invitation, though anyone privileged to observe how quickly the gloom had lifted from his brow would have known this hesitation was purely for effect. "Very well, Frederick. I shall put it to the touch. But you must run along now before you are missed."

"Splendid, sir! You won't forget about the cricket, will you, sir? We shall be going down to Cresswell ourselves at the end of the week, so we don't have much time." And with this parting shot he was gone, leaving Lord Mainwaring to stare pensively into the ashes of last night's fire.

"By God, the scamp just might be right. Kilson!"

Kilson, who had been standing suspiciously close to the library door, took some time before answering his lordship's bellow. "Yes, my lord?"

"Pack my bags. I think it's high time we found out how things are progressing at Camberly."

"Very good, my lord." Once outside the door again, Kilson's wooden countenance relaxed into a smile of heartfelt relief. "Bless you, Master Frederick," he breathed to himself.

Young Master Frederick was not at all above congratulating himself. "Cassie! Cassie, I say, where are you?" he bellowed up the stairs the minute Higgins had shut the door behind him.

"I'm up here, Freddie, with Ned. Whatever do you want?" his twin responded with some annoyance. She and Ned had just completed the laborious construction of an elaborate card castle, whose instant doom was imminent the moment her rambunctious brother appeared. Sure enough, he had only to enter the doorway of the drawing room for the entire structure to collapse. "Really, Freddie! You're worse than Wellington!" Cassie began disgustedly, but broke off at the sight of her brother's face. He was obviously bursting with information and quite obviously put out at finding her with company. Cassie was at a loss. On one hand, she was dying to discover what had put Freddie in such a state. On the other, she was very fond of Ned, and though wishing him to leave, knew that the last thing someone as quiet and shy as Ned needed was to be made to feel like a third party. "Ned is such a good castle builder, you can't think, Freddie," she began, seizing the first thing that came to mind. "He knows ever so much history, and so many stories that he's been telling me as we have been building this." Ned blushed uncomfortably. He appreciated Cassie's efforts to draw him into the group, but he would so much have preferred to be called a clever cricketer or a bruising rider.

"Does he now?" Freddie looked curious.

"Yes, he does, and what's more, he told me all about going to see the Horse Armory at the Tower with Nigel. Did you know they have effigies of all the kings of England, from George II back to William the Conqueror, mounted on horses and wearing their armor?"

"No." Freddie's interest was stirred. "Did you see all kinds of weapons too?" Fortunately, Ned had an excellent and exact memory. This, coupled with his true interest in the subject and a talent for narration, soon had Freddie listening with rapt attention, his momentous visit completely forgotten.

"Perhaps we can go together again sometime before we all go back to the country," Cassie suggested. Ned looked gratefully at her.

"That would be famous," her brother agreed enthusiastically.

"But who would take us?" They all agreed that this was indeed a puzzler, and all three of them realized, not for the first time, how seriously they missed Frances. Ned soon made his exit, promising to hint to Kitty so that she might hint to Lady Streatham that a second excursion to the Tower might be in order.

"Now, what has happened to put you in such a state?" demanded Cassie the minute he had gone. "I feared that if you had to wait another minute you might burst your buttons."

"Now, Cass," her twin began heatedly. Then, adopting a tone more suitable to the important nature of his mission, he continued coolly, "It's nothing. I've just been calling at Mainwaring House and thought you might be interested in how Lord Mainwaring is getting on."

Cassie was suitably impressed. "Freddie, you didn't! Weren't you dreadfully afraid? After all, he hasn't come to call in weeks."

"Well, I thought that might have to do with Fanny's being so mad at him in the park. I thought he mightn't understand that she doesn't stay mad long and she's always willing to cry friends, so I thought I'd tell him that."

Cassie was awed into silence by this worldly pronouncement. She soon recovered and added thoughtfully, "You're right, of course, but I'm not sure Fan would like us meddling in her affairs."

"I'm not meddling!" he retorted indignantly. "But I don't see why we should lose such a bang-up friend just because of a silly little brangle. You know how grown-ups are. They think the least little thing is terribly serious and important."

"You might be right," she began dubiously. "But what did he say he would do?"

Freddie tried to recall his lordship's exact words. He didn't remember Lord Mainwaring actually promising anything, but from somewhere he had come by the impression that Lord Mainwaring, feeling a great weight lifted from his mind, was on the point of immediate departure for Hampshire.

In fact, Lord Mainwaring's departure was forestalled in a slightly frustrating manner by the most amiable of friends, Bertie Montgomery. Bertie had an innately sympathetic nature, a quick, observant eye, and a finely tuned sense of social situations. Perhaps sooner than anyone else, the dowager Marchioness of Camberly and Lady Streatham included, he had foreseen Frances' and Julian's friendship developing and continuing into something more. He sensed, even before they did, the understanding that had grown up between them. Without being party to their last two disastrous encounters, he had a fair sense of what might have occurred. He had visited Frances not long after the episode in the park and had instantly noted the change in her and put it down to his friend's account. From her subsequent transformation he was able to surmise that somehow another woman, presumably Vanessa Welford, had been involved. Mainwaring, of course, had been out of town, so Bertie had had to wait some time to see how the situation was affecting him. Because he was fond of both Frances and Mainwaring and continued in his original conviction that they would suit each other very well, it was with some satisfaction that he observed the restless behavior Mainwaring had exhibited upon his return to the metropolis. The man who ordinarily scorned the social for more weighty affairs now haunted the opera, the theater, routs, balls, and even Almack's. To the casual observer, Mainwaring remained as aloof as ever, cutting the presumptuous and the insipid with his usual quelling hauteur, but there was a look in his eyes that spoke volumes to Bertie of his friend's unhappiness.

For a while it had seemed as though Frances, under the tutelage of the Comte de Vaudron, not only had recovered but also was discovering and truly enjoying the delights of society. Bertie was delighted. He had long thought she was dreadfully unappreciated and was glad to see her coming into her own. Perhaps even more gratifying was that she seemed to be enjoying herself immensely as well—a rare but well-deserved state of affairs. Still, a small part of him was sad that she seemed to have outgrown her friendship with Julian so quickly. Frances was so convincing in her role as a young lady enjoying taking the *ton* by storm, indeed she had almost convinced herself, that Bertie was unaware how much she too missed Mainwaring's companionship.

Then came the night of the Duchess of Devonshire's ball.

Bertie had been part of the general circle around Frances and had happened to glance up at the precise moment Mainwaring had entered the room. He saw the look that Mainwaring had been unable to hide completely, read the admiration, the jealousy, and the longing in it. He also observed, by the way she studiously avoided looking in Mainwaring's direction, that Frances was as intensely aware of his movements in the throng as Mainwaring was of hers. Having thus established that neither one of them was as indifferent as he or she hoped to appear, Bertie set himself to watch them closely. Thus it was that out of the corner of his eye he saw Frances go out on the terrace, trailed by young Wolvercote and shortly followed by Julian. When the only one of the principals to reappear was Wolvercote, he developed fairly accurate suspicions as to the nature of the scene and its outcome. The suspicions were confirmed the next day by Higgins, who informed him, "Lady Frances has gone to the country, sir. Urgent business at Cresswell required her presence, you understand." Though a confirmed lover of London, Bertie was well enough aware of country life and Frances' excellent managerial abilities not to be fooled a moment by this flimsy excuse to escape a difficult situation. Furthermore, he knew that it would not fool the sharper members of the *ton* either. Partly out of a true desire to offer her sympathy and companionship, and partly out of a desire to offer the type of support that would mislead the rest of the world and ensure her continued good standing in society, he gathered together a house party of the most witty and socially brilliant of his friends and, to his mother's complete astonishment, retired posthaste to his own nearby estate.

It was just as he was about to embark on this journey that he encountered Mainwaring. Both were caught in the crush of traffic on Park Lane. Mainwaring, on a handsome but nervous bay, was on his way to work off some of its skittishness and his own impatience as well. He was astounded and slightly alarmed to see his friend ensconced in a traveling coach. Knowing that Bertie never willingly left the bustle of the city, he inquired his destination with genuine concern. His amazement grew when he learned that Bertie was actually returning to his ancestral acres. "Is Lady Montgomery ill, then?"

"Oh, no. Quite the contrary, chipper as ever. I just felt in need of rustication and have invited Alvanley and some others to bear me company."

Lord Mainwaring might not have been as socially aware as his friend, but he was no fool. He was well aware that Bertie's friendship with Frances arose from the proximity of their estates. He had always thought of Bertie as a perennial bachelor, never the type to become serious over a woman, but as he quickly reviewed the past months, he realized uncomfortably that, aside from himself, Frances' most constant companion had been Bertie. The more he thought about it and of the warm way in which Bertie always spoke of Frances, the more jealous and suspicious he became. His face darkened as he said shortly, "Enjoy yourself." This ill temper was not lost on Bertie. It had not been part of his plan in the least to make Mainwaring jealous, but if he were, so much the better. Jealousy sometimes drove intelligent men to take steps they might otherwise avoid.

Bertie's visit to Hampshire was at least partially successful. He had managed, via his customary grapevine, to keep the *ton* informed of the picnics, the excursions, and the fêtes in which Frances always played an important role. Certainly Frances enjoyed all the company and the activity, but Bertie, catching her in unguarded moments, saw such sadness in her eyes that he longed to comfort her, to offer her anything—himself even— that would dispel it even the tiniest bit. And Bertie was someone who had a pure and unadulterated horror of the married state. Still, he advised himself, if one had to marry, Fanny would be the one to choose. She was so easy to get along with. But fortunately, before he moved too far in this vein, he realized that however comfortable it would be for him to live with Fanny, it would not be the least bit comfortable to live with the other Cresswells. Nor, when he thought about it, would Fanny be happy with him. She needed someone as intelligent and articulate as she was—someone like Lord Julian Mainwaring. In fact, he became so much more convinced of this than ever that he soon found himself returning to town in the hopes that he could effect some sort of reconciliation.

On the slimmest of pretexts, a totally false interest in the affairs at Camberly, he presented himself at Mainwaring House.

"Place is looking a bit run-down, you know," he reported to a surprised Mainwaring. "Wouldn't dream of telling you how to run your affairs, old fellow, but I know you've got so many of them you can't be everywhere and, well, I know Frances never trusted that rascally agent of yours."

"Oh, you saw Lady Frances, did you?"

"Oh, certainly. Called on her almost every day." Mainwaring's brows lowered threateningly. "She was perfectly charming. Always an addition to any party, and there were a good many of them. But she seemed a bit pulled."

"Oh?" Mainwaring would allow himself to reveal no more than that of his intense curiosity.

"Yes. She seems quieter than usual, almost worried. Something's upsetting her. 'Course, knowing her, she'll take care of it, but I don't like to see her tackling so many things on her own." The seed successfully planted, he rose to go. "Just thought I'd drop by and let you know how things are at Camberly. Might not be a bad thing for you to go down with Ned and Kitty when they return, and cast an eye around." And having given his friend the perfect excuse to pursue his happiness on his own, he departed, well-satisfied with his morning's work.

Bertie was more successful than he could have hoped. In fact, he was almost too successful. Mainwaring at first was infuriated by the thought of Frances flirting and enjoying herself with such a gay crowd while he suffered in London, tortured by an uncomfortable conscience. This brought back thoughts of the confrontation that had driven her from London in the first place. Bertie had mentioned her fatigue. Was she still upset over his unpardonable behavior? Or was it really some problem at Cresswell Manor that was wearing her down? Bertie's concern, damn him, had seemed almost proprietary. Mainwaring wanted someone to share and ease Frances' burdens, but Bertie Montgomery was not the person he had cast in the role of her supporter. Bertie was too much the gay dog to take on such burdens. Still, and there a shattering doubt crept in, Bertie cared a great deal for Frances, was an old friend, and possessed the kindest heart in London. Perhaps, despite his horror of anything remotely intellectual, he was the very person for her. Bertie, in any event, never upset her, never made her angry or acted reprehensibly toward her. How could he, Mainwaring, outstanding for his calm diplomacy, have forced his attentions upon her out of pure jealousy and anger? Again he cursed himself for having treated her so roughly at the Duchess of Devonshire's ball. She would never forgive him. At least, he consoled himself with a bitter smile, his further alienation of her brought with it the memory of her in his arms, a memory so intense that he ached with the longing to feel the softness of her, to bury his hands in her delicately scented hair and kiss her until she was forced to respond, to admit that he had been correct in interpreting that brief instant of yielding as passion for him. But no, Lady Frances had too much pride and independence. She would never allow herself to become a victim of passion. Even in her greatest moment of anger she had always been in command of her thoughts, her words. What had she said? "You seem to forget I am not Lady Welford." A passionately involved woman would not have been able to respond with such presence of mind. A woman less completely in control of herself would have raged at him or wept. Not Frances. Always mistress of herself and her surroundings, she had left rather precipitately, but in full possession of her faculties. Perhaps she did love Bertie. He was another one who never allowed his passions, if he possessed any, to obscure his delicate social sense. Yes, perhaps Bertie was the man for her. He, Mainwaring, should stay away from Cresswell and allow them a chance to pursue their friendship in peace. No! his mind and body protested. She is too vital, too spirited, too adventurous for him. She would be wasted on Bertie, bored within a month. They won't do together. He can't have her! Worn out with thinking, he poured himself a glass of brandy, and another, and another, savoring the burning in his throat as he slouched in his chair, head in hand.

He decided at last to set out for Camberly. But first he resolved to do something for Frances—and Freddie as well—that would please her, no matter what the outcome of future encounters. He fulfilled his much-longed-for promise and took Freddie, Nigel, and Ned to a cricket match at the grounds recently set aside by Mr. Thomas Lord. The boys were ecstatic. Even Ned, who ordinarily was more interested in bookish pursuits, his only outdoor activities centering around horses, was enthralled. The marquess himself had a surprisingly enjoyable afternoon. Though he'd since transferred his athletic interests and prowess to the boxing salon and equestrian pursuits, he had not forgotten his own days of glory on the cricket pitch. It was refreshing to return to those scenes, to discuss it all with such eager spectators, to talk with people too young to dissemble, to pretend interest that they didn't feel or feign boredom. Infected by their enthusiasm and undisguised admiration, he found himself unbending and enjoying himself in a way he hadn't since he had returned from his travels in the colonies.

He was not alone. Freddie, seeing that Lord Mainwaring was the true sport he had expected him to be, was more determined than ever to reestablish easy terms between the Cresswells and Mainwaring. This resolution extended even to the inclusion of Ned in his conversation. Ordinarily he would have written him off as a rather dull stick as he had in the past, but Cassie had seemed to see something in him. Now, as he got to know him, he realized that this dullness stemmed from a natural reserve and being raised in a feminine household. Ned wasn't necessarily unadventurous. He had just never had anyone to encourage him. Freddie resolved to visit Camberly more often in order to offer him the boon of male companionship. Of course, the chance to bring himself and his family to Lord Mainwaring's attention did nothing to weaken this admirable resolve.

28

The subject of these various machinations continued in her routine, totally oblivious of the stratagems of those interested in her welfare. In spite of admitting to herself that she was in a fair way to being in love with, or certainly attracted to, Lord Mainwaring, Lady Frances had never entertained the least thought of marrying him. She had never even seriously considered marrying anyone, and she would have been astounded and probably highly annoyed to learn that no fewer than all of her nearest and dearest, with the possible exception of Aunt Harriet—and the Comte de Vaudron was working on that redoubtable lady—not only pictured her married to Lord Mainwaring but also were actively promoting the match.

She was glad to welcome Cassie, Freddie, Aunt Harriet, and the staff home. In truth, after the first few days when she had relived past events, reinterpreted various scenes, and wrestled in general to put her thoughts and emotions in order, she had begun to find her solitude more upsetting than restful. Bertie's house party had certainly provided diversion. It was delightful to discuss antiquities with Lord Alvanley and match wits with Bertie's more brilliant friends. She had even enjoyed the blatant admiration of some of the younger members of his group, who trailed her everywhere, hanging on every word. And she had been warmed and comforted by the support and sympathy she read in Bertie's bearing toward her. But instead of dispelling unwelcome thoughts, these people, so closely connected with the life she had led in London, brought back the memories even more vividly. She longed for the simple trust and companionship of her family. Thus when one beautiful June afternoon the dusty carriage finally appeared, she greeted them all with unusual warmth.

"Fanny, Wellington, Nelson! We're here!" Cassie yelled, leaning perilously from the coach and waving vigorously as it rounded the bend in the drive. The twins were bursting with energy, eager to get back to the freedom and delights of the country.

"Has Jim arrived yet with the ponies?" Freddie wanted to know. "And has Ned come home yet?"

Frances was somewhat surprised by this last query, as Freddie had been less than interested in his neighbor before.

"I don't believe so, but I don't know when they plan to return."

"Oh, soon, I expect. He told me the other day it would most likely be sometime this week."

Frances' curiosity increased. "Oh, did you see Ned and Kitty while I was away?"

"Oh, yes. Lord Mainwaring took Nigel, Ned, and me to see a cricket match at Lord's. And, Fan, it was the most bang-up thing ever." Her brother had begun blithely, but observing the slightly rigid look that came over his sister's face, he broke off abruptly. "Wellington, Wellington! Come on, you silly mongrel," he called. "Let's go to the stables and see what's up."

"He's not a mongrel," Cassie protested indignantly, but then, recognizing the meaningful look cast in her direction, realized that Freddie had purposely chosen a taunt that never failed to rouse her, with the sole object of getting her attention. She trotted off obediently with him and Wellington to the stables.

Once out of earshot, her twin hissed, "She's still angry at him, so be sure you don't let on that he's coming down here."

She nodded, looking at once mischievous and approving. "What a strategist you are, Freddie."

"Nothing to it," he responded loftily, but spoiled his superiority the next minute by adding confidently, "Grown-ups aren't at all difficult to manage, you know. They aren't any better at covering up their feelings than children are. They just seem to want different things. Though why they want them, I can't understand." He frowned disapprovingly at this after-thought. In fact this had been puzzling him a great deal. Except for Fannie and Cassie, who were both great guns, awake on every suit, and pluck to the backbone, he had no use at all for females. They were weak, silly things who never knew when to be quiet and had no interest in the finer things of life—dogs, guns, horses, boxing. In fact, he had decided in a meditative moment that he liked his sisters precisely because they didn't act like other members of their sex. Given this misogynistic outlook, it was only natural that he should look upon love and lovers with the highest scorn. Most boys of eleven would have been totally oblivious of the existence of this phenomenon, but Freddie was a medievalist at heart. He delighted in tales of knights and dragons and bemoaned the cruelty of a fate that had caused him to be born in a civilized age when even duels were illegal. He read voraciously, anything and everything, even tackling Froissart and Malory in his enthusiasm. Though he skipped over the parts concerning fair ladies and concentrated only on the incredible feats required to rescue them, he was aware that their approval was a motivating factor in knightly conduct. Much as he loved and admired Lancelot and Arthur, he deplored their apparent foolishness over Guinevere. And now, another, more fleshly hero seemed to share their only weakness. Not only had Freddie been disgusted that such a nonpareil as Lord Mainwaring should want to spend time with someone as clinging and languishing as the lady who had been hanging on his arm that day in the park, but he had even found it difficult to believe that his lordship could prefer driving Frances around the park to joining him and Nigel on a return trip to the Tower.

At first he had thought Mainwaring escorted Frances so that

she would not feel left out when he returned to the more manly
companionship of Freddie, Nigel, and Ned. But it had soon been
borne in on him that Mainwaring enjoyed his sister's company,
in fact actually preferred it to his. It was not to be supposed
that Freddie could overlook this flaw in his hero, but in view
of his other outstanding qualities, he readily forgave it. And,
after all, Lord Mainwaring was not acting foolishly over just
any female. Just before the unfortunate encounter in the park,
Freddie had begun to recognize the advantages of this otherwise
disturbing state of affairs. Lord Mainwaring was increasingly
to be seen at Brook Street and could always be relied on to lend
a sympathetic ear to the problems of perfecting one's cricket
techniques or to offer advice on the management of recalcitrant
ponies. And then that overdressed lady with the mean eyes had
somehow ruined everything. Freddie didn't quite understand
it, but he knew that his elder sister was very angry. He also
knew that though she was seldom upset, once she was, she didn't
give in easily. He also knew that a man who had successfully
dealt with pirates in the West Indies and angry natives in Africa
would not be the least bit worried by a furious woman, even
if she were Lady Frances Cresswell. He was far more likely
to ignore her and sooner or later forget all about her and her
family. And Freddie certainly did not want that to happen. He
felt that the best course to reestablish relations was to take a
leaf out of Malory's book and hope for some situation that would
offer Mainwaring adventure and challenge, while at the same
time rendering a service to Lady Frances. In this boring day
and age, such dramatic situations were not readily available,
but Freddie felt certain that time and some ingenuity on his part
could produce one. In the meantime, it would be better if the
two principals in the drama were kept apart and not allowed
to annoy each other further.

At his wits' end as far as the creation of such a situation went,
he decided to enlist the aid of his twin. Cassie listened
breathlessly while he outlined his plans. Sympathetic as she was,
she was no more forthcoming with ideas than he had been. "If
only all the dragons hadn't been killed or died off," she sighed.

Wistfully, Freddie thought so too, but there was no use in
wasting time and energy lamenting the glorious past. "Come

off it, Cassie. Think!'' he ordered. And the two of them sat
in the hayloft with furrowed brows until Wellington summoned
them to tea. Ferreting out the twins in all their many hideaways
was one of Wellington's prime duties. Aided by his sharp eyes
and no less acute nose, he was justifiably proud of his skill,
for Cassie and Freddie were past masters at hiding in out-of-
the-way nooks and crannies.

Meanwhile, the object of all these plans was worrying over
the state of affairs himself. Well aware that it behooved him
to tread carefully where Lady Frances Cresswell was concerned,
Lord Mainwaring did not take Bertie's suggestion and escort
Kitty and Ned into Hampshire. Lady Frances was too damnably
self-assured as it was when trapped in the most unexpected and
uncomfortable confrontations. He certainly did not want her to
be forewarned of his presence at Camberly. He made certain
of arrangements for his wards' journey and bade them a warmer
farewell than anticipated. Really, he had almost grown fond of
Kitty's enthusiasms and Ned's youthfully serious air.

He then retired to business of his own—reports to be made
to Lord Charlton, problems with a greedy maharajah who was
making trouble with his agents in the East, and recalcitrant
tenants closer at hand on his smallest estate in Buckinghamshire.
He dealt with all of these in his usual incisive manner, but at
times his mind would wander back to Lady Frances and conjecture on a variety of possible receptions at Cresswell. His
shipping agent found him unwontedly cautious and several times
his solicitor was forced to recall his errant thoughts. Both
instances were so uncharacteristic of his lordship that these
worthy men were slightly dismayed.

"Hit's as though 'is 'eart wasn't in it,'' the agent complained
to an overripe widow of indeterminate age who shared his
predilection for the Mermaid tavern in Cheapside.

"I can't think what must have been worrying him. Everything
has been settled most advantageously,'' Mr. Wilkins confided
to his worthy mate as they sat over their dinner in Russell
Square. Both of these ladies, springing from backgrounds as
dissimilar as one could have imagined, had no difficulty in
interpreting this behavior. "It's a woman, sure as I'm
breathin','' sighed Nell gustily.

So it was that the Cresswells and their neighbors enjoyed a week of activity unconstrained by the presence of Lord Mainwaring. In fact, only Lady Frances would have been uncomfortable in his company. A Season in London had taught Kitty that formidable though he might be, her guardian was well-versed in the ways of society. In the main, Lord Mainwaring, concerned with more important problems than the latest style of tying a cravat or the tailor best capable of fitting a coat to perfection, spent too much time in diplomatic and financial circles to be acknowledged as a leader of the *ton*. However, his excellent taste in all the arts, coupled with tremendous wealth, pleasing personal appearance, and undoubted prowess in athletic pursuits of all types made him sought after by hostesses eager to lend cachet to their various functions, damsels aspiring to distinction or a great catch, sporting bloods in search of an amateur who posed a serious threat to the nation's champions, and hoary members of the Foreign Office in search of a well-considered opinion. In short, better than being one of its leading lights, Lord Mainwaring commanded the respect of the fashionable world, which was no mean feat. And in doing so, he had won the grudging admiration of his ward, uncomfortable as she occasionally still was in his awe-inspiring presence.

Ned, who could have cared less about society, or even whether or not his guardian noticed him at all, had first been impressed by his lordship's library. Not only was it well-stocked, it appeared to be well-used. Its shelves were never dusty and the volumes stood irregularly enough on them that even the most casual observer must recognize that they were frequently consulted. Ned was thrilled to have access to such a place. And, being a sensitive lad, he could see the trouble the marquess, obviously a busy man, went to to make certain his young charges enjoyed themselves. Though quiet, Ned was well aware of all that went on around him, and he grew to admire his uncle as he had never admired anyone else. He envied his calmness and assurance, the analytical approach he took to complications, and the way he interested himself personally in any problem, no matter how trivial.

Of course, Freddie and Cassie would have welcomed such a knowing 'un as the marquess. They had never stood in the least awe of him and were more ready than the others to recognize the qualities that made him an intriguing companion for even the most imaginative of eleven-year-olds. They were vociferous and frequent in lamenting his absence, and were carrying on in their usual manner one day to their sister. "Lord Mainwaring would let us go to see the Gypsy fair. I know he would," protested Cassie.

"You know he wouldn't allow Squire Tilden to convince him that it was dangerous. He would know what an old woman the squire is," her brother scoffed.

"That may very well be," Frances retorted. "But Lord Mainwaring is a man, fully able to scare respect into a band of Gypsies. No matter how well I am able to look after Cresswell, not to mention you two hellions, I don't scare Gypsies. And besides, he isn't here," she concluded triumphantly.

Here she received unexpected help from Kitty, who had ridden over to visit at the earliest opportunity. "You know, Freddie, everyone says that all those wonderful feats—sword-swallowing, fire-eating, conjuring, and the like—are the basest trickery. They don't really do it at all, but rely on their own quickness and the *stupidity* of their audience." She looked meaningfully at the twins, then concluded with a master stroke: "I am told they are hideously cruel to their animals. They beat their poor ponies unmercifully and they're too nip-farthing to feed their dogs properly. That's why they steal dogs wherever they go, because theirs are always starving to death." Kitty's cheeks pinkened and her large velvety eyes glistened with tears. In her earnestness, she remained oblivious of Frances' quizzical smile.

Lady Frances by no means believed these hair-raising stories, but if they kept the redoubtable twins from a situation bound to land both of them in some sort of trouble, so much the better. "Come," she said briskly, taking pity on their very genuine disappointment. "We must plan a great picnic instead to welcome home Kitty and Ned."

The twins were mollified with this idea, and when Frances discovered that the elder brother of the youngest housemaid added knowledge of a few magic tricks to a far-reaching reputation as an accomplished juggler, they were almost completely reconciled to the loss of the Gypsy fair.

The day chosen for the outing dawned clear and warm but not hot. In short, it was a perfect day for an expedition to Shooter's Hill, a spot beloved by picnickers for its commanding view of the surrounding countryside. Frances and Kitty had planned to travel sedately in the barouche, but the day was so fine and both of them had missed their long country rides so much while they were in the city that they chose to join the children on their ponies. Aunt Harriet had been offered a place in the carriage but had responded acidly that moments of such peace and quiet as this were too precious to waste, and besides, she must see to her precious plants after their upsetting journey. So the only traveler in the carriage was the well-stocked picnic hamper.

Ned, mounted on a recently bought chestnut his uncle had helped him select at Tattersall's, was the envy of the twins. And Freddie, seeing how well he sat a mount that was quite obviously full of spirit, was impressed. He wanted to know Xerxes' history, parentage, and fine points in minutest detail, and once again was surprised to find himself enjoying Ned's company so much. More inclined to conceal his accomplishments than call attention to them, Ned at first resisted Freddie's urging to "Show us what he can do, Ned." But when Cassie begged, "Oh, Ned, please do put him through his paces," he showed himself and his animal as proudly as though he were in the ring at Astley's. The twins then could no longer contain themselves, and itching for some violent exercise, galloped on ahead at breakneck speed, doubling back every once in a while to admonish the others, "Do hurry, we'll never get there at this snail's pace, and we're so hungry. Do come and look at Farmer Stubbs's new bull, Fan. Isn't he the most monstrous mean-looking beast you have ever seen?"

Ned fell back to listen to his sister and Frances discussing the progress of Frances' book. "In truth, I neglected it sadly while I was in London, and of course the first few days I was back at Cresswell I had my hands full, but I now am coming along better." Ned shyly asked what period of history she had chosen to present to the public first. "I've decided to try the most difficult first, the Greeks, and then, if I can make a go of that, I shall be so encouraged that I shall try the easier things—the Crusades, the Wars of the Roses, the Tudors. But, Ned, how have you come on with your own Greek studies? I know you had set the most ambitious plan to fill your days in London."

The boy flushed with pleasure. He had always regarded the twins' sister with awe. That she could be so learned, but so warm, adventurous, and gay, seemed a miracle to him. For years he had secretly envied Cassie and Freddie their close relationship with someone who could teach them so much. Dearly as he loved Kitty for her sweet and affectionate ways, he recognized that her mind was not as keen or inquiring as his. And here Frances was talking to him as a fellow scholar. He was in heaven.

Kitty rode on, amused by his admiration and happy in his pleasure at being treated as an equal. She was the only one of the party who seemed to feel anything but relieved to be back at home. Such an attitude was understandable in one who had exchanged exquisite ball gowns for a riding dress, a constant throng of admirers at a variety of dazzling social occasions for a family outing, and letters and bouquets for the complaints of the housekeeper and her elderly cousin. But the air felt so fine, the country looked so fresh, that she was content to ride along enjoying the fineness of the day and the peace and quiet of the countryside. She would have been astounded to learn how often Lady Frances' thoughts strayed back to the gaiety of the past Season and that her "Do tell me about the rest of your stay, Kitty," was as much to indulge the listener as the regaler.

Kitty was only too happy to oblige with dance-by-dance descriptions of the last of the Season's balls, as well as repeating word by word the conversations and detailing flounce by flounce the gowns at the final routs and fêtes. Young Lord Willoughby's name was featured rather frequently and always alluded to in such an offhand manner that Lady Frances was able to gratify her narrator by remarking on the apparent interest of that young peer. "Oh, yes, I daresay we did see a good deal of each other. He seems to enjoy the same things I do," replied Kitty with her adorable blush much deeper than usual. "He is all that is gentlemanly and attentive, not like so many of them, who only care whether one is impressed with the set of their coats, the intricacies of their cravats, or their athletic prowess. The tone of his mind is extremely nice. I think you would like him, Fan. At least, I hope you would. I do. I don't think I could like anyone else half so well," she concluded in a rush, with such a glowing look that her friend refrained from the obvious observations on the extreme youth and inexperience of both parties.

And, she thought to herself, just because I would not be happy with someone as naive and innocently optimistic as Willoughby doesn't necessarily mean that Kitty wouldn't be. Experience of the world does not ensure freedom from bitter disillusionment any more than naiveté assures it. After all, there was never a more naive and sentimental pair of lovers than Kitty's parents, nor a happier one. No need to be hard on them or her because they weren't to my taste. This last thought brought forcefully to mind the deep blue eyes and tanned face of one who was infinitely wise in the ways of the world, an image which, despite its instantaneous banishment, caused a warm fluttery sensation in the pit of her stomach and a certain breathlessness that had begun to affect her recently.

Kitty could not divine any of this complicated thought process, but she could recognize and correctly identify Frances' own blush and distracted air, and was instantly intrigued. For a while it had seemed to her that her guardian and Lady Frances had shared some special understanding, and she had hoped, not very optimistically, that something would come of it. She did not set such store by the relationship as Lady Streatham and her great-grandmother did, but then, she was not as well-acquainted with her uncle as they were. At any rate, she had been far more impressed with the *ton*ish group paying court to her friend just before her abrupt departure from London. Perhaps one of Bertie's friends? She began her investigation adroitly, she thought. "But you were quite gay down here yourself. Didn't Bertie Montgomery host a large party of friends directly after the Season ended?"

"Yes, he did," was the totally unsatisfying reply. There was no betraying consciousness, and the air of abstraction still remained. Kitty was at a loss to explain, but renewed her efforts. "Who was here?"

"Oh, Lord Alvanley, Lord Petersham, the usual, you know." Frances was patently uninterested in this select group.

The thundering of hooves ended any further questioning. "Do come on! However can you be so slow?" demanded Cassie.

"Women!" Freddie muttered, looking at Ned with all the world-weariness of an eleven-year-old who had just come home from a London Season. "Can you believe they would rather talk than ride or eat? Come along, Fan, we're so ravenous we've got pains in the breadbasket."

"In your what?"

"Well, that's what Jim calls it. Ain't it a great expression?"

"It is, I admit. And it's all very well for Jim, but it isn't for you."

"But, Fan, you're always telling us to write descriptively and enrich our vocabulary."

"Freddie Cresswell! You know very well that I refer to refined richness and not some stableboy cant," she retorted crossly.

Her brother grinned engagingly. "Come on, Ned. Cook made some delicious game pies and we must get to them before Cassie does or there won't be a crumb left." Having provoked both his sisters to his satisfaction, Freddie dashed on ahead to oversee the laying-out of the picnic.

The rest of the afternoon passed in the deliciously lazy way a perfect summer afternoon should. The children, under the critical eye of John Coachman, put their mounts through their paces, and Freddie even essayed the feat that had brought him to grief earlier. After many unsuccessful attempts he was able to stand on Prince's back long enough to ride in a circle at the end of the rein. "Fan, Fan! Look at me, I say," he was able to shout just before beginning to lose his precarious balance, but he was able to keep dignity intact by turning a slip into a jump off his mount's back and finish with a flourishing bow.

There was nothing for it then but for the others to try. Frances resumed her reading of *Guy Mannering*, just received from

Hatchard's in the morning post. Kitty was once again, after the Season's absence, busy with her sketchbook. Frances found the companionable silence and the hum of the bees very restful after the emotional turmoil of London and her own recent feverish activity at Cresswell. Slowly she drifted off and, for the first time in several months, fell into a deep sleep unbroken by any dreams or thoughts.

She was awakened by the rattle of tea things being set about and the arrival of William, complete with top hat and pet rabbit. The children spent a blissful hour stuffing themselves with jam tarts and exclaiming in delight as he made various articles disappear and reappear in the twinkling of an eye—and in the strangest places. He totally mystified the sharp-eyed Cassie with card tricks she thought she knew completely, and dismayed them all by making a dear little rabbit vanish altogether. He won all their admiration when, keeping five fresh eggs in the air, he reached deep into his empty hat and produced the rabbit, contentedly munching some dandelion greens. All in all it was a splendid afternoon and the Gypsies were totally forgotten.

29

W hile the Cresswells and their neighbors were thus enjoying the summer, the marquess was tidying up a few last details in town before descending on this unsuspecting crew. At last, two weeks after Kitty and Ned's departure for Hampshire, he was tooling toward Camberly, savoring the freshness of the country air and the chance to spring his grays after the crowds, noise, and claustrophobic atmosphere of the city. He did enjoy the wealth of interesting companions and the variety of entertainments to be found in London, but feeling sated with sophisticated pursuits, he welcomed the exhilaration of the drive, the test of his physical rather than his mental skills. For a while he gave himself thoroughly to the managing of his horses and the challenge of driving to an inch, but it wasn't long before unwelcome thoughts began to intrude. How was he going to convince Lady Frances to see him? And even if he were able to, what would he say? "I love you"? She would laugh in his face. No, that was not true. She would never allow herself to be unkind or vulgar. She would merely look at him in patent disbelief. How would he ever show that he cared about her? Well, then, should he tell her that she was the only woman he had ever wanted to marry? Despite the truth of this he knew her disbelief would turn to sheer incredulity. He would show her, make her see that he loved her, but how? In his frustration he took a corner much too fast and nearly locked wheels with a lumbering farm cart. Cursing himself, his stupidity, and his mismanagement of the entire situation, he gritted his teeth and drove the rest of the way, concentrating rigidly on nothing but the road ahead.

Before he was halfway to Camberly, Lord Mainwaring, for all his years and experience, was in no better shape than any young man in love. I was resisting matchmaking mamas and determined young women and carrying on liaisons with dozens of delightful ladies while she was still in the schoolroom, and now I am no better than someone in his salad days—or perhaps I'm already in my dotage, he thought bitterly. Humiliating as it all was, he reflected ruefully, it must mean he was in love. He had never in his life put himself out for a woman, and now he was allowing one to inflict agonies of self doubt—a hard lesson for a man who had been accustomed to holding his own alone in any situation, anywhere, for so long.

These serious reflections occupied him so that it seemed no time at all before he was in the yard at the White Hart, claiming the attention of several eager ostlers and the genial Crimmins. "Well, my lord, it's been some time since we've seen you here." Beaming, he ushered Mainwaring into a private parlor. "How are they all at Camberly? I fancy Miss Kitty did fairly make them stand up and take notice in London. We heard she's just come back. A lovely lass. And will you be staying on at Camberly or just passing through?"

"Thank you, Crimmins." The marquess gratefully accepted a mug of his host's best home brew. "Actually, I was hoping you could put me up. I'm sure they're all at sixes and sevens at Camberly, having just gotten back. I don't know how long my business here will take, and I don't want to put them out."

"You're more than welcome here, my lord." Crimmins completely accepted this barefaced lie. If he suspected that his wife's excellent cooking and his genial hospitality were luring Lord Mainwaring from Cousin Honoria's parsimonious housekeeping and smoking chimneys, he was welcome to. Mainwaring was not prepared to admit to anyone, even to himself, the real reason for his choice of accommodation. His presence in the neighborhood was much less likely to be brought to Frances' attention if he were at the White Hart than if he were at Camberly.

He had not reckoned on the sharp eyes of Master Frederick and Miss Cassandra Cresswell. The twins had just escaped from their lessons and had ridden straight to the village to see William's latest crop of baby rabbits. Since his performance at the picnic and subsequent offer to teach them the simplest of his tricks, that young man had become quite the favorite of the schoolroom set. William was at work mending fences in Squire Tilden's lower fields, but he had instructed his mother to show the rabbits to the children. He had not told her to regale them with freshly baked currant buns, but this offer was eagerly accepted and Cassie and Freddie came away more than satisfied, despite having missed their friend. They promised to visit Mrs. Tubbs next week when they came to check on the progress of the dear little bunnies.

As they rounded the bend in front of the inn, Cassie said, "Look, Freddie, there's Lord Mainwaring's curricle. Isn't it beautiful?"

"It couldn't be. He's doing business in London. You must be mistaken." The brotherly scorn in his voice implied that no mere girl could be capable of distinguishing one equipage from another, no matter how magnificent it was.

His twin was not so easily dismissed. "You are an odious boy, Freddie Cresswell. I can recognize Lord Mainwaring's grays just as well as you can, and well you know it! You might as well own up, Freddie. You know I'm right."

By now they had come abreast of the vehicle and there was no question as to whom they belonged. "Well, you may be right," her brother conceded unwillingly. Then he resumed with his superior air, "But don't tell Fan, whatever you do. I don't want you upsetting her."

Which, Cassie thought indignantly, was outside of enough and just like her toplofty brother. He never could stand to be bested at the least little thing. After all, *she* had not fallen off her pony and given her sister a week of worry in London.

But when they reached Cresswell in time for tea, both Frances and Nelson looked so agitated—an extremely uncharacteristic frame of mind for both of them—that they completely forgot this interesting turn of events. "I can't think where Wellington has got to," worried Frances. "Cook says he didn't show up for breakfast, and he hasn't bothered me for a walk the entire day. You know he always appears at teatime to tussle with Nelson and upset things as much as possible. Besides, Nelson has been meowing and trying to get my attention since I got up. And you know he's become so fat and lazy he wouldn't stir a paw if his life depended on it unless Wellington were playing with him."

"Mrrow," her companion agreed dolefully.

"Perhaps he found some stoats," volunteered Freddie. "Farmer Stubbs told me he thinks there's a family of them living in Hanger Wood. He's been meaning to go after them, but he's just too busy."

"Perhaps you are right," His sister agreed with little conviction. "He usually is here dropping them in my lap the minute he's caught one, though."

"Maybe they're very clever stoats and he's having difficulty catching them," ventured Cassie skeptically.

No one wanted to be the one to suggest what they all feared and suspected most. It was Cook, bursting in wrathfully to inform them that the chicken she had planned to dress for dinner had been stolen, who articulated their worst fears. "It's them rascally Gypsies, buffer nappers all of 'em, miss. They'll take anything that isn't tied down and locked up."

Frances interrupted soothingly. "It may have just gone off to find a nice private nesting place, or maybe a fox got it."

Cook was not to be mollified. "Humph. I don't believe no such thing, and it's my belief that they've stolen that pesky cur as well."

"You've no right to call Wellington that when you sneak as many scraps to him as anyone," protested Cassie. "But, Fanny, what would they steal Wellington for? They wouldn't . . . they wouldn't . . ." Cassie couldn't go on.

"Lord, no, you silly clunch," her brother exclaimed. "They've kidnapped him to turn him into a performing dog. They know that terriers like Wellington are very good at that sort of thing. And anyone looking at him can tell he's highly intelligent. That stupid nit has probably forgotten all about us and is having himself a fine time learning all sorts of tricks. You know how he likes to show off. He certainly enjoyed it when I tried to teach him some of the things I saw the dogs doing at Astley's.''

Hearing the name of his friend, Nelson howled and got up to scratch at the library door.

''Not tonight, Nelson. But if he's not back tomorrow, we'll go find him,'' Frances promised. ''Now, what do you say? I think a little of Caesar's *Gallic Wars* to take our minds off this.''

The twins groaned more out of habit than anything else, for they realized as well as Frances that since nothing could be done for Wellington that night and they were more likely to fret impatiently if they were unoccupied, they might as well direct their energies somehow. ''But,'' Freddie pointed out, ''there are lots more pleasant ways to drown our sorrows or forget them.''

''Yes,'' his sister agreed. ''And none of them is nearly as productive.'' All resistance squelched, the lesson began.

Freddie was wrong about one thing. Wellington was not enjoying himself in the least. In fact, he could not remember a time in his short life when he had been more miserable, he thought to himself as he sat morosely under one of the Gypsy caravans. He'd been happily following the fresh scent of stoat when he'd been roughly snatched up and thrust into a foul-smelling bag. He must have been tied to a saddle, because there was a distinct smell of horse and he was jolted quite dreadfully. It must have been an underfed pony. Wellington had ridden occasionally with Frances and he'd been behind the marquess's team of grays and he knew full well that no horse of any breeding would have as rough a gait as the one to which he had just been subjected.

They had bounced along for some time and then the air was suddenly alive with commotion. Women and children were shouting, dogs barking, ponies whinnying, and babies crying. The bouncing stopped. Wellington was jerked from his bag and pawed by a thousand curious hands, pulled and mulled like some object instead of a purebred West Highland Terrier of impeccable lineage, he thought huffily. Then, as if this man-handling by the common herd weren't enough, he was subjected to the final indignity—a dirty rope was tied around his neck and he was rudely pulled under a caravan, to be ignominiously tied there alone with his thoughts under the baleful eyes of the ill-assorted mongrels of the camp. One by one the fires were put out. The appetizing smell of stew died out, and as the cold evening fog descended, he sat alone, miserable, hungry, and sorry for every time he hadn't come when Frances called, hadn't sat down when one of the twins told him to, had nipped Nelson a little too hard when they were wrestling. With a gusty sigh he buried his nose in his paws and tried to sleep.

"Mrrow."

One ear lifted cautiously. Just a dream, he told himself, shaking his head.

"Mrrow."

This time, both ears shot up. "Arrph," he responded cautiously. A soft, furry body snuggled up next to him and purred loudly in his ear. Unable to persuade Frances to look for Wellington that evening, Nelson, his partner in crime and adventure, had set off to do so himself. Following the elusive trail and relying on a good deal of feline instinct, coupled with the conversation he had overheard at tea and a natural distrust of Gypsies, he had found him at last. All Wellington's loneliness and misery vanished, but it would never do to show Nelson how overjoyed he was to see him. Not only did someone now know where he was, but he had a friend and ally of his own. He had stuck out his square little jaw and showed himself completely unimpressed by those ravenous Gyspy dogs, even though all the while his insides were quaking. Together he and Nelson worried the rope, but it resisted all their determined efforts. They were at last forced to abandon the project, and Nelson slunk off in the dark, promising to round up reinforcements.

He arrived back at Cresswell only a few hours before dawn—just enough time to take a catnap at the end of Frances' bed before waking her. This he promptly did, just as the faintest streaks of morning light appeared in the east. He was loath to let her complete her entire morning bathing ritual, and complained loudly when she sat down in the breakfast parlor for some muffins and chocolate.

"Nelson, I *am* coming, but I shan't be able to help anyone on an empty stomach," his mistress admonished. "And what's more, you won't be able to either. Come, have some breakfast." She poured some cream in a bowl and laid on a saucer the kipper that Cook insisted no breakfast table be without. Despite the dreadful state of his nerves, Nelson succumbed to the delicious aroma of the kipper. Once that was finished, he needed the cream to wash it down. Much of his anxiety vanished once his stomach was full, and he was able to wait with a reasonable amount of patience for Frances to finish her repast. This she did with dispatch, fearing the descent of the twins and the inevitable delay while she told them her plans and dissuaded them from coming with her. As it was, she left the briefest of notes informing them that she and Nelson had left to search for Wellington, but not giving the slightest indication of their direction. In this way she hoped, without much confidence in the effectiveness of her stratagem, to prevent them from following her.

It was still quite early when she and Nelson set out, Nelson running a few feet ahead of her, tail waving proudly. It was a beautiful hour of the day, bathed in the golden glow of early-morning light. The grass, wet with dew, and the air, unsullied with the dust of the day, were fresh with the just-washed newness of a summer morning. In spite of her anxiety over Wellington and the emotional strain of the past few weeks, Frances felt glad to be there and alive with the sheer delight of ripening fields, singing birds, and trees in full leaf.

She was just a bit glad no one else knew of Wellington's disappearance, because it did seem a trifle absurd to be so upset over a mere dog. How Wellington would scorn her for such a heretical thought. And he would have been right to do so. To her, he wasn't a mere dog. He'd been a constant companion as she walked or rode the estate. He had sat up nights with her while she pored over the accounts or agricultural journals. When she had longed to rest her head on the shoulder of a parent or friend, he had snuggled up to her, beaming loyalty and encouragement out of his bright black eyes, and licked her face.

Absorbed in her thoughts, she tramped several miles, always keeping her eye on Nelson's tail but otherwise not paying a great deal of attention to her surroundings. All of a sudden Nelson stopped so abruptly that she almost tumbled over him. She looked about. Several hundred feet away was the Gypsy camp. In the early-morning light with the smoke rising from breakfast fires, it looked like some ghostly caravan from an Oriental tale. Frances stood taking in the scene a moment before collecting her thoughts to plan the next step. She had barely begun to do this when there was a rustle behind, a sharp pain at the back of her head, a flash of light, and then darkness.

30

"Freddie, Freddie," shouted Cassie as she raced up the stairs two at a time. She was usually an earlier riser than her slugabed brother, who remained warm and cozy under the bedclothes until the last possible moment. Today her matinal energy had been rewarded, as she was the first to discover Frances' note and was able to impart the news with an important air to the rest of the household that her sister had gone to look for Wellington.

Cassie had already apprised her Aunt Harriet of the news as that lady frowned over a botanical journal in the breakfast parlor while she absently crumbled a muffin into her morning chocolate. "Gracious, even Frances can't have been so pigheaded and independent as to have gone off to tackle those Gypsies alone," she remarked before returning to the latest theories for propagating orchids in England's inclement atmosphere. But an inquiry among the staff revealed that Frances appeared to have done exactly that.

Armed with this illuminating discovery, Cassie tore off to rouse her somnolent twin. For a moment he gaped owlishly at her from under a rumpled thatch of blond hair. "All alone, was she? That was dashed selfish of her to go off on a splendid

adventure just like that when she knew we were dying to
see . . . ahem, when she knew we would be worried to death
about her. Perhaps we should go help her," he suggested.
Galvanized by the prospect of such excitement, he leapt up and
pulled on his clothes.

He was forestalled by the venerable Higgins, who, knowing
his young master's mind better than anyone else, appeared just
in time to put a stop to any such plans. "Now, Master Freddie,
you know as well as I do that Lady Frances doesn't want any
interference from you." He silenced the indignant objections
that burst forth with an admonitory gesture. "No! You know
that anyone who is capable of standing up to that villainous Mr.
Snythe is not to be put off by a few vagabond Gypsies. No,
Master Frederick, and Miss Cassandra too, don't try to gammon
me. You know it's as good as my position is worth to keep you
here even if it means tying you two up and locking you in the
schoolroom. If Miss Frances had wanted company, she would
have asked for it. Now, that's an end to the matter." Determination was written large in every line of his countenance.
The twins sighed and contented themselves with topping each
other's speculations as to Frances' probable course of action
once she reached the Gypsy camp.

The day dragged on. Noontime came and went. Cook
reluctantly served luncheon, but there was still no Lady Frances.
By this time the twins were beginning to worry. It was so unlike
their elder sister to be gone so long on an errand that should
not have taken outside of an hour or two. "Perhaps she stopped
in the village," Cassie suggested. "I heard her say that Mrs.
Stubbs's youngest had the mumps." The only response she got
from her brother was a look of pure scorn.

By teatime they were seriously alarmed, but they allowed
Higgins to serve it as usual, just in case Frances should arrive
tired and thirsty, looking forward to it. But both of them felt
they couldn't eat a bite. Just as Higgins was setting down the
bread and butter, there was a scratch at the door and in bounded
Wellington and Nelson, both rather the worse for wear, but
ecstatic to be home again.

"Wellington, you scamp," cried Cassie, hugging the bedraggled body close and surreptitiously feeding him a thickly buttered scone. "Whatever have they done to you? Freddie, look. The rope has rubbed his neck raw, and look at this cut over his eye. You look dreadful, Wellington, you really do."

The little dog was disappointed to hear her say so. He'd evaded no fewer than two Gypsy mongrels, nasty snapping beasts with gaping jaws and sharp teeth. He thought the cut gave him quite a rakish appearance. It lent a definite air of distinction. Nelson's game eye was also slightly puffy. He'd been dealt a swipe by one of the dogs in the fray. His already tattered ears looked to be even more so, but he seemed to be quite cheerful, and ever so proud of having discharged his old debt in rescuing his friend. It had been his perseverance and sharp teeth that had finally severed the rope and freed his companion.

The animals allowed themselves to be welcomed and fussed over for a little while, but it soon became plain that theirs was unfinished business. Wolfing down a final scone, Wellington headed for the door and barked peremptorily. "Freddie, he knows where Frances is. He's going to show us," whispered Cassie excitedly.

"Of course he does. Just a minute, Wellington. I must get a gun."

"Freddie Cresswell! When did you ever learn to handle a gun?" his sister demanded suspiciously.

"Well, I don't say I've ever killed anything, but I can hit a target most of the time," came the defensive reply.

"Stuff! Those Gypsies can throw their knives farther and faster than you can hit anything with that. I tell you what. I think we want a grown-up."

Her brother protested. "Cass, they'll just rant and rave about how children don't know what's to do and that their place is in the schoolroom, and then we'll never get to Frances before the Gypsies. Besides, we'll miss all the excitement because they'd never let us join them in looking for her."

"We don't want just any adult. We want . . ." Cassie thought for a moment. "We want Lord Mainwaring!" she exclaimed triumphantly. Much as it cost him to admit, Freddie grudgingly agreed that Mainwaring was the perfect solution, and the two, having scrawled a brief note intended to reassure Aunt Harriet and the staff, headed off toward Camberly with Wellington and Nelson in tow.

The marquess had just stepped into the library to go over some household accounts when the butler Chamberlain announced, "Master Frederick Cresswell, Miss Cassandra Cresswell to see you, sir." He hid his surprise quite creditably as he ushered them to chairs and asked the butler to bring some tea. "What? You've had yours, have you? Never mind, then, Chamberlain. Oh, yes, hello, Wellington . . . hello, Nelson. Of course I'm delighted to see you all, but if I'm correct, this looks like a deputation with a mission. How did you know I was here?"

Freddie explained their having seen his curricle a few days before and then began hesitantly, "It's about Fan, sir."

The marquess raised one mobile eyebrow, a gesture that seemed more indicative of surprise than interest.

"Well, it's like this, sir. We think the Gypsies have kidnapped her."

Both brows went up. There was no doubt as to the expression now. It was one of patient disbelief.

"I know it sounds like nonsense, sir, but Wellington disappeared and, having heard that Gypsies were in the area, Fan thought, we all thought, they might have stolen him. So she went to look for him. And they must have—stolen him, I mean—and done something to Fan, because here he is and Fan hasn't shown up for luncheon or tea and her note said she left very early this morning to look for him. So you see, I think Wellington escaped but she's a prisoner somewhere because just look at the rope around Wellington's neck. Both he and Nelson appear to have been in a scuffle, and now they keep trying to get us to follow them."

"Arf!" Wellington confirmed the veracity of Freddie's suspicions.

During the discussion, Lord Mainwaring had gone from being slightly incredulous at such a wild tale to thoughtful, and now he looked distinctly forbidding. "I think, wildly improbable as this seems, you may be right. Now, and don't argue with me, I shall take Wellington and Nelson with me. You and Cassie must return to Cresswell on the off chance that Frances returns.

No! I know you feel you should come with me, and in any other
instance I would be glad to have two such plucky companions,
but I think it's best if I go alone. It's much easier for a single
person to surprise the enemy and rescue someone than it is for
a crowd.''

The twins, object though they would, were forced to bow to
superior knowledge and experience and admit the sense of this
plan. After wishing the marquess luck, they allowed themselves
to be persuaded to return to Cresswell. The unadventurousness
of this course of action was palliated somewhat by their being
driven in his lordship's curricle behind his famous grays.

In the meantime, Mainwaring, Wellington, and Nelson
repaired to the stable, where his lordship's powerful hunter was
quickly saddled. He would have preferred to take a carriage,
as Lady Frances might be in no shape to ride, but after nearly
a day's delay there was no time to be wasted. It had taken a
bit of doing to convince Wellington and Nelson that the twins
were putting the responsibility for the search for Frances into
the marquess's capable hands, but at last they understood and
were soon bounding along a few feet in front of him and Brutus,
feeling extremely important.

The early evening was as lovely as the morning had been when
Lady Frances set out. Soft light was slanting across ripening
fields, bathing them in gold, and a light breeze was stirring the
leaves. The marquess, his eyes fixed on the small figures leading
him, barely noticed his surroundings. The grim set of his jaw
and worried line of his dark brows revealed the unpleasant turn
of his thoughts. If only she had gone to the squire or one of
the local farmers instead of charging off completely on her own.
How foolish and how very like her, in the interests of efficiency
and speed, to take the entire problem immediately on herself
without stopping to consult anyone. Though he cursed her for
having put herself in such danger, Julian admired the spirit that
had prompted it. His face softened as he thought of the self-
reliance and the willingness to tackle and solve whatever
unpleasantness came her way. And once again he, who could
do so much to help her, had been unable to spare her. At least
this time he could still do something. But what state was she
in? Had the Gypsies, fearing the law, decamped already and

taken her with them? How had they kept her from escaping?
A lady as resourceful as Lady Frances would be difficult to
detain without resorting to some sort of violence or drugs or
both. He could not bear the thought of any of it.

After what seemed miles and hours of agonizing over Frances'
possible state, he and Brutus nearly stumbled over Wellington
and Nelson, who had stopped to reconnoiter before advancing
cautiously on a tumbledown shack that at one time must have
held laborer's tools. The four approached carefully, but there
was no sound or sight of any guard. There was no sound of
Frances either. Most likely, the marquess thought bitterly, the
Gypsies, panicked by what they had done, had gone off as
quickly and inconspicuously as possible, leaving her to her fate.
From Wellington's eager look it appeared as though she were
still in there. Mainwaring dismounted, tied Brutus to a tree,
ordered Wellington and Nelson to remain out of the way, and
advanced warily on the hut.

There was a rusty lock hooked through an equally rusty hasp
on the door, but these were easily broken with one well-placed
kick. The door burst open and the marquess stood aside, fists
raised. His powerful shoulders and businesslike stance proclaimed him more than a match for any Gypsy guard. None
appeared, so he stepped in. As his eyes became accustomed to
the gloom, he saw Frances in the far corner. Her hands and
feet were bound, and a dirty handkerchief gagged her, but at
the sound of an intruder she struggled into as combative a
position as possible, her eyes blazing defiance.

"My poor girl," he exclaimed. With one stride Mainwaring
crossed the hut and knelt beside her to untie the gag that was
painfully tight around her head.

She gasped for air and then in her coolest drawing-room voice
inquired, "Whatever are you doing here, my lord?"

"I *thought* I was rescuing you," he replied, busy with the
cords at her hands and feet.

It took all her willpower not to collapse when they were
loosened, but she was damned if she were going to reveal the
slightest weakness to her rescuer. In the past few minutes
Frances' emotions had run the full gamut, from fear, to relief,
to something else that she refused to recognize.

When she had first come to her senses after her capture, Frances had been too weak to do anything. Her head throbbed so much it had been impossible even to think. Gradually, though, she had felt better and had done her best to try to undo the ropes at her hands and feet. All her twisting and wriggling of her extremities had only succeeded in chafing the skin badly and not loosening them the slightest bit. At the outset she had been certain that the Gypsies would eventually recognize her and release her, but as no one came, she concluded they must be writing a ransom note of some sort. She had not been too afraid, only uncomfortable and thirsty. The day dragged on. She had kept track of the sun's passage through a hole in the roof, thinking hopefully of the note she had left back at Cresswell. Surely someone there would rouse the neighborhood and come to the camp in search of her. Still no one came. When far away came the sound of horses stamping, dogs barking, and harnesses jingling, she concluded in despair that the Gypsies were leaving to put as much distance between them and Cresswell as possible before her disappearance was noticed. Try as she would to think of some way to escape or to make her presence known, she could come up with nothing. She could only hope that somehow Freddie or Cassie would remember where the Gypsies had been camping and organize a search party. Certainly they would. Frances had settled down to wait with as much fortitude as she could muster, but her spirits, aggravated by hunger and thirst, would sink, and despite her best efforts, despair would creep up on her. It was when she began to feel her courage at its lowest ebb that the door had burst open and a tall, powerful figure strode in.

Frances had done her best to put on a face of defiance for the intruder, but she was quaking inside. Her biggest fear was that the Gypsies had come to take her off with them in order to thwart any search parties. When she recognized the square jaw and fierce blue eyes of Lord Mainwaring, she had nearly burst into tears of relief. Just in time she had recalled their last meeting and was able to summon up, with her last bit of energy, enough anger to restore her calm. In fact, she was quite proud of her coolness as she asked him how he had come to find her.

"Freddie and Cassie had seen my curricle at the White Hart

in the village before. When they discovered you were missing, they came to Camberly first to find me as it is closer to Cresswell than the White Hart.'' Though he couldn't help admiring the indomitable spirit that gave Frances such calm composure after the ordeal, Mainwaring wished rather ruefully that for once she were less spirited. Looking at the white face and dark circles under eyes large with fatigue, he wanted more than anything to take her in his arms and kiss away the strain of the last hours. But one could hardly comfort a perfectly composed lady who was asking in the most rational way about the events leading to her release. For a moment he had felt sure he'd seen her face light up when she had recognized him. For an instant he had been sure the gladness he had seen in her eyes had been for himself and not just any rescuer. But now, agonizingly, he wasn't sure, and a corroding sense of disappointment and sadness washed over him. Could it be that he really was nothing more to her than just another London Corinthian to be danced with and then dismissed with scorn for his frivolous tendencies?

Fortunately for both parties, at this juncture Wellington, who despite Lord Mainwaring's firm command to STAY could contain his impatience no longer, burst excitedly into the hut, heading straight for Frances and covering her face with reassuring licks. It was too much. The strain, followed by the relief at being rescued, and now the joy at finding Wellington unharmed, completely overset Frances and she burst into tears. Mainwaring pulled her gently to her feet and gathered her in his arms, murmuring into her hair, ''Oh, my poor love. Hush, now. It's all over. My poor dear.''

Frances had had no idea that a solid chest and strong arms could be so comforting. For some minutes she stayed there giving herself up to the soothing effect of his strength and the feel of his hands as he gently smoothed her hair. At first she had been totally incapable of stopping the tears that poured down her cheeks, but gradually, under Mainwaring's comforting influence, she became calmer.

Julian felt the tension slowly drain out of her, but he continued to hold her thus, his cheek resting against her hair, relishing the feeling of her in his arms at last. But then, looking down at the tousled head on his chest, he asked softly, ''Why did you run away?" She remained silent, head bent. "Frances?" He forced her to look up at him, tilting her chin with long fingers.

She at last looked up to see him regarding her with a more serious expression in his eyes than she had ever seen before. Unable to sustain the intensity of his gaze, she dropped hers. "I . . .There was something at Cresswell that had to be dealt with right away." A slight blush crept into her pale cheeks.

"Frances, I have been managing businesses and estates since you were in the schoolroom. Nothing, no problem, is that urgent. It couldn't have been." There was a pause. "Surely it wasn't the Duchess of Devonshire's ball? Frances, please tell me. Did I put myself beyond reproach? I must know what upset you so much that you left without a word to anyone." Much as she wished to make some reply, Frances was simply incapable of saying anything. "Frances," he pressed desperately, "please, I must know. I must know because I love you."

That jolted her out of her bemused state. Her eyes flew to his in astonishment. "You what?"

"I love you. I have . . . oh, for quite a while now, you know."

"But you couldn't possibly!"

It was his turn to be astounded. "And why ever not?"

"Well, because . . . because I'm not the sort of person you fall in love with."

"And what brings you to that conclusion?" he demanded with some asperity.

"Well, I'm just not the type." The skeptical look on his face deepened. She tried again. "Well, I'm not that amusing, sophisticated sort of woman who would interest you." Frances still didn't appear to be making herself clear. "What I *mean* is that I'm not at all sensual and alluring like . . . like Lady Welford."

The skeptical look was replaced by one of pure amusement. "My dear girl! How do you know that you're not sensual or alluring? You have a great appreciation and enjoyment for beauty of any and every kind. You see it all around you, and you enjoy it. That is far more sensual than dousing yourself with perfume and draping yourself on pink satin pillows all day long."

Frances was intrigued. "Is that what she does? I must say, it doesn't sound nearly as interesting and exciting as I thought it would be."

His arms tightened around her. "And furthermore," he continued, ignoring her last remark, "I find you quite alluring. If you hadn't been so damned alluring, there never would have been that scene at the Duchess of Devonshire's ball. You were absolutely breathtaking, and I couldn't even get near you! I can't remember ever having felt jealous before that night. But when I saw you sparkling and laughing in one man's arms or another's, but never in mine, I was furious with jealousy. Then, when you disappeared on the terrace, that was more than I could take." His voice grew husky. "You looked so beautiful there that I hardly noticed that puppy on his knees. I just knew I wanted you more than anything in the world. I had to have you! I apologize for making you so furious, but I am *not* sorry for what I did."

Stealing a quick glance up at him, Frances was taken aback at the intensity in the depths of his eyes. "I wasn't exactly furious. I was more confused, upset. I—"

She wasn't allowed to continue. He pulled her to him fiercely. His lips came down on hers and began to kiss her with a passion that left her weaker and more shaken than all the rest of the day's events combined. For an instant Frances remained there, transfixed by a feeling she had never felt before. Then his hold slackened, his hands slid caressingly up her arms to her neck, his lips became warm, tender, insistent, and her arms crept around his neck and she molded her body to his, responding to the warmth that enveloped her as he kissed her eyes, the line of her jaw down to her throat, her shoulders. Somehow, it seemed she had never felt as alive, as aware of all her senses as she did at this moment, feeling the strength of his back and shoulders underneath her hands, the warmth of his lips against hers.

He lifted his head at last, breathing hard. "We'd best get married at the earliest possible moment. I don't want to wait any longer for you than absolutely necessary."

"Married?"

He cocked his head. "It *is* customary, you know." He saw

the doubt in her face and remarked with some exasperation, "My dear girl, a proper young woman does not kiss someone the way you just did unless she is planning to marry him."

"But I never thought . . . The children . . . I couldn't . . ." Her voice trailed off as she realized just how much she would enjoy life with someone who thought the same way she did, who was interested in the same things she was, who respected her judgment and would let her go her own way. Her eyes filled. "It sounds lovely, but I can't leave Freddie, Cassie, Wellington, and Nelson to Aunt Harriet."

"I would never ask you to do that, my dear one. I like the twins. In fact, if it weren't for Freddie I wouldn't be here now." She was puzzled. "Well, why do you think I happened to arrive in Hampshire at such an opportune moment?"

"I don't know. I suppose you came to check up on Camberly."

"Lord, Frances, don't be a cloth-head. I have an agent who can do that. I came at Freddie's special request. No need to look so astonished. That's a very perceptive young man. When I was in flat despair over you, he came to me at Mainwaring House and hinted to me that you might be more amenable to an apology than I had hoped."

"Freddie?" Frances looked incredulous.

"Yes, Freddie. He surmised, and quite correctly too, that we had had a falling-out. He reasoned that you would never waste your time being angry at someone you didn't like; therefore, anybody who truly made you angry must be someone you truly cared about. He urged me to come down here. I must say I wasn't all that convinced of the accuracy of his theory, but I was so desperate that I was willing to try anything. So, here I am. Here we are."

"But Aunt Harriet . . ."

"Aunt Harriet can stay exactly where she is. We can live at Camberly. It's large enough for all of us and more. We shall foist Kitty off on the first young man she becomes intractable over. Cousin Honoria can have the seaside cottage she's been pining for for her and that dutiful niece from Bath. And Aunt Harriet can turn all of Cresswell into a conservatory if she wishes. You won't be missed in the slightest. Any more foolish objections?'' Overwhelmed, she shook her head. ''Good! Then we had better get along to let the others know you are safe before they murder each other out of impatience. But first . . .'' He looked at her soberly. ''My girl, I don't want to push you into anything you don't want. It's a difficult thing to contemplate sharing your life with someone. I don't want you to do something just because I want it so much. I can understand your wishing to remain the same as always . . .'' He paused uncertainly.

She shook her head and smiled mistily up at him. That was all the encouragement he needed. He kissed her again—a long, hungry, demanding kiss that left them both breathless—before picking her up and carrying her out into the fading light to the waiting horse and her faithful companions.

Miss Cresswell's London Triumph

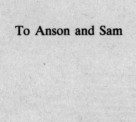

To Anson and Sam

CHAPTER 1

"Aunt Cathie, Aunt Cathie, letters from India!" Theodore shouted, rushing into the library as fast as his short five-year-old legs could carry him and waving two stained envelopes in his pudgy hands. "They're from Uncle Freddie and Ned," he added unnecessarily.

Cassandra looked up from her reading and smiled at the bundle of energy which had interrupted a morning spent rereading select passages of Homer. The small white terrier at her feet cocked his head expectantly at all the commotion. Fond as he was of Cassie, he had found life sadly flat since the departure of her rambunctious twin Freddie two years ago, but Theodore's eruption into the library promised some interest. Theodore was still too young to provide Wellington with as much excitement as the twins' adventures had brought the little dog, but he did appear to be cast in the same mold as the twins and therefore had a great deal of potential, which, if encouraged, was sure to bring activity again to a household that had become, in Wellington's opinion, far too orderly and serene.

"What do they say? Read them to me, pleathe, pleathe," begged Theodore, his eyes shining with anticipation as he plopped himself at her feet. Cassie opened the envelope that was nearly totally covered with her twin's disorderly scrawl. Knowing her nephew's bloodthirsty nature, she felt sure he would prefer the catalog of tiger hunts, elephant rides, and narrow escapes from murderous thugs certain to be in Freddie's letter to the probable discussion of the Hindu religion and its effect on British/Indian relations in Ned's.

His letters, filled with descriptions of temple architecture, Hindu customs, sculpture and painting had piqued her curiosity, stimulated her thoughts, and relieved much of the boredom she had suffered in the absence of her best friends and most constant companions.

"Does he say anything about any more tiger hunts? I wath hoping he would get a tiger at the next one tho we could have itth head here over the fireplace," Teddy announced, indicating the spot now graced by the portrait of a venerable ancestor which would be much improved by such a replacement.

Cassie looked down into his earnest chubby face whose missing front teeth only added to its endearing expression. "I'm sorry, Teddy, my wits were wandering. Let's see what is the latest news." She picked up Freddie's letter and began to read.

If Freddie were to be believed, India existed solely to challenge the skill and daring of adventurous young Englishmen. His wild scrawl related one colorful episode after another, the most important of these apparently having to do with a signal service rendered to the Nabob of Bhopaul, whose gratitude had been effusive and rewarding beyond their wildest dreams. Having amassed a vast sum and, as an aside, having accomplished what they had set out to do, he and Ned were heading home hoping to see everyone at Cresswell and Camberly in the not-too-distant future. At this last piece of news, Theodore let out a whoop and went running in search of his mother. "Mama, Mama, Uncle Freddie and Ned are coming home. Mama, Mama . . ."

Cassie listened to his voice echoing down the hall, remembering the day several years ago when Freddie's voice had echoed much the same way, "Cassie, Cassie, we're going to India!" How she had missed them! Her thoughts strayed back to the other letter and its writer. If she had missed Freddie's *joie de vivre* and his penchant for tumbling them into one mad scrape after another, she missed even more Ned's insatiable thirst for knowledge, and the smile that lurked at the back of his eyes as he teased her and challenged her to think and question as well. If Freddie had been exuberant at the thought of high adventure in the fabulous Indian subcontinent, Ned had been subdued over their departure—subdued and determined to overcome his unhappy memories and to change that part of his personality that had occasioned them in the first place.

Poor Ned. Cassie's image of her dejected friend remained as clear as it had been the day his misery began. She had been sitting reading, much as she was now, when he strode in, his blue eyes dark and hurt in a white, set face. "She won't have me, Cassie," he had groaned, throwing himself into the nearest chair.

Knowing full well who "she" was, Cassie had heaved a mental sigh of relief before urging him to pour out his tale of woe. Privately, she thought Ned well rid of the vain and spoiled Arabella Taylor, who had, in Cassie's opinion, remained as selfish and obstinate as she had been when she had insisted on tagging along after them as children and then refused to play any games that had not been proposed by her. But Cassie knew that she was the only person in the entire neighborhood who continued to retain these unkind thoughts in the face of Arabella's flashing dark eyes, riotous dusky curls, bewitching dimple, and lilting, childlike voice that only added to the enchantment of a mouth too often compared to a rosebud. Everyone, even the studious Ned, had been overcome when Arabella reappeared on the local scene, polished to perfection by an exclusive seminary for young ladies of gentle birth and high expectations. Even Freddie, inclined to dismiss all women except his sisters as useless and helpless creatures, seemed to have forgotten completely the whining, crying child who had always insisted on being the center of attention. She was no different now, Cassie reflected, just more practiced and charming at claiming that attention. But Cassie loved Ned nearly as much as she loved Freddie, and she felt his pain intensely, so it was with real sympathy that she heard him out.

"She wouldn't even listen to me, Cassie! When I"—he paused and gulped for air—"when I told her how much I admired her, she laughed me off. But when she saw that I was serious and wouldn't be fobbed off, she told me straight out that she was looking forward to a brilliant Season and was not going to be deprived of it by someone she had known this age. And then''—his fists clenched at his sides as he continued—''and then she said that we should never suit anyway because she had to have gaiety and parties and that everyone knew I was''—he drew a deep breath—''a prosy old bore.''

And that, thought Cassie, is the only intelligent observation Arabella Taylor has ever made. Empty frivolity is all that she understands and someone of Ned's intellectual capacities would be bored silly within a fortnight. However, she concealed her true feelings about her childhood playmate, generously defending her instead. ''She's young, Ned, and very pretty. Of course she wants to go to parties and be the reigning beauty. For her, the idea of settling down and giving all that up would make her reject even the most dazzling of Corinthians.''

He brightened somewhat, ''Do you really think so?''

''I am certain that it is more the loss of a brilliant Season than a distaste for your company that turned her against the notion,'' she reassured him.

''But she called me a prosy old bore. Am I a prosy old bore, Cassie?'' he asked anxiously.

Cassie smiled and stretched out her hand. ''No. You are our own dear friend who enlivens the dullest conversation at assemblies and parties and keeps them from being a complete waste of time.''

He stared fixedly out the window until what seemed hours later, when in a hard voice devoid of all emotion, he announced, ''No. She's right. I am a prosy old bore, but I shall change that. If Freddie can go to India, so can I! And when I return, I shall immerse myself in so many *ton* parties that no one will recognize me.''

Cassie could happily have killed Arabella for causing his brave smile to go awry. She was overwhelmed by a great rage at Arabella in particular and the type of women in general who seemed to have nothing better to do than dress for one social occasion after another so they could chatter empty-headed nothings and enslave as many luckless swains as possible. It was true that most of these victims were equally busy with their tailors and valets preparing to do exactly the same thing in return, so why couldn't it have been one of these fops dying for love of the toast of their Hampshire society that Arabella had rejected instead of poor Ned, who had so much greater a heart to lose than the squire's son and his would-be Corinthian cronies? Cassie knew there was very little comfort she could offer. In time he would bless Arabella for having been so blind to his good qualities, but for the moment it was best to put her out of his life and his mind.

"It would relieve me no end to have you with Freddie in India. He's a dear and he means well, but sometimes his enthusiasm gets the best of him and he doesn't think," Cassie remarked. This was a patently obvious observation, as the impetus for Freddie's departure had been an ill-judged prank at university. The master of Balliol had not found it amusing to return to a sow and six piglets rooting around his rooms and lapping up his best sherry, spilled from what had been a precariously placed decanter. So Freddie had been sent down. He wasn't repining, school never having been his strong point. When his attention was engaged, he was as good a student as the next man, but Oxford had offered too many distractions for a young man possessed of an abundance of high spirits and conviviality.

Rustication soon palled on someone as active as Freddie, and he began to toy with the idea of purchasing a cornetcy, having made up his mind he wasn't cut out to be a student, nor was he interested in taking up politics or any of the other occupations people took up. Before he could take more drastic measures to occupy himself, his brother-in-law hit upon a plan that offered an exciting alternative. Many years ago Lord Julian Mainwaring had inherited the fortune and far-flung concerns of a childless uncle who had been one of the Empire's first nabobs. For a long time Lord Mainwaring had looked after these interests himself, but his brother's untimely death, which had brought the burden of running several estates and the guardianship of his children, coupled with his subsequent marriage to the twins' sister, Lady Frances Cresswell, and his involvement in politics had left him with little time to do more than glance at the reports submitted by the agents appointed to administer these establishments for him. Julian Mainwaring liked Freddie and knew him for a decent and intelligent, if rash, young man. He seemed the perfect representative to send to remind the agents of Lord Mainwaring's continuing interest in their effectiveness in discharging their duties. Such a task would provide an outlet for the restlessness natural to an active young man, who had, since the beginning of their acquaintance, evinced a singular knack for tumbling from one scrape to another. As he had also demonstrated an equally strong propensity to overcome every mishap and emerge unscathed, Julian felt confident that Freddie would acquit himself admirably when challenged by truly adventurous situations.

So it had been decided that Freddie was to spend a year in India, or however long it took to visit and oversee Lord Mainwaring's operations. He had been preparing for an imminent departure to that mecca of every young man bent on winning his fortune when Ned had suffered his unhappy setback.

Ned, unlike Freddie, was a student—a scholar in fact—if enthusiastic masters were to be believed. Raised in a quiet household which, after his parents' death and before Lord Julian had taken over his guardianship, had been dominated by women, he had withdrawn to his grandfather's abundant library for companionship. He loved his effervescent sister Kitty dearly, but she had always turned to Lady Frances Cresswell for friendship, and the twins had been a little wary of one so quiet, well mannered, and clean as Ned. It wasn't until he'd accompanied Kitty to London for her come-out that he had really become acquainted with Cassandra and Frederick Cresswell, though there was little more than two miles between the gatekeeper's lodge of Camberly and the drive to Cresswell.

In London, deprived of their normal pursuits, the neighbors had been thrown together more often while Lady Frances accompanied Kitty and lent her moral support at social functions. The exuberant twins had taken to riding in the park as one of the few permissible ways of working off excess energy. It was during one of these rides that Ned had caught their interest. Oddly enough for one who was naturally quiet and reserved, he was a bruising rider and disported himself with ease on a mount that the twins admitted would have been too challenging for them.

When they had returned to the country, they had remained riding companions and friendship had blossomed. Freddie discovered Ned to be a far more expert judge of horseflesh than his louder, more boisterous acquaintances. Ned also possessed a seemingly inexhaustible knowledge of history, which was, at least the military and exploratory part, one of Freddie's true interests. Cassie liked him better than anyone else Freddie spent time with because he accepted it as natural that she should do everything her brother did—sometimes, as in the case of climbing trees, with much greater skill and daring. To her, their five-year difference in age made him practically an adult and she was flattered that he shared his thoughts with her as though she had been grown up. On his part, Ned had found Cassie to have a mind that exhibited all the curiosity and adventurousness of her tomboyish spirit.

The twins' parents, Lord and Lady Cresswell had been scholars of some note. They had traveled extensively with their family in Greece, haunting the important spots of the world until "that barbarian Bonaparte," as Lord Cresswell was wont to call him, had driven them home. In fact, they, along with their good friend the Comte de Vaudron, had been of inestimable service to Lord Elgin in ensuring that his priceless marbles were brought to England. Of all the children, Cassie had inherited her parents' scholarly turn of mind. Frances had put her excellent if unusual education to good use as an authoress of children's histories and continued to exercise an excellent mind as a brilliant political hostess and helpmeet to her husband, whose healthy respect for her intelligence made him bring his ideas to her for criticism and advice before he advanced them to the world at large. But it was Cassie who was the true intellectual, and her appetite for knowledge was as insatiable as Ned's. She was as well versed in the classics as he, and her more daring nature led her to question established opinion more readily. She did not hesitate to argue with him and challenge his opinions. To Ned, who rarely found anyone to share his interests, much less discuss them, this was as novel as it was refreshing, and they became fast, though occasionally argumentative, friends.

As time went by, some of the Cresswell exuberance rubbed off on Ned and he became more relaxed and ready to enter into new things. He, in turn, with his greater foresight and more levelheaded approach to life, kept the twins from falling into scrapes so disastrous that adult assistance was required to extricate them. They greatly appreciated this freedom from embarrassment and rewarded their new companion with their respect and occasional requests for advice.

But those busy happy days, for Cassie at any rate, had vanished with the boys. She and Lord Mainwaring had ridden with them up to London, where they had made some final purchases at S. Unwin's General Equipment Warehouse in Lombard Street before stowing their belongings on the ship that was to take them to Bombay. The captain was an acquaintance of Lord Mainwaring's, and Cassie had been glad to think that Freddie and Ned would have at least one friend on the long voyage. She had watched and waved as they sailed with the tide and then returned home, feeling lonelier than she ever had in her entire life. Freddie had always been more than a mere brother. He had been her constant companion, while Ned was the one person in the whole word who truly understood and appreciated her. It was true that Lady Frances encouraged Cassie's studies and her brother-in-law discussed them with her. Both of them included her as an equal in their conversations, but no one took the place of Ned, who teased her and delighted in challenging her ideas and stimulating her mind.

At least she had the mail, but it was slow and unpredictable. It could take ages for her replies to her letters to arrive—letters she had filled with thoughts on her reading, reflections on life in general, and questions about his experiences—but she reveled in his responses when they did come. His style, so very like him, made Ned seem present at the moment she was reading his letter. His reflections and comments, fashioned as they were to address her particular interests and tastes, made what could have been a mere traveler's description spring to life before her eyes. Thus, even though she sorely missed his companionship, she continued to feel the strength of his friendship. He had never mentioned Arabella again, but Cassie knew his sensitive retiring nature too well to think that she had been forgotten. For her part, Cassie had found it extraordinarily difficult even to exchange the politest of commonplaces with Arabella and was quite relieved when the girl had quit the neighborhood for what had been a predictably brilliant Season. Of course she had been hailed as an incomparable. How could anyone so devoted to herself and her toilette have become anything less than a diamond, Cassie had reflected cynically.

A belle who had enjoyed such success could not be expected to leave the scene of such triumph to bury herself in Hampshire, and many of those attending assemblies around Cresswell and Camberly that summer bemoaned the loss of their brightest star. Cassie, however, found such events to be much more enjoyable without Arabella's disturbing presence—a presense that seemed to have fostered nothing but dissension and jealousy as much among her envious female competitors as among vain young men.

Having seen what misery beauty, unaccompanied by heart or wit and bent solely on pursuit of its own pleasure, could cause, Cassie was not inclined to want a come-out of her own, but here she was having some difficulty. Her ordinarily levelheaded and sympathetic sister, who had suffered one miserable Season herself, was adamant that Cassie at least experience the world of the *ton* before condemning it out of hand.

"But Fanny," Cassie had wailed, "how can you, of all

people, insist that I waste my time in society when you were
so unhappy there yourself? You thought most of those routs
and balls excessively silly. And I daresay that I am less inclined
to society than you.''

"Yes, love. You are entirely in the right of it. I was
desperately unhappy, but that was my first Season when I was
under the aegis of Lady Bingley, who was as feather-headed
a female as you could hope to meet. Directly on bringing me
to a gathering she would retire to the card room, leaving me
to gaze around the room and wish intensely that I could become
part of the nearest pillar or bank of flowers. But when I helped
Lady Streatham chaperon Kitty, it was altogether different.
Lady Streatham's acquaintances were not the empty-headed
dowagers that comprised Lady Bingley's coterie; she made
every effort to put me as well as Kitty forward and make us
feel comfortable. And then the Comte de Vaudron made me
see that dressing beautifully and fashionably could be as much
an exercise of one's aesthetic sense and taste as any other sort
of creative expression and it need not be merely empty
competition to see whose dressmaker can make one resemble
the most stunning fashion plate in *La Belle Assemblée*. Besides,
Julian and his friends are in the *ton* and they certainly discuss
more serious subjects than the cut of their coats or their own
favored ways of tying a cravat.''

Cassie recognized the truth of this, but while she admitted
that Lady Frances Mainwaring and Lady Elizabeth Streatham
had found men who could carry more than one thought in their
heads at a time, she remained skeptical about the possibility
that there were enough such people to make a trip to London
worthwhile, especially since two of the few intelligent men were
at present on the high seas heading home.

CHAPTER 2

It was the Comte de Vaudron who saved the Season for Cassie as he had once saved it for her elder sister, though not in quite the same way. Cassie was again sitting in the library when the post arrived, but this time it was Frances who came rushing in waving a letter, which unlike the others, was on heavy cream paper and addressed in an elegant flowing script. "It's from the Comte de Vaudron," Frances announced, her eyes sparkling. "And he proposes a scheme that you are certain to like above all things. You know he is cataloging the marbles he and Papa helped Lord Elgin bring back from Greece. Having worked this age on them, he is beginning to realize what an enormous task it is and is feeling a bit overawed at the extent left unfinished. He is hoping that you will be able to help him, or at least act as his amanuensis when we arrive in Town. I rather think this should prove to be just the thing, don't you? Good heavens, the time! I promised Lady Taylor I would meet her at the church to arrange the flowers on the altar. I must dash." And Frances hurried off, leaving her sister to her thoughts. The idea of quitting the freshness, the quiet, and the freedom of the countryside for the frenzied, noisy pace and structured existence of London was detestable to someone whose neighbors had long ago ceased to comment on her long solitary walks with Wellington or her mad dashes across the fields on a horse that everyone from Squire Tilden to Sir Lucius Taylor had declared to be a "mount far too restive and totally unsuitable for a lady." Still, the idea of immersing herself in the beautiful artifacts brought back from Athens did have a certain appeal, and besides, she dearly loved the comte.

Never having had the good fortune of his friend Lord Cresswell, who had found a wife to share his enthusiasm, and being totally uninterested in living the stultified, formal life at Versailles required of France's aristocrats, the Comte de Vaudron had led a solitary existence until he had met the Cresswells. Lord and Lady Cresswell had shared their interests as well as their lively young family with him and he had grown inordinately fond of them all during their Grecian sojourn. When the revolution had made it impossible for him to return to his own country, and Napoleon seemed to be consuming all of Europe at an alarming rate, he had come to London and, after their parents' deaths, had once again established himself as a benevolent uncle to Frances, Cassandra, and Freddie. He had helped Frances enjoy herself during her second Season in London and had assisted her in the creation of her own special style, which had made her blossom into a witty and beautiful woman. While he had always been a favorite of the twins, ready at a moment's notice to get up an interesting excursion for their special amusement, he had not figured as prominately in their lives as he had in their sister's. Now it seemed he was turning his attentions toward Cassie's welfare and she looked forward to having him as a support in the ordeal to come—the intense social round demanded by the *ton* of one of its would-be members.

Her reverie was interrupted by a squelching sound and a brief cough. As she looked around, her gaze encountered three dripping wet and barely recognizable figures in the doorway. Wellington certainly more closely resembled a black Scottish than a white West Highland terrier while the distinctive black stripes of his erstwhile friend and companion, Nelson the Cat, seemed to have merged and spread to cover his white chest and paws. Theodore was distinguished from the other two by being covered in mud only to his waist and he was clutching another lump of mud to his chest, this lump's only distinguished feature being its quack. "We fell in the pond," he explained unnecessarily.

"Arf, arf," Wellington agreed. He was thoroughly enjoying himself. Theodore had proven himself to be a regular Trojan, and sooner than the little dog had dared hope. Today's adventure had been almost as good as any that Freddie and Cassie had tumbled into.

"So I see." As she spoke, Cassie had visions of a series of torn smocks and muddied breeches she and Freddie had presented to Frances in just such a manner.

"Cook said she won't have me in her kitchen, tho I came to the you. She said I'm to go thraight to the pump and take that 'dratted dog and cat' with me. I told her they weren't 'dratted' and she got ever tho red in the fathe and took a broom and here we are."

"Yes. Here you are," Cassie agreed, just beginning to understand the fortitude her sister had exhibited all these years in the face of Freddie's and her exploits. No disaster had been too dirty or bloody to upset her. Feeling the weight of her elder sister's example, she inquired as calmly and with as much interest as she could infuse into her voice, which now threatened to break into laughter, into the reasons for their condition. The trio, which truly did look disreputable, had now begun to appear somewhat shamefaced.

"Well, it was Ethelred's fault," Theodore explained, twisting one foot nervously on the pattern in the carpet.

"Ethelred?" Cassie inquired blankly.

The grubby quacking lump was extended for her inspection, revealing a bill and two small webbed feet. "Yeth. I named him Ethelred because he was unready jutht like the King Ethelred the Unready that Mama told me about."

This explanation clearly wasn't enough for his aunt, who continued to look puzzled. "Well, you thee, Wellington, Nelthon, and I were playing with my boat on the pond and we *truly* were being careful not to get wet, when we heard a crack and some peeping and then thith egg fell into the pond right near uth. Only it wathn't a whole egg becauth Ethelred'th head was thicking out. Then Wellington and

Nelthon ruthed in and tried to catch it but the waves they made jutht puthed in farther from thore, tho I had to wade in. We got him on thore and he got out of hith egg and made thraight for Wellington. There didn't seem to be any duckth around, so I brought him here. Can we keep him, please Aunt Catthie? I think he likes uth.'' The mingled chorus of quacks, meows and arfs that followed this statement seemed to bear out this assumption.

Cassie smiled. ''I expect you'd have a hard time getting rid of Ethelred now, but come along and let's wash all of you and dry you out.'' She led the trio out of the pump in the stable yard, where, under the watchful eye of John Coachman, they splashed happily until they more nearly resembled their former selves.

''Just like old times, you might say, Miss Cassie,'' John's weather-beaten face expanded in a warm grin. Like Wellington, he had missed the activity since Freddie had been gone, but being slightly more perceptive than the little terrier, he had worried a great deal that the sparkle had gone out of Miss Cassie when the boys had left. John loved Frances and he was proud of what a fine young man Freddie had become, but Cassie was his true favorite. Ever since she had taken her first spill from a pony at two years old and refused to cry, Cassie had won the critical coachman's heart, though he would have died rather than let on about his devotion. Young Master Theodore is proving to be just the ticket for diverting all of them, he thought, looking at Cassie's animated face and at the animals enthusiastically playing under the pump. Spending his life around them, John had been well aware of Wellington and Nelson's despondency since Freddie's departure. ''A good rubdown and you'll be right as rain,'' he announced, handing one towel to Cassie for Theodore and vigorously patting the rest with another. ''But you must ask Nurse to get you some dry clothes, Master Theodore,'' he directed as he gave a final wipe behind Wellington's ears.

''But what thall we do with Ethelred?'' Theodore wondered aloud. Ethelred, who had enjoyed the episode at the pump more than anyone, was quacking merrily and swimming in the barrel under the spigot, but as the others showed signs of leaving, he peeped anxiously and hopped out.

"He shall have a bed right next to Wellington's and Nelson's by the stove in the kitchen," Cassie replied. Seeing the mistrustful look on Theodore's face, she added, "Don't worry, Teddy, Cook does get exasperated when they get underfoot, but she loves them dearly and would miss their companionship sorely. Besides, what would she do with her scraps if she didn't have those two to take care of them for her? She knows that Nelson is the best mouser in Hampshire and Wellington won her heart when he caught the rat gnawing its way into her flour bin."

"All right," Theodore sighed, still somewhat anxious about his new pet's acceptance in the bailwick of such a domestic despot as Cook. "But may I help John make a bed for Ethelred?" he asked.

"Certainly, dear, but you must put on some other clothes first and I shall make sure these three finish drying out." Cassie smiled encouragingly at him as she shepherded the animals toward the kitchen. All were agreeably tired and needed no coaxing to lie quietly in a heap of fur and feathers under the stove while Cassie tried to convince Cook that really one more animal would not disrupt her domain so very much. Cook, who truly did have a soft spot for "her two rascals," demurred briefly before letting herself be won over.

"It's Miss Cassie and Master Freddie all over again," she remarked to no one in particular, shaking her head as she went back to rolling out pastry for a game pie. "Still and all, it's nice to have some activity around here once more," she addressed the kitchen clock, which remained obstinately mute.

Activity of a less drastic and certainly more social nature was the topic of discussion among the three ladies decorating the church for Sunday. Frances, Sir Lucius Taylor's wife, and his youngest daughter, the celebrated and, if Cassie's opinions were to be noted, infamous Arabella, were busily adding greens to complete the handsome arrangements in large vases of the church's rather severe altar.

"Will Cassie be joining you in London this Season?" Lady Taylor inquired, stepping back to admire the effect of a carefully placed sprig of lavender.

"Yes. We shall all be going up this time, though I fear we shall miss Freddie's company dreadfully. Brothers do come so in handy at a time like this—if not for their value as a partner of last resort, then for the friends they bring with them. Not that Cassie is in the least shy, but one always feels safer in numbers at first."

Arabella, always more than willing to discuss the resounding success of her first Season, broke in, "If I said to Mama once, I must have said it a thousand times last year before we left Hampshire, 'If only, dear Mama, you had been fit to provide me with older brothers instead of sisters, I should feel a good deal easier in my mind about my first ball.' I am sure I wished times out of mind that Edwina were an Edward before my first evening at Almack's. She is naturally very dear to me, but as a partner or friend of possible partners she was quite useless." Thus Arabella ruthlessly dismissed one of the *ton*'s most dashing matrons with a shrug of her pretty shoulders. It was a gesture that had once caused one lovelorn swain to label her "Cruel Disdain" and she seized every opportunity to practice it. "At any rate, I learned how to go on in no time at all and I had the most famous time. Didn't I, Mama?"

This was that worthy lady's cue to expound on the brilliance of her daughter's Season: how Lord such-a-one had hailed her as a diamond of the first water, how the Marquess so-and-so had disagreed, calling her instead an incomparable; how young Viscount this-and-that had been instantly struck by her beauty and positively haunted their house in Berkeley Square. All through the recital Arabella looked sweetly conscious until Frances was ready to wring the soft white neck which made such a perfect foil for the dusky curls. She was able to forbear, however, and with a great effort of will, she refrained from inquiring about any suitors, the absence of which had been quite noticeable during Arabella's return to Hampshire.

Such an unfair question would have elicited the gayest of inconsequential laughter and the amused reply that "of course Papa and Mama say I'm far too young to be settling down no matter how hard any gentleman may press his suit." The truth of the matter was that Arabella was aiming higher than any of the eligible but none-too-brilliant matches that had presented themselves. It had been a disappointment not to have netted a truly grand fish, but after all, it had only been her first Season, and these things take time. Arabella was determined to take no less than a marquess. After all, one had to have one's standards. But in spite of enjoying all the advantages of youth, beauty, and wealth, Arabella was laboring under the distinct disadvantage of being the daughter of a minor baronet and a woman who, though prettily enough behaved, had brought to her marriage a great deal of money earned in trade. It would have taken far more address and sophistication than Arabella possessed to erase these two flaws from the mind of a truly brilliant catch.

If Cassie, ensconced once again in her favorite chair in the library, could have been privy to all this, she would have felt a great deal happier about the projected Season, but knowing the type of person Arabella was, and knowing that she had been hailed as a great success in the metropolis, filled her with foreboding. For it seemed to her that a society which admired someone such as Arabella Taylor would never accept someone like Lady Cassandra Cresswell. Nor would she ever feel anything but uncomfortable or bored among such people. If only she had one friend and confidante, it wouldn't be so bad. Of course she did have Fanny and Lord Mainwaring, Ned's sister Lady Kitty Willoughby, and Lord Mainwaring's cousin, Lady Streatham, who had been so supportive of Fanny when she was in London for Kitty's come-out, but having them wasn't the same as having someone of one's own age and experience. It made her miss Ned and Freddie even more dreadfully. But she supposed that Frances was in the right of it. She couldn't molder forever in Hampshire with her books, going out in society less and less until she became nothing but an ape-leader.

Dearly as she loved her aunt Harriet, she could see that the lady's particular quirks and rather prickly personality had developed over the course of the years during her brother's absence in Greece, when she had been alone at Cresswell devoting herself to her orchids. It was not that she had been lonely, because her horticultural interests were her consuming passion. But this passion had led her to ignore all else, and so when she was forced into contact with society at large, she was most uncomfortable. True, she had little use for anyone, and even less use for fools, whom she considered to be the bulk of humanity, but Cassie had often thought it too bad that she didn't seem truly to love anybody. Of course, she cared a great deal about what happened to Frances and the twins, but she did not miss them when they were gone, and was only tangentially involved with them as their paths crossed at meals or during the course of the day. Though she knew Aunt Harriet was perfectly happy with her existence, and though it was a relief to know at least one woman whose entire life did not revolve around men, Cassie sometimes felt sad for her.

Not that her sister Frances's life revolved around men. She continued to write and publish her own books and maintained her own separate existence as an author, but Cassie could see that there were times when she gave up her own work to join Lord Mainwaring or Theodore in something that interested them. If only there were some middle ground between being an eccentric recluse or plunging headlong into society, but there did not seem to be. Men could enter politics or the army and thus pursue an interest among companions of similar dispositions, but there was nothing for someone like Cassie, who remained at a loss about how she was to go on in life. She supposed that Frances was correct, and that having lived buried at Cresswell with her books, she ought to try London to see what the alternatives were.

When Lady Frances returned for tea, Cassie was able to

tell her that having thought it over, she could now be easy in her mind about going to London.

"I'm glad, dear." Frances smiled at her younger sister's wrinkled brow and worried eyes. "I think you'll find enough there to interest you that you won't be forced to devote your entire existence to dressing and promenading at this ball or that rout. After all, Julian and I shall be there, and we have no more patience with worthless fribbles than you do. And not everyone is like Arabella. She came along with her mama this afternoon. What a frivolous thing she is, to be sure! I wonder at her success. But then, the only lips I have heard speak of her triumphs have been hers. At any rate, I shall write the comte directly and then see to it that the household has plenty of time to prepare before we depart. At least I do not have to worry about cajoling Aunt Harriet into coming or wonder how we shall transport her darlings to London as I did when we went up to London for Kitty's come-out. By the by, where are Wellington and Nelson? They never miss an opportunity to chase each other at teatime. Nurse said that Teddy had his tea early. When three such rambunctious characters are so quiet, I begin to have my suspicions."

Cassie regaled her with the afternoon's adventure, much to her sister's amusement.

"I can see that with Nelson and Wellington to egg him on, Tedfdy is bound to fall into as many scrapes as you and Freddie put together. Well, I must go meet this Ethelred, who has already managed to cause such a commotion in a household much accustomed to dealing with upheaval."

CHAPTER 3

Lady Frances' organization being what it was, the entire household was soon ensconced in Mainwaring House in Grosvenor Square. When Frances and Lord Mainwaring had first been married they had lived in the Cresswells' house on Brook Street, leaving his mother, the Dowager Marchioness of Camberly, to reign in state in Grosvenor Square. Lord Mainwaring had been more than happy to vacate what he more often than not termed "that gloomy pile" so his mother could entertain the other town tabbies to tea in style. It was Mainwaring's expressed opinion that more marriages had been made and more reputations launched or ruined in that stately drawing room than in any other in all of England. At this mother's death and upon his assumption of political duties, the marquess had reluctantly moved back—"But only on the condition that you make it fit for human habitation, my love," he had admonished Frances.

Frances, following the taste for simplicity, lightness, and elegance derived from her childhood spent among the glories of classical antiquity, had transformed the somber mansion into a dwelling that combined elegance with graciousness, and created an atmosphere which was both welcoming and restful to all and sundry—politicians, Corinthians, society matrons, and the select few among the Upper Ten Thousand whom the Mainwarings counted among their friends.

It was upon the threshold of this august residence one day in late March that the entourage from Cresswell descended to be welcomed by Higgins the butler and the staff, whom

26

he had assembled in the front hall. "Hurrah! Hurrah! We're here at last," shouted Teddy, who despite having been allowed to ride the entire distance on the box with John Coachman, still possessed an excess of high spirits.

"Arf! Arf!" echoed Wellington, who had also ridden on the box and, like his newly adopted playmate, was in fine fettle. Nelson, having endured the journey nursing a queasy stomach nestled against the squabs of the Mainwarings' beautifully sprung traveling carriage, descended in a more leisurely manner, tail aloft, delicately sniffing and evaluating the town scents which assailed him. At this point, Ethelred, who had slept quietly in a basket on Cassie's lap, woke up and demanded to be set free. With a loud quack and several flaps of yet unformed wings, he hopped down, beady eyes eager to take in all the new sights. Catching sight of their protégé, Wellington and Nelson instantly forgot their delight at being set free in the metropolis and, adopting the most jaded of airs, sauntered in a blasé fashion toward the stables with Ethelred and Teddy in hot pursuit.

"I daresay they shall have the place at sixes and sevens in no short while," Frances observed as she descended, a bandbox in one hand, to greet the staff. Cassie, clutching Ethelred's now deserted basket, followed suit, and with Higgins's assistance the travelers were soon ensconced comfortably in the drawing room in front of a well-laden tea tray and a welcoming fire.

In no short order, Wellington, Nelson, Teddy, and Ethelred appeared. Having explored the nether regions and discovered there that tea had already been sent upstairs, they had lost no time in hastening to the scene. Wellington and Nelson took up their accustomed places on either side of the fire while Ethelred padded around snapping at a curtain tassel here, pecking at a design on the rug there, until he was entirely satisfied with his new surroundings. He then joined his friends by the fireplace, where all three, along with Theodore, concentrated on the tea table.

As Theodore, consuming a hot buttered crumpet, expounded on the wonders of the stables, Frances absently nibbled a scone and perused a stack of gilt-edged invitations. Such abstraction made an ideal situation for the crumb-snatching brigade which watched every gesture of Teddy's that scattered bits of crumpet or every piece of scone that fell unnoticed from Frances's hand as she sorted through the mail. In fact, Cassie was the only one doing justice to the beautiful array that Higgins had brought in.

"Itth a bang up table, Cathie, though it doethn't hold a candle to the one at Crethwell," enthused Teddy, sending an irresistible shower of crumbs in Ethelred's direction. The little duck pecked happily until the other two, unable to restrain themselves, pounced at the same time on a large piece that had dropped beyond his reach under the cake stand.

"Cassie, my love, here is a card for Lady Delamere's rout tomorrow evening. That should do quite well for your first introduction to the *ton*," Frances remarked, not bothering to look up from her correspondence as she automatically caught the cake stand, which teetered precariously after Wellington's dive for the crumb. "Her affairs are always quite brilliant, though it's sure to be a sad crush so early in the Season. There is no time to have Madame Regnery make up anything new for you, but your white gauze with the blue satin pipings that we had made for the Alton assembly should do very well. It was fortunate that the snow made it impossible to attend."

"Teddy, if you eat another crumpet, you'll become ill," Cassie admonished before turning an anxious face toward Frances. "That dress may have done very well in Hampshire, but are you quite certain it will do for London?"

"Of course, love. It's very simple, but the lines are quite elegant and you're so lovely that you don't need rosettes and ruchings to disguise your flaws." Frances smiled fondly at her younger sister.

"Oh, give over, Fanny, do. You know that brunettes are all the rage and blondes sadly out of fashion now. At any rate, blondes are supposed to have complexions of peaches and cream." Cassie made a face in the gilt-framed mirror over the fireplace. "And despite the quantities of almond paste that Rose insists I use on them, my freckles will persist in appearing.'' Here Cassie wrinkled a beautifully straight nose, whose only flaw was its light sprinkling of freckles. Though it was not a face that exhibited the rosebud lips, velvet brown eyes, and delicately rounded chin that were all the rage, it was one that reflected far more character than those commonly encountered. The eyes were a brilliant dark sapphire, revealing a sparkle of humor in their depths which had disconcerted more than one self-satisfied young buck. Her hair was gold rather than blond and showed a definite tendency to break out into curls unless taken severely to task. The chin was a trifle determined for the taste of most amorous swains, but its challenge was softened by a generous mouth that hinted at a passionate nature below the surface. It was a vivacious face, which created a first impression of vitality and interest, and it caught the attention of those sensitive or clever enough to recognize the intelligence and strength of character that lay behind it. But even those who failed to appreciate the promise of a keen mind and a lively sense of humor rated Lady Cassandra Cresswell a very taking thing.

"Papa!" Teddy leaped up, threatening the equilibrium of the cake stand for the second time.

"Hello, Teddy, my boy. Did you have a good journey?" Lord Julian Mainwaring, Marquess of Camberly's somewhat forbidding countenance broke into a smile as he surveyed the little group around the fire. Handing his many-caped greatcoat to the hovering Higgins, he strode over to the fire, stepping gingerly around the menagerie.

"Oh yes, Papa! It was splendid and John Coachman let me sit on the box with him the entire way," Teddy assured him enthusiastically.

"Did he now? That was a rare treat. How were the new bays handling?" No one, seeing the fondness in Mainwaring's eyes as he looked at his son, could have guessed that not too many years ago he had considered children to be the worst possible sort of encumbrance. However, marriage to Frances and his necessary involvement with Ned and Freddie had taught him that they were not all little monsters who were better off seen and not heard. To the contrary, he had discovered during various outings to the Tower, Astley's Amphitheatre, and balloon ascensions that childish curiosity and enthusiasm could be quite enjoyable—enchanting even. So, much to his friends' astonishment, he had become a devoted, though by no means doting, parent, participating personally in much of his son's education and activities.

His son's eyes shone as he reassured his father, "They're a bang-up pair and John says they're very sweet goers."

"I am delighted to hear that they're all I thought they would be. Hello, my love," Julian bent to plant a kiss on Frances's forehead as she handed him a cup of tea. "Everything in good order when you arrived?"

"Yes. We're settled in nicely, thank you, and John has been able to find an eager young lad to help out in the stables. He's a cousin of Lady Streatham's groom Thompson and seems quite anxious to learn. How was your meeting with Canning?"

"Excellent. I admired Castlereagh's grasp of affairs on the Continent, but it's time we took to problems at home, and George Canning is the man for that. He has a far greater sense of what must be done in the way of financial reforms. But he needs support. He lacks the charm of Castlereagh and there are many who greatly distrust him."

"I am persuaded, Julian, that you, with acquaintances among both factions, can bring about some understanding." Frances raised a quizzical eyebrow and handed him the last remaining crumpet.

"I shall certainly do my utmost, love. But on to more immediate and pressing matters. I see a stack of invitations in your lap and I have the foreboding feeling that I am to be called upon to help ensure that Cassie is successfully launched toward the dubious pleasure of taking the *ton* by storm." He grimaced in the mirror at his sister-in-law. Having seen Lady Frances blossom during a Season from one who disdained and avoided the fashionable world to one who could charm it at will, he felt confident that Cassie would do the same, but he understood and sympathized with her reluctance.

"How fortunate you should mention it, my dear. Lady Delamere holds a rout tomorrow evening. It's sure to prove a dreadful squeeze, but we should attend it," his wife replied, eyeing him hopefully.

"Ecod, catched already. Well, you may count on me to escort you both and to defend you from dandies, fribbles, court cards, overeager young men, and all the other bores that plague these affairs. Furthermore, I shall order Bertie to join us and lend us éclat."

"That would be famous," Cassie thanked him, visibly relieved at the prospect of this support. Bertie Montgomery, longtime family friend of the Cresswells, had been at school with Lord Mainwaring. A perpetual bachelor, possessed of the most discriminating taste and a kind heart, he was an escort to ease the mind of the most nervous of damsels encountering the *ton* for the first time. An exquisite dancer, up on all the latest on-dits, he could be counted on to smooth the most difficult of social encounters and win the hearts of the *ton*'s most demanding dowagers.

"That's settled then," Frances remarked, propping the invitation up on the mantel. "We shall make our first appearance this Season tomorrow night. I must send a note to Elizabeth to ensure her presence and Nigel's." Frances, knowing the perceptive and kindhearted nature of Julian's favorite cousin, Lady Streatham, felt sure that the matron, well aware of the pitfalls awaiting a young woman entering society, would make certain that her son attended and brought along some of his brother officers from the Guards.

CHAPTER 4

So it was that Cassie, mounting the curving staircase at Lady Delamere's imposing residence in Portman Square, was well protected in her first engagement with polite society. His sister and brother-in-law preceded her up the stairway and Bertie Montgomery, resplendent in an exquisitely cut swallowtail coat and satin knee breeches, lent a supporting arm. Surrounded as she was by family and friends, Cassie was not particularly nervous, but as she surveyed the glittering throng she could not identify one among the turbaned dowagers, the overanxious young women, the self-important tulips of the ton whom she would not find a dead bore within no time at all. Sighing inwardly, she made her curtsy to her host and hostess and allowed Bertie to lead her into the set that was forming for the quadrille.

"Don't look so Friday-faced, Cassie. Know you don't like this above half, but it ain't all that bad, you know," admonished Bertie, who, correctly interpreting her thoughts, strove to reassure her. "Most of 'em haven't a thought in their cock lofts beyond cutting a dash or getting leg-shackled, but there's nothing to say you have to join their ranks, and there's nothing to say you can't be amused by it all instead of upset."

A faint smile lit Cassie's features. "You're in the right of it, Bertie," she agreed. "What a gudgeon I am. After all, Frances contrives to keep herself tolerably amused. It's just . . ." Her voice trailed off as she caught sight of Arabella Taylor, who, surrounded by a group of young bucks, was laughing delightedly and flirting behind her fan.

Bertie's eyes followed hers. "That girl may think she's an out-and-outer, but mark my words, none of 'em will come up to scratch," he observed, nodding sagely. "Kirkby will never get caught in the parson's mousetrap. Pierrepont's whole future depends upon his great aunt's fortune and she would never countenance his marrying someone who smelled of the shop, no matter how remote the connection. As for Fortescue, he hasn't a feather to fly with and it would take a larger fortune than Arabella's to keep the duns off his back. Besides which it's one thing to trifle with a pretty ninny-hammer and quite another to marry her. A man wants a woman of sense for his wife." He held up a hand at Cassie's mutinous expression. "Not that serving as a marriage market is all that society has to offer, but that is what Arabella is hoping for, which is why she and others like her can cause a stir—they think of nothing else and devote their energies solely to that." Here the set broke up and he returned her to Lady Frances, who was politely listening to the complaints of a hatchet-faced woman in a towering purple turban.

"Disgraceful!" Lady Buffington exclaimed, her dewlaps fairly jiggling in indignation. "What the young bloods won't do these days! Why we ended up in the ditch all because the stage driver had allowed one of them to take the ribbons. He came through Witney at such a pace that no one could have stopped him. Of course he took the turn at far too great a speed, overset the coach, and forced us off the road. You would never catch my Charles in such tomfoolery." Here she thrust forward a limp youth, declaring that Frances and Cassie must meet her youngest, who had vowed that he refused to rest until he had met Cassie. The unfortunate Charles smiled in a sickly fashion and, after a none-too-subtle push from his mother, asked Cassie to stand up with him.

"Dear Charles, such a good boy." His mother smiled fondly. "Though I worry that some flighty young miss may set her sights on his fortune. He's so tenderhearted that he can never refuse a lady and then he'll marry her so as not to hurt her feelings." She sighed gustily.

Abject fear rather than excessive sensibility seemed to be

"Dear Charles's" overriding emotion as, holding Cassie loosely in a sweaty clasp, he shoved her around the floor. After enduring some minutes of this painful exercise, Cassie could bear the silence no longer. "Have you just arrived in Town, then?" she inquired encouragingly, not caring in the least whether he had or not, but anything was better than this mute shuffling.

"Er . . . um . . . yes," he managed to gasp as, his brow creased in concentration, Charles narrowly missed careening into the couple next to them.

Thinking that perhaps the banality of such small talk had put him off, Cassie tried again, this time with a more leading question, "Have you read *Waverley* yet? I own I am quite partial to Mr. Scott's work."

As this produced no more animated response than the first question, she gave up and allowed herself to be led woodenly around the floor. Keeping Bertie's strictures in mind, she allowed her gaze to travel around the ballroom. There certainly was enough to entertain even the most jaundiced of observers—a plain-whey-faced damsel obviously hoping to compensate for what she lacked in address by adorning herself with rivers of diamonds, an aged dandy who creaked by, his corsets laced to give him a wasp waist that nearly deprived him of breath, a bracket-faced dowager in an immense green turban who fixed each hopeful young woman with an eagle stare and then turned to comment in an audible whisper to her mousy companion.

After what seemed an interminable period she was restored to Frances and Julian. Just then Bertie appeared bearing glasses of ratafia for the ladies and followed by a tall man whose languid air proclaimed him an habitué of such brilliant gatherings.

"Dear Lady Mainwaring, delightful to see you," he drawled, bowing low over Frances's hand. "What ever can have persuaded two such sensible people as you and Julian to subject yourselves to such a crush?"

Frances raised one mobile eyebrow. "But our reasons are unassailable. We are accompanying my younger sister in her first introduction to the *ton*. Allow me to present Lady Cassandra Cresswell. Much more to the purpose is what are you doing here, Lord Dartington?"

"*Touché*, Frances. You always were far too awake on every suit for my poor wit." Lord Dartington looked to be amused. "Is Cassandra as fearful a bluestocking as you, I wonder," he quizzed her.

Frances laughed. "You are doing it much too brown, my lord, but you must find out for yourself."

Lord Dartington smiled at Cassie. "May I have the very great honor, Lady Cassandra," he begged, holding out a slim white hand with a flourish.

"Do go on, Cassie," Bertie urged. "Once you are seen with Dartington, your reputation is assured. Only think of it! Why, being seen to amuse him for the duration of a boulanger is worth your successful appearance at several soirees. You may now absent yourself from these affairs for the next fortnight and still be remembered as a *succès fou.*"

The sardonic gleam in Lord Dartington's eye gave Cassie a moment's unease, but being one who could never resist a challenge, she put up her chin and replied in a dampening tone, "You are too kind, sir."

"Like your sister, you are unimpressed with such frippery fellows as we who haunt London's ballrooms," he teased as he led her on to the floor.

"That depends entirely upon the way you occupy your time outside of such hallowed halls," Cassie retorted. There was something in his tolerant air that piqued her and she resolved to remain unimpressed by one who clearly considered himself to be a nonpareil.

"Well met, young Cassandra," he responded. The kindling look in her eyes warned him that he had gone too far and he relented, adding in a kinder tone, "I am not an ogre, you know. But if one doesn't appear to be completely bored with everyone one encounters, one runs the risk of being accosted by every encroaching mushroom and toadeater who ever aspired to establish himself in society. A cut direct here and there, a general air of cynical boredom, and

I am left entirely free to choose my friends as I will. If Frances had followed my lead, she would never have had to endure a half an hour's conversation with that odious Lady Buffington, nor would you have been forced to risk life and limb on the floor with the young whelp she so fondly refers to as 'my youngest.' '' Here he imitated the patronizing accents of the doting mother with such accuracy that Cassie could not help laughing. ''Much better,'' he approved. ''Think of the damage to my character if a mere green girl had remained poker-faced during the entire dance with me.''

Cassie relaxed to some degree and found herself relating the perils of sharing a closed carriage with a dog, a cat, and a duck, all of whom seemed to feel entitled to space equal to or larger than that allotted to the human occupants.

He laughed in turn. ''And now you have amused me, for which I thank you.'' Dartington guided her skillfully around. ''When the two tabbies pounce on me, I shall pronounce you 'refreshing' and your success is ensured. Never forget, my dear, that no matter how many male hearts are laid at your feet, you are not assured of a place in this world until you thaw that organ in one of the icy dowagers who rules it.'' With these sage words, he restored her to her companions, who joined by Kitty and her husband Lord Willoughby, made a gay little coterie. Cassie was delighted to see these reinforcements, but the sight of Kitty, recalling as it did the thought of the absent Ned and Freddie, brought a lump to her throat.

''La, Cassie, how prodigious elegant you look—the first stare of fashion and you've not yet been on the Town a week,'' Kitty greeted her enthusiastically.

Cassie would happily have sat out the next few dances to exchange news of friends and hear about Kitty's new baby, ''the sweetest thing you can imagine, Cassie,'' but they were interrupted by the arrival of a portly young man whose fussily tied cravat threatened to strangle him.

''Ah, Willoughby. I haven't seen you this age. Been rusticating, old man?'' the young man inquired, subjecting Cassie to a thorough scrutiny that began with the wreath of flowers in her hair and traveled insolently to the tips of her white satin slippers. Cassie flushed angrily and turned away as much as possible to concentrate more on the conversation with Kitty. "You simply must introduce me to your charming friend," he continued, fixing Lord Willoughby with a meaningful stare.

Looking acutely uncomfortable, Kitty's husband bowed to the inevitable and muttered, "An old school acqaintance, Basil Weatherby, Lady Cassandra Cresswell."

"Utterly charming. Lady Cassandra cannot have long been on the Town, I am sure as I should have instantly been aware of such beauty come amongst us. I really must have this dance," he drawled.

Though Lord Willoughby looked not to be best pleased and Cassie was less than enthusiastic, there was no help for it but to be led out to the floor. Cassie needn't have worried that she would not have a thing to say to such an insufferable young man. In his own estimation, Basil Weatherby needed no one else to carry on a brilliant conversation. He seemed to feel it incumbent upon him to point out the ridiculous quirks in the leaders of the *ton*, winking knowingly as he spoke of Lord Petersham's collection of snuffboxes and repeating Lord Alvanley's latest witticism as though it had been addressed solely to him. In short, he did his best to intimate that he rubbed shoulders with the very tulips of the *ton* and that no social gathering would be complete without "Wily Weatherby"—here he smiled in a knowing way and contrived to stroke Cassie's hand while gripping it tighter in his fleshy palm.

The dance seemed endless. No matter where Cassie looked, he managed to bring his face with its pulpy lips and protuberant eyes into view. After what seemed an eternity they headed toward Cassie's group, which had now been joined by Lord and Lady Streatham and their son Nigel. Divining Cassie's ill-concealed distaste for her partner, Lady Streatham, a perceptive and kindhearted soul, immediately rushed forward, exclaiming, "Cassie, my dear, how delightful to see you! You must come tell us about Freddie. Nigel is absolutely dying to hear his latest adventures."

Cassie smiled gratefully, took a gulp of air, and began to share the latest news of her twin. After the dreadful Basil and the inarticulate Charles it was a relief to see Nigel's bluff open-faced countenance and take a moment to share the descriptions of the splendor of maharajahs' palaces, villainous thugs, murderous dacoits, perilous tiger hunts, and all the other exotic details she had gleaned from Ned and Freddie's correspondence.

Nigel, who was between Freddie and Ned in age, had been their constant companion when they were all in London. Being with him was almost as good as being with her brother and Ned. He was a cheerful giant given to claiming that he made up in size for what he lacked in his brain box. He was perfectly happy to leave the thinking to clever fellows like Ned, and though he wouldn't have been caught dead with a book, he had inordinate respect for Cassie and Ned, who not only read them, but actually enjoyed them.

"You're looking bang up to the nines, Cassie. I hardly recognized you in such fancy toggery. I see that old Basil was trying his best to charm you. That man gives me a pain in the bread basket. Fancies himself an out-of-door, does old 'Wily Weatherby,' but I must say I don't like him above half—nasty weasely sort of fellow," Ned remarked.

"He's the most odious toad," Cassie rejoined hotly. "Trying to make out that he's all the crack and condescending to me as though I were a complete rustic, and all the time ogling me as though I were some prime bit of blood. Disgusting!"

"Don't fly into the boughs, Cassie," Nigel soothed. "We'll keep a weather eye out for him next time. I expect he caught poor Willoughby off guard and there was nothing else he could do but introduce you. Basil will make a good catch for someone who can stomach him. He's well breeched. Got a wealthy aunt who dotes on him, but to my mind he's a nasty piece of work. Trouble is he's such an eligible bachelor, he gets invited everywhere." Here Nigel caught a meaningful look from his mother. "Ahem, Cassie, would you like to dance," he asked, responding dutifully to his mother's unspoken urging.

Cassie, who had intercepted the look from Lady Streatham, smiled and replied, "Thank you, Nigel, but I would just as soon sit this one out." When she saw the relief on his face, her smile deepened, "Let's sit down and you can tell me all about life in the Guards, which is sure to be more interesting than anything I have encountered at Cresswell or here at the Marriage Mart."

While Nigel was not an extraordinarily bright young man, he was kind, and he detected the wistful note in Cassie's voice. "Is it too dreadful having to attend all these routs and balls and things? I should hate it. Lord, one quadrille and I'm done for. But I thought females like that sort of thing—not that you're like other females—thank goodness. You're a great gun, Cassie. If I could find someone like you, it wouldn't be half bad to go to these sorts of things." His brow furrowed as a thought struck him. "You wouldn't like to get married, would you, Cassie? If you would, then neither one of us would have to stand this nonsense. You've got more pluck than most men. We could have a bang-up time. And . . ."—he added the clincher in a rush—"I don't know anyone who's a more bruising rider or a better judge of horseflesh."

Cassie smiled fondly at him, replying gently, "That's very sweet of you, Nigel, and you're a dear to think of me, but I really don't want to be married, and neither do you." Her quick eyes caught the barely perceptible relaxation of his posture at her reply and the slight sigh of relief as he realized his narrow escape, and she had to struggle to keep her countenance. "But I hope you will stand my friend and rescue me as you did tonight. Now tell me, did you purchase that bay you saw at Tattersall's not long ago?"

Thus engaged in one of their favorite pastimes, comparing

the points of various bits of blood they had known or seen
and describing the ground over which they had been on
diverse hunts, Nigel and Cassie managed to wile away the
remainder of the evening most enjoyably.

CHAPTER 5

The next day Cassie was awakened by Frances hard on the heels of the maid who brought in the morning chocolate. Having correctly interpreted Cassie's reactions to her various partners the previous evening, Frances thought it time to call upon the Comte de Vaudron before her younger sister's opinion of London and the *ton* descended so low as to be irredeemable.

"Cassie, my love," Frances began, pulling her wrapper closer as she settled herself at the foot of Cassie's bed. "We must call on the comte as soon as possible. Today bids to be fair and I think we should beg Julian to drive us around the park and drop us off at the comte's before repairing to Brooks's. What do you say?"

Cassie, who had been somewhat daunted by visions of galas similar to that of the previous evening stretching endlessly, cheered up considerably. Her face regained some of its former animation and she replied, "I should like that of all things."

"It's done then. As soon as you're dressed, we shall be off," Frances concluded briskly, rising from the bed and making for the door.

Inspired, Cassie instructed Rose to select her newest walking dress. Indeed, she looked quite charming when she descended sometime later. The lavender tint of her zephyrine silk pelisse intensified the blue of her eyes and the lace-trimmed capuchin brim of her bonnet framed her curls, which, ordinarily kept ruthlessly smoothed and pulled into a knot, were allowed to escape in golden profusion. Even

41

Lord Mainwaring, that noted connoisseur of feminine
fashion, remarked that she looked complete to a shade as
he handed her into his curricle.

Wellington, who fancied himself a coaching dog, had run
out eagerly when the elegant equipage was brought around
to the door. Hating to disappoint him, Cassie did her best
to explain why he wasn't being lifted onto the driver's seat.
"Not today, Wellington, we're not going for a long ride,
you know. We're off to visit some very dull friezes which
wouldn't interest you in the least." The little dog's ears and
tail drooped but were soon restored to their usual perky
posture when Nelson, who had been sunning himself on the
front step, reminded him that Cook had just finished making
a game pie and there were sure to be some delicious scraps.
With a farewell arf, Wellington sent them on their way and
trotted around to the kitchen to see what he and Nelson could
round up. Besides, he consoled himself, on such a fine day
Theodore was certain to ask John to take him to the park
on his pony and he was bound to invite Wellington along.

The curricle bowled through the park, pausing briefly as
they exchanged salutations with Nigel and some brother
officers then stopped to speak to his mother, who was taking
the air more sedately in her carriage. "You're up betimes
for someone who just survived her first ball," she greeted
Cassie warmly. "I'm only sorry you were subjected to so
many poisonous partners. I shall instruct Nigel to keep an
eagle eye on you." Under no illusions about her offspring,
she added, "He doesn't like dancing above half, but he must
learn and he'd as lief have you as a partner as anyone else.
Girls who simper alarm him intensely and he's likely to tread
on their toes or, worse yet, their gowns. And his brother
officers, though they are rather more ill at ease on the dance
floor than they are in the saddle, can be relied upon to make
pleasant enough partners. At any rate, they are not likely
to try to lead you into some secluded alcove as I'll be bound
young Weatherby would have." She smiled in sympathy at
Cassie's involuntary shudder of revulsion. "Exactly, my

dear. He's a nasty character, make no mistake. You did well to keep him at arm's length."

Bidding adieu to Lady Streatham, they drove toward Hanover Square, Mainwaring deftly maneuvering among the crush of carriages. The comte was delighted to see them. *"Ma cheré* Fanny *et ma très chère* Cassie, *comme je suis enchanté de vous voir,"* he exclaimed, bending over their hands. "But come, I am eager to have you see my work and the proof of the most pressing need I have for the assistance of my brilliant Cassandra." He led them to a library littered with books and papers, the odd fragment of a frieze or statue scattered here and there among them.

A young man rose to greet them as they entered. "Ah, I must introduce you to my other assistant. Horace here has had the great good sense to resist all his family's attempts to provide him with a military career. He had decided to become a classicist instead. I have told him that from my experience I find it to be a far more rewarding and undoubtedly a safer form of existence since I should certainly have been one of Madame Guillotine's first lovers had I not been more enamored of the glories of Athens. Lady Mainwaring and Lady Cassandra Cresswell, may I present the Honorable Horace Wilbraham."

Cassie found herself liking the square-jawed serious face and steady gray eyes of the young man who took her hand. Her heart was further won by his next words. "I have been longing to meet the daughters of so noted a scholar as your father. I have read everything Lord Charles Cresswell ever wrote and I am a fervent admirer of his. How I envy your upbringing," he concluded with a wistful note that Cassie found somehow quite touching.

"The Earl of Amberly is undoubtedly a man of excellent principles, but he does not understand a son who prefers books to sport," the comte explained. "Horace, show Cassie what we have been doing while I inveigle news of that young rapscallion brother of hers out of Fanny."

Horace led Cassie over to a pile of papers at which he had

been working. "We are describing everything Lord Elgin brought over. It is a monumental task, but so rewarding. You, who have been there, cannot imagine the feeling it gives me to be able to touch the past and to try to capture the magnificence of these marbles in words so that others may share them. We hope to be able to publish a catalog which will be of inestimable value to scholars everywhere."

Here, the comte interrupted scornfully, "Yes, Fosbroke claims that his *Encyclopaedia of Antiquities, and Elements of Archaeology, Classical and Medieval* is the first of its kind, but it is a mere compendium. We intend to produce a work of much greater detail and thus of far greater use to scholars than his desultory attempt."

"Ours is a truly enormous enterprise," Horace continued enthusiastically, "and having someone such as you to assist us will be the greatest help imaginable. The comte speaks very highly of your accomplishments, Lady Cassandra." Horace's eagerness was infectious and Cassie found herself warming to this earnest young scholar, so different from anyone else she knew—except, of course, for Ned, but Ned was special.

"Do call me Cassie, please," she begged, smiling at him. "And do show me how you have been proceeding. Papa would be so pleased to see that his work was being carried on so carefully by such authorities."

The next two hours flew by as Horace and the comte explained what they had done, what they had hoped to accomplish, and the process they had been through thus far. Cassie found herself relaxing and entering into the conversation in a way she had not since the departure of Ned and Freddie. Indeed, Horace was as learned as Ned and certainly far less argumentative—a point which stood greatly in his favor. The awe in which he held Lord Charles seemed to extend to all the Cresswells and the admiration in his eyes as he listened to Cassie was balm to her lonely spirit. They discussed not only the cataloguing of Lord Elgin's marbles, but the new edition of *Tacquot's Latin Scholar's Guide* and various translations of Homer, though they both agreed that Chapman's remained the best.

"It is wonderful to find a lady who thinks of something beyond the latest drawings in Ackermann's *Repository* or *La Belle Assemblée*. In general, I have no conversation. I never seem to find anything to say at the routs and balls my mother insists I escort her to. My presence never adds anything and it continually reminds her what a disappointment I am to them," he confided.

Cassie snorted. "You must find it equally difficult to converse with men as well because I find that if they have anything in their heads beyond sport, it has to do with the set of their coats or the intricacies of their cravats. It would be amusing if one were allowed merely to remain in the background observing, but no one allows one to do that." She sighed audibly.

Horace nodded. "Very true," he agreed. "Though I admit to being a mere observer at Lady Delamere's rout. I saw you there and thought how very elegant you looked without all the fussy frills and silly gewgaws that most women seem to need to wear to lend themselves consequence."

At this Cassie turned quite pink with pleasure. She was not a stranger to flattery, but this speech was delivered with such ingenuousness that she felt truly complimented. "Why thank you. It is wonderful to be recognized as an individual in such a situation when one is ordinarily judged by one's social address or position."

"I know. I realize that I am more often the second son of the Earl of Amberly at these affairs than I am Horace Wilbraham, scholar, though I suppose it makes little difference because most people would rather know the former than the latter," Horace concluded somewhat gloomily.

"I find Horace Wilbraham infinitely preferable to and far more interesting than the second son of the Earl of Amberly," Cassie declared stoutly.

"How kind you are," Horace thanked her, smiling gratefully.

"And have you two decided how you would like to divide up your work? I have more than enough for the three of us, and if we ever finish with Lord Elgin's collection, we should do the same with the Towneley Marbles and the sculptures from Bassae," the comte remarked as he and Lady Frances strolled over to the window where Cassie and Horace were sitting.

"Come, Cassie. John should be here shortly. I instructed him to call for us before nuncheon. I daren't leave Teddy, Ethelred, Wellington, and Nelson alone together for too long a stretch. Cook and Nurse are worth their weights in gold, but neither one of them has the strength of character to resist the blandishments of those four," remarked Frances as she pulled on her lemon kid gloves.

Cassie agreed ruefully. "Nor the resourcefulness or strength of character to rescue them from the scrapes they are likely to fall into."

The butler came in to announce the arrival of the ladies' carriage, and after arranging to come the next day and gratefully accepting Horace's invitation to escort them to a concert at the Academy of Ancient Music, they departed, well satisfied with the morning's outing.

Lady Frances, sneaking a glance at her sister's profile, was pleased to see a happier look than had been on her face for some time, but refrained from any comment. She was correct in her observations. Cassie was delighted. After having endured so many dull and pointless conversations she had found it refreshing and revitalizing to share her deepest interests with someone who could appreciate them. She looked forward with pleasure to the next evening and to the days ahead, which no longer seemed to stretch emptily and endlessly before her.

CHAPTER 6

Cassie's expectations were not disappointed. She truly enjoyed the concert, but what made it even more delightful was having Horace there. He was so attentive to her slightest wish, making certain she was comfortably placed in the most advantageous seat possible. Occasionally during the performance she caught him glancing at her to reassure himself that she was enjoying herself to the utmost. No one, except Ned, had ever paid such attention to her wishes or had seemed to be so concerned for her happiness. She felt immensely touched and flattered by such thoughtfulness, particularly since it provided such a marked contrast to the treatment she had received at the hands of her dancing partners at Lady Delamere's rout. It heightened her enjoyment that much more when in the carriage on the way home he inquired in an endearingly diffident way, "I do hope the concert pleased you?"

"Oh, yes. It was entirely delightful. I do so love music, but I have had little chance to hear anything but ill-rendered pianoforte recitals performed more for the opportunity they afford to demonstrate that the performer would make someone a delightful and accomplished companion than for the sake of the music. Thank you ever so much," she replied gratefully.

He laughed. "You are too critical, Cassandra. That poor young woman undoubtedly has nothing else to show for herself, but I, too, have endured too many similar tedious evenings to be much in sympathy with the performers. It is one of the true delights of the Town to be able to hear pieces

47

as they should be played. I attend many such evenings. They
give me such a great deal of pleasure that I am afraid I must
admit them to be one of my true vices. My parents often
accuse me of neglecting my social responsibilities for such
evenings of self-indulgence. I hope I shall be able to convince
you to join me again. But what did you think of the Handel?''

"I especially delighted in that. One rarely gets an
opportunity to hear it so well performed. But here we are.
Thank you so much. I enjoyed myself tremendously." Cassie
had been so engrossed in their discussion that she was
astounded to find the carriage had come to a stop and the
footman was waiting patiently to hand her down.

Not all evenings could be as certain to appeal to Cassie
as the one with Horace. Certainly she looked forward to her
first appearance at Almack's with a notable lack of
enthusiasm. "It is certainly less elegant than any other
gathering you'll be asked to attend," Frances warned. "It
makes up in the selectness of its elected guests what it lacks
in amenities. Truly, the entire experience is a study in the
pretensions of anyone with social aspirations. If the tastes
of its patronesses were not so omnipotent, it would be a dead
bore. But their social hegemony so governs the imagination
of the *ton* that it becomes extraordinarily amusing to see how
people allow themselves to be affected by entry to its
hallowed portals and the whims of those who rule it. Those
who dominate in the political or military arenas become putty
in their hands and are properly subservient. The Iron Duke
himself was sent home to change into proper attire before
being allowed admittance and he submitted without a word
of protest."

Cassie looked doubtful. "I don't see the slightest need to
make a push for the approval of such people. After all, I
don't intend to spend my life in the *ton*, so its opinion matters
very little to me."

"That's as may be," Frances agreed. "But the patronesses' approval can do you no harm and their sanction allows
you the opportunity to appear at any social function you
should wish, thus giving you the liberty of selecting

whomever you will as social companions. And besides, such acceptance becomes a social cachet to your own special activities and interests, which might otherwise not be found to be socially acceptable.''

Begrudgingly Cassie acknowledged the wisdom of her elder sister's views. Personally, she would have preferred to do without such ceremony, but she was realistic enough to be aware that such social recognition could smooth her way in other areas more dear to her heart. So, with as much enthusiasm as she could muster, she instructed Rose to select her the approved raiment of a young lady in her first Season—a white muslin gown with cerulean blue trimming— and allowed her to dress her hair in the simplest of styles with a matching wreath of blue flowers.

The rooms were already crowded when they arrived, and the Mainwarings were immediately hailed by several acquaintances as they made their way through the crush. Lord Mainwaring's political crony Lord Charlton, looking most uncomfortable and out of place, hovered awkwardly near a capable-looking woman conversing animatedly with Princess Esterhazy and a blushing young damsel who seemed on the verge of expiring at being recognized by such an august personage. ''Ah, Julian''—he greeted Lord Mainwaring with the eagerness of a drowning man seizing a buoyant object— ''have you seen Canning lately? I know you and Castlereagh were as thick as thieves in Vienna, but mark my words, George Canning is your man for the moment. With your views on our financial situation, I should think you and he should rub along happily together.'' He drew Julian aside, leaving Frances and Cassie to shift for themselves, a situation which was soon remedied by the appearance of the Streathams.

Nigel was the picture of discomfort as he towered over his vivacious mother. Cassie, correctly interpreting the emotions at war within him—a desire to please his mother by partnering Cassie and his loathing for the dance floor— burst out laughing. He reddened self-consciously. ''Relax, Nigel,'' she reassured him. ''I shall be more than happy if you procure me a glass of that dreadful lemonade and then share your latest adventures with me.''

Relieved, Nigel practically stumbled over himself in his eagerness to cater to her wishes. They spent the next half hour exchanging reminiscences and ignoring the quizzical glances sent their way by the inveterate matchmakers who frequented the place.

Their *tête-à-tête* was brought to an end by Nigel's exasperated mother, who turned from observing the dance floor to exclaim, ''Really, Nigel, it's too bad in you. Cassie will never lack for partners. You must stop monopolizing her and ask Amanda Billingsley to dance. She's such a dab of a girl, no one will notice her unless someone makes an effort. Off with you. There's a good boy.'' A firm hand in the small of his back accompanied these words. Nigel rose dutifully and lumbered over to the corner where Miss Billingsley, keeping close to her mama, was timidly observing the scene.

Once Nigel had departed, Cassie found herself approached by several young gallants eager to discover all they could about one of the Season's more attractive new faces. She conversed dutifully with them, but her mind was on a thousand other things—the latest piece of work she was doing for the comte, a scratch on her horse's fetlock which seemed to be developing an infection—and all of her partners remained an indistinct blur to her. At last she was able to welcome a moment of respite between dances when she could stand quietly in the shadows and observe the throng around her. The lights and the crush of people made her yearn for the green fields of Hampshire and the exhilarating feelings of freshness and freedom as she galloped across them. How she longed for that solitude. In no time at all the moment of peace was interrupted by conversation behind her.

''My dear, you must tell me who that divine man is,'' drawled an affected voice.

''I have not the remotest idea, but he looks just like Byron's Corsair. Do let us stroll in that direction,'' replied her companion with a fashionable lisp easily identified as belonging to Arabella Taylor.

Try as she might, Cassie could not refrain from glancing toward the end of the room where something appeared to have attracted a throng of people. Involuntarily she found herself drawn toward the center of the commotion, which she judged to be a tall dark-haired man whose broad-shouldered back was toward her. He was speaking to Lady Jersey, but as Cassie approached he turned toward the center of the room and she found herself looking at a tanned hawklike face whose swarthiness was rendered even more striking by the dark blue eyes under black brows. Their gaze alighted on Cassie and a singularly attractive smile erased the cynical lines around the well-shaped mouth and softened his somewhat sardonic expression. "Cassie," he exclaimed, holding out a hand.

Bereft of speech, Cassie extended hers, wondering how this stranger could possibly know her. The mystery was solved in an instant as another much beloved face appeared at the stranger's elbow. "Freddie, Ned," she shouted joyfully, gripping the hand that lifted hers to his lips.

One eyebrow lifted quizzically. "Am I that changed then, best of playmates?" Ned inquired in an amused voice.

"N-no, not exactly," stammered Cassie in an unusual state of confusion. But he was changed! True, the shock of dark hair that *would* fall over his forehead seemed in danger of doing so again despite his elegant crop. The eager, intelligent glance remained, but it was altered somehow by an ironic gleam that seemed to mock its owner as much as it did the company around him. The finely chiseled lips were firmer and less inclined to smile, while the lines at either side indicated that most of these smiles were more likely to result from derision than genuine amusement.

Ned, looking down at his companion, found a less physically noticeable but equally disconcerting transformation. The hair, done *à la couronne*, a style much admired by Horace, seemed too severe for the unruly curls he

remembered. The teasing sparkle in the eyes had been
replaced by a more serious, almost somber expression. Ned
found himself wondering what could have happened to
quench the rebellious spirit he remembered.

This mutual examination was broken by an exuberant
Bertie Montgomery, who strode over exclaiming jubilantly
as he wrung Freddie's hand, "Freddie, my boy!" He nodded
in Ned's direction. "Wonderful to see you both. Quite the
nabobs, I hear. London will be agog to learn of your exploits.
Do let me be the first to hear 'em, as then I shall be lionized
and shall be able to lord it over all the rest."

At that, the world, or at least the world of the *ton*, closed
in around them. Lord Mainwaring shook their hands,
wondering how they'd left everything in India. Lady Frances
kissed Ned and clung to Freddie, remarking that since they
were in evening attire, they must have been at Mainwaring
House and wondering if Cook had given them anything to eat.

Freddie smiled fondly at his sister. "Lord, Fran, can you
imagine my even bidding good day to Cook and not having
some tasty morsel thrust upon me? In fact, Ned and I would
have been here hours earlier if John Coachman hadn't fussed
so over the horses, or if Higgins hadn't insisted on unearthing
Mainwaring's best port." This last was said with an
apologetic look toward his brother-in-law. "And Cook. Cook
knew for certain that we'd been existing on 'that outlandish
heathen fare' for so long that she insisted we have at least
one good English meal inside us before we went gallivanting
all over Town. So, you see, we have been a good deal
delayed in paying our respects to you all." Freddie indicated
the rest of the fashionable world, which had by now joined
the crowd, with a breezy wave of his hand.

During this interchange, Lady Jersey, always alive to an
attractive young man with an interesting background, had
managed to wean Ned away to partner her in a waltz. And
Horace, who had eschewed such useless social gatherings
until he had met Cassie, suddenly noticed that the object of
his attention was bereft of company and led her off into a
quiet corner where they could discuss the merits of the

translation of Euripides which had just appeared in Ackermann's *Repository*.

Cassie was naturally delighted to see Horace, but despite her consuming interest in the topic, she discovered she could not keep her mind on it. Try though she would to concentrate on Horace's eloquent and admirable defense of someone whose works he had heard Cassie criticize severely, she found her eyes wandering to the center of the room, where Ned, a teasing smile on his lips, was bending over Lady Jersey, apparently enthralled by the latest on-dits that "Silence" was recounting in her own inimitable fashion. Where had the shy and self-effacing Ned acquired such an assured and positively flirtatious manner? That aside, where had those broad shoulders and the confident manner come from? Struggling to analyze the transformation, Cassie could barely muster the monosyllables to answer Horace. "Very true," or "Of course," or "Without a doubt," she rejoined at appropriate moments, trying to nod sagely, while the entire time her mind was in a whirl.

Cassie was not the only one to be taken aback at the changes in the two travelers. Limpetlike, Arabella Taylor clung to Freddie Cresswell's arm as he strode over to claim his sister as a partner. "Oh, Freddie, you're so very grown up!" she cooed. "What exotic scenes you and Ned must have encountered! Why, I should never have recognized either one of you if you hadn't appeared together and sought out the Mainwarings. You're both so brown! I expect that dealing with all those heathens has made men out of both of you." She sighed audibly. "I am so tired of the same old beaux one finds in Town. All they think about is their tailors. There is not a true man to be found among them. I grant you I have been paid some very pretty compliments by leaders of the *ton*"—here she blushed becomingly and lowered her eyes. "But one becomes bored with such trifles and longs to meet someone who is a man of strength and a leader in society instead of a mere hanger-on."

Her eyes followed Ned as he restored a laughing Lady Jersey to her coterie. Freddie and Arabella were just close enough to hear her as she tapped his cheek with her fan, scolding him coquettishly, "Naughty boy. Your travels have taught you wicked ways. You must take me for a drive in the park and tell me more."

"And," pursued Arabella, keeping a close eye on Ned as he leaned over to respond to Lady Jersey's latest sally, "I've heard you have both become disgustingly plump in the pocket, veritable Golden Balls, if ballroom gossip is to be believed."

"Don't believe a word of it, Bella," admonished Freddie, trying desperately to pry himself loose from her clutches. "You know what the town tabbies are." He at last succeeded in pulling away from her to join his sister, whom he greeted with visible relief. "Cassie, at last! Will you grant a poor fellow, desperate for intelligent female companionship of any sort, even if it is his sister's, this dance?"

Cassie laughed. "Of course, Freddie, with all the pleasure in the world." The two strolled off, leaving Arabella and Horace to deal with each other as best they could.

CHAPTER 7

It would have been a gross exaggeration to say that all of London was intrigued by the reappearance of the two travelers, but their return certainly formed the main topic of conversation the next day in several select drawing rooms. The floor of one of these in particular was littered with exotic trifles as Freddie distributed acquisitions from his travels to his nearest and dearest. "Freddie, how lovely! You are rigging me out in the latest fashion whether I will or no," exclaimed Cassie, surveying the effect of a cashmere shawl draped artistically over her shoulders while Frances slid numerous delicate gold bracelets onto her wrist. Theodore, totally entranced by a set of elephants and their mahouts beautifully carved in ivory, was arranging them on the floor before an interested audience. Nelson, Wellington, and Ethelred were divided in their opinions—Nelson wishing to bat the pieces around on the carpet, Wellington feeling it would be more amusing to chew them, while Ethelred, unready as usual, sat regarding them suspiciously with beady black eyes.

Lord Mainwaring was ensconced in a chair by the fire reviewing the reports Freddie had brought back. Agreeably surprised by the thoroughness of the observation and the degree of detail with which they were recorded, he remarked, "Well done, Freddie. Your recommendations about replacing the *banyans,* who can charge what they will for their services as brokers of goods to unsuspecting foreigners, with knowledgeable Englishmen is certainly well founded. I hope you will help me in effecting the change."

Freddie, accustomed to holding his formidable brother-in-law in some degree of awe, flushed with pleasure, replying modestly. "That's very kind of you, sir, but even the veriest neophyte can see how these men are able to take advantage of those unfamiliar with the commodities so as to charge whatever price they wish and exact whatever-percent commission they desire."

Cassie, beaming proudly at her brother, disagreed. "That's as may be, Freddie, and I daresay that's a common enough topic in the coffee rooms all over India, but your suggestion of setting up an exchange where such abuses can be remedied shows an active intelligence that is lacking in so many people who merely listen to hearsay and add their own complaints to the general conversation but do not bestir themselves to discover a solution."

Unused to such praise in a family whose talents usually outshone his, Freddie was visibly flattered but disclaimed any credit in his most offhand manner. "Oh it was nothing, Cassie. Any gudgeon could see what needed to be done."

Cassie refused to be convinced. "You are far too modest, Freddie, truly. You must make a push to ensure that your recommendations are heard." Privately she was relieved to hear how well her twin had conducted himself. Cassie had always had faith that he had more bottom and sense than his peers. Even though his talents had failed to assert themselves during his school years, she had remained certain that given the proper opportunity, Freddie would prove himself brighter and more steady than he was credited by most people, who were inclined to dismiss him as a lovable chap but sporting mad and devoted to nothing more serious than his stable.

This reverie was broken by Higgins, who announced, "Lady Taylor, Miss Arabella Taylor."

Cassie gave a start of surprise. Never intimate with Arabella in the country, she had not sought her out in the city, and had been annoyed at herself for being piqued at Arabella's failure to acknowledge her existence when their paths had crossed at various social functions. Wise enough in the ways of the world to recognize that Arabella never entered into friendships that did not profit her, Cassie perfectly understood that someone determined to be labeled an incomparable would rather die than admit a connection to a young woman who, to all intents and purposes, was a country nobody and content to remain exactly that. Furthermore, running an eye recently educated in the shops of Bond Street modistes over Arabella's walking dress of jaconet muslin under a richly worked open robe with a mulberry-colored spencer that showed off to perfection the flawless skin and dark eyes, Cassie was puzzled by the visit and the obvious care Arabella had lavished on her toilette. The plaited front of the gown enhanced a generous figure and the cornette of lace under her hat framed her face delightfully.

"La, Cassandra, you are looking vastly elegant, I am sure," Arabella declared, tripping across the room. Modifying this uncharacteristically generous praise, she continued, "I vow I wouldn't have recognized you at all."

A casual observer might have been pardoned for being confused over the intended recipient of this speech as Arabella, ostensibly addressing Cassie, never looked in her direction but smiled and dimpled at Freddie instead the entire time she was speaking.

"You must think I showed a sad lack of conduct in not calling on you directly you arrived in Town. I am sure I meant to call times out of mind, but one has so many engagements, so many pressing social obligations . . ." She trailed off, hoping to be asked to elaborate on these.

Cassie, who found more to comment on in this sudden appearance than in her neglect, was cudgeling her brains for an explanation for this sudden solicitude and wondering how best to discover the reason for the visit in order to bring it to a close as expeditiously as possible. Town bronze, in her opinion, had done nothing to improve the dubious charms of Hampshire's reigning belle. "Do not refine too much on it, Arabella. Having been about a bit, I can see that someone as sought after as you must have many more urgent

engagements," Cassie replied, adopting what she hoped was
an interested enough tone of voice to encourage Arabella to
state the purpose of her visit.

However, Arabella was not to be led. Her eyes surveying
the room, she disposed herself elegantly upon a chair and
smiled intimately at Freddie, remarking, "What a stir you
and Ned caused at Almack's! Everyone has a different story
to explain how you made your fortunes and what you plan
to do to dazzle us with your wealth. Do tell me all your
adventures. I feel certain you and he outshone everyone there.
You certainly did last evening—both of you brown as natives
and looking as though you had a hundred hair-raising tales
to relate. Do tell me." She looked up expectantly, her whole
being expressive of eager anticipation—an attitude that had
won the hearts of numerous swains happy to recount the least
little exploit to such a charming listener.

Freddie had known Arabella too long to be overwhelmed
by the thought of so much charm and beauty waiting breathlessly to hang on his every word. Like his sister, he was
extremely curious as to what really lay behind the unexpected
call. Whatever it was, it had not been accomplished, because
Arabella's eyes never left off their restless inspection of the
room. In the midst of a truly gripping account of stalking
a man-eating tiger, he became aware that her wandering
attention was occupied elsewhere. "And so, the mahout and
I climbed down from the elephant and I was able to dispatch
the wounded tiger with a bullet between the eyes," Freddie
concluded.

"Very interesting. I am sure you did yourself proud,"
Arabella replied vaguely with a notable lack of enthusiasm.
"Was Ned with you? I vow he is vastly changed since I saw
him last. I overheard Lady Jersey telling Countess Lieven
that he left a trail of broken hearts in India and Europe. Such
a man of the world is sure to cast the other pinks of the *ton*
into the shade, such dull lives as they lead. Did you say he
stays with his sister?"

At last Freddie understood the impetus behind the visit and
was highly amused by it.

Cassie, on the other hand, was incensed. She could barely keep from ringing a peal over their visitor and was debating the wisdom of depressing their visitor's ill-concealed interest in Ned with a sharp retort when the object of all this interest himself was announced.

Ned Mainwaring in riding clothes was even more arresting than Ned Mainwaring in evening attire. The exquisite cut of his coat showed off his broad shoulders to advantage and the close-fitting breeches emphasized the powerful long legs that made him tower over other men. This height, which had made him a gangly and somewhat self-conscious youth, now gave him an air of command, which was further accentuated by his piercing blue eyes and resolute jaw.

"Hello, sir," he greeted Julian, extending a lean tanned hand to his former guardian and mentor.

"Ned, my lad. It's wonderful to see you. I hope you have come to enlighten us on the true state of things behind the undoubtedly highly embellished tales with which Freddie has been regaling us," Lord Mainwaring greeted his nephew with quizzically raised brows.

Ned barely had the opportunity to shake his hand and bend over Lady Frances's before Arabella pounced.

"Ned! How delightful to have you back. We've missed you this age. London has been sadly flat," she declared as she swept gracefully across the room, extending a hand and smiling at him in such a way that he received the full effect of charming dimples and pearly teeth.

Behind Cassie, Freddie, who was enjoying the scene hugely, snorted, "What a bouncer!"

And Cassie, unable to contain herself, gasped, "Why she never paid the least mind to him in Hampshire, let alone London!"

The subject of all this attention appeared unaware of it as he smiled broadly down at Arabella. "Arabella, you are as exquisite as I remember you. Though absent from London's salons, I have nevertheless heard news that you have taken the *ton* by storm."

If Freddie had snorted before, he fairly gagged now. Ned

was the best of good fellows and someone you could count on in the most desperate of situations, but this was doing it much too brown.

Cassie, too, was taken aback. How could Ned, her simple, direct, awkward Ned, speak such fustian?

Arabella, who did not share the twins' critical point of view, scolded him archly as he bent over her hand. "Flatterer. You know you never gave a rap about the latest on-dits."

Ned raised a mobile eyebrow, rejoining, "You will not let me forget the gaucheries of my past, I see, but where the on-dits concern you, I assure you, I listened very carefully."

This bantering exchange could have continued for some time, delighting some and boring others, if Lady Taylor had not recalled with a start their appointment with the dressmaker. "Arabella, come my dear, we must be off," she announced, rising majestically. "Lady Frances, I shall be sending cards for an affair we're having—nothing elaborate, you understand—just a pleasant evening with a card party for us and some dancing for the young people."

Cassie, who could barely keep her own lip from quivering at the thought of Frances and Lord Mainwaring relegated to the card room with the likes of Sir Lucius and Lady Taylor, wondered how her sister was able to keep her countenance. A surreptitious glance over her shoulder at her twin revealed that Freddie, quietly convulsed behind her, was even less successful than she at containing his mirth.

Arabella did not look best pleased to have her *tête-à-tête* interrupted, but she recovered quickly and followed her mother to the door. Just as Higgins was preparing to usher the ladies to their carriage she stopped and, as if struck by a sudden thought, exclaimed, "Ned, why do you not accompany us? Our appointment is not so pressing that we may not take a turn around the park before consigning ourselves to an afternoon with Madame Celestine."

If Ned was somewhat taken aback at being invited to leave directly he had arrived, he did not exhibit the least sign of discomposure. Instead he assisted each of the ladies into the carriage, remarking, "It has been so long since I have been in such a salubrious climate that I welcome every opportunity to enjoy it, especially in the company of two such charming companions."

Arabella simpered complacently and even her mother's somewhat wooden countenance relaxed into the semblance of a smile.

Those left behind in the drawing room were left to react as they would to Arabella's stratagems. "Well, of all the impudent . . ." Cassie sputtered. "She never gave Ned the slightest opportunity to speak for himself."

"Arf," agreed Wellington, whose own nose had been put slightly out of joint because his old friend had been so occupied by that fussy Arabella who had never liked dogs that he had not even acknowledged Wellington's furiously wagging tail and smile of greeting. "I should have barked to get his attention," he confided to Nelson. "But that would have displeased Frances." With a gusty sigh he dropped his nose between his paws and stared into the fire.

"Don't refine upon it too much, Cass," admonished Freddie. "He didn't seem to be the least put out."

"His wits must have gone begging then," Cassie snapped as she went to collect her bonnet and pelisse before seeking the more rational companionship of Horace and the comte.

CHAPTER 8

Cassie's spirits, which had been somewhat dampened by the alacrity with which Ned had gone off with Arabella, were restored by the warmth of her reception in Hanover Square.

"*Ma cherè* Cassie, how happy we are to see you!" exclaimed the comte as his general factotum, the lugubrious Jacques, ushered her into the study. "We have been arguing . . . no, discussing, the theme represented on this frieze. I believe it it be a procession from the celebration of the Panathenaea, but Horace here has his doubts."

Picking her way carefully among the bits of frieze here, a torso there, Cassie made her way slowly to the one clear patch of floor that the comte and Horace had left for themselves. Horace, who had been frowning in concentration over a section of frieze, looked up as she approached, remarking, "I don't believe it could be the Panathenaea because nowhere is there any representation of the olive wood figure of Athena which was essential to the ceremony. Furthermore, there are too many male figures for it to be the procession."

Cassie studied the figures, stepping first to one side and then the other and moving away from it as far back as the clutter would allow. For some time she remained deep in thought, her eyes fixed on the figure of a child handing something to an adult. Horace, glancing surreptitiously at her face, thought the way she bit her lip in concentration infinitely more charming than all the dimpled smiles and simpers cast his way at the various social affairs his mother had forced him to attend. He was far more attracted to her in her total absorption in the frieze than he had ever been to any woman, even those who had lavished their most seductive attentions on him. Here was someone as oblivious as he to the rest of the world, someone who was not only as uninterested as he was in the vagaries of fashion or the latest on-dits, but whose concentration was fixed on the same concerns as his. In all his years of study he had only found one person who shared his passiojn for antiquity—the Comte de Vaudron. For Horace, misunderstood by his family and ignored by his peers, this friendship had provided the most rewarding companionship he had ever known. Now here was someone his own age who, in addition to understanding his enthusiasm, entered into it as wholeheartedly as he. To Horace such a state of affairs was nothing short of a miracle and he regarded Cassie with a mixture of reverence and awe that he had never felt before in his life.

"Ah, yes." Cassie's brows cleared and she replied, "I regret that I agree with the comte, Horace. Surely this figure is that of a girl handing the new *peplos,* woven to cover the image of Athena, to a magistrate. I am sorry to disagree with you." Here Cassie flashed such a charming, apologetic smile at the young man sitting at her feet that it quite took his breath away. The admiration he'd felt toward a revered scholar's daughter suddenly metamorphosed into something more potent, and for the first time he was fully aware of Cassandra as a beautiful, vital woman. He sat stunned by the intensity of these new emotions.

Meanwhile, Cassie, oblivious to the powerful effect she was having, turned to the comte for confirmation of her theory as she speculated, "It is true that the figure could be either male or female, but the form looks to be more feminine, don't you think?"

The comte smiled at his protégé. "I had not previously thought of that as being the *peplos,* but that is an excellent interpretation. I quite agree with you *ma chère.*" He was looking at Cassie as he answered, but as his glance fell on Horace, transfixed by his private revelations, the smile deepened to one of amused contemplation. Aha, we have here the beginning of a passion for something other than the dust of antiquity, he muttered silently to himself. Such a situation will bear some watching.

Cassie took up a pen, looking expectantly at the comte. "How would you wish this described in the catalog, then?"

He waved a hand toward the manuscript of the catalog, responding airily, "Oh, I absolutely leave it to you, *ma chère,* as your reasoning behind your attribution of it as the Panathenaic procession has far more merit than our humble interpretations. Write what you wish." Turning to Horace with an impish twinkle, he remarked, "This Cassie is a scholar, *non*? I warned you she would put us on our mettle." A blank look was all the response he elicited, so he continued, "We must not get on our high ropes merely because she arrives and answers in a few minutes the question that has been dominating our discussion the entire morning, *hein*?"

"Yeeeeeees," Horace responded vaguely as he slowly returned to reality. He continued in a more punctilious tone, "But surely we should discuss this with others who are equally well read in these matters. It would be most dis-advantageous to put forth such an interpretation without having consulted many more sources and explored every avenue of thought in a work that is to serve as a guide for future generations."

"Relax, *mon brave,*" adjured the comte. "Who is more well informed than we? Who has spent more time with these *chefs d'oeuvres* than we? Remember"—he held up a cautionary hand—"the best, most judicious interpretations are those that mingle instinct with learning, and emotion with intellect. Cassandra and I looked at the figure presenting the object and both of us instinctively *felt* it was a girl. This then led us to the more refined and rational conclusion that it was a *peplos* that was being offered. You, on the other hand, looked at the procession and, applying only your knowledge, assumed the procession to be dominantly male and therefore could not explain the reason for such a procession or interpret the identity of the object. This is not to say, of course, that ours is necessarily the correct interpretation," he continued fair-mindedly, "but our trust in our immediate responses gave us perhaps a richer interpretation."

He laid a reassuring hand on the young man's shoulder, adding, "I can see you are disturbed. Do not distress yourself, *mon ami*. To cultivate the mind is all very well, but one must not do so at the expense of the other faculties. I think now we require some refreshment, *non*?" After ringing unsuccessfully for Jacques, the comte strolled off in search of him while Horace, prey to a variety of conflicting emotions, turned to stare out the window.

He was not the only one staring vacantly at the gardens outside the library. Cassie, who had been scribbling furiously at the onset of their discussion, had written progressively more slowly as unwelcome thoughts from earlier in the day returned. At first at a loss to explain her general malaise, she began to examine her feelings more closely and realized, much to her surprise, that she felt betrayed. She should have been glad that Arabella, who had so callously spurned someone as fine as Ned, should now be so eager to capture his attention. And you *are* glad, she admonished herself severely. He deserves, he always deserved, admiration. But how can he be taken in by such an about-face? she wondered. Surely he must see that she only wants his attention because he is the *ton*'s latest sensation. Can't he see that she is constant only as long as friendship brings social distinction? How can he not be disgusted by a nature that is only interested in someone who will lend social cachet to her.

But Ned had not only been disgusted, he had actually looked at Arabella with admiration. That was where the sense of betrayal arose. It came from the fact that someone as intelligent and sensitive as Ned, who had been her constant intellectual companion and ally at countless dull engagements, now seemed as taken in as all the rest by a beautiful countenance, a coquettish manner, and a frivolous mind. Did he value his own mind and interests so little that he would forgo them for the dubious excitement of a flirtation with a pretty ninnyhammer? His pursuit of Arabella seemed to be a rejection of all they had once appreciated and shared. Not only was Cassie genuinely puzzled by his fascination with someone whose existence was so antithetical to his former interests, she felt horribly alone—abandoned in some respects—by someone she had counted on above everyone else for understanding and sympathy.

So lost in thought was she that she did not hear Horace approach, nor did she hear his tenative, "Cassandra?" He tried again, a little more loudly this time.

Cassie came to with a start. "Oh, I do beg your pardon. I'm dreadfully sorry, Horace. I didn't hear you. I was wool-gathering, I'm afraid," she apologized.

Horace, still coping with his newfound appreciation of her, had crossed the room to invite her to Mr. Glover's recently opened exhibition of oils and watercolors in Bond Street, but the words died on his lips as she turned to apologize to him. The bright light streaming from the window behind her turned her hair to a golden halo framing a face whose half-amused, half-rueful expression at having been so distracted coupled with the remorse at having ignored him made her seem all at once so beautiful and so dear that he was overwhelmed with tenderness. Horace was ordinarily the most punctilious and reserved of men, but before he could stop himself, he had seized her inky hand and pressed it reverently to his lips.

Cassie was stunned. Though she had eschewed much of society and the attendant opportunities for flirtation, she had received her share of compliments. Ordinarily she dismissed such admiration as purely groundless flattery, but Horace had shaken her. The intensity of the genuine admiration she read in his eyes and the fervor with which he devoured her hand with kisses were something she had never before experienced. It was a novel and disturbing sensation to be the object of such attention. Her knees felt weak and she found it difficult to catch her breath.

Horace was the first to recall himself to his surroundings. Flushing a deep scarlet, he gasped, "Please forgive me . . .

I never meant to . . . I wouldn't for the world cause you distress. I can't think how I came to forget myself. It is just that I admire you so greatly, Lady Cassandra, and you looked so beautiful . . ." He blushed even more deeply, if such a thing were possible, and stumbled on, "I apologize for allowing my feelings to run away with me and subjecting you to such a vulgar display."

Cassie, once she had a chance to recover from the shock of it all, found herself wishing he would stop disavowing his actions. The idea of being truly admired by one whose mind was generally occupied by higher things was an appealing one and she found it most intriguing to be the subject of such passionate protests from a young man who, if the comte and others were to be believed, had hitherto had no thoughts for anything but his work.

Fortunately for both Cassie and Horace, struggling in the grip of new and strangely intense emotions, the comte and Jacques returned, bringing welcome distraction. Tea was set out and the bustle of serving allowed them time to recover their equanimity, but not before the shrewd eyes of the comte had taken in the entire scene and reconstructed with amazing accuracy the events that must have led up to it. So, the little Cassie is becoming a woman, he thought to himself. *Bon.* It will do her a great deal of good to be distracted from her books. Perhaps she will begin to be a little more pleasure seeking, and Horace, too. He smiled in satisfaction as he accepted a cup of tea from Jacques.

CHAPTER 9

Ned astride Brutus, a high-spirited bay that was the envy of all those who had seen him purchase it at Tattersall's immediately upon his return, was savoring the pleasure of accompanying the Taylor ladies through the park on such a fine day. The flowers were in full bloom, the air was newly washed from an early-morning shower, and the whole world seemed lush and filled with promise. Once again Ned was struck, as he had been so many times since his return, with how fresh and green it all looked. He reveled in it and all the wonderful smells of England in the spring, which, after the heat and dust of India, made it seem an even more wonderful season than it had before his departure.

"La, Ned, your wits are wandering a thousand miles away, I do believe." Arabella's liquid laughter broke into his reverie.

He glanced down at the face whose mischievous, teasing look only added to its charm.

"People will certainly wonder that I am unable to keep the attention of my old playmate for even a short drive in the park. What a lowering thought. I shall very likely go into a decline if you don't tell me immediately all your adventures. They are certain to be vastly amusing and far more interesting than the same tired *on-dits* the tulips of the *ton* trot out again and again in an effort to keep us all entertained. It must have been all so very different from anything here that I hardly know where to ask you to begin. Where did you live? Did you have armies of servants to cater to your every whim? Do the Hindu wives truly throw

68

themselves on their husbands' funeral pyres as we have heard? What a dreadful thought.'' She shuddered artistically.

"Stop, stop," Ned protested, somewhat taken aback by the barrage of questions. However, he reflected cynically, he ought to be enjoying this. Previously, Arabella had never shown the least sign of interest in any of the many more valuable topics of conversation he could have discussed at length, but now that he had something exotic to offer, some information which, if repeated, could set her apart from the *ton* and cause a stir, she was agog with interest. Still, Ned was not inhuman and the idea of a beautiful, sought-after woman demanding his attention and hanging on his every word would have won the heart of the most hardened of men, much less one who had spent more hot nights than he cared to remember recalling every feature of her lovely face, every charming little gesture, and dreaming of just such moments as this. So he began by recounting the voyage out, describing their slow progress around the cape with occasional stops at exotic ports, his eccentric shipmates, and his final arrival in Calcutta, where he had immediately been plunged into a world whose multitudinous, colorful population, bright hot sun, and pungent foreign smells had threatened to overwhelm him.

Arabella's eyes grew rounder and rounder as he painted a vivid picture of teeming bazaars crowded with vendors of every sort, and he found himself enjoying her rapt attention as he brought to life ponderous bullocks with their painted horns pulling rudely constructed carts, temple processions bearing flower-bedecked statues, and women dressed in flowing saris balancing unwieldy bundles on their heads.

"You must be exceedingly adventurous to visit such a place. How ever did you go on, surrounded as you were by so many strange people? No doubt they thought you some god," Arabella exclaimed.

Ned explained that the longer he remained, the better he understood their customs and the better he was able to function and accomplish what he had set himself to do. He could see that as soon as he began to discuss his research into the customs of the country and the mentality of its inhabitants with a view to comprehending them, her eyes glazed over and she lost interest.

"Oh, there is Sir Brian Brandon waving at us. We must stop, Ned. He is truly one of the leaders of the *ton* and I do so want you to meet him. He is a special friend of mine," she confided in an undertone as a handsome Corinthian on a powerful gray approached them.

Ned, who had his own ideas about whose social advancement would be furthered by such an encounter, allowed himself to be introduced. Nevertheless, if he, as the latest sensation, could make Arabella happy by dancing attendance on her and adding to her consequence, it amused him to do so.

"Arabella, my dear, you look more lovely every day," observed Sir Brian as he leaned down to kiss the dainty hand that was extended to him. "Lady Taylor," he acknowledged Arabella's mother briefly before returning his attention to her daughter who was urging Ned forward.

"Sir Brian, you may have heard of my very dear friend Ned Mainwaring, who was just returned from a sojourn in India where he conducted himself with great distinction." Arabella spoke as though entirely familiar with the events which had conferred fame and fortune upon Ned and Freddie and she presented him with the air of one solely responsible for the discovery and introduction of such an exciting person to society.

Not best pleased to be so quickly claimed as Arabella's exclusive property, Ned extended his hand with a distinct air of hauteur.

"Another of Arabella's famous protégés," Sir Brian inquired as he surveyed Ned with rueful sympathy. "I heard Crockford speaking of your exploits at the club last evening. It seems you and young Cresswell were involved in some extremely delicate negotiations. You must have had the upper hand in the affair, as I find it extremely difficult to picture old Rough-and-Tumble Cresswell in the role of peacemaker.

I should be most interested in hearing the details," he invited, leading Ned a little apart from the others as he spoke.

Pleasantly surprised to find Arabella intimate with a man of obvious sense and interests beyond the petty concerns of the *ton*, Ned allowed himself to be drawn into conversation on the complexities of dealing with an Indian rajah.

Absorbed in their discussion, the two men rode on, oblivious to the person who had introduced them. Arabella, who had completely failed in her object of becoming the focus of attention of two gentlemen instead of one and thus engendering a spirit of rivalry between them, leaned back in the carriage. A distinct pout obscured her dimples and wrinkled her brow in a most unattractive manner. However, she had not been a toast of London for nothing, and squaring her shoulders, she urged the coachman to catch up to the two men. With a tinkling laugh she turned to her mother, saying, "I am certain you are in the right of it, Mama. Times out of mind you have warned me that once men begin talking about affairs, they become deaf and dumb to the world around them. Such a glorious day should not be wasted in a discussion of the tedious machinations of some foreign potentate. Ned, here is all of England waiting to welcome you home and you can talk of nothing but the dirt, dust, and heat you left behind. And you, Sir Brian, are dreadfully provoking to force him to recall all those uncomfortable things when there are ever so many other more cheerful topics to discuss," Arabella scolded the two men archly as she tapped Ned's hand playfully with the ivory point of her parasol.

Once she had succeeded in attracting their attention, she unfurled this concoction so as to soften the unforgiving glare of the sun and cast a flattering pink light on her delicate features. Satisfied that she was presenting as delightful a picture as possible, she prattled on, dividing her dimpled smiles and silvery laugh equally between the two men, contriving in her own inimitable way to make each one feel that he alone was the focus of her attention. Juggling admiring swains was an art to which Arabella had devoted a great deal of effort until she was able to bring it off perfectly just as she was doing now. Even her mother, who had spent years studying the evolution of such a technique, found herself constantly amazed at her daughter's ability to keep two men completely engrossed.

By this time the little party had reached the edge of the park and Sir Brian, who was being eagerly hailed by some young bucks mounted on prime bits of blood, took his leave after securing a waltz with Arabella at the Countess of Wakefield's upcoming ball.

"I am so delighted you were able to meet him, Ned. If he takes a liking to you, you are certain to move in the first circles of fashion," Arabella remarked eagerly as she placed a gloved hand on Ned's arm and rewarded him with her most enchanting smile.

He raised one dark brow, demanding in an amused tone, "And am I destined to move in the first circles of fashion? I am not at all sure that I wish to."

A delicious little frown appeared as she pouted at him. "Ned, you are quite dreadful. Of *course* you wish to. Don't you want everyone to see how important you have become? And surely you would want your childhood companions to be proud of you."

Ned laughed. "When you put it so charmingly, how can anyone resist you?"

Sure of herself now, the beauty spoke earnestly, "Ned, you know you are destined to do great things. I feel certain of it. But you must be seen as intimate with those who are the leaders of the *ton* in order to succeed. I could see that Sir Brian was most taken with you and he has the most exacting standards."

Ned smiled down at her. "He must have if he chooses you as an object of his attention."

"Your travels have taught you to be a dreadful flatterer," protested Arabella happily as she blushed and did her best to look disconcerted.

She succeeded admirably. Ned had encountered coquettes

of every description on his travels and recognized a mistress of the art of flirtation. He was under no illusions as to Arabella's character, but he was forced to admit to himself that despite what must have been a great deal of practice, she still managed to look adorable. He grinned appreciatively, reined in his horse, dismounted, and tossed the reins to an eager young lad who was loitering near Madame Celestine's establishment for just such a purpose. He held out his hand to help her alight from the carriage, remarking as he did so, "I can see you are determined to advance my career. Very well, then, I resign myself into those dainty, but capable hands." He then kissed each one of them before turning to assist her mother.

Arabella was somewhat taken aback. She had always been confident of her ability to twist Ned Mainwaring around her thumb and had been delighted to discover that her former devoted admirer had acquired a delicious air of sophistication on his travels. But she had not expected him to be so accomplished in the art of dalliance. There was a disturbing glint in those dark blue eyes that made her less than certain of her ability to rule him, and the suspicion entered her mind, ever so briefly, that perhaps the tables had been turned.

CHAPTER 10

The understanding that had sprung up between Cassie and Horace deepened in the following weeks and they were seen a great deal in each other's company, attending the more intellectual social events the metropolis had to offer. The visit to Mr. Glover's exhibition was a great success. Cassie would have enjoyed the exhibit anyway, as she preferred landscapes to portraits and thought the *Ruins of Adrian's Villa, in the Campgna, Italy* particularly fine, but it added to her pleasure immensely to be able to discuss it with Horace. He had spent some time in Italy on his Grand Tour and was able to add information and an expanded critical view, which increased her knowledge, and therefore her appreciation, of the artist's skill. In fact, Cassie had been so much taken by this exhibition that Horace, who insisted that these paintings closely resembled the celebrated Mr. Wilson's works, offered to take her to visit Lord Humphrey Wycombe, an old family friend who collected the works of Wilson, Constable, and other landscape painters.

They made an outing of it, including Kitty and Frances in the expedition to their host's country seat, where they enjoyed a wonderful luncheon al fresco and a walk through his notable Italian gardens as well as viewing his truly magnificent collection of paintings.

Cassie was pleased to see Lord Wycombe's obvious enjoyment of Horace's conversation and the serious attention the old man gave to the younger's opinions. Later, strolling around the gardens with her host, she was highly gratified when he confided in her, "Horace is a very good lad. It is the greatest of pities that he receives no encourgement from his family. Why, if I had a son such as he, I should spare no effort or expense to help him pursue his studies. As it is now, he constantly meets with resistance from his parents and they allow him the merest pittance for his scholarly pursuits. If he were to become as enamored at faro or hazard as he is of Homer, he would have the family fortune, considerable as it is, at his disposal. What a waste."

His look of disgust brightened as he patted Cassie's hand, continuing, "Allow me the privilege of an old man who loves Horace more deeply than his own father does and let me say, my dear, that I am thoroughly delighted that he has found as fine and intelligent a companion as you. It does my heart good to see how much happier he is since he has had you as a friend." Noting Cassie's confusion, he added, "That is all I shall ever say on the matter except for one more thing. I knew both of your parents well enough to know they would be infinitely proud of such a bright and charming daughter as you are."

Cassie was too overcome to do much more than stammer, "Thank you." It was so rare that someone outside her family circle recognized and appreciated her talents that she felt a little overwhelmed at his praise.

Horace also squired the ladies from Mainwaring house to the opera several times while Lord Mainwaring was out of Town tending to political concerns. Though she appreciated his escorting her, Lady Frances was a trifle dismayed by his constant attendance. She was delighted that her sister had discovered someone she enjoyed, but Frances, a high stickler where the happiness of her family was concerned, found herself wishing that Horace was not quite so prosy. Cassie had always been one whose high spirits and sense of fun could be counted on to enliven the dullest of surroundings. Now these seem to have disappeared. It was true that Freddie's absence had deprived her of her source of support for her escapades, but Frances had noticed that since the beginning

of her friendship with Horace, Cassie had devoted herself
even more earnestly to intellectual pursuits at the expense
of the lighter side of her nature.

Accustomed to the brilliant political circles in which she
and Lord Mainwaring moved, Lady Frances knew very well
that a powerful intellect did not necessarily preclude a sense
of fun or humor. In point of fact, she would have staunchly
maintained that for all his vaunted scholarly interests, the
Honorable Horace Wilbraham was far less intelligent than
Lady Cassandra Cresswell. At the same time, he seemed to
feel far more certain of his intellectual superiority than she
did.

Yes, Frances concluded, Horace was eminently suitable
as a companion for her sister, but she was concerned lest
Cassie, surrounded as she was by empty-headed tulips of the
ton, give Horace more credit for intelligence than was his
due and come to view him as something more than a
companion. Having caught that young man, blissfully
unaware of anyone's scrutiny, gazing adoringly at Cassie,
Frances realized that he was besotted with her sister and she
felt certain that he would soon be approaching Lord
Mainwaring to ask for her hand. The prospect did not
precisely displease Frances, but by the same token it did not
please her either. Somehow she had hoped that the return
of Ned and Freddie would liven things up, but Freddie was
too busy reestablishing ties with his cronies and Ned seemed
bent on breaking most, if not all, the female hearts in London.
If he could be said to be spending time with anyone, it was
with Arabella Taylor. Often he could be seen riding beside
her carriage in the park, and if her expression were any
indication, his conversation was extraordinarily gratifying
to that young woman.

Cassie had also noted this interesting development of
events, and far from being pleased at her former playmate's
pursuit of the woman he had wooed so long in vain, she felt
rather put out by the affair. As they had entered their box
at the opera she had happened to glance over at the couple
several boxes away from them just as Ned had leaned over

to whisper something that had produced a most coy look and a playful tap on the cheek from Arabella's fan. Cassie had looked quickly away, but not before Frances had caught the expression of disgust on her sister's face. Cassie had remained rather quiet and abstracted the rest of the evening, though normally she would have been completely enthralled by Mozart's music.

It was not too many evenings later, at the Countess of Wakefield's ball, when Cassie, never one to mince words—especially when addressing someone she had known since childhood—articulated this disgust to Ned himself. Frances, also privy to the little scene, would have been as amused as always by watching the sparks fly between these two particularly strong-minded people, except that this time a more serious note had crept into their argument, though to do Cassie justice, it had been Ned who had precipitated the quarrel.

After spending much of the evening with Horace quietly discussing the relative merits of Mr. Gillies's translation of Aristotle, Cassie had been lured into an energetic country dance by her brother, who had begged, "Please, Cass, dance this one with me. Amanda Billingsley's mother keeps looking at me in the most meaningful way. It's not that I don't feel sorry for someone as dish-faced as she is, but must she simper and make eyes at me just because I give her a nod now and then?"

"Surely it was only a friendly smile such as she would direct at anyone she has known for some time," Cassie suggested.

"Perhaps," Freddie replied, though he did not sound the least convinced. "But does she have to look so desperate? It makes a fellow feel dashed uncomfortable, I can tell you."

Here Cassie noticed Ned in conversation with a dashing redhead who looked to be a good deal amused and gratified with their *tête-à-tête*. At any rate, she kept hanging on to his arm in the most intimate way, Cassie reflected huffily.

Not too much later, after Freddie had left her to ask a friend about a matched pair of grays he was eager to acquire, Cassie

looked about for Horace, who had gone off to the card room
to find his mother. As her glance swept the crowded ballroom
it landed again on Ned, this time with Lady Jersey. That
renowned coquette was positively draping herself all over
him and he seemed to be enjoying it hugely.

Thus, she was not in the best of humors when he strode
across the floor to her just as a waltz was struck up. Bending
over her hand, he looked up at her, quirking one dark brow
and asked, "Would you grant a poor supplicant the very great
honor, Cassie?"

Annoyed though she was, Cassie found it impossible to
resist the appeal in his dark blue eyes and, giving him her
hand, allowed herself to be led onto the floor. As they whirled
around the room she found herself wondering again at the
change in her old gawky Ned, who bore not the least
resemblance to the tall powerful man now guiding her skillfully among the maze of couples.

However, it was the same old Ned who broke into her
thoughts some minutes later in his usual direct manner.
"Now, Cassie, what's this I hear about your lending a hand
to the Comte de Vaudron? I should think that you would like
it above all things. And you, with the background Frances
gave you in history, as well as your own knowledge of Greek,
will do the thing right. Why, if some moldly old pedant got
hold of those marbles, he would want to bury them away
so only the most devoted scholars among us would have the
right to view them just as they have done with the zoological
collection at the British Museum. It don't bear thinking of."
Ned paused and regarded his partner thoughtfully. She was
in many ways lovelier than ever, but somehow the spark that
had made her what she was—awake on all suits and ready
for any adventure—seemed to have disappeared. The
thoughtful look on his face vanished as quickly as it had
appeared and he continued in a rallying tone, "And speaking
of pedants, I hear Wilbraham has joined the comte's
entourage. Take care, Cass, lest you cast him in the shade.
He doesn't take too kindly to competition, especially when
it comes from someone with true intellectual attainments."

Cassie did not look to be best pleased at this remark, and she defended her fellow scholar in a decidedly frosty tone. "I consider Horace Wilbraham to be quite the brightest young man of my acquaintance."

Ned snorted, "Freddie and I didn't return a moment too soon if you are forced to make do for companionship with that pompous—"

The calm disdain which Cassie had hitherto displayed dissolved in an instant as she retorted in a furious undertone, "Horace, at least, possesses a mind devoted to serious subjects, for which I admire him. He is concerned with higher things than causing a stir in the ballroom or at the opera. I am thankful to know someone who does not waste his time, as so many do, flitting from one person to the next, squandering his intelligence on idle flirtation and frivolous chatter. If there is a better man around, I am sure—"

"You don't know," Ned finished. His brows snapped together and now, equally furious, he took up the battle. "Have a care, Cassie," he warned, "or you will become as much of a dead bore as he is."

"Well, of all the wickedly unjust things," Cassie gasped. Too angry now for caution, she continued, "I should far rather be a bore than a silly heartless flirt like Arabella Taylor, whose only thought is to amuse herself, whatever the cost. I wish you joy of her."

"Thank you. I am sure I shall receive it from a woman who at least knows how to enjoy herself and entertain others," Ned answered grimly.

By now they were well within earshot of Frances and Kitty and somehow they managed to finish the waltz in hostile silence. With a curt nod to these two ladies, Ned restored his partner to her coterie and then, without a backward glance at Cassie, strode off, leaving them all openmouthed.

Frances was the first to recover. Seeing her sister's distress, she came quickly to her aid, saying, "Horace has come to tell me that as his mother is feeling a trifle fatigued he is taking her home." Privately she thought it was less fatigue which motivated Lady Wilbraham than a desire to make her son cater to her every little whim, but at the moment it suited Frances to believe this fiction. "She has the right idea," she continued. "This has become a sad crush and I would just as soon leave now that we have paid our respects to the countess. Besides, Teddy seemed fretful tonight and I am worried that he has caught something from the stableboy he has been spending time with."

Ordinarily, Cassie would have recognized this last farrago of nonsense as a stratagem of the most obvious sort—Lady Frances being a practical mother and never one to be unduly dismayed by the normal misfortunes of childhood—but she was far too upset to think clearly, much less recognize the ruses employed for her protection. With a grateful sigh she acquiesced and allowed herself to return to Grosvenor Square, where she sought the sanctuary of her dressing room as quickly as possible.

CHAPTER 11

Though escape from the crowds in the ballroom afforded her peace and quiet, it meant that Cassie had ample time to reflect on the entire scene that had passed and she spent a sleepless night going over and over again her contretemps with Ned. Try as she might, she could not erase the final image she had of him, his face taut with anger, blue eyes blazing as he accused her of being a bore. I am not in the least a bore, she told herself defiantly. I can discuss a vaster array of subjects than most of my acquaintances and I am truly interested in almost any topic. Well, most topics of a serious nature, she amended, remembering how insipid she found the conversation of Arabella and other damsels like her.

It is *he* who has changed. But irrefutable though her logic might be, she found herself wondering doubtfully if Ned might not be right. Perhaps her devotion to scholarly pursuits was making her rather serious and dull. Thus in the following weeks the two men laboring over metopes from the Parthenon in Hanover Square saw very little of Cassie. Instead, she threw herself into an orgy of activity.

It would have been too much to expect that she frequented every social event that was offered, but in her time off from serious endeavors, she took the opportunity to allay another worry of hers, which was that she had been neglecting Theodore. With this in mind, and remembering her own days in London when Frances had seen Kitty through her come-out, she inveigled Freddie and Nigel into taking her and Teddy to Sadlers Wells, where they spent several delicious hours under the spell of Grimaldi. The famous clown was a good deal older than he had been when Freddie and Cassie had last seen him perform, but his antics were as amusing as ever, and Teddy was enchanted.

Watching him as he sat enthralled, Cassie realized that it had been some time since she had done anything for the sheer pleasure of it. True, she loved the work she was doing with the comte. It was intriguing, challenging, and rewarding, but there was always a purpose behind it. Reflecting further, she became more conscious of the fact that everything she did in her life had some well-conceived reason behind it. Even the more frivolous activities of her come-out were for a purpose and became, therefore, duties which she felt it incumbent upon herself to fulfill. Thus she had found herself at balls and routs conscientiously asking herself if she had taken adequate advantage of each event to expand and enlarge her acquaintance, never giving a thought to enjoying herself. In fact she had, on the basis of her limited experience with the assemblies in Hampshir, journeyed to London with the expectation that the social events of the Season would be larger but equally mindless versions of these country gatherings. With this preconception she had not even stopped to consider the possibility that they might be entertaining or amusing, and thus they had not afforded her much amusement or entertainment. Nor had she, bearing Ned's criticism in mind, afforded much amusement or entertainment to those she encountered there, she reflected.

As always, Ned Mainwaring, with his keen perception and his ability to get straight to the heart of the matter, had started her thinking, and Cassie was far too fair-minded to let her anger or her disapproval of his behavior keep her from appreciating his insight. The very thought of losing Ned as a friend, a distinct possibility given the heated nature of their discussion at the Countess of Wakefield's, made her vow to scrutinize her own behavior and work to make amends, if possible.

Much the same thoughts that occupied Cassie were preying on Ned as well. He had returned home seething with rage at the condescending tone with which Cassie had criticized a childhood playmate who could be accused of doing nothing worse than the rest of the *beau monde*—dressing, flirting, chatting, and generally enjoying herself. A bottle of port later, some of the rage had subsided and the chief impression that remained, hazy though it was by this time, of the unpleasant scene in the ballroom was the hurt look in Cassie's eyes along with the sense that somehow he had let her down. Damn it, I don't owe her an explanation of my behavior, he fumed. And Horace Wilbraham *is* a pedant of the worst sort. But somehow, no matter how he vindicated his conduct, it didn't justify the pain he seemed to have caused an old friend. I shall make it up to her tomorrow, he resolved. It's been years since we went to Astley's. Certainly Horace won't have taken her there, he would not be caught dead frequenting such a place. And besides, Teddy would enjoy it. Feeling a trifle comforted by this decision, he promptly fell into a deep sleep.

It was with this laudable purpose in mind that he presented himself quite early one morning in Grosvenor Square only to find the place in a minor turmoil.

"Good morning, sir," the venerable Higgins greeted Ned with his usual stately demeanor, but Ned retained the distinct impression that he had come from somewhere in a great hurry. This feeling was just establishing itself in his mind when Teddy came tearing around the corner and screeched to an abrupt halt when he caught sight of a visitor in the hall.

Seeing who it was, he relaxed visibly exclaiming, "Oh, famous! You're jutht the person we want. You thee, Papa and Mama are out riding in the park and Freddie ith at Tatterthallth, and thereth jutht Cathie and me and I'm not tall enough." As Ned persisted in looking blank despite this illuminating explanation, Theodore, looking slightly exasperated at the occasional and inopportune obtuseness of adults, summed up the problem in a word. "It'th Ethelred."

At that moment, Wellington and Nelson came racing around the corner in the direction from which Theodore had appeared. Recognizing an old friend and source of aid, Wellington smiled his most gracious smile and plopped himself directly in front of Ned's gleaming Hessians. "Arf, arf," he barked significantly before getting up again and heading back around the corner, pausing to look meaningfully over his shoulder at Ned and Theodore. Considering it beneath him to dash around in such an undignified hurry, Nelson strode off in the same direction with the same significant backward look at them. Recognizing an imperative summons when he saw one, Ned followed the two messengers and Theodore with alacrity.

The reason for all this commotion at his arrival became immediately apparent as he descended to the walled garden behind the breakfast room. There was Cassie, a picture of the fashionable young lady in a morning dress of shaded yellow jaconet muslin with sleeves *en bouffants* perched precariously on top of the wall clutching a distressed Ethelred.

Entirely forgetting the unfortunate nature of their last encounter, she greeted Ned with obvious relief. "Ned, the very one! You have no notion how delighted I am to see you."

An appreciative smile lit up his tanned features as he strode over to the wall, remarking, "On the contrary, Cassie, I have a very fair idea of exactly how glad you are to see me. Oh, do be quiet, I shall get you down." This last, obviously addressed to Ethelred, seemed to reassure both parties. "Here, hand him to me," he directed. Taking the frightened duck in a firm grasp, he smoothed his feathers and managed to calm him down before restoring him to his friends on the ground and turning to assist Cassie.

"Pooh, I am not such a poor creature," she remarked indignantly, ignoring his hand and climbing down the thick vines which must have provided her the means of scaling the wall in the first place. "You see, Lady Telfair's odious pug somehow got into the garden and took great exception to Ethelred, in his own garden, if you can imagine such effontery. I daresay you think it's amusing"—Cassie fired up as Ned's eyes began to dance—"but you wouldn't if you were Ethelred, and it is truly a *nasty* little dog."

"Arf, arf," Wellington agreed wholeheartedly. Nelson declined to comment, but the look of disdain on his face provided ample evidence of his opinion on their neighbor.

"At any rate, neither Nelson nor Wellington was around to protect him, so, taking fright, he flew to the top of the wall, but he's not much of a flier. So he panicked, and began quacking dreadfully. This brought Teddy, Nelson, and Wellington, who routed the pug but could do nothing to rescue Ethelred. They went for James the footman, but it was beneath his dignity to rescue a duck—"

"But not beneath yours, I see," Ned interrupted. "I thought it would not take long before the true Cassandra Cresswell emerged from the proper young lady of the *ton* that I found upon my return." The air of injured dignity which Cassie invariably assumed at being caught in a scrape descended upon her countenance. Ned grinned and proffered one tan hand. "Cry friends, then, Cass," he begged.

Cassie's infectious smile lit her face as she in turn extended a slightly grimy one. "Friends, Ned," she agreed.

This satisfactory resolution to their quarrel was interrupted by Teddy, who insisted on discussing the finer points of Ned's bay with him. "He lookth to be a high-mettled, prime bit of blood," he observed, nodding his head with all the sagacity of a dedicated frequenter of Tattersall's.

Ned's eyes twinkled as he nodded. "Oh he is, I was assured of the purity of his lineage. He's a Thoroughbred from ear to hoof, and though highly strung, there's not an ounce of vice in him," he agreed. Recognizing the light of a fanatic in the boy's eyes, he offered, "Would you like to examine him yourself?"

"Oh, yeth," breathed Teddy, glad to see his belief that Ned must be a right one confirmed. He and Wellington began to head to the stables, where Higgins, seeing that Ned's visit was going to be protracted, had ordered the horse to be taken.

Teddy's headlong rush was stopped midflight by Ned, who suggested that his aunt, who was credited to be no mean judge of horseflesh herself, might like to accompany them. Teddy looked somewhat crestfallen at having the purely masculine nature of the party vitiated. Seeing this, Ned was quick to point out that many people, Nigel Streatham included, considered Cassie to be a far better judge of the finer points of equine quality than her brother. This was a piece of news, indeed, to Teddy, who looked curiously at Cassie for confirmation of this interesting opinion.

"Well, Freddie has been known to be more impressed by the more showy points of a horse than I am and he is sometimes less critical," she acknowledged, loath to disparage her twin.

"Cut line, Cassie," Ned commented. "You know if it weren't for you, he would have bought that gelding from Ponsonby and been taken for a complete flat. You saw immediately that it was spavined."

Cassie grinned at the memory of Freddie bouncing along on the gelding's back after she had suggested that it might be wise to put it through its paces before purchasing it. "You are right, as always, Ned. Freddie was certain he was striking a bargain. He insisted that Ponsonby was at the low-water mark and needed the blunt. He was, too, and it was a shame we weren't able to help him by buying the horse, but the price was too high to pay for that bonesetter."

Teddy looked from one to the other, round-eyed at these revelations concerning an uncle he had always considered to be something of a demigod, at least as far as the sporting world was concerned. Despite his high regard for Cassie's intelligence, he tended, like all boys, to dismiss female opinion, particularly in these matters, as so much chatter, and he was much struck by Ned's obvious regard for her horse sense. At this point they reached the stables and he became totally immersed in examining the horse, talking to it gently as he rubbed its nose and ran a remarkably experienced eye for one so young over it.

Watching Teddy and Brutus, Ned was recalled to the original purpose of his visit. "I say, Cass, remember how much we enjoyed ourselves at Astley's? How would you like it if I escorted you and Teddy there soon?" he inquired.

"Why, what a capital notion, Ned!" Cassie responded enthusiastically. "I am sure Teddy would enjoy it above all things." She smiled shyly and added, "And I should like it a great deal, too."

Looking down at her, Ned saw the little girl he had once known peeping out from behind the severely intellectual facade she seemed to have adopted and he felt a great rush of tenderness toward her. "It's agreed, then. I shall ask Freddie if he would like to join us and it will be just like old times," he said, surprised himself at how much he was looking forward to the outing all of a sudden.

CHAPTER *12*

It was just like old times, Cassie reflected, as several days later the four of them were ensconced at Astley's Amphitheatre, except that Philip Astley was no longer there to perform. As they witnessed one equestrian feat after another she couldn't recall when she'd enjoyed herself more. It was so comfortable to be with Freddie and Ned again, laughing and joking. She felt none of the constraint she sometimes did with Horace when, amused at some ridiculous pretension, she would laugh or make some sarcastic remark only to find him looking at her with a puzzled or faintly disapproving air. In fact, until now, completely at ease and accompanied by her oldest friends, she had been unaware that she had felt this way and she wondered at it. Loyalty to Horace immediately asserted itself and she banished such thoughts, recalling instead the intellectual stimulation she always enjoyed during their discussions.

"Cathie, Cathie," Teddy cried, tugging at her sleeve and recalling her to the scene at hand. "Do look at the way he standth on the horth ath it goeth. How doth he do it?" he wondered.

The small boy was totally entranced, and watching his absorption, Cassie could see that she would soon be hard put to keep him from emulating the famous trick rider Andrew Ducrow. Remembering another boy who had sat enraptured in much the same way many years ago, Cassie tried to save her nephew from disastrous experiences by cautioning him about the difficulties involved in attempting this particular feat. "I once knew someone who gave his head a nasty crack trying to do that very trick and he was in bed for weeks as a result," she warned him.

"You did?" Teddy looked up inquiringly. "Who was it?"

Cassie quirked a teasing eyebrow at Freddie. He grinned guiltily, admitting, "I was certain that it was easily done and tried it one day on Prince when no one was around to stop me. Unfortunately, it was in the stable yard, and when I slipped off his back, I hit my head on the cobbles. Everything went black, and when I awoke with a blinding headache, I found myself in bed, surrounded by anxious and disapproving adults. I was laid up for some time and was most uncomfortable, I assure you. But Cassie felt for me in my plight. She read adventure stories to me by the hour and was a famous nurse. Actually, old Ned here was a Trojan, too, because he retrieved his toy soldiers from Camberly, and when I was a bit better, Nigel was allowed to visit me with his and we had some famous battles. So you see, I was tolerably amused, but it was difficult being confined to a bed during such fine weather."

Seeing the disappointed look on her nephew's face, Cassie hastened to add, "But when we returned to Cresswell where there was nice soft grass, we practiced endlessly. And"—she smiled impishly—"I expect we could do the same thing now when we return to Cresswell."

"We could?" Teddy asked eagerly. "Would you help me?"

"Certainly," she replied. "I was able to ride several times around the paddock standing on Prince's back with no help and without falling. I should think I could do it again. I don't expect, after all, that once one has learned something like that, one forgets it very easily."

Looking over at her animated face as she discussed this with Teddy, Ned reflected how few of the women he had flirted with and encountered in society would have given a second thought to the pleasure of a small boy, much less have entered into it as wholeheartedly as Cassie did. Her unaffected enthusiasm had always attracted him, but now the contrast she presented to the sophisticated women of the *ton* made him cherish her even more. He was glad once again that the unpleasantness of the Countess of Wakefield's ball had not spoiled their friendship. Being an avid horseman himself, Ned was enjoying the evening as much as anybody. The horses were magnificent specimens, their riders no less so. He leaned over to Teddy, who, after this evening and the episode with Brutus, was now his ardent admirer, and explained to him how the equestrians were able to practice and to accomplish what seemed to be impossible feats.

Watching the rapt expression on Teddy's face as he listened to Ned, Cassie recalled an evening when she and Freddie had looked just such a way at Lord Mainwaring as he had introduced them to the marvels of Astley's. It was a rare man who was able to offer such a treat to a child, she reflected, and once again she was struck, as she had been so many times before, with Ned's kind and sensitive nature. The shock of seeing him as a man of the world—handsome, assured, sought after by ladies of all ages and descriptions—had wiped this original conception of him from her mind and she was glad to have it restored.

Thus it was that when he turned to her, a half-quizzical, half-amused expression on his face, and asked, "Enjoying yourself?" she thanked him warmly, her entire face glowing with enthusiasm. Looking down at her, Ned realized, as he had from time to time in the past, that his tomboy playmate was also quite a lovely young woman. And later, driving home, as Cassie continued to tease Freddie with his past adventures, Ned decided that he could not recall when he had enjoyed an evening more.

"What a bouncer, Freddie! You most certainly did *not* succeed in riding the entire way 'round the paddock at Cresswell the first time we tried standing on Prince's back," Cassie protested, laughing at her twin's extravagant claims that after his accident he had immediately mastered the art. She turned to appeal to Ned. "Don't you recall that you tore your second-best breeches when you fell off and that I didn't fall nearly as many times as Freddie?"

Ned, however, was not one to be completely won by feminine appeals. "Now Cassie, if you don't remember, I do, several pinafores that were all over grass stains," he argued.

She frowned, but remained undaunted as she asserted, "That may be true, but I only *slid* off. Freddie *fell*."

Ned choked, "You never could bear to be anything less than the best where horses were concerned." A darkling look from Cassie made her pause and admit, "Very well. You were in the right of it. Freddie did fall more times than you."

"There! You see, Ned agrees with me," Cassie crowed triumphantly as she turned to her crestfallen twin.

"Well, if that don't beat all," spluttered Freddie. "You defend a friend through thick and thin over all parts of the globe and at the least argument from a woman he betrays you."

Ned laid a palliative hand on his shoulder as he admonished, "Calm down, my boy. Cassie may have fallen fewer times, but you stayed on longer."

Cassie was outraged. "Why you traitor!" she blurted. "You know that's not true!"

By this time Ned was laughing so hard he could argue no longer. He held up a hand as he gasped, "Peace, you two. You'll be the death of me. I always swore you would be, and you will if you don't give over."

Theodore, scrunched into a corner of the carriage, was enjoying himself hugely. He had never seen adults scrapping like this before. Why, they were no different from him and Jem, Cresswell's stableboy, when they got into an argument. This had truly been a most instructional evening!

The night's experiences proved to be illuminating to more than one of the party's members, though their particular enlightenment dawned on Ned and Cassie later than it had on Teddy.

Ned had ample opportunity to reflect on Cassie's original, open, and friendly nature as he escorted Arabella to Lady Allsop's the next evening. As always, she was a vision of

loveliness. When he came to collect her and her mother, the
sight of her quite took his breath away. In a dress of
aerophane crepe over a white satin slip the silver Vandyke
trimming on her short sleeves matching the border of the
skirt also edged in silver, and pearls threaded through her
hair as well as at her throat, she looked like an angel as she
descended the staircase. Her smile as she took Ned's arm
was devastating, and the melting look that accompanied her
seductively murmured, "Oh Ned, you *do* look dashing,"
would have captivated a far less susceptible man than Ned
Mainwaring, who, despite his treatment at her hands and a
series of torrid *affaires de coeur* in the capital cities of
Europe, was predisposed to admire his former love.

However, as the evening advanced, it began to be borne
in on him that Arabella had allowed him to escort her as much
for who he was—the latest sensation in a Season that already
promised to be sadly flat—as for the pleasure she might be
expected to derive from his company. It was true that she
stood up with him for more than one dance and that she had
laughingly accorded him, from among all the eager admirers
clamoring for it, her hand in the waltz. But as he whirled
her around the floor he was aware that as much as she gazed
meaningfully into his eyes, she was constantly glancing
around the room to see just how many people were aware
of how very devoted the wealthy and extremely eligible Ned
Mainwaring was to the lovely Arabella Taylor.

Just as this slightly cynical thought entered his head she
looked up, cheeks flushed, dark eyes alight with happiness,
a bewitching smile beginning at the corners of her mouth,
and sighed. "Ned, you waltz divinely. Why, not even Sir
Brian Brandon dances as well as you and he is acknowledged
to be one of the best."

Ned, who had not the slightest wish to cut a dash either
on the dance floor or in society, did not know whether to
be flattered or concerned at being favorably compared to so
notable a Corinthian. His dark blue eyes twinkling with
amusement, he raised one mobile black brow remarking

sardonically, "I am certainly now set for life, for surely no one could aspire to greater heights of glory than that."

Arabella nodded. "Oh no, certainly not," she agreed seriously. "For he is top of the trees, you know," she assured him.

Ned's amusement faded as he realized that she was entirely in earnest. "I collect this means you now consider me to be an eligible *parti*," he commented ironically.

His acid tone was completely lost on Arabella, who looked up in astonishment. "But of course!" she exclaimed in some surprise that he should even be in doubt of such a thing.

Finding himself at a loss, he soon escaped to go in search of refreshments, leaving her in the eager hands of young Ponsonby, who was quite desperate to lead her in the quadrille. As he crossed the ballroom he found himself wishing that Cassie were there. He could just picture the way her big blue eyes would brim with amusement when he told her that he'd been adjudged a worthy member of the Corinthian set by no less a social devotee than Arabella. He could even hear the laughter gurgle in her throat as she protested, "Oh Ned, not even *Arabella* could be such a gudgeon!"

"And what has put such a cynical expression on the face of one so young and debonair?" a voice at his elbow inquired. Ned looked down into the dancing eyes of Lady Jersey. Here, at least, was someone witty enough to see the amusing side.

His teeth gleaming in his tan face, he replied, "I have just been informed that I can now consider myself a Corinthian."

Lady Jersey's eyes wandered to the other side of the room, where a besotted Ponsonby was gazing adoringly at Arabella. "But most assuredly, *mon brave*," she murmured wickedly. "Surely you don't think the fair Arabella would allow herself to be led in a waltz by anyone less than a nonpareil?" she inquired.

It was truly turning out to be an evening of revelations. Ned had never before viewed himself in this light, but he could tell from the alacrity with which his invitations to dance were accepted that he was apparently the last person in this ballroom to realize that he was an extremely desirable partner.

Arabella, who was keeping as eagle an eye on Ned's conquests as much as she was counting her own, was flushed with pride. So pleased was she at his success and the glory his attentions reflected on her that she allowed herself to squeeze his hand as he helped her into the carriage. "I told you that Sir Brian would have to look to his laurels with you around," she cooed delightedly.

Meanwhile, Cassie was undergoing an equally revelatory experience that evening at the theater. Horace, having heard her express a wish to see Kean's *Richard III,* had escorted her and Frances to Drury Lane. At first, Cassie had thought the famous actor to be somewhat melodramatic, but as the play progressed, she fell more and more under his spell until she became totally immersed in the action of the play, only to be brought rudely back to earth by Horace's whispered comment that he thought Kean a frippery fellow who rolled his eyes too much. Forgetting her first reaction to the actor, Cassie protested, "How can you say so? I think it is a most sensitive interpretation."

"My dear Cassandra," Horace began in a tone that to Cassie sounded almost patronizing, "the entire performance is sensational in the extreme. Shakespeare's language is overblown enough as it is, and this fellow exploits it for all he is worth. I am astonished that you can like it. For my part, I find it to be quite vulgar."

Cassie's mouth, which had dropped open in astonishment, shut with a snap as she turned her attention to the stage, totally ignoring Horace, who had been about to launch into a dissertation on the superiority of Greek tragedy. He subsided into hurt and angry silence. Frances, an interested bystander to the scene, was not sorry that he had revealed this side of his nature to Cassie. It would do her good to see just how stubborn and opinionated Horace Wilbraham could be. For her part, Cassie had never felt so out of charity with her companion. She was quite glad when Horace finally deposited the ladies at Grosvenor Square and she was free to discuss the performance with a more open-minded and stimulating conversationalist. She and Frances agreed that while Kean did tend toward the histrionic, his sensitive rendition of the hunchback had made them view the play and the characters in a slightly different light than they had before.

CHAPTER *13*

The next day when Cassie arrived at the comte's, her acknowledgment of Horace's greeting was rather frosty, but she was almost immediately mollified by his next words. "Cassandra, I had not the least intention of offending you last evening," he apologized. "I realize that I am inclined to be carried away by my enthusiams. You must forgive me if I react so strongly, but drama, and tragedy in particular, is one of my ruling passions and I find I cannot be lukewarm about it."

Cassie smiled as she replied, "Think nothing of it. I certainly shall not."

He heaved an obvious sigh of relief before turning back to the marbles he had been examining. Cassie was fast becoming an obsession with him. He had never been able to converse with a woman who comprehended what he was saying and could therefore truly appreciate him. That someone as lovely as Cassie paid attention to him and understood him was quite wonderful. Lately, he had begun to contemplate asking her to marry him. The more he thought about it, the idea of spending his life with this exquisite creature who would cherish his work and admire him made him quite drunk with happiness. Her coldness the previous evening had threatened this beatific vision and struck terror into his heart. Without understanding the cause of it, he was determined to overcome her displeasure. Her gracious acceptance of his apology convinced him once more that he was truly blessed in his friendship with her and he was more determined than ever to make her his.

Cassie, moving over to the materials she had been working on, was contemplating a less rosy picture of the future than was her companion, for it had occurred to her that while he had apologized for upsetting her, Horace did not in the least comprehend what he had said to do so. It was not that she was made uncomfortable because he did not completely share her opinions. After all, she and Ned had disagreed times out of mind and had spent many happy hours arguing with each other over an entire range of subjects. What bothered her was Horace's utter lack of appreciation for the myriad and conflicting emotions which Kean's performance, overdone through it may have been, revealed, as well as his total obliviousness to the sympathetic emotional response the actor managed to elicit from the audience. That he could be so caught up in the mechanics of the play's presentation as to ignore completely and absolutely its fundamental drama revealed a rather unsympathetic side to his character of which she had previously been unaware. This, coupled with his obstinate refusal to appreciate any of the good points at all in the performance simply because he had one criticism of it made him seem slightly narrow-minded.

To top it off, he had entirely misunderstood the cause of her displeasure. That he should assume that she would naturally be in complete agreement with any opinion of his and ascribe her distress merely to the fact that he expressed his opinions with such ardor thoroughly annoyed her. The more she thought about it, the more Cassie was angered by his blatant disregard for her individual critical faculties and taste. She remained in a most pensive mood for the rest of the day despite the fact that she was working on a truly exquisite section of frieze.

Over in his corner of the library, the comte, observing the angry set of Cassie's jaw, nodded sagely and thought to himself, She has spirit, that one. It will take someone with a stronger and more adventurous nature than Horace Wilbraham's to appreciate someone such as she. He is a good lad, but something of a dull dog and his mind is no match for hers. He certainly lacks the quick wit and charming conversation. We must see what we can do to find Cassie an intellectual companion worthy of her.

Much the same thoughts were going through Lady Kitty Willoughby's mind as she observed her brother and Arabella Taylor. Arabella had called at the Willoughbys on the slimmest of pretexts. She and her maid were on their way shopping and she simply *had* to know the name of the shop where Kitty had procured the perfectly ravishing ribbons for the bonnet she had been wearing in the park the other day.

Kitty was nobody's fool and was thus not the least surprised when Ned walked in, obviously dressed for a ride in the park, that a girl who not two minutes before had been determined to unearth the exact duplicate of Lady Willoughby's ribbons now had no thought in her mind beyond a refreshing stroll through Hyde Park.

Glancing coyly up at Ned from under the brim of a charming cottage-shaped straw bonnet, she laid one lavender kid-gloved hand on his arm, begging, "Do join your sister and me in the park. I had been planning to make some small purchases in Bond Street, but it is far too fine a day to waste. I should infinitely prefer taking the air and sharing some elegant conversation with some charming companions."

Kitty, far too well bred to reveal the least dismay at this abrupt change in plan, yielded to superior strategy as gracefully as she could, adding her voice to Arabella's. "That is a delightful idea. I shall just go and fetch my bonnet." And that, she fumed as she quitted the drawing room, leaves that scheming little hussy with Ned all to herself. No doubt she is counting on having the good quarter of an hour alone with him that it would take her to primp herself to perfection. Well, she shan't have it! Snatching a bonnet with more haste than usual, Kitty slapped it on her head without even consulting the mirror. No doubt I shall look the perfect quiz, she thought, but I won't leave poor Ned in her clutches a minute longer than necessary.

"Poor Ned," in fact, was tolerably amused by the entire situation. Knowing that Arabella bore no great friendship for his sister, who, as a dashing young matron, was apt to offer more competition than Arabella liked to encounter, he had surmised as he entered the drawing room that Kitty had been the victim of some stratagem.

It only remained to establish the exact nature of the vague excuse Arabella had invented to explain her unexpected visit. Ned had been too aware of the possessive light in Arabella's eyes as they had lighted on him to doubt that he was her real quarry. Watching her take in the significance of his attire and change her plans accordingly had been a very real entertainment. Consequently, he leaned his broad shoulders against the mantel, awaiting developments.

Arabella looked admiringly at these same shoulders, noticed that they were shaking suspiciously. Tilting her head at him coquettishly, she inquired, "Are you laughing at me?"

Unable to contain himself, Ned burst into laughter. "You enchanting little witch! Confess, you had not the least notion of going for a walk when you came here."

An uncertain look flitted across her features before she gurgled merrily and admitted, "Of course not, you silly creature. But you men are so elusive, we poor women are forced to adopt the feeblest of excuses in order to win your escort."

He heaved himself from the mantel and strode over to capture one small hand. Raising it gracefully to his lips, he murmured, "I should be loath to put you to such trouble and I doubt very much that so beautiful a creature as you is at all familiar with the shifts mere ordinary women are put to."

His tone was earnest, but Arabella saw the quizzical gleam in his blue eyes. "You are a dreadful creature to tease me so," she said, pouting.

He smiled at her. "And you know your pout is as enchanting as your smile, so I refuse to feel the least compunction at causing it to appear. But come, I hear my sister on the stairs."

As they sauntered along in the sunshine, Arabella chattering happily of this musicale and that ridotto, of the shocking quiz of a turban that Lady Ullapool wore to the opera and the truly ravishing riding habit Amanda St. Clair had ordered, Kitty saw the boredom begin to creep into Ned's eyes. She noted the mechanical responses that appeared to satisfy Arabella while her escort appraised the points of Lord Alvanley's hack, cast an experienced eye over the showy chestnuts drawing the barouche of a noted barque of frailty, and generally kept his mind occupied while leaving Arabella under the impression that he was attending solely to her.

This won't do, Kitty told herself. No matter how besotted he had been in the past, or how attracted he is now, he would be bored with her within a week and ready to strangle her within a fortnight. Confronted with a situation similar to that of the comte's, she arrived at the same conclusion—such intelligence and wit should not be condemned to pass the rest of its existence with mediocrity and self-centeredness as its companion.

CHAPTER 14

While some of their nearest and dearest were cudgeling their brains for ways to help Cassie and Ned recognize and free themselves from entanglements that were unlikely to prove enriching to either one, the two principals were continuing to pursue these same relationships with varying degrees of satisfaction.

A dreadfully boring evening at Lady Heatherstone's rout, where there was such a dearth of conversation between sets that Cassie would have been grateful for a partner who even wanted to discuss something as mundane as his shirt points or the weather, had left Cassie wondering if she had not perhaps been too critical of Horace.

Meanwhile, that young man, desperate at the coolness with which Cassie had been treating him lately, was inspired to more active and more sensitive behavior than was customary for his rather self-centered nature. Driven nearly to distraction at the thought that she might be losing her interest in him, he even included Teddy and Wellington in his next invitation, though he normally detested children and pets— lumping them all into the same category as noisy nuisances that were to be avoided at any cost.

However, he knew Cassie's fondness for her young nephew and he resolved to make the truly handsome sacrifice of taking her, Teddy, and any other companions for an outing in the park. That this generous gesture would also confirm the world's opinion that Lady Cassandra Cresswell and Horace Wilbraham were an "item" was an added advantage to the outing that was not lost on Horace, scornful though he might be of society and its predilection for gossip.

So it was that the next sunny day he presented himself at Grovenor Square. "I thought that since it was such fine weather you and Master Theodore might like to take the air with me in the park," he stammered hesitantly in response to the inquiring look Cassie directed at him as Higgins ushered him into the drawing room.

He was instantly rewarded with a brilliant smile. "The very thing!" Cassie exclaimed, jumping up. She had been penning, without much enthusiasm, a letter to Aunt Harriet, who, casual though she was about her nearest relatives, did like to hear from time to time how they were rubbing along. After relating everyone's general health, Cassie had been having great difficulty selecting a topic of mutual interest. Her aunt, who possessed unbridled intellectual curiosity in horticultural matters, was totally uninterested in any aspect of classical antiquity, and even less so in the fashionable happenings in London society at the moment. Knowing Aunt Harriet to be at least on speaking terms with the Comte de Vaudron, one of the three males of her acquaintance—the other two being Lord Julian Mainwaring and Ned Mainwaring—that she did not label a complete nodcock, Cassie filled a great deal of the letter describing his household and his current endeavors. She had written herself to a standstill, however, and had been gazing wistfully out the window at the sunlit square when Horace was announced. The prospect of a walk drove all the previous uncharitable thoughts she had harbored toward him from her mind and she accepted his proposal with alacrity.

Horace further endeared himself to her by suggesting that she might like to invite Theodore and any other interested parties to accompany them. At the first mention of an outing Wellington, who had been resting his chin comfortably on Cassie's slippered foot, perked up his ears. When he heard the full extent of the invitation, he bounced happily out of the room to go in search of Theodore.

Cassie smiled gratefully at Horace. "How kind of you to remember Teddy and include him. He amuses himself quite wonderfully here, but I am persuaded that the delights to be found in London pale in comparison to the freedom he has to explore the woods and ponds at Cresswell and Camberly.''

Horace was both charmed and relieved by her appreciation of his scheme and was just about to suggest that young Theodore was exceedingly fortunate in having an aunt so devoted to his welfare when Theodore himself appeared with Wellington at his heels.

''Did you with to thee me, Aunt Cathie,'' he asked, looking Horace over with all the unabashed curiosity of a five-year-old.

Horace, unaccustomed to enduring the candid scrutiny of the very young, fidgeted and looked the other way, only to encounter an equally appraising stare from Wellington's bright shoe-button eyes. The little dog, sensing the stranger's unease, smiled encouragingly, but as this seemed to render the visitor even more nervous, he gave up and looked at Cassie expectantly instead.

''Yes, dear, I did want to see you, though Wellington was beforehand in summoning you. Mr. Wilbraham has very kindly invited us to join him for a walk in the park.''

To Theodore, accustomed as he was to such noted Corinthians as Lord Mainwaring, Ned, and Freddie, the prospect of sauntering sedately through the park with someone he had no hesitation in stigmatizing as a very dull dog, was less than inviting, but he mustered as much enthusiasm as he could and accepted with tolerably good grace. ''Thank you, thir. That ith motht kind of you. May Wellington come, too?''

''Yes, my lad. Of course. Most certainly,'' Horace replied ingratiatingly, well aware that it behooved him in his courtship of Cassie to ensure that Theodore and Wellington were his allies.

Wellington, like Theodore, preferred the more invigorating company of such bucks as Freddie, Nigel Streatham, Ned, or Lord Mainwaring, even Bertie Montgomery, who, despite his not being a sporting man, was enough of a nonpareil to lend an air of fashion to any party, but he was grateful for

the chance to be out of doors. He trotted off happily to collect
Nelson and Ethelred while Cassie went to don her pelisse
and exchange her slippers for half boots and Theodore went
to retrieve his new sailboat, recently purchased by an
indulgent Uncle Freddie.

Horace looked to be a bit taken aback at the size and
composition of the party when they assembled sometime later
in the hall, but seeing Cassie's happy expectant look, he was
more than satisfied. As Cassie's maid Rose accompanied
them, neither he nor Cassie was obliged to pay close attention
to the more motley part of the group and Horace was free
to devote himself to retrieving his position with the object
of his adoration.

He set about to do this immediately, discussing the report
recently published by the trustees of the British Museum in
the *Edinburgh Review* and soliciting her opinion with
becoming eagerness.

Cassie, who had also read the report, was delighted to
comment on it, agreeing wholeheartedly with its author's
belief in the need for more care in the display and
preservation of zoological specimens. Thus she was in a
charitable frame of mind toward her escort by the time they
reached the recently erected statue of Achilles. Here, Cassie
stopped to explain to an openmouthed Theodore that it had
been cast from cannons captured from Napoleon at Toulouse,
Salamanca, Vittoria, and Waterloo and donated "By the
women of England to Arthur, Duke of Wellington." At the
mention of his namesake, Wellington, who had been sniffing
the statue with an entirely different interest, perked up and
regarded it with new respect.

Theodore, who had marched many of his toy soldiers
through some of these same famous battles, walked 'round
and 'round, envisioning the fields of glory that the lump of
metal must have seen. He was brought quickly back to reality
by a loud quack from Ethelred, who had spied the Serpentine
and was making directly for it.

"Your friend seems to prefer aquatic adventure to history.

Shall we follow him? Perhaps I can help you with your boat,"
Horace offered kindly.

He was immediately rewarded with a brilliant smile from
Cassie and a rather subdued "Thank you, thir" from
Theodore. Theodore, having observed Horace precariously
balancing teacups and looking nervously at the prime bits
of blood that happened to come close to him, had little
expectation that he would be of the least use, but he
acquiesced. He and Wellington watched in some amusement
as Horace managed to tangle the string in the riggings and
to capsize the boat as he set it in the water, but they held
their tongues until he had quite finished and turned to address
Cassie.

"Now we can really sail it and have some fun," Theodore
confided to the little terrier.

"Arf. Arf," Wellington barked as he ran precariously
along the edge, watching as the little craft caught the wind
and gained speed.

"Quack. Quack," Ethelred proudly escorted the sailboat
around the pond.

All was going famously until an unexpected and violent
puff of wind tore at the sails, causing the little craft to shoot
forward so rapidly that the string attaching it to Theodore
broke and it sailed proudly into the middle of the Serpentine.
"Oh, no!" Theodore wailed. "Cathie, Cathie, my boat.
What shall we do?"

"Never mind, love," Cassie comforted him. "We shall
look for a gardener and see if he can help us."

"You mustn't sail in such heavy weather, young Master
Theodore," Horace commented with ponderous humor.

Meanwhile, Wellington was surveying the scene,
disgustedly thinking to himself that if it were left to his
landlubbing companions, they would never retrieve the boat.
Without a moment's hesitation the little dog hurled himself
into the pond with a terrific splash.

"Quack. Quack." Ethelred steamed up, intrigued by all
the commotion and enchanted to be able to share quite the

most delightful thing he'd seen in London with his best
friend.

In no time at all, Wellington had paddled out to the craft,
which was now becalmed in the very center of the Serpentine.
Seizing the frayed end of the string in his strong terrier jaws,
he paddled back to what was now a crowd of spectators
surrounding Cassie and Horace on the bank. Always one to
appreciate an audience, the little terrier found himself in
somewhat of a dilemma as he found it impossible to smile
winningly at the onlookers and keep the string between his
teeth. He settled instead for adopting a valiant expression
as he towed the boat to shore, Ethelred behind him, quacking
encouragement all the way.

His efforts were rewarded by Teddy, who clapped gleefully
before grabbing the string and praising him. "I knew you
could do it, Wellington. You're smarter than all the dogs
at Astley's Amphitheater put together."

Wellington smiled modestly, but when a fashionably clad
young buck exclaimed to his friend, "Gad, did you see that?
What spirit. Damme, that dog's a regular Trojan!" he was
ready to burst with pride. With a mighty shove, he clambered
up the wall and onto the bank, where he was greeted
enthusiastically.

"Quack! Quack!" Ethelred cheered, beaming praise from
his bright little eyes.

"Well done, Wellington!" Cassie congratulated him as
she sought a dry spot on his head to pat. The little dog
was so drenched that it was rather difficult to locate one,
and unfortunately for her, he decided at that moment to shake
himself dry. Spraying muddy water in all directions, he
thoroughly spattered Cassie's gray kerseymere pelisse. As
she was trying to wipe the spots off with her pocket handkerchief, Ethelred hopped out and waddled over to her,
shaking out his feathers and indicating in no uncertain terms
that he was tired and wanted to be picked up. Never one to
refuse a friend, Cassie stooped over and lifted him in her
arms.

At this moment, an amused voice intruded on the scene.

"I should have known when I heard the commotion and saw a crowd gathered that somehow Cassie would be at the bottom of it," remarked Ned, sauntering up with Arabella on his arm.

Cassie had been conscious, even as she had donned it that morning, that though the gray pelisse with ruby trim was infinitely becoming, it was definitely outmoded. Now, seeing Arabella's exquisite silk pelisse in the latest shade of *peau de papillon* with the delicate ruff and sleeves *à l'Espagnole* which emphasized her dainty beauty, Cassie felt doubly aware of her dowdy appearance.

Her humiliation was complete when Arabella fluted, "Oh, Cassie, how perfectly dreadful! You're soaked and your pelisse is all over mud. I wonder that you bear it so calmly." Arabella laid a hand on her arm with a meltingly sympathetic look which, Cassie thought to herself, was all for Ned's benefit. She doesn't care a rap how I look, only that she looks a great deal better. In spite of this salutary little speech to herself, Cassie could not help feeling like a scrub of a schoolgirl, thus confronted by her elegant friends.

Help came from an unexpected quarter. "Cassandra always looks beautiful," Horace defended her. "She has an elegance of mind and spirit that render her beautiful no matter how she is clad."

"Why, thank you, Horace," Cassie exclaimed in surprise, her smile appearing like the sun after a shower.

Arabella's jaw shut with a snap, making her mouth an unbecomingly thin line in her face. She was not accustomed to hearing others than herself praised with such gallantry and it did not please her in the least.

But Theodore spoke staunchly in defense of his aunt. "Cathie ith the most beautiful lady I know, and what's more, she'th a great gun, too."

"Arf! Arf!" Wellington joined in, not one to be outdone by a couple of humans when the reputation of his mistress was at stake.

"Well done, all of you," drawled Ned, highly amused at the spirited defense accorded his playmate.

Arabella, mightily put out by the turn events were taking, interrupted sweetly, "Why yes. With such good friends as these, one doesn't need to be fashionable or win the approval of the *ton*. And speaking of the *ton*, I am certain I see Sir Brian waving to us. We should leave Cassie to go home and change into some dry clothes." Laying a possessive hand on Ned's arm, she led him off toward the spot where Sir Brian, astride a magnificent gray, was conversing with Lady Jersey and her companions in an elegant barouche.

The schoolroom party wended their way home, where no one was the least surprised at their dishevelment, Higgins having welcomed Cassie and Freddie over the years in far grubbier attire than anyone was in now. Without blinking an eye, the butler instructed them, "You go on into the drawing room. I shall have a fire lit there and tea brought in to you directly." Cheered at the prospect, the entire party hurried upstairs.

In no time at all, tea and cakes were brought in and Frances, who had appeared from an hour spent with the dressmaker, was regaled with tales of Wellington's quick thinking and heroic action. The little dog sat blissfully munching a cake surreptitiously slipped to him by Theodore, and allowed himself to be led to the best spot in front of the fire and generally fussed over.

"We saw Ned and Arabella, too," Theodore volunteered, "and I mutht thay, I don't think she wath very nice to Cathie. She didn't say anything particularly nathty, but they had mean eyeth."

Here, Horace deemed it prudent to interrupt. "You're looking much more the thing, Cassandra. I confess to some relief at that. I had meant to give you an outing that would afford you some relaxation, but instead it became far more taxing than the writing you were engaged in when I appeared."

The darkling look that had appeared on Cassie's face at the mention of Ned and Araballa vanished and she smiled warmly. "Oh no, Horace, I had a lovely time," she contradicted him. Then, lowering her voice confidentially, she admitted, "I do so enjoy a bit of adventure, you know."

Privately, Horace thought that someone as elegant as Lady Cassandra Cresswell should avoid adventure at all costs, but unwilling to disrupt their reestablished harmony, he contented himself with remarking simply, "I'm glad."

"Thank you so much for thinking of it and including all of us, especially when we proved to be more of a charge than you anticipated." Laying a hand on his arm, Cassie smiled gratefully at him.

She looked so charming and Horace had felt such a thrill of pride at her gratitude when he had championed her in the face of Arabella's comments that he resolved to speak to Lord Mainwaring at the soonest possible moment. He then took his leave, but not before securing the first waltz at the upcoming ball in Cassie's honor.

Horace sauntered home, will satisfied with the day's events, picturing himself the center of attention at intellectual soirees with a beautiful vivacious wife on his arm. At first he had been so taken with Cassie that he had not thought beyond his attraction, but later, as he had observed her at various social gatherings, it had been borne in on him that having such a woman as his wife would do a great deal to further his advancement in the scholarly community. Having realized that, he frequently congratulated himself on having had the forethought to be attracted to the daughter of such noted classicists as Lord and Lady Cresswell.

CHAPTER 15

Cassie was not the only one to see her companion through slightly different eyes. Ned, reflecting on his latest experience, however, was coming to view his in a less propitious light. Beginning with his first youthful adoration of Arabella, he had suffered disillusionment. But the several intervening years that he had not seen her had dimmed the first sharp pangs of disappointment and he had come to see her as Cassie had first characterized her—a social creature who craved gaiety. Picturing Arabella in that light, he had taken some of the blame for his dismissal upon himself, realizing that a raw, reserved, and serious youth such as he had been could hardly have appealed to someone who aspired to the pinnacles of social success. As he had moved from one princely court to another in India, Ned had acquired diplomatic skills and social polish. This, and the fact that as a single, attractive male in a foreign land he was much sought after as a companion by the ladies connected with the British enclave, had given him a great deal of experience in the art of dalliance and increased his self-confidence enormously.

He had gradaully lost the natural shyness and reserve which had obscured a keen wit and charming conversation and discovered that he was someone who could entertain and be entertained by society. Added experience in the capitals of Europe, where his facility with languages and his sensitive nature recommended him to some of Europe's most beguiling coquettes, had turned him into a man who was admired by women of taste everywhere. By the time he returned to

London, Ned was so much the master of any social situation that he had entirely forgotten his pettish resolve to prove himself to Arabella Taylor.

The ease with which he had captured her interest had amused him. Never one to rate himself very high, he was under no illusions that it was his character or intellect that attracted her. Full well Ned realized that he was one of the Season's sensations and that it was in this role that he commanded Arabella's attention. He had so far recovered from his infatuation with her that he could be amused by her transparent attempts to win him as her cicisbeo, being well aware that as soon as another, more fashionable conquest presented itself, he would lose much of his attraction for her. There was not the slightest doubt that Arabella was a very beautiful, very skilled young woman who could be counted on to charm any escort and to make him feel as though he were the very center of her existence. So, Ned had acquiesced in all her various schemes and, though fully cognizant of her machinations, had allowed himself to be taken in by all her little ploys, viewing them as diverting but harmless manifestations of her devotion to fashion. It frequently amused him to see how important the opinion of the *ton* was to her, and though he considered this slavish worship of the tenets of the beau monde to be a weakness in her, it was, nevertheless, a weakness which rendered her charming.

All this had changed, however, when he witnessed her encounter with Cassie in the park. What had been a charming, if frivolous, propensity for following fashion's lead suddenly appeared a selfish desire to be the sole focus of attention whatever the cost. The self-centeredness that had heretofore seemed amusingly childlike now became unattractive at best, not to mention unkind.

Disgusted at himself as well as Arabella, Ned began to eschew social gatherings, concentrating instead on furthering his political aspirations. Having experienced firsthand in India the way England's mercantile interests influenced her foreign policy and military affairs, he had become quite concerned that these far-flung mercantile interests be given the proper attention and direction by the government at home. The advent of Canning and Huskisson in the government, men who were scrutinizing colonial policy and reappraising the Navigation Acts, encouraged him to believe that there were people in power who shared his interests.

Convinced that he was too young and too reserved to be successful in Parliament, Ned concentrated on attaching himself to the proper people. He was decidedly fortunate to have Lord Julian Mainwaring as an uncle, for not only did the marquess move in the correct political circles and have the ears of the most influential men, he was able to offer a fair assessment of Ned's character and capabilities to these political allies.

Thus Ned became a more frequent visitor in Grosvenor Square and at Brooks's, where Lord Mainwaring had been kind enough to sponsor him. There, he found, thanks to his connection with Lord Mainwaring, that some of the government's leading lights were increasingly happy to include him in their discussions. Even Lord Charlton, a man whose enormous power was usually hidden from the view of the uninitiated, favored him with his opinions one day after a large repast.

Strolling over to the table where Ned was regaling some of the younger men with colorful descriptions of his more lurid exploits, Lord Charlton launched without ceremony into a political discussion. "Fenton tells me that you're in favor of the relaxation of the Navigation Acts," he charged.

Ned nodded a cautious assent.

"Are you daft, lad? With Spain allowing the world to trade with her colonies and the opening of Brazilian ports we need to protect ourselves against competition," he insisted.

"That is true, sir, but keeping the Navigation Acts as they are won't accomplish that. Portugal, Prussia, and the Netherlands are benefiting from trade with Brazil, San Domingo, and the others, but in order to protect themselves, they are raising their dues against British vessels. This will not only injure us, but worse, it hinders our colonial trade," Ned defended himself.

"You may have a point there, my boy. Fenton warned me that you were almost as extreme as Bentham on the subject of the Colonies," Lord Charlton remarked, wagging an admonitory finger at him.

Ned laughed, "Never that, sir. But I do believe that we must rid ourselves of the notion that the acts exist purely for the profit of the mother country. We ought to recognize that what is in the Colonies' best interests will ultimately be in our own best interests and act accordingly."

"Good lad," Lord Charlton approved. "I was merely teasing you, though. Bentham is a fine man with high ideals, but he sometimes becomes so involved in what should be that he completely loses sight of what is."

Ned nodded. "We need high-minded men with vision to keep us headed in the right direction, but we also need others with a more pragmatic bent to ensure that these reforms are carried out."

"I agree. I agree. It's all very well to carry on about the need for reform in government, but most of those who advocate it so strongly haven't the least notion how to go about accomplishing it. We need men like you who are intelligent enough to grasp the theories, and the principles of these improvements, but whose experience has trained them to succeed in getting such changes carried out. From what I hear, you and young Freddie Cresswell were able to make a goodly number of changes in India without setting up anyone's back and causing resistance. We need young men like you. I must make sure to introduce you to Canning one day. He's a busy man, but not so busy that he doesn't realize he needs supporters—especially bright young men who are too few and far between these days for my liking. Everyone is too caught up in cutting a dash for himself in society to worry about politics or the state of affairs here and in the Colonies. Now that Boney's no longer a threat, they seem to have forgotten that such things as governments and armies exist, much less realize that they need people to run them. But I won't run on. You must come and see me. I shall see what I can do to bring you to Canning's attention."

"Thank you ever so much, sir." Ned was visibly gratified at this unexpected vote of confidence and support. In fact, he was so elated at the prospect of moving in such exalted political circles that he quitted Brooks's immediately after Lord Charlton and strode over to Grosvenor Square to share the news of this propitious encounter.

He would have preferred to share it with Cassie, who had been privy to all his political aspirations through their correspondence, but since the episode in the park, she appeared to have been avoiding him. And when she did encounter him, she was noticeably cool in her manner. In all likelihood, Ned reflected disgustedly, she would be off somewhere with that tiresome fellow, Horace Wilbraham. Being entirely correct in his assumptions, he was forced to content himself with relating it all to Freddie, who, though he listened with interest, was not as fully conversant with Ned's ideas and dreams as his sister.

Aware of the importance of Lord Charlton, though, he was suitably enthusiastic. "Most impressive, Neddie boy!" he exclaimed, giving Ned a hearty buffet on the shoulder. "In no time at all you'll be moving in such exclusive circles you'll be quite above my touch."

Ned quirked an amused eyebrow at him. "You always were given to exaggeration, Freddie. After all, you and I are interested in accomplishing the same things, and you have your own ideas as to what should be done."

Freddie looked skeptical, protesting, "That's as may be, Ned, but I haven't got nearly as much in the old cock loft as you. Why, if you hadn't gone gallivanting off to India with me, you'd be at Oxford now ruining your eyesight, your nose eternally in some musty old tome like the rest of those scholarly fellows." A darkling look settled on his normally sunny features as he continued, "And speaking of scholarly fellows, I wish I knew what Cassie saw in Wilbraham. Fellow haunts the place. I tell you, that disapproving studious look he constantly wears is enough to put anybody off. To tell you the truth, Cassie is becoming almost as bad as he is.

She says she enjoys his company because it improves her mind. Hah! If you ask me, I don't think he's half as bright as you or Cassie. All he is, is a prosy old windbag." He lowered his voice conspiratorially. "I can tell you, Fanny doesn't like the connection above half either. Of course she doesn't *say* anything, but you can see it, nevertheless. Why even Teddy and Wellington don't care for him in the least."

Cathing Ned's amused glance, he defended himself. "Laugh all you want to, but Teddy and Wellington know a right 'un when they see him. If you ask me, there's something dashed smoky about him. Can't put my finger on it at the moment, but there's something queer there, I'll be bound."

Further commentary on the character of the unfortunate and defenseless Horace was interrupted by the headlong entrance of Teddy, closely followed by Wellington, Nelson, and Ethelred. "Uncle Freddie, Uncle Freddie," Teddy burst out. Catching sight of his idol, he came to a screeching halt, causing the companions following close behind him to tumble into a disorganized heap of fur and feathers. "How glad I am to thee you, thir," he exclaimed. "Did you ride Brututh? May I go thee him? I promith you Wellington won't bother him. He'th ever tho good with hortheth," Theodore begged, looking worshipfully up at Ned.

Ned laughed, but he was touched by the blatant admiration he saw in Teddy's eyes. "It's Ned, Teddy. And, yes, I did ride Brutus and of course you may go see him. I expect he would enjoy it as I have been a rather dull companion to him lately."

"Oh, thank you, thir . . . I mean Ned," Teddy added shyly. On the point of a departure as precipitate as his entrance, he recalled his original errand and turned back to Freddie, asking, "Uncle Freddie, could you come and pitch for me? I want to try my new cricket bat, but John Coachman can't spare Jim at the moment, tho . . ." Teddy's voice trailed off disconsolately.

"I'm sorry, Teddy," Freddie began apologetically,

glancing at the clock on the mantel, "but I promised Fortescue I would meet him at Tattersall's. Why don't you ask Cassie?"

"Cathie?" Teddy sounded doubtful.

"She's a much better pitcher than I am, you know," Freddie admitted generously. Always loath to let his twin take all the glory, he couldn't resist adding, "But she's hopelessly cow-handed with a bat."

Teddy remained looking dubious until Ned added, "Don't underestimate your aunt Cassie. She and Freddie played together as children and she always could do everything he did—sometimes better." He grinned at the sputtering sound behind him.

Convinced that if his hero said it, it must be so, Teddy wasted no time in racing off in search of his aunt while Wellington, Nelson, and Ethelred, having learned from their recent experience, followed at a more judicious distance.

CHAPTER 16

As Ned had surmised, Cassie was with Horace busily working at the Comte de Vaudron's. Feeling guilty about having abstained from visiting the comte because she had wished to avoid Horace, Cassie had thrown herself back into their endeavor with renewed energy and had happily spent her morning amid friezes and fragments of statues. She enjoyed the quiet of the comte's library after the constant bustle of Mainwaring House, but even more, she enjoyed the feeling of silent companionship as she, Horace, and the comte sat working, each absorbed in his or her own particular project.

There had been more commotion than usual in Grosvenor Square that morning as Mainwaring House girded its loins for the ball in honor of Cassie's come-out. Frances, ordinarily the least ostentatious of hostesses and the most sympathetic of sisters, this time had turned a deaf ear to Cassie's remonstrances.

"Fanny, there's not the least need to go to all that bother," Cassie protested. "I've been introduced to most of the *ton* already. They know and I know I shall never cut a dash, so there's really no need to bring me to their attention further. I've met enough of them to feel certain that I don't wish to spend my entire life in society. I'm happy as I am, so a ball is really to no purpose." She did not add, though she might have, that since she also had an extremely eligible prospect, there was no longer any reason for her to be introduced to marriageable young men. It was common knowledge in the household that since Lord Mainwaring's return, Horace had been assiduous in his efforts to seek the marquess out but had met with little success. With unerring instinct he always seemed to arrive at Grosvenor Square just minutes after Julian had left.

"And a good thing, too," Higgins commented, unbending a little to confide in Cook. Ordinarily the most dignified of mortals, who would never indulge in anything so far beneath him as to gossip, especially with his inferiors, Higgins found this matter to be of such serious concern that he relaxed his rigid principles. "This Horace Wilbraham is not the match for her. Our Cassie wants someone who's awake on every suit. He is far too dull for her. She would be bored within a month and she could never get along for long with someone made as nervous by horses as he is."

Cook nodded sagely as she handed him another slice of plum cake. "Aye, you're in the right of it, Mr. Higgins. Our Miss Cassie's much too lively for the likes of him. She wants someone who knows all about them Greek fellows she's so interested in as well as someone who will help her cut a dash. Leastways, she's much too pretty to waste her life as a spinster. She needs a man who is adventurous as Master Freddie but with a little more in the brain box." She paused for a moment, fixing a ruminative stare on the remains of the plum cake. "She needs someone like Master Ned," she announced at last.

Higgins appeared to be much struck by this idea. "Master Ned," he murmured thoughtfully. "You may have something there, Mrs. Wilkins. I must see what I can discover about this situation. Certainly the prospect of young Mr. Wilbraham as a husband for Miss Cassie doesn't bear thinking of."

But for the time being Higgins had to set aside this concern for his young mistress's future as he was far too busy doing his best to ensure that the ball to be given in honor of Lady Cassandra Cresswell would be the most talked of event of the Season. He threw himself into the supervision of silver polishing and chandelier washing, spending more time than he cared to think of ordering the proper quantities of champagne and flowers, making sure there were enough link boys engaged, and worrying over the procurement of the miles of red carpet to be laid out to the street. And though he left the preparation of the quantities of lobster patties, jellies, chantillies, ices, and sweetmeats to Cook, he kept a proprietary interest in it all and made certain, having spent much time discussing such matters over a pint of ale with contemporaries from other great houses, that nothing but the best was being served at Mainwaring House.

On a smaller scale, Rose, Cassie's maid, was putting forth her best efforts to make sure that Cassie was in her best looks for the big event. She watched her mistress with a more observant eye than usual to make certain that she didn't set a foot out of doors without a bonnet and a parasol. "Because you know Miss Cassie," she confided in Lady Frances's maid, more intimately known to Rose as her eldest sister Daisy. "If I didn't keep a sharp eye on her, she would forget either one or both and be brown as an Indian in no time."

It was at Rose's urging that a protesting Cassie went more than her usual one time to Madame Regnery to be fitted. When Cassie pointed out to her that Madame knew her figure and all its flaws better than its owner did, Rose turned mulish. "It's as much as my position is worth, Miss Cassie, to see that you do us all proud. It is already outside of enough the airs and graces Miss Arabella Taylor's Susan puts on. I've borne with them for years because we all know your mind is on higher things, but allowing her to have the least cause to put on airs because her mistress criticizes your toilette at your own ball is something I will not do, no matter how much it displeases you. I have my pride, after all, and no mistress of mine is going to be outdone by that creature."

"Very well, Rose," Cassie sighed. "I had no notion I was such a trial to you, but I can see that you have had to put up with a good deal all these years."

"Not at all, Miss Cassie," Rose contradicted her stoutly. "You're far more beautiful than Miss Araballa. Aye, you may stare, brunettes being all the rage, but your nose is much better and your chin won't run to fat the way hers will, mark

my words. What's more, your skin and curls owe nothing
to art.'' Seeing Cassie's look of patent disbelief, Rose
defended herself. ''Well, everyone is aware that she paints
. . . or at the very least she uses the rouge pot and blackens
her lashes. It's common enough knowledge, but Susan is
forever complaining of the hours she has to spend with all
sorts of lotions and powders, making her mistress look her
best. Why you would be astounded at the goings-on.''

''Arabella?'' Cassie was horrified. The idea of painting
conjured up an image of a sophisticated woman far more
exciting than the person she had seen skin her knees and fall
off her pony times out of mind.

''Yes, Miss Arabella,'' Rose maintained firmly. ''And
what's more, her curls aren't natural either.'' Again Cassie
appeared to be completely taken aback by this revelation.
''The amount of time Susan spends to make those ringlets
would make your head spin. Why her hair is as straight as
a board!'' Rose shook her head.

''Gracious, this certainly has been a most enlightening
afternoon,'' Cassie commented. Still too bemused by this
surprising information to absorb it all, she allowed herself
to be helped into her pelisse and hustled off to Madame
Regnery's elegant establishment on South Moulton Street,
where she meekly endured a tedious hour of being pushed
and prodded while Madame's minions draped and pinned.

CHAPTER 17

The extraordinary efforts of all the staff were well worth it, and those waiting to be helped out of carriages the next evening in front of a Mainwaring House ablaze with the light from quantities of flambeaux were already labeling it a dreadful squeeze even before they mounted the great marble staircase. There was such a crush of vehicles that the link boys, John Coachman, and the lads from several of the neighboring stables had their hands full helping the carriages maneuver up to the doorway to deposit their occupants.

Cassie, standing at the head of the stairs with Frances and Lord Mainwaring, couldn't remember when Mainwaring House had looked so elegant.

"It certainly outdoes the way it looked for my come-out," Lady Kitty Willoughby assured her as she greeted Cassie warmly. "And that was voted the event of the Season."

Cassie was astounded at the sheer numbers of beautifully clad women, their shoulders glittering with splendid jewels, accompanied by elegant men in satin knee breeches who mounted the stairway to greet them before proceeding to the ballroom, where the banks of flowers, masses of candles, and musicians all contrived to overwhelm the senses.

Rose finally had her way, and Cassie who had submitted to many more hours in the preparation of her toilette than she would have ordinarily allowed, was in her best looks. Wearing a round dress of Urling's net over a white satin slip, the skirt trimmed with flounces of lace, she looked ethereal and innocent among the brightly colored assemblage. Her mother's magnificent baroque pearls emphasized the creamy

smoothness of her skin. Pearls also anchored the lozenges
of her corsage and were sewn in the rouleaux of satin that
trimmed the short puffed sleeves. Rose had prevailed upon
her to allow her hair to be dressed in a more elaborate style
than the simple ones preferred by Horace. At Cassie's
protests that these were the types he favored, Rose had
snorted, "Hah! And what does Master Horace know, I'd like
to know. He's head over heels in love with you as it is.
Besides, it's the ladies you want to impress. They're the ones
who gossip. Except for a few very elegant gentlemen like
Mr. Bertie Montgomery, men don't give a fig for such things,
but they do notice them if a woman points out to them, and
rest assured, people like Miss Arabella Taylor take every
opportunity to do so."

So Cassie had given in and permitted Rose to dress her
hair in the French style with the back hair brought up to the
top of her head and held in place with a garland of white
roses, while a profusion of curls, "nat'ral, every one of
them," Rose had declared with satisfaction, framed her face.
"Just you watch, Miss Cassie," she had admonished her
mistress, "if that Miss Arabella dares to wear curls this
evening, they'll go limp with all the heat, because it's bound
to be a sad crush." With that, she had given a final pat to
her mistress's coiffeur, twitched a flounce on her dress, and
sent her on her way.

If she had been able to see her mistress leading off the
first dance with Lord Mainwaring, Rose would have been
reassured that her ministrations had not been in vain. Though
she did not rate it high on her favorite list of activities, Cassie
was possessed of a natural grace and coordination which
made her a beautiful dancer. To see her coupled with as adept
a partner as Lord Mainwaring, whose powerful frame
elegantly clad in black evening clothes provided the perfect
foil for her slim figure encased in shimmering white, quite
took the breath away of even the most casual of observers.
No matter that brunettes were all the rage, Cassie's cloud
of golden hair and her dark blue eyes fringed with dark lashes
only emphasized the freshness of her complexion. Compared

with the gaudy sophisticates around her, whose faces were pictures of weary boredom or self-interest, she presented such a contrast of innocence and vitality that it caused the pulses of more than one male bystander to quicken.

Even Freddie, who ordinarily remained blithely unaware of the competitive spirit rampant in the fashionable world, remarked to his twin as he led her through the quadrille, "You're looking fine as fivepence, Cass."

"Why thank you, Freddie," she responded, surprised and touched by this brotherly encomium.

Freddie nodded as sagely as if he had been an acute observer of the social scene for years instead of the past hour. "Tell you what, you take the shine out of every lady here. Even Fortescue told me he thought you looked to be in prime twig, and you know Forty, you have to be a horse, and a sweet goer at that, to rate such praise from him," he volunteered.

"That is praise indeed. I am truly overcome," Cassie agreed, her eyes dancing. "If you say any more, I shall fear you're offering me Spanish coin and that you're angling for something like borrowing my horse Chiron or wanting me to do some disagreeable task such as writing a letter for you."

Freddie looked aggrieved. "Lord, Cass, can't a fellow offer you a compliment without your being so blasted suspicious?"

His sister laughed. "Forgive me, Freddie. It's just that you are so much in the way of pointing out what's wrong with my seat as I take a jump or the way I hold a cricket bat that I'm not accustomed to your praise and I don't know how to react properly. I *do* appreciate it, and your approval means more to me than most because you are often odiously candid about my flaws. Thank you."

"Now *that's* more the spirit a compliment should be received in," her twin remarked, accepting this handsome apology with an air of noble condescension.

Their *tête-à-tête* was interrupted by Ned, who strolled over to claim his dance. He led Cassie so energetically around the floor that she was quite out of breath when Bertie

appeared to claim her in the waltz he had reserved the minute
he had received the gilt-edged invitation.

Casting an experienced eye over her toilette, he nodded
approvingly. "That's an exceedingly elegant rig, Cassie.
Madame Regnery outdid herself this time . . . not that she
didn't have an inspiring model."

"Why thank you, Bertie," Cassie responded in a highly
gratified tone. "Coming from such an *exacting* arbiter of
taste and fashion as you, that is high praise indeed!" And
Cassie was flattered. Constant and true a friend though he
might be, Bertie Montgomery never allowed his exquisite
sensibilities to be blinded by loyalty. Indeed, he considered
that the several occasions he had rendered the greatest
assistance to his friends had been when his obstinate criticism
had helped them to avert sartorial disasters.

He shuddered even now to think how close old Ponsonby
had actually been to wearing a waistcoat of a particularly
violent shade of yellow had not Bertie fortuitously appeared
just as he was leaving the house in Curzon Street. Even such
a nonpareil as Lord Julian Mainwaring, Bertie's oldest friend
and schoolmate, had been known to have second thoughts
when Bertie, upon encountering him, had looked vaguely
troubled and asked, "Are you sure you want to be seen in
that cravat, old man?" Thus his approbation was an accolade
of which Cassie could justifiably be proud, and though she
normally did not devote a great deal of thought to her
appearance once she had dressed, she did feel a glow of
confidence knowing that the others considered her to be in
her best looks.

The exertions on the dance floor added a becoming flush
to her cheeks and the humidity of the crowded ballroom made
the few golden tendrils escaping from her coiffeur curl so
delightfully around her animated face that more than one
bracket-faced dowager remarked that the youngest of Belinda
Carstairs's daughters was a remarkably pretty gel. And
among the male observers, bored by Seasons of new faces
entering society, more than one young buck was heard to

say that Freddie Cresswell's sister was turning into a "demmed beauty."

By the end of the dance, Cassie was breathless and her feet were beginning to ache, so it was with relief that she realized her next dance was promised to Horace. She knew he could be counted on to prefer sitting quietly on the sidelines to maneuvering around a crowded floor. But when Bertie, casting an eye around the ballroom, remarked, "And now, having had the great honor of dancing with the belle of the ball, I shall take you to your next partner, wherever he is," Horace was nowhere to be seen.

After searching the assemblage for some minutes, Cassie finally identified him amid a clump of men earnestly discussing something intriguing enough to render them totally oblivious to their surroundings and their social obligations. "There," she pointed him out to Bertie.

"Well, I call that pretty cavalier behavior," Bertie commented, taking her arm. "Yes, and foolish, too. If he don't take care, one of the many pinks of the *ton* who's been admiring you all evening is likely to steal you from under his nose. Horace always was a slow top."

Cassie laughed. Nevertheless, she flushed with pleasure as she replied, "Doing it much too brown, Bertie. I'm no incomparable, but you certainly make me feel like one."

It was Bertie's turn to blush, but he was saved from making any response as they had reached the group that contained Horace, Ned, that noted classicist and president of the Society of Antiquaries, the Earl of Aberdeen, and several others whom Cassie did not recognize.

"Ah, *ma chère* Cassie," exclaimed the comte, turning to take her hand. "Come, you must take my place. Milord has been asking how our work progresses. You must tell him while I go in search of Lady Montague, to whom I promised a waltz."

The Earl greeted Cassie courteously. "I heard that you are following in the footsteps of your estimable father and mother. You were fortunate in having such diligent and devoted scholars as parents. They were an inspiration to us all and we miss them sorely. But at least we have someone equally brilliant in the Comte de Vaudron to carry on their valuable work. And your colleague, Horace here, bids fair to joining their select group. He has been telling me how his interpretation of the object on one of the friezes as a *peplos* establishes the sex of a previously unidentified figure and thus makes it clear that the procession represented is a celebration of the Panathenaea. A brilliant piece of deduction. I saw the frieze myself and was at a loss, but now, applying Horace's theory, I see it makes perfect sense.''

All thoughts of her gay surroundings vanished and Cassie felt a cold chill wash over her. A knot hardened in her stomach. She felt as she once had when Freddie, in one of their few true fights, had sought to tip her a leveler and had punched her in the stomach instead, knocking the wind out of her. The shock of Horace's deceit and betrayal left her cold and shaking. Mustering all her courage, she gritted her teeth, smiled brilliantly, and replied, ''Yes we discussed it at some length and it does seem to be the most reasonable way to look at it. Horace is very quick to adopt new ideas.'' She looked around, desperately searching for some excuse to leave, but seeing none, fixed her eyes on a pillar, remarking, ''But I see my sister beckoning me. I must go to her. I do apologize for leaving such an interesting discussion.'' With this she fled as precipitately as possible, trying not to reveal her anger or her pressing wish to be somewhere by herself.

The only escape lay in the garden. Glancing quickly around to assure herself that no one would notice or remark on her exit, she slipped through the open French window and into the peace and quiet outside. The glow from the ballroom made the obscurity of the yew-lined walk around the perimeter walls appear even darker than usual. It was here she fled to lean against the cold mossy wall, her breath coming in gasps as she clenched and unclenched her hands and tried to blink back the tears of rage that sprang to her eyes.

Her disappearance had been swift and quiet enough to
escape everyone's notice except that of someone whose quick
perception and sensitivity had seen her first start of surprise
and had hazarded a fairly accurate guess as to its cause. Years
of debating intellectual arguments with Cassie had closely
attuned Ned to her mind and her ways of thinking. He had
been several years ahead of Horace Wilbraham in school,
where he had known him as an earnest, but plodding student
who lacked the intellectual brilliance and creativity or the
curiosity to become a true scholar. Familiar with the pedantic
and unoriginal cast of his mind, Ned had been more than
a little surprised that he had come up with such a well-
constructed and intriguing interpretation of the frieze. In fact,
Ned had just been criticizing himself for having judged
Horace too quickly when he happened to catch sight of
Cassie's face. One glance and he knew the reason for the
look of shock and betrayal registered there. His initial disgust
at such intellectual dishonesty faded quickly when she left,
replaced by an urgent desire to catch up with her and assure
her that *he,* at least, recognized the stamp of her intellect
even if others did not.

Waving to an imaginary acquaintance across the room, Ned
bowed to the group and headed for the French windows,
where a swirl of white flounce was all that gave away
Cassie's place of retreat.

He stepped across the threshold and into the shadows.
"Cassie?" he called softly, walking toward the farthest
corner of the garden. "Cassie?" He tried again with no
success. This time, though, he heard a faint rustle and saw
the vague gleam of pearls caught in the light from the
ballroom. As he approached, he heard the gasps and saw
the shaking of the delicate shoulders as Cassie fought for
control.

Ned's heart went out to her. One swift step brought him
to her and he pulled the slender form into his arms. For some
time he held her there, stroking her hair and murmuring over
and over, "My poor girl. Hush, Cassie."

The sobbing subsided. Cassie gave a gulp, pulled herself

away, and looked up, apologizing angrily, "I can't think why I was so overcome. I'm usually not such a poor creature. It's just that—"

A lean bronzed hand reached out to push back a stray tendril as Ned soothed, "I know. I know. You couldn't fathom how anyone could lay claim so baldly to your ideas."

The dark blue eyes bright with unshed tears regarded him in astonishment. "But how did you know?" she demanded with some surprise.

Ned smiled fondly down at her. "Cassie, my girl, I know your mind as well as I know my own, and I also know Horace Wilbraham's. You were at daggers drawn with me once for casting doubt on his capabilities, but he doesn't hold a candle to you in any field. He no more could have dreamed up that interpretation than he could ride Chiron."

She smiled weakly at him. "Will you forgive me for being so angry at you that time I acknowledged that perhaps you were in the right of it?"

An answering smile glimmered as Ned raised his eyebrows in disbelief, exclaiming, "An apology! From the redoubtable Cassandra? You must be more distraught than I had realized."

This sally was rewarded with a watery chuckle.

"That's better, my girl. It takes more than a poor pedant to get the better of Lady Cassandra Cresswell."

Cassie's smile was erased as another thought came to her. Eyes dark with hurt and anger, she looked up at Ned as she wondered aloud, "But how could he . . . how could he lie like that?"

And take the credit from someone he professed to admire so extravagantly and pursued with such dogged determination, Ned remarked privately in disgust. But he kept his thoughts to himself, saying instead as he took her hands in a firm but gentle clasp, "I don't know why, Cassie." A flash of grin broke the gravity of his expression. "But it's a brilliant interpretation. You can hardly blame the poor fellow for wishing he'd thought of it," he conceded.

She smiled shyly at him. "Thank you, Ned. How kind of you to say so."

Looking unwontedly serious, he cupped her chin in his hand and gazed deep into her eyes. "It's not kindness, my girl. It's the truth. You have a mind filled with ideas that can compete with the best of them," he assured her.

She returned his look gravely, questioningly.

They stood some time gazing at one another until a burst of laughter from the ballroom recalled them to their surroundings.

"Will you be all right?" Ned asked in some concern, gathering both her hands gently in his.

Cassie dropped her eyes to look at her slim white fingers linked with his long tanned ones and nodded.

A tender look stole into Ned's eyes. He dropped a light kiss onto the golden curls. "That's my Cassie. Come." He drew her hand through his arm. "It wouldn't do for someone to be missing too long at her own ball, much as she considers such things to be the most frippery of occupations." This last remark, spoken as it was in a rallying tone, restored some modicum of vivacity to Cassie's countenance.

"That's the ticket," Ned approved. "Come. Waltz with me. It's the thing to do, you know. Sally Jersey vows I am the best waltz partner this side of the Channel." He quizzed her wickedly as he led her onto the floor.

To those who cared to observe, Lady Cassandra Cresswell, having danced continuously that evening, was now being whirled gaily around the room by one of the Season's biggest matrimonial prizes and enjoying herself immensely.

CHAPTER *18*

For Cassie the rest of the evening passed in a blur of assorted partners and conversations. Freddie and Bertie kept her plied with glasses of champagne and delicacies from the supper room, but she could no more than take a sip here and a nibble there. Somehow, she was not quite sure how, she managed to smile and nod in the appropriate places. Certainly she was able to satisfy eager partners or doting mamas with her conversation. At any rate, Arabella, who had magically appeared at Frances's elbow the moment Ned led Cassie back to the Mainwarings' coterie after their dance, seemed to find Cassie's abstracted response of, "Yes, lovely . . . no, truly, did she?" to her questions about the elegance of her own toilette and the raptures of Madame Celestine over her favorite partroness entirely satisfactory.

At last the evening ended and she was able to fall into bed, alone at last and at peace, to try to marshal the welter of thoughts, impressions, and emotions that had occupied her mind the latter part of the evening.

First and foremost were anger and disgust at Horace's appropriation of her ideas as his own. She then fell prey to a variety of emotions ranging from abhorrence of his duplicity and his sycophantic need for admiration whatever the cost, to hurt pride at his assumption that she would not notice or care that her inspiration fed his glory, to disillusionment at the discovery of dishonesty in someone she had admired and given her friendship to, to rage at her own stupidity at having been so blind to his weaknesses.

But thoughts of that dreadful moment in the ballroom when

130

revelation struck her also brought with them the memory of
Ned's kindness. And the feelings stirred by that were even
more varied and complicated than those precipitated by
Horace's betrayal. She had always thought of Ned Mainwaring as an ordinary part of her life just as she had considered
Freddie, Frances, Julian, and Teddy to be, but his sudden
appearance in the garden had changed all that. He had
invariably been extraordinarily sensitive to her moods and
needs, and on the occasions when Freddie's bracing ''Buck
up, Cassie,'' had not had the desired effect, his sympathetic
ear and advice had always brought solace. But this time something had been different. At first when he had taken her in
his arms, she had felt nothing more than the comfort and
security she had felt when as a child she had run to her parents
or to Frances with a skinned knee. But as he had stroked
her hair and comforted her, she had relaxed, and other,
different feelings had washed over her.

Gradually she had become aware of his lean strength, the
solidity of his chest, and the tightening of the muscles in his
arms underneath the material of his jacket as he held her.
When he had looked down at her, encouraging her and
rallying her back into better spirits so she could reenter the
ballroom with some degree of equanimity, she had realized
for the first time what a singularly attractive man her old
playmate had become. There had been an intensity in the
dark blue eyes that she had not seen before and this had
evoked a quiver of response in her that she could not quite
place. All of a sudden she had become vividly aware of his
nearness, of the warmth of his fingers on her bare arms and
the feel of his breath in her hair. When he had kissed the
top of her head, the response became a warm languorous
tide sweeping over her and threatening to suffocate her. It
had subsided somewhat by the time they returned to the
ballroom, but her heightened awareness of Ned had not.
During their waltz she had been conscious of nothing so much
as the warm hand at her waist holding her, guiding her, and
the agility with which he moved as he led her deftly around
the floor.

Cassie lay awake for some time recalling in precise detail all these feelings and the moment that had brought about each one of these new sensations as she tried to identify and analyze the responses they evoked. But cogitate as she would, she could not come up with any satisfactory explanations for the puzzling sense of vague disquiet which excited her and made her extremely anxious all at the same time. She at last fell asleep just as the first rays of sunshine stole between the curtains, but it was a restless sleep, and it was not long before she woke, impatient to see if the daylight and quotidian duties would prove these new sensations to be mere figments of her imagination.

On his part, Ned was just as disquieted. Though no less confused than Cassie, having had more worldly experience than she, he was somewhat less in the dark as to the causes of the intense emotions he had experienced that evening. Unlike Cassie, he had not even made any attempts to go to bed or to seek the oblivion of sleep, but instead had sat in front of the fire swirling a glass of brandy in one hand and staring into the flames. When he had returned from his travels, having moved in society in India and Europe as well as London, Ned had begun to see Cassie from a more social perspective and to realize that she had become a lovely young woman. He had become more accustomed to this new picture of his former playmate as an attractive member of the opposite sex than Cassie had.

The revelations he was undergoing now were not of that nature, but they were no less disconcerting. Despite an initial sense of shock, Ned had gradually adjusted to the idea of a beautiful grown-up Cassie, but he had continued to regard her in this light as a fond brother might have. When she looked particularly elegant or charming, he had felt nothing more than the pride that Freddie or Frances might feel that their sister was admired, and he had been pleased to see her so well accepted by the *ton*. He had been less pleased by her attachment to Horace Wilbraham, but again, that had been the same feeling of disgust that Freddie experienced seeing his sister wasting her attention on someone who was inferior to her in every way.

However, when Ned had pulled Cassie into his arms that evening, something had occurred to make him realize that Cassie affected him in a way that had nothing to do with brotherly affection.

The vision of her, his intrepid playmate, trying desperately to stifle heartbroken sobs, had torn at his heart, and as he stared into the flames, it continued to move him. Because she had always been so ready to take on any challenge or adventure that Freddie, Nigel, or Ned could devise, Ned had always pictured Cassie as stronger and larger than she really was. It had been a shock to discover as he had pulled her close to him how small and fragile she felt in his arms. As he had looked down into her tear-filled eyes, huge in her delicate face, an overwhelming surge of protective rage had swept over him. He wanted to hold her close and do battle with anyone or anything that threatened her equanimity. The fact that, independent as she was, Cassie would have scorned to accept such protection made him doubly eager to spring to her defense and act as her champion.

As the sobs had subsided and Ned's immediate concern for her distress had lessened, he had gradually become aware of how she felt in his arms—the softness of her skin under his hands, the delicate scent of her hair brushing his chin— and he had wanted to pull her even closer to him, to hold her there forever, reveling in the depth of tenderness that welled up within him. He had held many other women in his arms, a good number of them more seductive and more voluptuous than Cassie Cresswell, but the feel of her body against his, lithe, slim, and trembling from her distress, had stirred emotions in him that he had never experienced before. A bewildering array of sensations had swept over him. Foremost had been the yearning to comfort her, to wipe away her distress as easily as he smoothed back her hair and to make everything all right again. Following that, dawned the awareness of how beautiful and desirable she looked. And last came the realization of how wonderful and yet how natural it felt to hold her in his arms and how much more he wanted.

Thinking over it all, reliving every gesture, every sigh, he longed to hold her again. His arms ached to go around her, to comfort her, to protect her from the world in spite of her constantly and vociferously expressed wish to take care of herself. You must be in your dotage, Ned, old boy, he admonished himself. That's Cassie you're thinking of. She's practically your sister. People don't feel such things about their sisters. It's just the concern you have for her happiness that makes you respond this way. She is not the type of woman to appeal to you—too damnably sure of her own mind, too prickly in her independence, too caught up in her interests to relax and enjoy herself. You don't want or need someone like that when those are already your natural proclivities. You should have someone charming and sophisticated who can introduce you to the gaieties in life and help you indulge yourself. You might be able to tolerate a sister who tells you that you have nothing in your cock loft or that your opinion on some issue is bacon-brained, but it don't make for an amusing companion. So why do you want to waste your time on someone who would lead you on such a merry dance?

This last question was so unanswerable that he tossed off the last of the brandy and tumbled into bed, hoping that total oblivion would erase those tantalizing but disquieting memories of the evening and allow him to pursue the less taxing, more pleasurable society of people such as Arabella and Lady Jersey, who could be counted on to demand so much flattering attention from him that he could give himself up to the pursuit of agreeable sensations. He needed someone whose gaiety and coquettishness would counteract his naturally serious personality, not someone who would exacerbate it. Flirting with beautiful worldly women from India to the capitals of Europe had taught him that life could be pleasurable. He had learned to appreciate the beauty, wit, and the delights of civilized society. It had made him more aware of the social needs of others and of his own desire and capacity for taking pleasure in the more sensual aspects of life, including fine food, wine, music, and art, all of which, in his headlong pursuit of his studies, he had rejected as wastes of time. These discoveries had expanded his perspective, enhanced his faculty for enjoyment, and had made him a richer person emotionally.

Upon returning to London, he had resolved not to become like the old reclusive Ned, who had shut himself off from the rest of the world in devoting his attentions to his scholarly pursuits to the exclusion of all else. Along that path lay shallowmindedness and self-centeredness. Unlike Horace Wilbraham, he resolved to avoid those at all costs. Somewhat to his surprise, he had succeeded so well in this resolve that he had been avidly pursued by the *ton*. Courted at first because he was a novelty who exhibited those perennially popular attributes of bachelorhood and wealth, Ned eventually came to be sought out because he was good company.

Ned and Cassie were not the only ones subject to post-festivity reflections. Bertie Montgomery was also pondering the evening's events as he sat at his ease swathed in a gorgeous dressing gown and sipping brandy in front of a fire. For all his insouciance and his intense devotion to fashion, Bertie was a sensitive and perspicacious observer. After having delivered Cassie to Horace that evening, he had hovered protectively on the edge of the group, fearing that one of the participants at least was so caught up in the discussion that he might completely ignore his previous social commitments. Bertie's quick ear for the nuances of social discourse had, on hearing the Earl of Aberdeen's infelicitous remark, immediately noticed Cassie's shocked expression of disbelief, quickly banished though it was, and the stiffening of her spine, more eloquent of her displeasure than any possible facial expression could have been. Not wanting to break in on the conversation, he had left her with Horace, but had lingered long enough to witness her departure from the ballroom closely followed by Ned. His curiosity aroused, he had kept a close watch on the French windows long enough to witness their subsequent reappearance.

To any other observer, nothing would have appeared at all amiss, but to Bertie, who had watched Cassie metamorphose from an adventurous tomboy to a vivacious young woman, she had seemed unwontedly subdued the rest of the evening. Bertie Montgomery was not completely the amiable brainless fop that all of society believed him to be. Though quick to admit that he did not have as much in his upper story as his friend Lord Julian Mainwaring, he did maintain that he was not entirely cork-brained. In fact, he had more than once astounded that exacting peer with his incredible grasp of the art of antiquity. He had not, as he had responded in his own defense, wholly wasted his youth, and his friendship with the Cresswells had sprung up more because of a common interest in classical Greece than from physical proximity. Though his ancestral estate was not far from Cresswell, he had spent more time with them while they were in Athens than he had when they were in Hampshire. It was only after Lord and Lady Cresswell had died that he had become such a frequent visitor to their household as to seem to be another brother to Frances and uncle to the twins.

It was his familiarity with both classical scholarship and the mind of Lady Cassandra Cresswell that had led Bertie to hazard some very accurate guesses as to what had happened. As someone who shared a common interest in antiquity, Bertie had become acquainted with Horace Wilbraham, but finding him to be a less than original scholar with no appreciation whatsoever for aesthetics, he largely ignored him. In fact, Bertie had been astonished to find Horace under the Comte de Vaudron's aegis, for the comte was someone he profoundly respected both as a brilliant scholar and as a man of the world, but he had known the comte to be overworked and thus surmised that whatever Horace lacked in brilliance, he made up for in pedantry and could therefore be counted upon as an amanuensis. Bertie had been less surprised at Cassie's friendship with Horace, knowing her dislike of fashionable bucks and her often expressed wish to find a friend who could share her interest. There was no doubt that Horace Wilbraham was well connected and well enough to look at. Bertie had wondered how long it would be before Cassie discovered her infinite superiority to him both in education and intellect. If his guess were correct, she had discovered it that evening along with several other rather unpleasant truths. Though not inclined to become romantically involved himself—he shuddered at the thought of running the risk of messy entanglements which invariably made one lose all sense of social grace and propriety—Bertie had a tender heart. He sympathized with Cassie's disillusionment and unhappiness and resolved to do something to help her get over it. I shall take her for a ride in the park tomorrow, he decided. Having cleared his conscience in this manner, he swallowed the last drop of brandy and buried himself luxuriously in a mound of pillows.

CHAPTER 19

Daylight did not bring further enlightenment to those who had fallen asleep the previous night mulling over the implications of the scenes at the ball. However, each one arose with a heightened awareness, looking forward to further revelations or understanding that the next day might bring. The only person who did not awake to a sense that somehow the world, or his perception of it, had altered was the precipitator of the entire thing—Horace Wilbraham.

Though intelligent enough, Horace had devoted himself to scholarly passions more because of his interest in classical antiquity and a concerted application of this interest than because of any high degree of brilliance, sensitivity, or natural aptitude. This singleness of purpose which had allowed him to progress as far as he had in his studies had also completely blinded him to the people and events around him. He moved through life in a state of unconsciousness that would have been fatal to anyone who did not have servants and a family, disgusted though they were by his chosen occupation, to look out for him. Thus he remained totally oblivious to the offense he had given his lady love. In fact, he had not even noticed that she had never danced the dance she had promised him. So it was in a state of happy insensibility that he presented himself at Grosvenor Square the next morning. At the ball the Earl of Aberdeen had graciously suggested that Horace and Cassie visit him to discuss their work, and never one to lose the slightest chance of advancing himself, Horace was quick to accept the invitation. He would have preferred calling on this learned peer alone, as lately the creeping suspicion that Cassie might be more accomplished than he in their field of endeavor had occasionally caused him some uneasiness. However, he had reassured himself with the excuse that in acquiring the expertise, Cassie had the advantage of having been immersed since infancy in the world of classical antiquity and had been constantly in the company of its brightest scholars. This had made him feel somewhat better, but he continued to find her natural quickness and brilliance of conversation rather unsettling, especially when other parties were present. However, the earl had spent time in Greece with the Cresswells and become a close friend of her parents, so there was no help for it but to include her.

Cassie, sitting in the library flanked by Ethelred, Nelson, and Wellington, was forewarned of Horace's approach by Teddy, who, on his way to claim his aunt's assistance in cricket practice, had seen Higgins greeting Horace in the front hall. In an effort to avoid condescending pats on the head and ponderous questions about the progress of his Latin, Teddy had beaten a hasty retreat, calling, "Cathie, Cathie, that man ith here, but you promithed me that you would help me with my batting today, remember?"

Fully aware of who "that man" was, Cassie frowned. Teddy, who ordinarily possessed the friendliest of natures, had so little regard for Horace Wilbraham that he could never remember his name and usually referred to him as "that man who took me to the park the day Wellington saved my boat." This had proven to be such a mouthful that it had eventually been shortened to "that man."

"Don't worry, dear," Cassie consoled him, touched by his confidence in her prowess and his crestfallen face. "He isn't going to be staying long. I shall be with you directly."

Teddy looked dubious. Horace was a frequent enough visitor at Grosvenor Square that every member of the household was fully aware of his tendency to hold forth at length and keep Cassie unavailable to the rest of Mainwaring House for hours.

" 'That man,' " Higgins often grumbled, adopting

Teddy's epithet as he complained to Cook. " 'That man' kept me holding the door for an age while he prosed on at Miss Cassie.''

Or Freddie, in a fit of exasperation at having been made late once again to his appointment with Gentleman Jackson because Horace insisted on proving in minute detail the superiority of Chapman's *Iliad* to Pope's or some equally dull theory, would exclaim, "Lord, Cassie, ain't that fellow ever quiet?''

Even Lady Frances, the essence of graceful manners, had been unable to restrain herself from yawning in his company.

Nevertheless, all these people loved Cassie, and critical though they were of Horace's extended discussions, if they pleased her, well they were willing to put up with a good deal to make her happy. Teddy, subject to the unequivocal likes and dislikes of the very young, was the only exception.

Pleasure could not have been further from Cassie's voice and countenance now as she greeted Horace. Totally oblivious as usual, Horace ignored her rigid posture and frosty tone as he plunged into the reason for his visit. "Cassandra, the Earl of Aberdeen has been so kind as to invite me to call on him and he has most graciously asked you to accompany me.''

Cassie's eyes darkened. "No doubt he wishes to learn more about your theories of the Panathenaic procession,'' she replied in a voice of dangerous calm.

"Why yes, I expect so,'' Horace responded, still unaware of the signs of Cassie's rising temper. Even Wellington and Nelson, blissfully asleep at the beginning of the encounter, and Ethelred, who had never seen Cassie angry before, recognized the danger signals and uneasily awaited further developments. Horace continued with becoming modesty, "He certainly appeared to be much struck with all my thoughts on the subject and desired to discuss them at greater length.''

"Doing it much too brown aren't you, Horace?'' Cassie inquired. If there had been any uncertainty as to Cassie's state of mind before, there was none now. She was coldly furious. "What a bacon-brain you must think me not to recognize my own ideas. And how you can appropriate them as your own so calmly without even acknowledging their origin, especially after you ridiculed them to the comte, is beyond comprehension!"

Horace looked to be genuinely surprised and hurt. "But Cassandra," he began in an aggrieved tone, "I did come to agree with you about the theory of the Panathenaic procession, you know. Besides, I thought we shared everything."

"That's precisely the point, Horace Wilbraham," she snapped. "You're not sharing the slightest thing, not even recognition for something that wasn't your idea in the first place."

"Cassandra, be reasonable," he begged. "Even if I were to acknowledge that you had some hand in it, no one would credit a woman, a mere girl moreover, with such ideas."

By now Cassie was so furious that she could hardly speak. Wellington, sensing this, was beginning to growl under his breath while Ethelred and Nelson had fixed Horace with baleful stares. "You seem to have completely forgotten that my mother was regarded as equally brilliant as my father whom you profess to hold in such deep respect and he always accorded *her* the acclaim due to her work."

Still ignorant of the danger he was in from all quarters, Horace went blithely on, "But that was because she had your father to guide her and she was able to be of use to him in his work."

Cassie looked murderous. Not too many years ago she would simply have planted Horace a facer as Freddie had taught her. But, she told herself, you're grown up now and you must not allow such a miserable excuse for a man make you lose your dignity. She straightened up, drew a breath, and adopting her most imperious voice and manner, she ordered, "Horace, I think you had better leave now."

"But Cassandra," he protested in bewilderment, "we're expected at the earl's."

"That is of little interest to me, Horace, as I don't wish

to see or be seen with you ever again," she replied haughtily.

"Cassandra, what maggot have you got in your brain?" Horace asked uneasily as he finally realized that she was truly upset.

"If you haven't fathomed it by now, you never shall, Horace," Cassie reponded. Her dignity began to disintegrate as he continued to stand there transfixed, staring at her stupidly. "Oh, *do* go away, Horace," she said crossly.

He might have remained that way forever had not Wellington, seeing that his mistress did not like "that man" and was having trouble getting rid of him, intervened. Looking significantly at Ethelred and Nelson, he growled viciously and, frowning ferociously, approached to snap at Horace's feet, closely followed by Nelson, who looked truly alarming with his ears back and teeth bared. Ethelred, unable to adopt such a dangerous mien, nevertheless managed to appear quite threatening. The fur-and-feather contingent succeeded where Cassie had failed, and Horace fled.

Though Horace was unaware of any witnesses to his ignominious rout, there had been two who had enjoyed it hugely and shared it with the other members of the household. Higgins had been across the hallway in the dining room buffing silver when the door had opened and Horace emerged, looking harassed. From behind him issued the sounds of growling, hissing, and a muffled quacking. Curious, the butler shot a quick look in the library as he went to open the door and caught a glimpse of the phalanx of vicious and victorious animal defenders. It was with some difficulty that he was able to preserve his countenance as he bid Horace good day and closed the door behind the unfortunate young man. As it was, the minute he pushed the door to, he broke into a grin.

"And that's the last we'll see of that young man, I'll be bound, Mrs. Wilkins," he confided to Cook. Once again, Higgins's devotion to the Cresswells and his recognition of a similar attitude on the part of the rest of the Mainwaring House staff, made him overcome his customary aloofness and sit down to dinner with them later in order to share the good news that, if he had interpreted the signs correctly, the Honorable Horace Wilbraham would no longer be calling at Grosvenor Square.

"I shall have to give Wellington and Nelson the remains of that joint I served last night," declared Cook. "And Ethelred shall have the rest of the poppyseed cake. Those good-for-nothings have certainly earned their keep this time."

"Ooooh, I *am* glad!" Rose exclaimed. "He wasn't up to snuff in the least. Miss Cassie deserves a real out-and-outer, she does." Rose, who had the most exacting standards for her mistress, had never been pleased with Horace, but familiar with Cassie's distaste for most of the young bucks, she had been grateful to him at least for escorting her mistress to the places where she might encounter gentlemen more her style. A high stickler where fashion was concerned, Rose had not appreciated Horace's influences on Cassie's toilette, as he encouraged her to wear the plainest of coiffeurs and the most drab colors, which contrived to make her look as dowdy as anything could make Cassandra Cresswell look. While Rose had not been privileged to observe her mistress in society, and therefore could not judge his influence on her character, she suspected that it was similar to his effect on her appearance, for it had seemed to her that since Cassie had met Horace she had been more quiet and serious and less vivacious than before.

"And good riddance to him," Rose concluded. But his departure did leave a gap and Cassie's maid was worried. "But *now* who will take her around?" she wondered aloud. "She's so particular about gentlemen and there are few who are fine enough for her."

Higgins smiled smugly. "I've a feeling that Master Ned will take care of Miss Cassie," he replied, nodding sagely.

Rose looked up in surprise. "But Miss Arabella," she began.

Adopting an even more astute expression, he elaborated,

"Miss Arabella has overstepped herself this time, mark my words. And Master Ned isn't one to live under that cat's foot."

Rose frowned doubtfully. She was agog to know where the butler had come by this notion, but it wasn't her position to question the oracle, so she let it pass, remarking merely that she would like it above everything if Miss Cassie were to find herself a nonpareil like Mr. Ned.

Another witness to the humiliating scene in the library was Teddy, who had been hanging around the door in hopes that his aunt would be true to her word and not spend too much time with "that man."

"You thould have theen it, Jim," he confided later to his bosom buddy in the stable. "Wellington wath a real Trojan. He'th a fearth one all right. Ethelred and Nelthon were right behind him. 'That man' wath scared out of hith witth. I always knew there wath thomething havey-cavey about him. What a chicken heart," he concluded scornfully.

Off in an other corner of the stable, John Coachman muttered to himself as he mended a harness. "Well rid of that one she is. He's cow-handed, I'll be bound, and our Miss Cassie would never be able to stand with that for long."

CHAPTER 20

While the various members of the household were rejoicing at Horace Wilbraham's decampment, each for his or her own particular reasons, Cassie remained in the library deep in thought. In fact, she wondered at herself. It seemed as though, given the attachment between Horace and her, and all that they had shared together, she should be feeling desolate. Instead, her chief emotions, as nearly as she could sort them out, appeared to be anger and . . . could it be relief? The more she considered it, the more she realized that relief was just what it was. Though Horace had provided her with a companion who had participated in her interests and had proven that she could be appreciated beyond the requirements set by the *ton*, she had been aware, unconscious though it may have been, of a niggling sense of doubt about their friendship. As she examined it, the reason for this unease became clearer. It had not, she decided, been a true friendship because, to Cassie at least, friendship meant something shared between equals. Though they had enjoyed common interests and were alike in their rejection of the purely fashionable life of the *ton* for more serious pursuits, they had not been an even match. Though Cassie had reveled in having an escort who, instead of dismissing her as a bluestocking, could, on the contrary, understand and appreciate her ideas and could converse knowledgeably about them, she realized now that Horace had never challenged or stimulated her. Rather, he had resembled a sponge—soaking up her knowledge and her vivacity without giving a great deal in return.

At first she had rejoiced in his admiration and appreciation of her, but lately this appreciation had come to pall on her to a certain degree, for it had begun to seem as though the attributes he admired in her somehow redounded to his credit. It had happened so slowly as to be unnoticeable at first, but now it dawned on her that gradually he had begun to irk her. She had refused to recognize this irritation, putting it down instead to the natural change in feelings that occurred as a result of increasing familiarity. Of course the excitement one felt upon first discovering someone who could partake of one's views of the world would decrease as one became accustomed to it and began to take it more for granted. And naturally the first unquestioning enthusiasm one felt for this person and this friendship would cool as one became better acquainted. Cassie realized now that it had not been the normal lessening of ardor as infatuation was replaced by the less exciting but more long-lived emotion of friendship, but that her irritation had been caused by her slow and virtually unconscious awakening to the fact that while Horace provided her with an escort who appreciated the same things, he gave her little else. Furthermore, as she had discovered at the ball, not only did he not provide her with much, he took from her.

As she reviewed all this in her mind, Cassie began to realize all the things she had been missing in their relationship. For all their similar interests, she had felt no sense of intimacy. She would have felt less inclined to confide in Horace than she would have in Freddie or even Rose. And though he could speak with more knowledge than most people on a very few isolated subjects, beyond those, Horace did not offer much in the way of conversation, and even less in the way of wit. As she considered it, Cassie concluded that he had no humor whatsoever. It was this lack of humor that led to a certain rigidity of mind that had made her uncomfortable. All in all, she was well out of it, and though the discovery that he and his friendship had failed to fulfill her initial hopes and expectations made her sad, she was glad that she had awakened to her delusion soon enough to avoid committing herself to him further. Still, it was a somewhat melancholy thought that perhaps there was no one out there who could offer her what Horace had appeared to offer.

That's enough moaning, my girl, she scolded herself. Falling into a fit of the dismals won't help you in the least, and it certainly won't help Teddy with his cricket. Giving herself an admonitory shake and calling to Wellington and the others, Cassie arose and went in search of her nephew.

Teddy was soon located in the garden aimlessly thwacking the ball around and whistling tunelessly. He broke into a grin the moment his aunt appeared. "Oh, famous! I knew you'd come!" he exclaimed happily. His face fell slightly when he saw her companions.

Recognizing his concern, Cassie reassured him, "Don't worry, they won't interfere. Let's make some wickets and set up a pitch. Once Wellington sees them, he will understand what we're about and will keep the others in line."

In this she was entirely correct. Once the sticks Teddy hunted up in the stable were in place, Wellington planted himself firmly on the sidelines. He ran a practiced eye over the proceedings and kept a stern watch on Ethelred and Nelson to make sure they didn't stray onto the pitch.

"That's the ticket, Wellington," Cassie approved, smiling at the little dog as she loosened up her bowling arm.

Teddy took up the bat and went to stand before the wicket. Cassie let fly the first ball and Teddy was so bemused by the sight of his studious aunt bowling with such speed and accuracy that he forgot even to lift the bat. The ball hit the ground and rebounded in an unexpected direction. A look of astonishment came over his face. "Aunt Cathie, you put a spin on it!" he declared indignantly.

"Well, of course I did, you gudgeon. It wouldn't be helping you to improve your batting much if I were to bowl directly to you, now would it?" she retorted.

Acknowledging the justice of this, Teddy gripped the bat firmly, planting his feet and awaiting Cassie's next pitch with a determined set to his jaw and his eyes squinting in concentration. It was a fast one, but he was able to connect with a satisfactory thwack, and Cassie, transforming herself in an instant from bowler to fielder, had to scramble to retrieve it.

Breathless from her exertions, she returned to her place to wind up for another bowl, panting, "It would be a good deal easier if we had someone to act as wicket keeper."

"And thus, your prayers are answered, fair maiden. Behold a willing and obedient wicket keeper," a deep voice spoke behind her.

Cassie whirled around. "Ned!" she exclaimed. "I'm that glad to see you. You're the very person!"

Ned winked at Teddy. "If there were more people, I should be flattered into thinking you wanted me for my cricketing prowess, but given the meagerness of your numbers, I suspect you'd be glad to see anyone who had more grasp of cricket than Ethelred," he said, laughing.

Surveying the small group of onlookers at the sidelines, Cassie's face brightened. "Of course, the very thing!" she cried. "Wellington can field for us!"

"Arf, arf," Wellington agreed enthusiastically.

"Still the same old Cassie who could never bear to see anyone sitting comfortably," Ned teased as he stripped off his coat and tossed it onto a bench. He strolled over to the wicket, remarking, "Very well. Your wish is my command, but see that you bowl so well that Wellington and I don't have to work too hard."

Cassie made a face. "And now who doesn't want whom to be comfortable?" she taunted. "Here, Wellington." She walked over to a spot and snapped her fingers. With a backward glance of triumph at his less skilled companions, Wellington proudly took up his place.

Cassie hurled the ball. There was another crack and Cassie yelled, "Fetch!"

Wellington jumped with alacrity, fielding the ball before it hit the ground.

"Aha, caught. Good job, Wellington," she cried as he raced to the wicket with the ball.

Teddy was disgusted. "You traitor, Wellington. Dithmissed on my second try," he grumbled.

Further commentary on his pet's loyalty was cut short by his mother, who called, "Teddy, Teddy, you must come do your history lesson now before I have to go out."

"Botheration," Teddy declared, hunching a mutinous shoulder. "Just when I was getting the hang of it!"

"Don't refine on it too much, Teddy," Cassie consoled him. "Wellington and I will be happy to practice with you whenever you like, and if we can prevail upon Cook to make her famous Dundee cake, I am certain that we can count on Ned as well. Run along, now. I promise you Ned and I will stop playing and talk of the dullest things imaginable so you won't be missing anything."

"Can we try tomorrow?" Teddy begged, knowing full well the vagaries of adult schedules.

"Certainly. I shall be happy to," Cassie responded, smiling reassuringly at the anxious face turned up to hers.

Teddy collected the ball and bat and scampered off. But just before disappearing into the house, he turned to call, "Thank you, Aunt Cathie and Ned. You're great guns, both of you."

"You couldn't hope to win higher praise from the most besotted of admirers," Ned rallied her.

"Of which I have countless numbers, naturally," Cassie replied, smiling impishly at him in such a way that he wondered why she didn't have hundreds of them haunting her doorstep.

He looked down at her, taking in every detail of the way the sun made the curls surrounding her flushed face glow like spun gold, how the thick dark lashes fringing her eyes made them look an even deeper blue. Even the smudge of dirt on her chin emphasized the smoothness and softness of her skin. He stood thus bemused until her expression changed and an inquiring look wrinkled her brow. Giving himself a mental shake, he apologized. "I am sorry. My wits have gone begging. I hadn't thought to be pressed into service so quickly and I clean forgot why I came, which is to bring you this." He pulled a small bundle out from under his coat as he spoke.

"Why Ned, a present . . . for me." Cassie looked so eager in her anticipation that he was touched. Ned had presented far more expensive-looking boxes embossed with the names of famous jewelers to far less effect than this simple packet done up in plain brown paper and string.

"Well, I just saw it and thought you might find it inspiring," he replied offhandedly.

She tore off the paper to reveal the works of Epictetus translated by Elizabeth Carter.

"Do not for a moment think that I doubt your ability in the least to read it in the original, Cassie. I just thought you would like to see that women such as you *are* taken seriously and that they *can* succeed at their endeavors. And I believe that this represents the second printing."

Cassie was greatly touched. "Ned, how very kind you are. I can't wait to read it. And thank you for, for . . ." She fumbled for the words to express how much it meant to her for someone to have faith in her abilities and to treat her as one would treat any scholar with aspirations.

Living as she had in such a talented household, Cassie had never been fully aware how little respect she could command outside it—even from those who comprehended and applauded her interests—simply because she was a woman. She had resigned herself to being misunderstood and labeled "blue" by the rest of the world, but having no social aspirations, she had not been bothered greatly by it. She had, however, expected to be taken seriously by those who could appreciate her scholarship. Horace's attitude had dealt her a severe blow and she was just now realizing how much it had hurt her. This demonstration of support expressed by such an appropriate gesture and from someone who was truly capable of appreciating and judging her abilities meant more to Cassie than she was able to express. She blinked rapidly as she extended her hand, trying to find some way to articulate her gratitude. "I wish, I wish you could know how much this means to me, but . . ." Her voice cracked and she found she could not go on.

Ned raised a mobile eyebrow. "What? Cassandra

Cresswell at a loss for words? Things *have* come to a pretty pass," he teased. "Don't refine on it too much. I just thought you could use an example of feminine scholarship right now. But that's not the entire purpose of my visit. I also came to inform you that there is to be a balloon ascension next Tuesday and I thought you, Teddy, Freddie, and I might enjoy going. If it's a very fine day, we could make a picnic of it."

"What a lark! I should like it of all things and so would Teddy!" Cassie exclaimed. "He's been teasing Freddie and me to take him ever since Freddie read the announcement of the ascension and the exhibition in the *Times*. I've only been to one balloon ascension when I was quite small and couldn't see a thing because the crowd kept pushing so. A nice man put Freddie up on his shoulders so he was able to describe it to me, but that's not the same thing at all."

"That's set, then. You ask the others and we'll hope for a good weather. Now, I must be on my way as Canning has asked me to call on him." Ned added this last bit in as offhand a manner as possible, but it was with great difficulty that he kept the pride out of his voice.

Cassie lit up immediately. "Oh Ned, how perfectly splendid!" she cried. "However did that come about? I *am* so proud of you."

Ned recounted his discussion with Lord Charlton at Brooks's. Good as his word, Lord Charlton had spoken to Canning about Ned. The statesman had been intrigued by Ned's background and experiences and had very graciously invited him to call on him.

"That's wonderful beyond anything! You are certain to impress him with your views on conditions in India. Not only have you been there and worked with the system, such as it is, but you have reflected seriously on it and have devised your own particular plan for what should be done to improve things. Everyone declares him to be rather temperamental, but I believe that it's because he refuses to suffer fools gladly. You are quick and clever and, I should think, would be just the sort to appeal to him. I heard him speak in Parliament and I must say that I thought him brilliant, though his sarcasm, amusing though it is, must make him many enemies. Do please come tell me everything afterward.''

Ned smiled at her exuberance, as he demurred modestly. "You are prejudiced in my favor. I should take you along as my advocate. How could he fail to think I am a coming man after hearing you on the subject? However, with you espousing me, I shouldn't be able to get a word in edgewise." His tone was teasing, but secretly he was pleased and touched by her support and her unbounded faith in his abilities. Cassie better than anyone comprehended his ideas and understood his political aspirations. Her opinion was more important to him than anyone else's, as she could best appreciate what it meant to him to have these ideas recognized by such men as Lord Charlton and his peers.

Cassie's enthusiastic reaction, her happiness at his recognition, and her passionate support were all he had hoped for and he headed off to Canning's chambers in Stanhope Street buoyed up by the knowledge that she would be thinking of him.

CHAPTER 21

Ned was not able to share the details of his visit to the foreign secretary until the next evening when he joined Cassie, Frances, and Julian in the Mainwarings' box at the opera. Frances had for some time expressed a wish to see Rossini's *Otello*, particularly as the composer was conducting his own work. Her husband had ruthlessly turned down several important invitations from his political cronies in order to spend a peaceful, enjoyable evening in the company of his family and free from the brilliant government circles in which they ordinarily moved. Knowing that Ned was also very fond of Rossini, Frances had urged him to join them.

Her motives were not entirely unselfish. Ever since the ball she had noticed a change in her sister. Cassie seemed restless and disinclined to fix her interest on anything for any length of time—an unusual state of affairs for one who often had to be pried loose from the library to attend meals. At the same time Frances was aware that Cassie had ceased her regular visits to Hanover Square. This unusual circumstance coupled with the notable absence of Horace Wilbraham led her to suspect that the friendship had ended, but being the good sister that she was, Frances would have died rather than mention this state of affairs to her sister.

She was indebted at last to her maid Daisy, Rose's eldest sister, for her enlightenment. Daisy, having been with Frances since both were barely more than twelve, was not one to stand on ceremony. "And though I am sad to see Miss Cassie lose any admirer, mark my words, she's better off without that Horace Wilbraham. Can't hold a candle to her,

he can't, and he's always bragging about his learning. Pooh!
Why Miss Cassie could run circles around him. Learning!
That's his excuse for being such a dead bore. Miss Cassie's
well rid of him, I say. Why he was such a dullard he was
making Miss Cassie into one, too. Not many a man could
bear to have a companion who is gayer and wittier than he
is. For all his mealymouthed ways he's as selfish as he can
stare. Anyone can see he must always have the first consideration. As I see it, Miss Cassie needs somehone who can keep
up with her, someone who is a true out-and-outer.''

Aware that Daisy's sources of information were impeccable, Frances didn't question her knowledge but acted
accordingly to ensure that Cassie would have some sort of
escort even if it were a person she'd known since she'd been
in pinafores.

There had been no time for discussion before the opera,
but at the close of the first act Cassie turned to Ned. ''Do
tell me what transpired with Canning, I've been bursting to
know. What did you talk about? Were you able to tell him
any of your notions for improving trade?''

Ned held up a well-shaped hand to stem this impetuous
outburst. ''Hold on, my girl. One question at a time. Yes,
we did discuss my ideas. And I must say we dealt excellently
with each other. We both agree that we must work to improve
our colonial trade and direct our policies toward strength-
ening the Colonies, even if that means modifying our
Navigation Acts and freeing England from the Holy Alliance.
We have involved ourselves too long in the affairs of Europe
to the detriment of our mercantile interests in other corners
of the globe, and now something must be done about it.''

Cassie nodded. ''And what with Napoleon no longer on
the Continent to cause wars and require armies and supplies,
we need other markets for our merchants to supply.''

''Just so,'' Ned replied, reflecting on what a refreshing
change it was to be able to relate his ideas to someone who
grasped them and responded, instead of treating him to a
bored pout or changing the subject immediately to something

that forced his attention to revert solely to his charming companion.

Suddenly he was forced to do just that as Frances interrupted to point out that his attention was being demanded by just such a charmer. "Isn't that Arabella beckoning to you?"

Sighing inwardly, Ned glanced over to the box opposite, where Arabella, resplendent in diamonds and a revealing décolletage, was beckoning purposefully to him. Her attire was in fact a trifle daring for a young unmarried woman, but Arabella, who had detected a lessening in Ned's attentiveness, had not cared. Inquiries from her maid, who had grown up with Rose and continued the friendship in Town, had revealed that the Mainwarings were planning to attend the opera that evening, and the beauty had bullied her parents, neither of whom could bear opera, into taking her. She was confident that her bright poppy-colored muslin gown with sprigs of gold and ornamented with gold lace was certain to make anything Cassie wore seem pale and insipid by comparison. She was also certain that no young woman in her first Season would dare expose such a creamy expanse of beautifully rounded bosom and shoulders as she was now displaying to the delight of the besotted young men who hovered around her. Secure in the knowledge that she was in her best looks and drawing appreciative stares from all over the theater, she positively glowed.

Attired perfectly correctly in a white *gros de Naples* round dress which was becoming enough but certainly not distinctive, Cassie breathed a wistful sigh. As long as she was well groomed and wearing something that was not noticeably out of fashion, she ordinarily discounted her appearance as unimportant, but for once she longed to be more than acceptable; she wished she was dazzling. Not that she wouldn't have been heartily bored by the insipid conversation of men such as those surrounding Arabella, but she did for a moment wonder what it would be like to be so fatally attractive, so confident of one's beauty and power

to be admired for it. She had been acquainted with Arabella
all her life and knew that her intellect was not strong, nor
was her conversation particularly witty and charming. It
seemed dreadfully unfair that something as simple as big dark
eyes, dimples, dusky curls, and a voluptuous figure could
command the total attention of so very many gentlemen. And
just once she wished she could change places with her. But
only for a moment, she said to herself. I should be bored
silly within the hour.

Ned, who had responded to Arabella's summons with a
slight nod and was debating whether or not he could ignore
her obvious wish for him to join the devoted little group of
admirers, caught Cassie looking at her. Her expressive face
revealed a good deal of what was going on in her mind, and
Ned was both amused and touched by it—amused that his
feisty little playmate, who had never spoken of fashionable
women who devoted themselves to their appearances except
in tones of deepest scorn, should now look so thoughtful at
the sight of someone who thought of nothing else, and
touched by the wistfulness of that look. The irony of it was
that though Arabella cultivated every art to attract while
Cassie remained largely oblivious to such guile, Cassie's
natural liveliness, her genuine interest in those to whom she
was speaking, combined with the wit and intelligence of her
conversation made her far more appealing to all but the most
superficial of the *ton*.

An urgent desire to rally to Cassie's defense and honor
her qualities made him decide to ignore Arabella's summons.
He turned instead to his companion, inquiring, "Did you
read the account of the subscription to help the Greeks in
the *Times* last week?"

Cassie's eyes sparkled. "Yes, I did. And I'm glad that
someone is at last doing something for those poor people.
How anyone can say that they are as barbaric as the Turks
I simply cannot comprehend. What could be more uncivilized
than storing ammunition in one of the greatest artistic feats
of mankind? I only thank heaven that Lord Elgin, Papa and
Mama, and the Comte de Vaudron were able to save as much

of the Parthenon as they did. It's a dreadful shame that the
marbles had to be taken from their proper place and the nation
that created them, but if it inspires people who would otherwise never have the opportunity to see and appreciate the
monuments from classical antiquity, then I am all for it. And
you must admit that the decorative arts in general have
improved because of this very appreciation."

"Gently, my girl," Ned teased. "Don't get on your high
ropes with me. I am as devoted as anyone to the Greeks,
past and present. I was merely curious to know if you were
aware that at long last a movement is afoot to—"

But whatever the movement was to accomplish was lost
as the door to the box opened. There was a rustle of skirts,
a breath of seductive perfume, and then Arabella broke in
gaily, "How delightful to see you!" Her dazzling, but
perfunctory smile included the entire company; however, the
languorous look accompanying it was directed to Ned alone.
Unwilling to brook Ned's ignoring of her invitation, Arabella
had been overjoyed when Sir Brian Brandon had appeared
in her box, for she could hardly visit the Mainwarings' box
alone and Sir Brian was the perfect escort to rouse envy in
the breast of any female and dismay in any male's. Let Ned
see that she was sought after by the very pinks of the *ton*.
That would put him on his mettle!

Smothering his annoyance as best he could, Ned inclined
his dark head as he acknowledged them. "Arabella, Sir
Brian, good evening. And how do you find the opera? Cassie,
here, is a severe critic, you know. She has been telling me
that while she admires Rossini and finds *Otello* particularly
delightful, she does not find the performers equal to the
music—a sad state of affairs, don't you agree?"

Cassie's jaw dropped as she had said no such thing, nor
could she have the least idea why Ned would let fall such
a plumper, but a conspiratorial wink brought her to her
senses. Trying to sound as world-weary and sophisticated
as possible, she sighed. "Yes, I find it quite upsetting when
the singers cannot do justice to the work. If the corps de ballet
is as uninspired in the dance to follow, I am sure I shall be

frightfully *ennuyée*. And I most certainly object to the tampering with Shakespeare's masterpiece. The happy ending is beyond all things absurd."

She was rewarded by another wink and a lopsided grin. Unaware of this private interchange, Arabella struggled to regain control of the scene that Ned had so successfully stolen from her. He had succeeded far beyond his wildest hopes, which had merely been to rob Arabella of some of her infernal confidence in her ability to dominate the center of every stage, because upon hearing Cassie's remark, Sir Brian, whose gaze had been slowly sweeping the theater, now fixed upon her with some interest.

"Are you a devotee of opera, Lady Cassandra, or merely of Rossini?" he asked, moving closer to her chair as she spoke.

Cassie smiled. "Oh opera, certainly," she replied. Then, lowering her voice conspiratorially, she added, "I know that one shouldn't admit to such a thing when Italian opera is all the rage, but I find that Mozart appeals more to my tastes."

He nodded sagely. "I should have known."

"Oh dear," Cassie sounded rueful. "Do I look so *démodée*? My entire family is hoping I shall acquire some town bronze and I shouldn't want to disappoint them. It's not for myself that I care about being au courant, you understand," she concluded somewhat defiantly.

"Not in the least." Sir Brian was amused. "I had expected that a composer as refined and subtle as Mozart would be more appealing to someone who has such an elegant mind."

"But you have no notion of my mind," she protested.

His brown eyes dwelt on her appreciatively as he responded. "On the contrary, the clothes you wear, the way you carry yourself, your voice are all very elegant. How could your mind fail to be so?"

Cassie's eyes opened wide as she exclaimed, "I, elegant!"

"Don't let it go to your head, Cassie," Ned teased. "There are those of us who remember you with mud on your nose and grass stains on your pinafore. Be aware, Sir Brian, that underneath that elegant exterior you describe, there lurks the best tree climber and one of the most bruising riders in all of Hampshire.''

If they had not been in polite company, Cassie would have stuck her tongue out at Ned, but she contented herself with shaking an admonitory finger at him. ''Have care, Ned. As the Marriage Mart's biggest catch, you have a greater reputation to be ruined by childhood reminiscences than I do. And if you can dredge up my past, I can certainly recall some inglorious moments in yours.''

He grinned appreciatively. ''Wretch!'' he responded, laughing.

Arabella, who had been forced, and with very poor grace at that, to maintain a desultory conversation with Lady Mainwaring and the marquess, could bear it no longer. Laying a possessive hand on Sir Brian's sleeve, she cooed, ''Come. We must be going or we shall miss the next act.'' Then, bending toward Ned and treating him to the full benefit of her décolletage, she whispered intimately, ''I hope to see you at Lady Portman's masquerade.''

''I expect so. I shall be there, I suppose,'' he replied carelessly as he quickly turned his attention to the stage. Left with nothing to do, Arabella swept out as grandly as possible, clinging seductively to her escort.

CHAPTER 22

The projected outing to the balloon ascension had met with Theodore's instant and enthusiastic approval. "What a bang-up plan!" he exclaimed when Cassie relayed Ned's invitation to him. He looked up at her, adding shyly, "I like Ned. He's a regular Trojan, isn't he?"

Cassie smiled fondly at him. "Yes, he certainly is." The warmth in her smile was as much for the man who had made the boy so happy as for the eager boy himself. Dear Ned, he always was there offering advice, distraction, support, whatever she needed and whenever she needed it most. Few people could count themselves as fortunate as she in having a friend like him. She thought of how consoled she had been by his quick understanding and sympathy, how comforting and secure it had felt to be in his arms, and her smile became even more tender.

Her reverie was interrupted by a grubby hand tugging at her sleeve. "Aunt Cathie, I thay, Aunt Cathie."

She came to with a start. "Yes, Teddy?"

"Will we be able to get clothe to the balloon? I would so like to thee what ith like."

Cassie looked uncertain. "I don't know, dear. It may be a sad crush, but we shall certainly try."

The day of the balloon ascension dawned clear and warm. Ned had borrowed his sister's barouche and also availed himself of her cook, who had packed a tremendous hamper of game pies, cold chicken, and cheese, as well as tarts and cakes of every description. Teddy's eyes bulged at the sight of it as he climbed in the carriage and settled himself in anticipation of a day of unprecedented delights.

Wellington sat happily on the box by the coachman. Ned was an old crony of his, and when the little dog had seen his best friends about to depart in a carriage without him, he had looked so miserable that Ned had relented. "Very well then, Wellington, but you must stay on the box because we wouldn't want to lose you in all the crush. Hackney is not the genteel area of London that Mayfair is. No telling what mongrels will be abroad."

"Arf," Wellington barked obediently. He had no intention of leaving his seat, not because he was afraid of even the fiercest canine, but because he did not want to miss the slightest detail of the ascent. Besides, fancying himself an equestrian sort of dog, he was never happier than when he was seated on the box next to the coachman.

Ned had drawn the line at Nelson and Ethelred, however. Nelson had not really wanted to go, as the idea of sunning himself on the front steps was infinitely more appealing than perching way up in a swaying open carriage amid throngs of people, but it would never have done to let on to Wellington. Ethelred really did not care one way or another, but not liking to be separated from his hero, he looked mutinous at Ned's decision.

"I'm not certain they would understand about ducks as pets in Hackney," Ned explained. "And you would undoubtedly prefer to remain here than end up in someone's stew pot."

"Arf," Wellington agreed, settling the matter, and Ethelred, sighing sadly, waddled off to join Nelson on the steps.

A silent observer of Ned's kindness and understanding toward the trio, Cassie couldn't help comparing him to Horace, who had ordinarily been rendered acutely uncomfortable by the menagerie. He had always trodden awkwardly and uneasily when they were around and more than once had remarked in exasperation, "Really, Cassandra,

I don't understand why they are allowed the run of the house.
Animals in a drawing room are absurd, not to mention most
improper." Well aware of his unpropitious attitude, and
hoping to discourage such a caller, the three had invariably
made it a point to hover around his feet when he called, and
they had been as relieved as everyone else that Horace's visits
to their mistress had ceased.

The party arrived in the Mermaid Tavern, Hackney, in
time to view the balloon and equipment which was on exhibit
to the public in the assembly room. As they walked around
inspecting it, Ned explained the principles of ballooning to
an enrapt Theodore. "And we are fortunate to be able to
see such a noted balloonist as Mr. Green. He has made
several innovations in ballooning, inventing the drag rope
go make the descent slower and smoother and using coal gas
instead of hydrogen. Though it's much more likely to catch
fire, it's a great deal cheaper."

Pleased by the rare occasion of having a truly knowledgeable spectator and one who was a nonpareil, by the look of
him, Mr. Green himself came over to explain the science
of ballooning to the little party. Teddy was thrilled by his
description of his more daring exploits and was so excited
by the outing and the opportunity to meet the famous
balloonist that he hardly touched the picnic which had
captured his eye when they first set out.

"What a knowing one you are, Ned, old boy. Never knew
you was so into the scientific stuff as well as the classics,"
Freddie commented through a mouthful of game pie.

"I'm not, but I've always been intrigued by the idea of
being able to fly. The idea of gliding peacefully along over
the countryside above all the hustle and bustle and the horrors
of country lanes appeals to me mightily," Ned averred.

They were interrupted by a gasp from the crowd as Mr.
Green and his assistant pulled in the anchors and the gaily
striped equipage rose slowly and majestically above them.
Wellington let out a startled "woof" while the rest of them
sat silent gazing at the magnificent sight.

"Oh, how I should love to ride in one!" Cassie exclaimed. "How wonderful it would be to look down on everything while sailing along free as a bird."

Ned smiled fondly at her. With her face alight with enthusiasm and the stray golden curls catching the sunlight as the wind gently blew them, she looked more like the Cassie he used to know—passionate, vital, and adventurous—than the serious and proper person who had lately been appearing at all the fashionable haunts of the *ton*. It was as though her true spirit had broken through some restraint and was reasserting itself. Ned was glad to see that it was still there and hoped that somehow he had been instrumental in bringing about the transformation.

He felt a great rush of tenderness toward his old playmate as she sat there rapt in the excitement of the event. You're too young to be getting nostalgic, Ned, my boy, he admonished himself. You've only just kicked off the dust of the schoolroom yourself not so many years ago and have all those fascinating women out there to amuse you. You must be all about in the head to be so happy at the thought of being with someone you spent your boyhood rescuing from one scrape after another. She has no more idea of how to go on in the world than she did when she was falling out of trees. But he couldn't help remembering how she had looked at him the night of Horace's betrayal, and how comfortable she had felt in his arms. He gave a snort of disgust at his sentimentality over a childhood companion.

Cassie was enjoying herself too thoroughly to be paying much attention in return to this particular childhood companion, but on the drive home she was strangely silent. While Ned and Freddie hotly debated the relative merits of the matched bays Sir Charles Pierrepont had just purchased, she sat quietly reflecting on the day's outing.

She realized that it had been an age since she had felt as comfortable and at ease in a group of people as she had felt today. With Horace she had enjoyed the conversation, but had always been conscious of some constraint, knowing how

high-minded his principles were, lest she say something that
offended his sensibilities. Often she had caught a look of
disapproval in his eyes as she had waxed enthusiastic over
something. And frequently he had made her feel as though
her love for adventure was, if not improper, certainly
hoydenish and unattractive. The consequence had been that
she had always held back and examined every thought before
expressing it. Ned, on the contrary, not only did not act
disapproving, but he encouraged her to express herself and
explore her interests no matter how unusual.

"I'm delighted that you enjoyed yourself, Teddy," Ned's
voice broke into her thoughts. "We shall have to plan another
outing in the near future before your aunt can acquire too
much town bronze to enjoy such things." He turned and
winked at Cassie, amending, "Not that she is in much danger
of preferring a ballroom to a chance for adventure."

Cassie grinned at him and he thought how wonderful it
was to have the impishness back again breaking through the
air of reserve she had worn since he had been in London.
"What do you say to an excursion to the Egyptian hall to
see the reindeer and the wapiti on exhibit there? I have read
that the horns of the wapiti are very curious."

Teddy could hardly breathe in his excitement at the thought
of another such outing. He was in seventh heaven sitting
alongside Ned conversing with him as though he were a true
grown-up. Aunt Cassie and his mother were great guns, but
though they knew their history backward and forward and
were practically on speaking terms with all those Greek
fellows, they did show a sad lack of interest in things
scientific and mechanical, any detail of which was of
passionate interest to the little boy. Uncle Freddie was a
trump and could be counted on for his knowledge of any type
of sporting endeavor, but if Teddy were to ask him about
some point of science such as why stars twinkled, or how
water became steam, Freddie would look rueful and reply
apologetically, "You know, Teddy, you'd better ask your
father. I haven't got all that much in my brain box, my lad."

Lord Mainwaring, when he could be found, could be counted on to supply satisfactory answers, but he was often away or busy, and besides, he was his father. It was so much nicer to have a friend with whom you could discuss things.

Seeing the worshipful light in Teddy's eyes, Ned was touched. He remembered his own admiration of Lord Mainwaring, who had proven to be a similar friend and mentor for a bright inquiring boy raised in a household of kind but unintellectual women, and he resolved to spend more time with the lad. There was another aspect about Teddy's eager expression that moved him. It reminded him strongly of the look Cassie wore when some question or some new thought had struck her. That constant desire to learn and to discover new things or new ways of thinking about things was what he loved most about her.

At this thought Ned stopped dead. How long had he loved her? Consciously he had always been inordinately fond of Cassie. She had been his best friend and playmate for almost as long as he could remember. His life before her was a jumble of small insignificant memories, but after he became her friend, it had taken more shape and purpose. Knowing her had made him more aware of his interests and propensities, so that he was better able to pursue and develop them. But when had this sense of companionship changed to something deeper? He supposed it had come about quite gradually as he moved about in society flirting and enjoying liaisons with the sophisticated women of the *ton*. They had been amusing and seductive and he had been attracted to them in a way that had gratified his senses, but he had never felt the least concern for their happiness, had never wished so desperately to protect them from hurt, had never wanted to help them grow and flourish the way he wanted to take care of Cassie. Though these entertaining coquettes of the fashionable world had stimulated the sensual side of his nature, not even the most charming and accomplished of them had challenged his mind or inspired such a feeling of tenderness in him as she did.

As he watched her entering into the discussion of Pierrepont's bays, it suddenly came to him that he had never been so at ease with anyone as he was with her.

"They may be sweet goers, Freddie, but they haven't enough wind. They won't last. You and Ned may think he got a bargain, but the two of you are forever being taken in by these showy high-spirited bits of blood that have no strength," Cassie maintained, glancing impishly at Ned, daring him to contradict her.

Recognizing that challenging glint in her eye, Ned realized that of all the women he had ever known, Cassie was the only one whose interest in him was so purely friendly and so utterly disinterested that she could tease him. He felt strangely gratified by this proof that she paid attention to him for himself and not for the social cachet his companionship could bring her. Other women to whom he was important because of his wealth or his status as an eligible bachelor and nonpareil could never risk giving offense by laughing at him or mocking him. In fact, most of the time, though he had enjoyed his flirtations immensely, he had felt as though he were a mere actor in a carefully orchestrated play where anyone else of equal economic or social status would have been equally acceptable in the leading male role. With Cassie, it was different. She reacted to him as Ned Mainwaring and liked him for all his own particular interests and accomplishments, not for his social position.

These revelations, while they brought a wonderful sense of discovery and excitement, were also somewhat disturbing because he was not altogether certain of Cassie's state of mind. Could she possibly feel that same special way toward him or was he nothing more to her than a family member, someone like Freddie, who was loved because he had been a part of her life for as long as she could remember? Was she comfortable and natural with him because she liked and trusted him for himself or because he was like her favorite chair in the library at Cresswell, something that she had become so accustomed to having around that she was unaware of it in itself? This was such an upsetting notion that he was glad it was time to leave so that he could be alone with his thoughts and the turmoil of emotions they had aroused.

CHAPTER 23

Lady Portman's annual masquerade could always be counted upon to be one of the highlights of the Season. Anybody among the Upper Ten Thousand who had the least claim to fashion could be counted upon to be there. For weeks before the big event seamstresses and Bond Street modistes cast aside pictures from *La Belle Assemblée* and worked on costuming multiple Mary Queen of Scots, Queen Elizabeths, shepherdesses, and Titanias. Conversations over teacups in drawing rooms from Brook Street to Hanover Square centered around which member of the *ton* was going to appear as what fictional or historical figure that year.

Weary of all the thought of the upcoming masquerade and of how she had already been forced to dress this Season, Cassie seized this opportunity to select a character whose attire would be simple and comfortable, and she directed Madame Regnery in the creation of a costume of the Greek goddess, Diana. Madame, an old friend of the comte's from prerevolution days, had been dressmaker to the Cresswells since she had so successfully created the gowns which had helped Lady Frances establish her own special style the year she became Marchioness of Camberly. Madame, who had understood and sympathized with Cassie's reluctance to become just another fashionable young woman dividing her time between preparing her toilette and then parading it at social functions, had done her best to ensure that the creation of Cassie's wardrobe was a process that was as simple and swift as possible, with the result that Cassie liked her and trusted her judgment implicitly. At last, she and Madame could enter into a project for which Cassie could evince some degree of interest and she and Madame spent several happy hours at Madame's shop in South Moulton Street going over the details of the costume.

Madame was delighted to see Mademoiselle Cassie entering into its creation with such enthusiasm and was suitably impressed with her knowledge of Greek culture and mythology. "Mademoiselle has chosen well. Such a simple style and the gracefulness of the drapery will show off her *taille élégante* to perfection. There are not many young ladies who could wear such things without looking like a pudding bag tied in the middle," she remarked with satisfaction. The classical elegance of the Cresswell ladies' figures was always a great source of gratification to her, for it did justice to her creations. She felt fortunate to be free to design instead of having to struggle to cover her patrons' deficiencies as so many other modistes were forced to do.

Madame was entirely correct in her opinion. The chaste pleated white silk tunic secured with gold cords emphasized Cassie's slender figure while the flow of the drapery called attention to the gracefulness of her movements. As she stood in the archway of Lady Portman's ballroom clutching a golden bow, the light from the chandeliers catching the glow of the golden crescent moons in her fair hair, she did look as ethereal as if she had just stepped down from Mount Olympus. She was accompanied by her sister and brother-in-law, who, attired as Helen and Paris, made a fitting backdrop. The trio had dressed with classical simplicity that only called attention to their elegant bearing and they presented a marked contrast to the fantastic multicolored assemblage before them.

Standing off in one corner with her parents, Arabella felt a pang of envy. No, it couldn't have been envy for someone like Cassie Cresswell, still a scrubby schoolgirl despite her presence in Town this Season. It was certainly not envy, but all of a sudden Arabella, who had been confident of her capturing all eyes dressed as a shepherdess in a costume that contrived to look demure while revealing as much of her

charms as possible, felt less certain of these charms.
Compared to Cassie's, her costume seemed fussy and overly
elaborate, the décolletage obvious and slightly tawdry when
put beside the subtle charm of Cassie's draperies, which only
hinted at instead of blatantly revealing the beautiful figure
beneath them. It didn't help matters in the least when her
roving eye discerned Ned Mainwaring off in another corner
of the ballroom flirting with Lady Jersey, for Ned, clad in
a tunic which only served to emphasize his height and athletic
physique, a lion skin draped over his broad shoulders, was
dressed as Hercules—the perfect foil for Diana and a
ridiculous partner for a shepherdess.

Ned's abrupt departure from Lady Jersey when he
recognized the party from Mainwaring House did nothing
to improve Arabella's temper, and she watched, seething,
as she bent first over Lady Mainwaring's and then Cassie's
hand. To one whose existence was defined by the least little
nuance in any social gesture, it seemed that he clasped more
of Cassie's hand than the requisite few inches of finger and
held it for longer than politeness dictated. Arabella, who had
for years taken his admiring glances for granted and had only
this Season come to recognize and value them as something
to be envied by other women, was now truly annoyed to see
the warmth in the look he directed at Cassie and the intimacy
of his smile as he teased her about something. Such a situation
would never do! No one must be allowed to outshine such
a diamond as Arabella Taylor, much less supersede her in
someone's attentions, especially not an unfashionable
bluestocking like Cassie Cresswell. Marshaling her considerable powers of seduction, Arabella prepared to do battle.

Pinning a charming, if totally false smile on her face, she
glided over to the little group, exclaiming, "Oh, I am so
glad that I did not come as Aphrodite after all because it
would have been quite dreadful if there were two of us."

Catching the amused glint in Ned's eye at Arabella's
misreading of her costume, Cassie found it difficult not to
laugh, but managed to respond without a quaver, "What a

fortunate circumstance. To have been caught in similar attire would certainly have been a social disaster.''

"Yes, I'm so thankful that I realized that people might think me shockingly blue if I were to appear as a character from Greek mythology,'' Arabella replied with a triumphant smile.

Cassie's eyes danced. "That would never do, certainly,'' she agreed seriously. "How perfectly dreadful to be mistaken for a person of culture.''

Even Arabella had the grace to blush as she recognized the full import of her words. "But Cassie,'' she protested, "you don't understand. I have my reputation to consider. The whole of the *ton* knows you to be a bluestocking, so what can it signify what you wear? Whereas I am reckoned someone of taste and fashion among my acquaintances. One should never appear too serious, you know,'' she added in a confidential tone. Then, warming to her favorite theme, she continued a trifle defiantly, "Sir Brian Brandon, whose knowledge and experience in these matters I rely upon entirely, has even said he considers me to be an incomparable.''

Here, Freddie, as he had done since they were children, stepped in and thwarted Arabella's plans. "I say, Arabella, you and I don't fit in with all these lofty Greeks. Why don't we leave them to their own intellectual devices and join the set that's forming for the quadrille. Nothing could show off your costume to better advantage than being a partner to a pirate.'' And it was certainly true that Freddie, who had utterly refused to wear a namby-pamby tunic like the rest of his family, did make a most fearsome pirate indeed, complete with cutlass and a wicked-looking scar that Cook had helped him concoct with flour and water.

Poor Arabella could do nothing but thank him prettily and allow herself to be led onto the floor, though her eyes continued to follow Ned and Cassie as they chatted and laughed with Lady Frances and Lord Julian.

Arabella's ill humor was considerably mollified when Sir

Brian Brandon, gorgeous to behold as Apollo, solicited her hand for the waltz, but the pleasure of being seen to captivate such a leader of fashion was soon spoiled when she saw Ned take Cassie's hand and lead her into the waltz as well. The fact that they perfectly complimented each other—he, tall and dark, she fair and slender, wearing costumes that showed their figures to the best advantage, and were so perfectly suited to each other—did nothing to improve her mood. Nor did the graceful way they moved together, oblivious to everyone but each other, improve the situation.

Cassie herself was commenting on this. "I had no idea you waltzed so well, Ned Mainwaring. If you don't make a go of politics, you could be a first-rate caper merchant," she teased.

Ned grinned. "You have no notion of the skills I've acquired in my travels," he replied airily.

"Oh"—she laughed—"Freddie has been hinting darkly at beautiful Italian contessas, Austrian baronesses, and Spanish marquesas, but I thought it was all a hum because the Ned I knew would have been off buried in some library or seeking out some desiccated scholar in all of those places."

One mobile eyebrow shot up as he looked down at her, smiling in such a way that her heart began to beat quite fast and it suddenly became difficult to catch her breath. "Not all scholars are desiccated, you know," he said. His gaze became more intent as he added softly, "In fact, some of them are quite charming and *very* beautiful. Those are the ones I waltz with." Observing the blush that rose in her cheeks, Ned decided that there were few, if any, times when he could remember Cassie disconcerted and he found it adorable.

Even more enchanting was the delighted surprise in her eyes as she raised them shyly to his, whispering, "Why, Ned, how kind of you. Thank you."

Her innocent astonishment at his remark brought to mind so many others who, with far less reason, took such compliments for granted. In fact, they often pouted if such pretty sayings were not regularly forthcoming, and he thought again what a rare unspoiled creature Cassandra Cresswell was and how infinitely dear to him. Recalled from his reverie by the other couples leaving the floor, Ned smiled fondly at Cassie and led her back to Frances and Julian, who had been joined by a monk so large that it could be no one but Nigel Streatham.

After her dance with Freddie, Arabella had stuck like a limpet to the Mainwarings, and the moment Ned returned, she pounced. "Ned, I hear you were at a balloon ascension of all things. What a charming notion! One does become so very tired of the constant social whirl and long for a divertissement to relieve one's boredom. But I fear that I should become quite dizzy watching such a thing," she protested, contriving to look interested but fragile all at the same time.

"Then it's most fortunate I didn't invite you," Ned responded equably.

Rapping him across the knuckles with her fan, she laughed playfully. "You're a dreadful wretch, Ned Mainwaring, and you must make up to me by dancing this next with me or I shall never speak to you again."

Fairly caught, Ned bowed and led her out onto the floor, though his eye followed Cassie as she laughed merrily at some disparaging remark her twin had made. Soon she, too, was on the floor, following the inexpert lead of Nigel, who had desperately sought her aid.

"Dance with me, please, Cass," he had begged. "M'mother's looking daggers at me, and if she don't see me on the floor with someone soon, she'll carry on dreadfully. It's not that I don't like dancing, but I feel like a regular chawbacon in this toggery. And it's not that I don't like women exactly, but why must they giggle so? I know I ain't a great wit, but my cock loft ain't completely empty, and no matter what I say to these young girls, they just look at me and simper. I've chosen the most unexceptional subjects of conversation, too," he complained. "I tell you"—he lowered his voice confidentially—"it's enough to turn a fellow off women completely. Why can't they be regular fellows like you and talk about something sensible like horses? Speaking of which, I've been meaning to ask you what you think of Bedford's hunter. I've been needing a hunter and I saw his at Tatt's the other day and I tell you, it was as pretty a piece of horseflesh as one could hope to see." Warming to his favorite subject, he continued, enthusiastically cataloging every one of the horse's features in minutest detail.

Cassie listened and nodded at the appropriate moments, but she was only half attending. Her thoughts were all on Ned, her waltz with him, and the odd rush of feelings that had come over her when he had looked at her in that special way. She had never thought a great deal about her appearance one way or another so long as it was presentable, but now, having been told she was beautiful, all of a sudden she cared a great deal how she looked and she wanted desperately to be truly as beautiful as he might think her—as beautiful as anyone he knew.

This was such a novel thought that fond of Nigel though she was, Cassie was glad when the dance ended so she could seek the peace and quiet of the garden to be alone with these disturbing new thoughts.

She stepped through the doors out onto a gravel path, but the solitude she sought was not to be hers, as another couple, also in pursuit of privacy, had preceded her. As Cassie stood there wondering what to do, the woman leaned toward the man and he caught her in a close embrace. Embarrassed at her unwitting intrusion into such an intimate scene, Cassie turned to go, but her feet scrunched on the gravel.

Alerted by the sound that their privacy had been invaded, the man looked up, and in the split second as she turned and hurried to leave, Cassie recognized Ned. The image of the woman locked in his arms rose before her and she realized that it was Arabella. It had all happened so quickly that she was stumbling back into the ballroom only moments after she'd left it. But in that short space of time, Cassie's entire world had changed.

Unfortunately, she had not stayed long enough either to see Ned look up or to see him unwind Arabella's arms from around his neck. In fact, Ned had been almost as unwitting a participant in the scene as Cassie. Certainly, he was as much a victim of Arabella's machinations as Cassie, though when Arabella had plotted to lure him into the garden, she could not, even in her wildest imagination, have hoped to find a way to ensure that Cassie would witness the entire scene.

Once Arabella had maneuvered Ned into soliciting the dance, the rest had been quite simple. Ned had kept up only the most desultory of conversations, all his thoughts on Cassie, so she was able, by dint of holding her breath, to become charmingly, but alarmingly flushed. Once that was accomplished, she turned her big eyes imploringly up to his, begging breathlessly, "Oh, Ned, I do feel so giddy . . . the heat . . . the crowd. I vow I am quite overcome. Do take me to some fresh air or I shall surely faint."

Ever the gentleman, Ned had led her to the doors and out onto the path, making for a small stone bench at the end of the garden. But they had barely stepped outside before Arabella collapsed against him, gasping, "I'm quite unable to stand." What could even the most callous of escorts do but come to the aid of a stricken lady? So Ned had put a supporting arm around her. No sooner had he done this than she had thrown her arms around his neck, exclaiming gratefully, "Dear Ned, so kind, so strong. The constant demands of the Season have quite worn me to a thread. I am such a poor weak creature." Here she looked up at him in an adoring way that had been the undoing of everyone who had been the object of it.

But Ned had not flirted with the beautiful women in all the capitals of Europe for nothing, and he knew very well that far from exhausting her, the frantic social round of the *ton* was tonic to Arabella. Suspecting that he was being

manipulated for some unknown purpose, he was about to
extricate himself when he heard footsteps on the gravel and
looked up to see Cassie framed in the light streaming from
the ballroom. Before he could utter a syllable of her name,
she had turned and vanished, but not before he had perceived
the stricken look on her face.

Already annoyed at having been forced into an unwanted
embrace, Ned was now furious at Arabella, and it was with
some difficulty that he was able to address her with any
civility at all. Frowning, he declared, "This is quite serious.
I am persuaded you should return home and lie down. Come,
let us find your mother." And without giving her time to
protest, Ned took her arm and led her forcefully over to the
pillared alcove where a portly Queen Elizabeth who was the
image of Lady Taylor was comparing notes with Mary Queen
of Scots, equally obviously Lady Billingsley, on their
charitable activities in their respective parishes.

"Good evening, Lady Taylor. Arabella is feeling faint.
She is quite done up by the hectic pace, so I've brought her
to you so you may take her home," Ned remarked, bowing
to Arabella's mother and her companion.

Lady Taylor immediately began to fuss over her daughter.

It was difficult for a lady seething with frustration to
maintain the appropriate air of lassitude that would render
her story convincing, but Arabella had been such a
consummate participant in the social scene for so many years
that she had become an extraordinarily convincing actress.
She murmured faintly, but heroically, "You're too kind,
Ned. I would feel dreadful if anyone were to leave on my
account. If I may just make use of your vinaigrette, Mama."

These last remarks were addressed to Ned's retreating
back, as once he had assured himself of Lady Taylor's
attention, he had beat a hasty retreat and gone in search of
Cassie.

She, however, really did feel faint and so alarmingly ill
that Frances was all concern when she saw her sister.
"Cassie, you look quite done up. Shall we go home?" she

asked the instant her sister had rejoined their little group.

But all of a sudden, Cassie, who only minutes before had been wishing to do that very thing, took a deep breath, straightened her shoulders, and forced a glittering, if totally false smile on her lips, and replied, "No thank you, Frances. For a moment the closeness of the ballroom was too much, but I would not miss this for the world."

Something inside of Cassie had snapped at the sight of Arabella and Ned. The stamina and desire to prove herself that had kept her from shedding tears and had inspired her to get up and try again after falls from trees and tumbles from horses had promptly asserted itself. If someone as stupid and vain as Arabella Taylor can become an incomparable, there must be something wrong with you, Cassandra Cresswell, because you have twice the wit she does, Cassie scolded herself. There is not the slightest reason that she should have things entirely her way and capture all the attention for herself, she continued. It's not that you want that attention, mind, but it just doesn't seem fair that someone as selfish and undeserving as she should be allowed to dominate and win the admiration of everyone.

Cassie, despite this reflective mood, was not willing to admit even to herself that it was the admiration of a particular someone rather than the world at large that she begrudged Arabella.

In the grip of this salutary anger, Cassie was unaware that she was being watched by one of society's most inveterate and acute observers, Bertie Montgomery. He had seen her return from the garden followed closely by Ned and Arabella and thus had a fair estimation of what had occurred. Oddly enough, thoughts quite similar to those going through Cassie's mind were going through his, and with the vague notion that he could help put things to rights somehow, he sauntered over to the alcove where Cassie, Julian, and Frances were standing.

"Hallo, Julian, Frances," he said, acknowledging Cassie's companions before turning to her. "Cassie, I see you've had a chance to catch your breath after all your exercise on the floor. Would you care to stand up with me? I've endured several toe tramplings in my attempts to sponsor the success of Lady Warburton's and Lady Hathaway's youngest and therefore I richly deserve a partner who not only will do justice to my dancing ability, but will reply to any of my poor attempts at conversation with something more than a monosyllable."

"Why, thank you, Bertie," Cassie accepted his invitation gratefully.

After some minutes of silence during which Cassie, busy with her thoughts, performed her steps abstractedly, Bertie interjected in an injured tone, "I say, Cass, at least those blushing damsels had a mumbled response to my sallies even if they confined it to a mere yes or no."

Cassie looked up, conscience-stricken, "Oh, I am sorry, Bertie. I was not attending. What did you say?"

He looked amused. "Nothing as yet, but you were so deep in your thoughts I could see that anything I could say would be to no purpose."

"Oh dear," she replied. Then, impelled by the look of sympathetic interest on his face, she plunged into a rather tangled speech. "Bertie, why is it that some people who have more hair than wit and aren't very nice besides can become all the rage? How can people like people who only have a pretty face and nothing else to recommend them when there are so many other people who are much nicer but seem to be less admired?"

Despite his amiable and open countenance, Bertie was no fool and he did not for one minute believe that Cassie's question sprang from a purely general and dispassionate curiosity concerning the workings of the *ton*. He reflected for a moment before answering, "Well, Cassie, I ain't a particularly clever fellow, but I think it has to do with interest."

"Interest?" Cassie looked blank.

"Yes, interest," he replied. Warming to his theme, he

continued, "Most people ain't all that sure of themselves, so they watch what everyone else is doing and then do that. That's called 'fashion.' " He beamed triumphantly at his own perspicacity. "Now someone who spends a great deal of time thinking about fashion is someone these people understand. Moreover, someone like, like . . . Arabella Taylor, for instance, knows that fashion comes from everyone's doing or liking the same thing, so she spends an enormous amount of time and effort working to win their approval and demonstrate how much she cares about what people think of her. Much of her day is devoted to choosing a toilette that will be universally pleasing, and she can always be seen in the most approved places. She does her best to converse only on topics that are of the most general concern. All this attention to the opinion of society flatters people, and because she makes them feel that she attaches great importance to their judgment, they decide that they like her. Then they tell their friends that Arabella Taylor is a nice gel, and before you can say jackstraws, she's all the rage." Here, proud of this unusually long speech, Bertie stopped to catch his breath.

"But what a two-faced thing to do!" Cassie protested.

"It ain't two-faced. She truly is interested in those things and she truly is interested in people, in her own way of course. Now someone, say like you, enjoys many things and your whole existence don't begin and end with others' opinions of you. People know that being liked and admired by them ain't the most important thing in your life. They're never certain of what you're thinking. Makes 'em uncomfortable."

"Do you mean to say that someone like me could become all the rage if she cared to do so?" Cassie demanded in disbelief.

"Might do." Bertie looked thoughtful.

Cassie was silent for a while and then, glancing shyly up at him, asked, "If I were interested in cutting a dash, do you think you could help me, I mean show me how to go on?"

"Happy to," Bertie beamed at her.

"Could . . . could we start tomorrow, do you think?" she wondered.

"No time like the present," he declared stoutly. "I'll call for you tomorrow morning and we can begin with a drive in the park."

"Oh, thank you, Bertie. You're the kindest friend in the world," Cassie breathed.

He blushed, disclaiming, "It's nothing. Happy to do anything to be of service to you and the family."

Bertie led Cassie back to the alcove where Sir Brian Brandon had now joined Frances, Julian. and Freddie. Sir Brian claimed Cassie's hand, closely followed by her brother-in-law and her twin, so that Ned, try though he might, was unable to get near her for the rest of the evening.

CHAPTER 24

The next day found Ned riding north with Lord Charlton to visit Lord Haslemere, an aged peer who, though now retired in the country, nevertheless retained powerful political connections and was in many ways more aware of what was occurring on the political scene than those participating in it. They left so early that Ned was unable to call at Grosvenor Square and was thus forced to wait with as much patience as he could muster to offer his explanation to Cassie.

As he rode, he reflected on this odd state of things. Accustomed to living his own life and pursuing his own interests wherever they led him, he was one who highly prized his freedom and resented the slightest interference in his affairs. Previously he had conducted all his liaisons with women who had understood and completely respected his dislike of feeling obligated or having to answer to anyone. There had been one person who had inspired him to give up his freedom, one person he had spent his life dreaming of. Now, not only was he irked at her proprietary attitude, he was wishing desperately that a childhood playmate he had laughed at, teased, and argued with would demonstrate just such an interest in him. More than anything he wanted to wrap his arms around Cassie as tightly as Arabella had clung to him and reassure her concerning the scene she had witnessed in the garden. He sighed.

When he had first learned of Lord Haslemere's wish to meet him, he had been overjoyed at the opportunity. As Lord Charlton had said, "Any man who has Haslemere's stamp of approval will go far, no matter what his political party."

Now Ned was longing to be back in London, all because he wanted to explain himself to someone he'd known since childhood, someone who, for all he knew, may not have cared whether or not he reassured her. I must be in my dotage, he thought. Why am I worrying about her feelings when in all probability she hasn't given a second thought to seeing Arabella and me, or if she has, she is, if anything, amused?

Here he was entirely wrong. Not only had Cassie given second thoughts to the intimate moment she had intruded on, she could not get the tableau of Arabella wrapped in Ned's arms out of her mind. She was still too upset to realize that it was Ned who had been wrapped in Arabella's arms despite his heroic efforts to extricate himself gracefully. At this moment, Cassie's valiant efforts to erase the memory and direct her energies into more productive channels were taking the form of a ride in the park in Bertie's new phaeton.

Even the friends who had known Bertie since schooldays were constantly amazed that a man who spent so much time on his wardrobe and seeking out and repeating fashionable on-dits in London's most select drawing rooms, all the while completely ignoring such male haunts as Manton's and Gentleman Jackson's, could be such a notable whip. It seemed incongruous that the languid and willowy Bertie could possibly have the strength to keep a spirited pair in control. Yet somehow, without disarranging his exquisite attire or overcoming his loathing for any sort of exertion, he managed not only to handle the most restive of high-spirited teams, but drove with all the finesse of the most noted member of the Four Horse Club. He had recently purchased a beautiful pair and a new phaeton with yellow wheels, a combination destined to cause a stir in the park and arouse envy in the breast of every admirer of fine horseflesh.

Certainly his equipage had caused a favorable sensation at Mainwaring House. Teddy and Freddie had agreed that the turnout was slap up to the echo. Bertie and Cassie could have waited forever for them to finish examining and enumerating the fine points of the entire rig, if both Teddy and his uncle had not had too much respect for such a mettle-some pair to keep them standing.

Even Cassie forgot her unpleasant thoughts long enough to exclaim over them as they bowled along. Excellent horse-woman that she was, she kept silent while Bertie maneuvered through the streets, and refrained from commenting on the smooth gait and the well-sprung ride until they reached the park. "You do drive to an inch, Bertie," she commented admiringly as he skillfully negotiated his way between two wagons and through the gate.

"Thank you, Cassie." Bertie, knowing that Cassie's own driving skills were something beyond the ordinary, looked gratified. "But," he began as purposefully as Bertie Montgomery did anything, "we ain't here to pass judgment on my driving. We're here to help take your rightful place in the *ton*."

Cassie looked dubious. During her sleepless night she had thought about her expressed wish to become all the rage with some misgiving. She now gave voice to these reservations. "I'm not at all certain that I can simper, smile, and act bird-witted as though I am in the greatest need of someone who can tell me how to go on and explain everything to me. Nor can I admire some overeager buck that I don't care a rap for."

"Whoa, Cassie. I ain't saying you have to do any of those things. You don't have to bamboozle anyone. Just enjoy yourself. If you're dancing with some blade who can only talk about the way he ties his cravats, it's Lombard Street to a China orange he has taste and can dance well, so you should take pleasure in the graceful way he executes his steps and appreciate the care he has taken with his toilette the way you would appreciate the skill of any other artist. If you're stuck with some beefy-faced squire who can speak of nothing but horses, why you can enjoy yourself discussing that without thinking that you would die of bordeom if you were condemned to spend your entire life with him. People don't want flummery. They just want someone who is interested in their particular passions and can share these, as well as someone who knows how to converse with them on their favorite subjects.''

Cassie was quiet. The more she thought about it, the more she realized that this was exactly what Bertie did. Every member of the *ton* liked him and sought out his company, not for his brilliant wit or overwhelming charm, but because of his amiable adaptability and the ease with which he could enter into any discussion. "That's all very well, but to be a diamond or a nonpareil one must be well looking and have an air of fashion," she objected.

"Well, one certainly can't be an antidote," he conceded. "But again, it's enjoying oneself that is important. Whatever rig one chooses, one should look upon selecting it as an artistic experience and take pleasure in using it as a way to express oneself.''

Cassie looked puzzled.

"Take you, for instance. You wear your clothes as though choosing them were a duty. You always look elegant, but you don't appear as though you relished preparing your toilette. In point of fact, you take this all too seriously. You look at it the way you would some task of Greek translation, as though it has some underlying significance. You don't need to know the meaning of everything to take pleasure in it. You like beautiful things, don't you—paintings, sculpture, music?''

Cassie nodded.

"Then why not enjoy wearing beautiful things and using them to make yourself feel and look beautiful?''

Cassie sat silently as they rolled along, nodding mechanically to familiar faces here and there. She realized that Bertie was echoing a criticism, once voiced by Ned, that she considered everything too seriously. She sighed. It was all so very confusing and difficult to think about. Had she been wrong in the way she looked at things for so many years?

They had completed the circuit before Bertie interrupted these rather melancholy reflections. "Cassie, you mustn't look so blue-deviled. We'll take you to Madame Regnery, choose some new togs for you, and you're bound to feel much more the thing. You must begin with a riding habit.''

''A riding habit?'' Cassie echoed blankly. ''But I have a perfectly—''

''I've seen it and it's all that's suitable, but that ain't enough,'' Bertie interjected firmly. ''You have the best seat of anyone I know, man or woman. You should wear something that calls attention to you in a situation where you show to advantage and most females don't—Arabella Taylor for one. She'd be terrified of a cart horse while you can manage a prime bit of blood with ease. It's time the *ton* was aware of that.''

Cassie, much struck by this idea, meekly allowed herself to be deposited at Madame Regnery's while Bertie found a boy to take care of the horses.

The next few hours flew by in a blur as Bertie, conversant with feminine fashion down to the last furbelow, ordered up gowns that would be an accurate reflection of the true spirit of Lady Cassandra Cresswell.

''And that hair,'' he concluded severely, subjecting her modest style to a critical examination, ''positively must go.''

''What's wrong with it?'' Cassie demanded a trifle rebelliously. She had submitted with tolerable good grace to being pushed and pulled, fitted, evaluated, discussed, and gone over as though she were a prime piece of horseflesh, but she was now beginning to feel rather tired of being treated as though she didn't exist.

''It makes you look like an ape-leader,'' Bertie responded with unusually brutal frankness.

''It does no such thing! Besides, it's dignified. I detest the odiously fussy way everyone is wearing theirs now,'' Cassie objected mutinously.

Ignoring her completely, Bertie waved to Monsier Ducros, Lady Frances's hairdresser, who had been hovering unobtrusively in the background. ''You see what I mean?'' he inquired despairingly.

"*Mais oui,* Monsieur is entirely correct. Mademoiselle looks *un peu sévère,*" he agreed. "*Oui, c'est trop sévère.* Mademoiselle must be *moins sérieuse, je pense.*"

Cassie sighed and gave herself up to the ministrations of Monsieur. When he was finished, she was forced to admit that Bertie and Monsieur Ducros were entirely correct. Her previous coiffeur had been too severe. With her hair cut shorter, her curls were freed to fame her face, adding piquancy to her expression, emphasizing the large blue eyes, the generous mouth, and the delicately but firmly molded chin. It felt lighter, freer, and made her feel just that much lighter and gayer herself.

Bertie nodded sagely as she pirouetted in front of the mirror. "What did I tell you?" he asked, unable to keep a trace of smugness from showing. "Put on that new walking dress and you'll feel a different person. No one should underestimate the importance of becoming clothes and coiffeur to one's sense of well-being. Anyone who tells you differently is a slowtop." He then directed Madame's assistance to help Cassie into the most dashing of the walking dresses and to wrap up the sober carriage dress she had been wearing. The cerulean blue spencer cut tight to the shape revealed Cassie's graceful figure and the matching gauze lining the very fashionable watered *gros de Naples* bonnet brought out the intense blue of her eyes.

As they strolled along to the carriage and Cassie caught sight of herself in shop windows she reveled in the moment of startled recognition when she realized that she belonged to that exquisitely fashionable reflection. This in turn made her conversation and expression more animated and sparkling. The air of gaiety and confidence, as much as her very real beauty, caused several passersby to stop and take a second look at the lovely young woman with Bertie Montgomery—a circumstance he was very careful to point out to her. This admiration increased Cassie's sense of well-being, so that she positively glowed with her enjoyment of the fineness of the day, her companion, and herself.

It was not only those on the street who were struck by

Cassie's newfound *éclat*. Freddie and Nigel, strolling along after an agreeable sojourn at Tattersall's, halted in their discussion of the auction taking place there. "I say, that's a dashed pretty girl," Freddie remarked.

At which Nigel, who had observed more carefully than his companion, nearly doubled over with mirth. "Freddie, you cawker! That's your sister!" he bellowed.

"Why, so it is," Freddie agreed in mild surprise. "Hallo, Cass. What have you been doing to yourself? You look fine as fivepence."

"Why, thank you, Freddie." Cassie turned quite pink with pleasure. Freddie, the best of brothers a girl could wish for and unfailingly kind about including his twin in every kind of lark, was totally oblivious to the niceties of feminine fashion. To have her toilette penetrate his consciousness was a coup indeed! Even Nigel, who had been as unconscious as Freddie until his service with brother Guardsmen inclined to ogle any woman between the ages of sixteen and thirty had taught him the niceties of feminine fashion, was looking at her admiringly. Bertie is in the right of it, she thought to herself as she promenaded along surrounded by these escorts, wearing fashionable clothes does affect one's frame of mind.

CHAPTER 25

It would have been too much to say that the transformation Bertie had effected in Cassie stunned the fashionable world, but the members of the *ton* were more aware of her presence. Captain Walworth, upon seeing her in the park mounted on Chiron and wearing a close-fitting lavender riding habit with its dashing hat, remarked to Major Dowling that Lady Cassandra Cresswell was a remarkably pretty girl. "Excellent seat, too," he observed, watching her with a critical but admiring eye.

Major Dowling repeated this to his bosom companion Henry Ffolke-Smythe, a noted clubman, who of course shared it with his fellows, and slowly Cassie found herself beginning to be scrutinized with a deal of interest and approval.

Taking Bertie's advice to heart, she relaxed and began to interest herself in the particular attributes and passions that each new admirer had to offer. Somewhat to her surprise, she truly began to enjoy herself in a way that she hadn't for a long time. She learned a great deal as well. As she sat next to him at Lady Waverly's musicale, instead of scorning the Honorable Winston Denham's obsession with his tailor, Cassie listened to his catalog of the agonies suffered over the perfect fitting of his coat and the creation of a new style of tying his cravat. She gained a new appreciation for the creativity that inspired this particular passion. Not that she could ever become the greatest of friends with someone who spent such an inordinate amount of time selecting just the right waistcoat and snuffbox to match his attire, but instead of discounting such attention to toilette entirely, she began to perceive it as a mode of self-expression and to have more sympathy toward him. This sympathy communicated itself to the Honorable Winston, who relaxed in its warmth and found himself opening up and speaking far more naturally and freely than he ordinarily did. In fact, he couldn't think when he last had a more delightful conversation. Later, recapping the evening to some of his closest friends, he pronounced Lady Cassandra Cresswell to be simply charming.

As Cassie pursued this new program she discovered that it put people more at their ease with her, and feeling comfortable, they were less likely to converse on the safe and boring subjects of the weather, the latest *on-dit*, or their health. Instead they began to share more topics that were their own particular concern, and this all made for much more enlightening and intriguing discussions. Cassie even began to look forward to some of the festivities of the Season and to take pleasure in social encounters. This new attitude expressed itself through the sparkle in her eyes and the vivacity of her expression. Those around her, attracted by this vitality, gravitated toward her naturally. The change was a gradual one, but it was distinct, nevertheless, and those near and dear to her remarked on it with pleasure.

"Is that knocker never silent, Mr. Higgins?" Cook demanded as she served the butler his supper one evening.

"Hardly. There is a constant succession of bouquets and eager young bucks, top-of-the-trees, some of them. At last Miss Cassie seems to have taken the *ton* by storm, though it was a long time coming. I began to wonder if they had eyes in their heads." If Higgins had not heard from Lady Kitty Willoughby's butler that the lady's brother was in the country, he would have been concerned over Ned's conspicuous absence as he still firmly maintained that of all Miss Cassie's London beaux, Master Ned was the only one capable of handling her. "She's a rare handful," he remarked reminiscently to Mrs. Wilkins. "There are very few with the wit and spirit to keep up with her. Mark my words,

Master Ned is the one for her. He's one of the few people she has ever listened to."

Rose, though less vocal in the servants' hall than her superior, was also relishing her mistress's new attitude, perhaps more than anyone else. Born with a strong creative streak, the young maid had always been sorry that her mistress, dearly as she loved her, did not care enough about her toilette to utilize Rose's talents to their fullest degree. Now, however, instead of looking askance at her hair when Rose had finished and asking hesitantly if she could make it a trifle smoother and less frivolous, Cassie would glance appreciatively in the glass at her maid's artistry, remarking, "You are as much a genius as Monsieur Ducros, Rose. I am indeed fortunate to have you to take care of me."

Rose would smile secretly to herself, but could not refrain from remarking, "It's that glad I am to see you enjoying yourself as you should do, Miss Cassie. It's good to see you at your old ways again."

"My old ways?" Cassie asked curiously.

"Why yes, miss. Ever since Master Freddie and Master Ned left you've been so very serious. When they came back, we all thought you would be your old gay self, but you weren't. I suppose it was that you spent so much time with that Horace Wilbraham, who always wore such a Friday face and filled your head with all those Greeks, so it was not to be wondered at that you didn't enjoy yourself."

Goodness, Cassie thought to herself, Bertie rescued me just in time. It seems as though I was on my way to become the deadest of dead bores.

That evening she threw herself with such renewed effort into the gaiety that people, seeing her vivacity, wondered if there was to be some special forthcoming announcement that would account for it.

In the meantime, far removed from the frivolity of the capital, Ned had ample time on his own to reflect. Lord Haslemere, never the most sociable of men even when young, now retired very early in the evening, "to save what little strength I have in this desiccated frame,'' he explained. ''Never get old, lad. Being treated as an oracle isn't worth the cost in the aches and pains of growing old and wise.''

So Ned was left to his own devices and he spent a great deal of time sitting in front of the fire, a glass of brandy in hand, thinking of Cassie. He always began by wishing she were there so he could recount the day's discussion and hear her views. As he warmed to his topic he would envision her sitting with the firelight catching the golden highlights in her hair, her head tilted to one side, her forehead slightly wrinkled in concentration, and he would long for nothing so much as to have her in his arms.

He would imagine so vividly how it would feel to hold her against him, her head resting on his shoulder, that he could practically smell the rosewater in her hair. But then the image of her face as she saw him with Arabella would always intrude and shatter the delightful vision.

''Damn and blast! I must get back to Town!'' he would fume in frustration. But there was no help for it. He couldn't leave such a golden opportunity to absorb political wisdom from ''the oracle,'' as Lord Haslemere so ironically dubbed himself, so he remained in the country with as good grace as he could muster, learning all Lord Haslemere had to offer and advancing his own ideas for criticism and discussion. Warmed by the approbation he heard in his mentor's voice and stimulated by the day's conversation, he would retire at night to be tortured anew by the sequence of events which kept him away from Cassie and this strange new longing to be with her, to hold her and feel her close to him.

Cassie, on the other hand, was keeping herself far too busy to be suffering such agonies. At the back of her mind was a part of her that looked for Ned as she entered every ballroom or stepped into the box at the theater or the opera, but such unwelcome thoughts were speedily banished by recalling the scene with Arabella. If Cassie missed having her best friend to share things and laugh with, she soon

overcame that with the thought that no one who lived in
Arabella Taylor's pocket could have the discrimination and
sensitivity to be dubbed her closest friend.

Still, amidst all the gaiety and the bevy of young men
soliciting her company for every sort of entertainment, she
felt a small empty space and knew that something was missing
to keep her happiness from being complete. It was not a big
enough hole that she was constantly aware of it, but in the
quietness of the carriage returning to Mainwaring House
from some brilliant soirée, or as Rose was helping her to
undress, the little feeling of incompleteness would insist on
intruding. Cassie would quickly shake her head, telling
herself that she was just tired, but as she drifted off to sleep,
her mind wandering aimlessly, she would admit to herself
that it wasn't exhaustion but the wish to have, if not Ned,
someone who could be exactly as he had been for her before
Arabella had taken him over.

Ned and Cassie were not the only ones suffering disturbing
thoughts. Arabella, though she did her utmost to avoid
serious reflections of any sort, was undergoing some
unpleasant revelations of her own. These had been prompted
by the reactions of a dancing partner, a callow youth that
she only suffered to lead her on the dance floor because he
was the youngest brother of a highly eligible marquess who,
in Arabella's opinion, had remained unattached or even un-
attracted to any single woman for far too many Seasons. As
they went through their figures she noticed his attention
wandering. Accustomed to being the sole focus of anyone's
interest, the beauty was considerably miffed and followed
his gaze, which seemed to be fixed on a group of young
blades at the other end of the ballroom. Realizing that
Arabella was aware of his distraction, her partner looked
somewhat uncomfortable but asked eagerly, "Who is she?
I know you know everyone who is anyone so you must know
her, but I don't ever recall seeing her."

Neither did Arabella recognize the particular slender
vivacious blond girl with a decided air of fashion about her
who somehow seemed vaguely familiar. She looked again

more closely only to discover that not only was she acquainted with what appeared to be society's newest interest, but she had known her since they had been in pinafores instead of ball gowns. Trying to keep herself from audibly grinding her teeth, Arabella responded with an air of sweet condescension. "Why that's little Cassie Cresswell. It must be her first Season. How time flies! It seems no time at all since she was the biggest tomboy for miles around."

And that was not to be the last of it. The next day a tactless young gallant whose protestations of undying affection had become something of a bore because his constant hounding of Arabella had begun to discourage more sophisticated and more eligible admirers, further annoyed her by remarking to her that the Hampshire air must be extraordinarily salubrious as it had produced two of the Season's reigning beauties: Arabella Taylor and Lady Cassandra Cresswell. Seeing the frown settling on his deity's brow, he had hastily added that of course everyone knew brunettes were all the fashion and that he himself found blondes a trifle insipid for his taste. But it was too late. The damage had been done and Arabella was now were aware that that upstart Cassandra Cresswell, who was a tomboy and a bluestocking besides, had become a force to be reckoned with. She retired to plot her course of action, for it would never do to have the *ton* linking their names just because they happened to have the misfortune of having grown up together.

CHAPTER 26

At last Ned was able to break away from Lord Haslemere's most flattering hospitality and return to London, where it was not very long before it was borne in upon him that some changes had transpired during his absence from the capital. He had barely changed clothes and washed the dust of travel from his person before he presented himself in Grosvenor Square, requesting to see Miss Cassie.

Now Higgins, wise in the ways of the world and the Cresswells in particular, though he had long ago decided that Master Ned was just the person to keep his mistress in line, had also decided that it would never do for Master Ned to take her for granted. He was pleased, therefore, upon hearing the object of Ned's visit, to inform him that this object had just departed in Sir Brian Brandon's elegant curricle.

Ned was forced to cool his heels with ill-disguised impatience, which only increased when his valet reminded him that he was promised to his sister for her card party that evening. Knowing that the group from Mainwaring House was far too dashing to frequent card parties and were far more likely, it being a Wednesday night, to be gracing Almack's select assemblage, he was forced to contain his frustration until the next day.

Having been beaten out the first time, Ned was careful to present himself at Mainwaring House at an early hour the following morning. Hearing the slightly anxious note in his voice when he asked again for Miss Cassie, Higgins was happy to inform him that she had just left for the park mounted on Chiron and accompanied by Nigel Streatham and his fellow Guardsmen. Concerned lest such an old friend as Miss Cassie be unappreciated because her familiarity and eager for her claims to fashion and popular acclaim to be recognized and properly respected, Higgins was delighted to note Master Ned's reaction upon receiving this news with no little satisfaction. His jaws tightened, his shoulders tensed, and his blue eyes darkened—all very propitious signs to one who wished him to wake up to the fact that his Miss Cassie was crucial to his happiness and that her presence was not necessarily to be taken for granted. He's the one for her, all right, the butler chuckled to himself. But our Miss Cassie will give him a run for his money and that's no bad thing for someone who has had women shamelessly pursuing him, if the tales Master Freddie tells are to be believed.

Not having anything better to do, Ned decided to go to the park anyway by himself. He had no very clear-cut plan in mind beyond the wish of at least seeing Cassie even if he couldn't talk to her—a wish that had grown stronger with every obstacle put in his way. Hoping to accomplish this, he rode off toward Stanhope Gate and began a slow circuit of the park. It was a fine day and the place was crowded with beautiful women in elegant equipages and bucks of the first stare mounted on the finest bits of blood England had to offer.

At long last, after much fruitless searching, he located Cassie, the center of a group of Guardsmen who seemed to be enjoying themselves hugely, if their guffaws of laughter were any indication. However, there was a press of horsemen and carriages surrounding him and his progress toward her was slowed considerably. Controlling his mounting irritation, Ned resigned himself to observing the crowd around him and sizing up their mounts. He had just finished mentally going over the points of the handsome bay in front of him when its rider leaned over to address his companion. "I say, who is the Aphrodite on that great black horse?"

The companion looked at him in some surprise as he replied, "Where have you been, old fellow? She's the latest sensation. That's Lady Cassandra Cresswell, Freddie's sister, and, if Nigel Streatham is to be believed, it's the greatest shame that the rest of us are only privileged to see her trotting sedately along in the park. Says she's a bruising rider. Got the best seat he's ever seen in a woman and what she don't know about horses wouldn't fill a thimble.''

Ned's ears had pricked up at the mention of Cassie's name and he urged his horse forward so he could hear better.

"By God, she's magnificent!" the first rider exclaimed.

"It won't do any good, Ferdie," his friend warned him. "She has scores of men dangling after her. Small wonder, she's the most taking thing. Arabella Taylor grew up with her and declares her to be shockingly blue, but she ain't a bit high in the instep and makes anyone feel comfortable. She talks to a fellow as though she were his brother—none of the mealymouthed flirting and simpering that so many girls seem to have to do. I've never heard Fortescue speak so many words at one time to a female in his life, but not only did he converse with her, he even stood up with her at Almack's the other night—enjoyed himself, too. Says he's never met a woman before who had anything to the point to say about horses. And young Buckingham's besotted. He can talk of nothing else. Making a cake of himself, I can tell you. If I have to hear him describe her dimples when she smiles once more, I shall do violence to him, I assure you. But there's something special about her, make no mistake. Tell you what is—she's kind. Got a sense of humor, but she laughs with you, not at you. You don't ever get the feeling she's passing judgment on you or seeing if you measure up to some standard.''

The rest of the conversation was obliterated as another group of Guardsmen went clattering past, hallooing to those in the group surrounding Cassie. Suddenly Ned had lost all enthusiasm for a ride in the park and the day which had seemed to promising felt quite flat. He decided to head off to Brooks's in search of distraction and more serious conversation. Once there, he made a praiseworthy attempt to immerse himself in deep political discussions, but he could not get his mind off the scene in the park. He told himself that he was delighted to find that Cassie was at last being recognized. In fact, she appeared to be all the rage, and who could be more deserving of praise and admiration? But it had shaken him to hear her, his Cassie, being spoken of so familiarly.

Hitherto, Ned had felt somewhat proprietary about her because he alone had known how unique she was. He alone had made her relaxed and comfortable enough that she revealed her wit and charm. Now, apparently, she was sharing them with the entire *ton,* and Ned was not best pleased about it. Don't be a dog in the manger, he admonished himself. Isn't that the very reason you paid such attention to her? You wanted to help bring her to the notice of society so she would be given the admiration and acclaim that was her due.

As he examined his motives and the turmoil of emotions he was now experiencing, Ned realized that he had been acting in his own interests all along. Face it, you've been in love with her since you were in short coats, you fool, he told himself. Arabella was the merest of infatuations and only now when you're at a standstill do you recognize all this. You're a nodcock, Ned Mainwaring, and now you must do your best to retrieve your position with Cassie and set about the task of convincing her of all this. He sighed. Complicated as this process of discovery had been, it was nothing compared to the task he was now setting for himself. It was extremely difficult to know how to proceed, especially when he could barely get near her, constantly surrounded as she was by a crowd of beaux.

Ned knew that Cassie was likely to be at the ball at Rutland House that evening, and since it behooved him to act as quickly as possible before she was more distracted by the attentions of other admirers, he resolved to try to approach her there in the hopes of explaining himself.

He dressed with uncommon care, taking more time than customary on his cravat and assuring himself several times

that his coat fit without a wrinkle. Observing these prepar-
ations, his valet, a taciturn individual who had long ago
realized that his master's interest in clothes was, at best,
limited, knew that something of importance was in the wind.
But, having been hired just because he catered to Ned's
preference for silence and solitude, he refrained from
revealing by the slightest gesture that he was aware of
anything at all unusual in his master's conduct.

The extra care taken in Ned's accouterment had its effect,
and more than one head turned as he entered the ballroom.
Many hearts fluttered at the sight of his tall, well-knit form,
the breadth of his shoulders, and the strength of his arms
and chest, all heightened by the severe elegance of his attire.
More than one woman sighed at the firm jawline and the dark
blue eyes set deep under black brows in a countenance
rendered more attractive but more forbidding by the contrast
between the snowy whiteness of the cravat and the dark coat.

Unaware of the admiring glances he was attracting, his
eyes swept the room, anxiously looking for the gleam of
candlelight on gold curls. At last he found Cassie, an ethereal
yet provocative presence in silver net over a white satin slip,
her delicate grace emphasized by the somber lines of the
costumes of the men surrounding her. As Ned watched she
laughingly disengaged herself from the cluster around her
and headed toward an alcove whose gently billowing curtains
suggested an open window or balcony beyond them.

So intent was Cassie on gaining the sanctuary of the alcove
that she did not notice that she was being followed by young
Buckingham, whose besotted expression showed him to be
as unconscious of the rest of the occupants of the ballroom
as she was.

That puppy! Ned ground his teeth, as much annoyed by
Buckingham's obliviousness to everything but Cassie as he
was by the fact that the enamored swain was going to intrude
on the moment of respite she was so obviously seeking. With
no very clear idea of why he was doing so, except to keep
Cassie's chance for a minute of peace and solitude from being

ruined by an overeager young buck, Ned started toward the alcove himself.

Unfortunately, his progress was impeded by several friends who insisted upon learning the consequences of his sojourn in the country, so it was some time before Ned succeeded in gaining his objective. By the time he arrived, there was no sight of either Cassie or her follower. Deciding that it must be a balcony rather than an open window that was responsible for the breeze, he pushed the curtains aside and stepped out, only to have his gaze met by a scene straight from the most romantic of novels to be obtained from the circulating libraries.

Cassie stood, one hand on the railing, her slender form outlined in the moonlight. Directly in front of her, young Buckingham was smothering her hand with kisses and endeavoring to pull her into his arms.

Ned, normally a coolheaded man of sanguine temperament and a peace-loving nature, was suddenly seized by a murderous rage. The scene was blurred by a red mist of anger that rose before his eyes and his hands clenched at his sides as he accused her furiously, "So, not content with being the Season's latest sensation, you are now trying for the title of the biggest flirt in all of London!"

Cassie snatched her hand away and turned toward him, her eyes blazing with indignation. "I am *not* a flirt, Ned Mainwaring. And if I were, I don't see that it's the slightest concern of yours," she responded, her voice trembling with anger.

"And you, my lad, you ought to be ashamed of yourself, intruding upon a lady's solitude like that." Ned grasped the now quaking Buckingham by the cravat.

"Yes sir, of course, sir," the youth quavered. Released abruptly as Ned turned back to Cassie, he fled as quickly and quietly as possible, only too glad to escape the unpleasant scene.

Looking at him, Cassie couldn't think when she had seen Ned more angry. His countenance was truly alarming: the blue eyes were dark in his white set face, the firm lips were compressed into a thin line, and his black brows were drawn together in a dreadful frown. All the frustrations of the past week overwhelmed him and Ned's control snapped. He grasped her shoulders roughly and pulled her to him, gasping in a curiously grating voice, "And you . . . if you are determined to be a coquette and steal kisses in the moonlight, you ought at least to do so with someone who knows what he is doing."

With that he pulled her to him and brought his lips down hard on hers. He was furiously angry and at first his kiss was brutal, punishing, but as he felt the softness of her lips underneath his and sensed the warmth of her body against him, caressed the silkiness of her skin beneath his hands, his fury drained away. His lips relaxed. He sighed and gathered her closer to him, kissing her lingeringly, caressingly, as he traced her jaw with his lips, moving them down the smooth column of her neck. Through half-closed eyes he saw the net of her corsage straining as she gasped for breath and he longed to tear it aside and cover her with kisses.

Too taken aback at first to do anything but respond to the anger in his attack, Cassie struggled to escape, but the more she strove to free herself, the more tightly Ned pulled her to him. Dimly she was aware of her surprise at the strength of his arms and the hardness of his chest. As his lips became gentler and more persuasive, a wave of warmth and languor swept over her. The rigidity seeped out of her body and she found it molding itself to his, her lips opening under his insistent pressure. A haze swam before her eyes and she felt dizzy and weak.

But just as her senses threatened to be overwhelmed by the intensity of these new and disturbing sensations, a warning flickered inside her head and the ever-present voice of reason asserted itself once again. What ever are you doing, Cassie Cresswell? It's Arabella he wants. You've only made him angry. It's just that he doesn't like the idea of an adoring playmate growing up and paying attention to someone else.

It's not that he wants you. He is angry at you, not attracted to you. Gathering the last reserves of strength and self-esteem, Cassie pulled herself away, gasping, "How could you, Ned! Oh how could you treat a friend so?" With a swirl of skirts she fled.

CHAPTER 27

Somehow Cassie gained the staircase without being seen and located a footman to go in search of the Mainwarings' carriage. John, who had not expected to be called for hours, had been dozing happily, and came grumbling at the footman's summons. Catching sight of Cassie's white face, he was immediately all concern and threw the reins to a link boy so he could hand her tenderly into the carriage himself. "There, there, Miss Cassie. We'll have you home in a pig's whisper," he reassured her gently as he helped her in and shut the door.

Tears strung her eyes at his solicitude and as she settled back against the squabs, they began to trickle slowly down her cheeks. Wiping them furiously away with her hand, she muttered to herself. This will never do. It's only Ned after all. You've been angry at each other before. You'll see. You'll both come 'round and be merry as grigs in no time. She sighed, knowing full well that this time it was different and the difference was in her reaction to him. It's not Ned that's upsetting you, my girl, she told herself. It's you. You know you wanted him to go on kissing you, to crave you as much as you longed to stay in his arms and feel him close to you and holding you. That's what's upsetting you. You're disturbed because your body recognized before your head did that you're in love with him. In love with him, she repeated softly to herself. Yes, I suppose that's it. And he's in love with Arabella.

The carriage halted. Sighing wearily, Cassie gathered her

skirts around her and descended slowly with none of her characteristic quickness.

Higgins, opening the door and observing her wilted form, was all concern, ushering her in and sending Rose scampering to her mistress with a cup of hot milk and a soothing touch as she helped her out of her clothes and brushed her hair.

"Something is dreadfully wrong with Miss Cassie. I've never seen her so quiet before. She's in a bad way," Rose confided to the worried little group clustered in the kitchen. "I wish I knew what to do." She sighed heavily. "But you know Miss Cassie, never one to share her troubles and always wanting to fix them herself."

While the discussion was going on belowstairs, Cassie lay in bed staring wide-eyed at the pattern in the bed hangings. I must get out of here, away from all of this, back to Cresswell where I can be myself again, she thought. But she knew that she would never quite be the old, saucy, independent Cassie again.

She traced her lips with the tip of her finger, feeling the tingling that still remained there from his kiss. How could I have been so blind? she wondered. Thinking over the empty way she had been feeling since Freddie and Ned had gone to India, she realized with a start that she'd been missing Ned. Why I've been in love with him for ages, I just never knew it, she marveled. But why did I discover this tonight?

As she considered it, she became aware that until he had kissed her, she had thought of Ned as a dear friend. He was someone whom she was fond of as she was of Freddie or Frances, someone she felt comfortable with, someone she could confide in. But tonight she had recognized that he was someone who aroused far deeper feelings than that. She desired him. She wanted to be close to him, to feel him against her. And she wanted him to desire her.

For a moment when he had looked at her with such intensity, she had thought perhaps he did, but she knew that was just an illusion. She was not the type of woman men

desired. Despite Bertie's tutelage, she knew she wasn't at
all seductive. She could not be like Arabella and tantalize
men until they craved her above everything else. She was
just Cassie Cresswell, someone people enjoyed because they
felt comfortable with her. She could talk on any subject, share
any interest, make people relax and confide anything to her,
and amuse them with her unexpected comments. Until now,
thta had been enough. She had been more than happy to be
sought out and enjoyed because he was good company and
everyone trusted her. Now she wanted more, and she wanted
it from someone who longed for someone else just as she
longed for him.

She tossed restlessly, thinking and thinking, revisiting the
scene until her head ached, but she could come up with no
solution other than escape. Yes, I shall go down to Cresswell
and I shall begin my studies again. In time, if I'm not wildly
happy, at least I shall be at peace and I shall be able to occupy
my mind and my time with something useful. That settled,
she fell into an uneasy sleep just before dawn.

Meanwhile, Cassie was not the only one for whom sleep
was an impossibility. Ned had only remained on the balcony,
staring aghast at the empty space she had just left, a few
minutes longer than Cassie before he, too, left the ball.
Hoping to clear his head, he had dismissed his carriage and
walked home, cursing himself for a fool all the way. What
a cow-handed gudgeon you are! Instead of telling her that
you loved her, you raged at her like an idiot and then mauled
her like some importunate youth. And now you've alienated
her completely. If she used to hold you in mild affection,
she certainly won't any longer.

He had been walking along at a brisk rate, suiting his steps
to his thoughts, and he arrived home even before he was
aware of having turned in to Brook Street. His valet was
waiting for him, but after requesting him to bring up a bottle
of brandy, Ned dismissed him and sat down, staring moodily
into the fire.

Despite the blackness of his thoughts, he smiled tenderly

as he recalled the brief moment when he had felt Cassie relax in his arms and her lips open beneath his. He had wanted that feeling to go on forever. Over the years he had kissed countless women and had held and caressed scores of voluptuous bodies in all states of dress and undress, but when he had felt the quiver of response in Cassie as her body moved to fit itself to his, it was as though he had discovered love and all the wonder and delight of it for the first time. In truth he had. He had certainly been attracted to women before, had desired them, been aroused and stimulated by them, even fancied himself in love with them, but he had never before undergone the variety and intensity of emotions besieging him now. He wanted Cassie desperately. He wanted to talk to her, to tease her, to discover and learn things with her. All at the same time he wished to protect her, cherish her, seduce her, and ravish her until she ached with the same fire that was torturing him.

He laughed bitterly to himself as he emptied a second glass of brandy. For so long he had been her closest friend, and though he had considered her and their friendship special, he had taken it somewhat for granted. Now, just as he was discovering all that she meant to him, she had suddenly blossomed and become all that he had always known she could become. Now, just as he realized how much he wanted her and that she was the only one for him, he was faced with the very real possibility that she might choose to spend her life with one of her many other admirers. And the thought of this, of life without her, was unbearable.

"Hell and damnation!" he exclaimed aloud as he tossed down yet another brandy. "I'll go and see her tomorrow. I'll *make* her see me. I'll *make* her listen and understand that I must have her, that we belong together. I must . . ." He slumped down in his chair, overcome by the intensity of emotions and the unaccustomed amount of brandy.

CHAPTER 28

If the morning did not bring counsel, it did bring resolve. Cassie got out of bed at an early hour, determined to put London, the Season, and all thoughts of Ned Mainwaring behind her. Throwing on a wrapper, she hastened to her sister's dressing room, where she knew she would find her alone at her writing. Busy wife and mother that she was, the Marchioness of Camberly still found time to write the children's books that had been the cause of her visit to London years ago when she had accompanied Kitty Mainwaring for her come-out and fallen in love with her uncle. Now the only time she could be assured of the peace and quiet she needed was early in the morning before the rest of the household was awake and making demands on her time and attention. She was unvarying in her schedule. No matter how late she had been out the night before, Frances always arose at six o'clock or earlier and sat down at her desk.

Cassie rapped softly on the door.

"Come in, Cassie," he sister replied, recognizing her knock.

Frances had been aware that something was wrong the previous evening when one of the footmen had delivered the message to her that Cassie had returned home, but familiar with her sister's penchant for solitude, she had left her alone, knowing that when she was ready to talk, she would seek her out. Forewarned as she was, she was still unprepared for the white strained face that greeted hers as she opened the door.

"Come in, love, and have some chocolate," she invited,

leading Cassie to a chair by the fire. She handed her a cup of the morning chocolate that Daisy had brought her and waited patiently for her sister to initiate the conversation.

"Fanny, I . . ." Cassie began, and then stopped. Where should she start? Cassie's eyes filled with tears. She was so worn out with thinking that she could not put two words together much less explain the state of her feelings.

Frances remained silent, allowing Cassie to collect her thoughts.

At last, feeling the weight of the silence, Cassie looked up, and seeing such a wealth of understanding and sympathy in her sister's hazel eyes, she could not hold back the tears any longer. "Oh Fan, I'm so tired . . . I mean, I need to get away . . . I mean, I need to go to Cresswell," she sobbed.

Frances nodded. She had seen Cassie stumble into the ballroom, and not long after, she had caught a glimpse of Ned, his face white and set, coming from the same direction, and had put two and two together. Having suffered a smiliar disastrous encounter once herself, she understood completely her sister's need to be alone, to draw into herself to reassess her sense of who she was and rebuild her inner strength.

"Would you like to take Teddy? Nurse will see to it that he doesn't bother you and then we shall put it about that he was feeling poorly and you, knowing I couldn't leave Julian to face the tender mercies of our political hostesses alone right now, kindly offered to take him there for me." Frances offered this suggestion in the calmest of tones, but she was truly worried about her sister. She had seen Cassie upset before, but ordinarily her sunny and resilient nature managed to reassert itself within an hour or two. The dark circles under her eyes and the stunned expression on her face showed that she had been awake and in this state of distress most, if not all, of the night.

Cassie's tired eyes lit up and some of the strain disappeared at her sister's quick grasp of the situation and ready sympathy. "I should like that above all things, Fran. And could Wellington, Nelson, and Ethelred come, too?" she asked hopefully.

Frances smiled. "I expect you couldn't keep them from accompanying you even if you would. I shall have Nurse prepare Teddy and his things and ask Cook to pack a basket for you. Now you run along and have Rose get you ready. Just ring for Higgins on your way out, would you, so that I may ask him to inform John and Cook that they are to get the carriage and a hamper ready for the journey."

"Oh thank you, Fan," Cassie replied gratefully as she planted a kiss on her sister's cheek before running off to find Rose.

That devoted minion was more outspoken than her sister had been. "It's running away you are, Miss Cassie," she accused her mistress sternly. "It's not like you and it won't mend a thing, mind you. Now I've had my say and I won't carry on any further, but it's my belief you should stay and have it out. No problem was ever solved by pretending it wasn't there."

"I know, Rose, but I must have some time alone to think first," Cassie sighed.

Seeing the misery in her face, Rose relented. "There, there, Miss Cassie," she consoled her. "You just wait and see. He'll come 'round. Now I must go and ask James to bring down the trunks." The maid bustled out of the room, leaving her mistress to stare after her in astonishment, wondering how much the rest of the household had guessed the true state of affairs.

For such a large household, Mainwaring House was run with incredible smoothness, and the staff, always efficient, responded with alacrity to Cassie's wish to return to Cresswell. Unable to express their sympathy with her unhappiness, they rallied 'round and saw it in that "our Miss Cassie" was on the road to Cresswell as quickly and comfortably as possible.

"And, mark my words, some fresh air and long walks in the country are just what she needs," Cook remarked to Higgins as she put the finishing touches on the hamper and assured herself that she had included some of Cassie's favorite delicacies.

Teddy was beside himself with excitement. Though he had been entranced with all the wonders London had to offer, he missed the liberty that he enjoyed at Cresswell and he longed to explore the woods and fields again, free to become as grubby as he wished. He ran through the house, shouting, "Hooray! Wellington, where are you? We're going to Crethwell! Hooray!"

"Arf, arf!" Wellington responded, as delighted as his master at this prospect. He went off to round up Nelson and Ethelred and lead them to the stable yard, where they waited patiently until the last box had been strapped onto the back and they could climb in. Nelson and Ethelred, who were made slightly ill by the swaying of the carriage, found safe places wedged under the seats while Wellington sat happily aloft on the box next to John.

They were soon off, and by the time Ned, suffering from an aching head and dry mouth had doused himself in cold water, drunk several cups of strong black coffee, dressed, had his horse brought 'round, and ridden over to Grosvenor Square, they had been on the road the better part of an hour.

"What do you mean she's not here?" he demanded querulously of Higgins upon being informed of Cassie's absence. "It's not even noon yet and she was at a ball till all hours last night!" Ned was indignant. Even a constitution as strong as that of his intrepid Cassie would have been taxed by the events of the previous evening. But not only was she not relaxing at home in an effort to recover from them, she had been up betimes. To one who was himself exhausted by the emotional turmoil he had suffered in the past twelve hours and was seriously in need of recuperation, this energy and apparent unconcern was daunting in the extreme.

"Neverthelelss, she's up and gone, Master Ned," Higgins responded firmly. Having worried that much over Miss Cassandra's state of mind, he was secretly pleased to see Master Ned looking so haggard and blue-deviled this morning.

"Gone?" Ned repeated stupidly.

"Gone," Higgins reiterated patiently.

"But where?" Ned was beginning to sound worried.

"She's taken Master Teddy to Cresswell," Higgins replied. Before Ned could remark on this unusual state of affairs, he added, "He was feeling poorly, poor lad, and as it's difficult for Lady Frances to leave just now, Miss Cassie volunteered to take him."

Ned was too bemused by the turn of events for it to register that when he had last encountered Master Theodore not two days ago, he had been as healthy as a horse. There was nothing to do but ride off again, but he was at a loss as to how to proceed.

The more he thought about it, the more Ned began to realize that it might be Cassie and not Teddy who needed the restorative peace and quiet of the countryside. And how am I ever to explain everything to her if she is so intent on avoiding me that she flees to the country? he wondered in despair.

The rest of the day went by in a fog. He had an appointment with Lord Charlton, but he was so distracted that the eminent peer, looking at him with some concern, asked if he had been driving himself too hard. "It won't do to wear yourself to the bone, my lad. Why, we old men are counting on your youth and energy to give us all new life."

Ned smiled faintly, but he was barely attending. He couldn't keep his mind on any one thing for very long. No matter how he tried to concentrate on other matters, he kept going back to the moonlit scene on the balcony, remembering how wonderful it felt to hold Cassie in his arms, and hearing the anguish in her voice as she cried, "Oh, how could you treat a friend so?"

The more he thought about it, the more he longed to hold her and kiss her just once more, and the more he worried that in his anger he had ruined any chances he had of ever doing it again. At last he could stand the torture of uncertainty no longer and he resolved to go down to Cresswell immediately and force her to listen to his apology, prove to her that she belonged with him for the rest of their lives.

That settled, Ned tried to contain his impatience as best

he could. He managed to get through the rest of the day, but it was all he could do to make himself go to the opera. However, he had promised his sister weeks before that he would take her, as Lord Willoughby, devoted husband that he was, declared that there were limits to conjugal affection and the opera was one of them. Being a fond brother and one who shared his sister's love of opera, Ned had volunteered to take her. He couldn't back out now, but his heart wasn't in it.

They had not been there above half an hour before Arabella was waving at them from her box and beckoning to Ned. Though he was able to cope with escorting Kitty, Ned felt unable to face the cause of all his difficulties. Knowing that he would be far more uncivil if forced to speak to her, he turned his head and concentrated on discussing the performance with his sister, ignoring Arabella completely. Between acts he rushed out of the box in search of Lord Charlton, who, given the eagerness with which he had been sought out, was then somewhat mystified by the desultory nature of his companion's conversation. Again, he put this down to the strain caused by Ned's immersing himself so wholeheartedly in politics as well as attending to the demands society placed on such an eligible bachelor.

At the end of the last act, Ned hustled his sister to her carriage with such speed that she barely had time to wave to any of her friends. "Gracious, Ned, there's no need to get me home with quite so much dispatch," she protested. "John is at his club and won't be home for hours." Then, catching sight of Arabella, who was watching their departure intently through narrowed and speculative eyes, she subsided, smiling to herself as she divined the reason for their flight. That will teach her to think she can make him dance to her tune, Kitty remarked to herself with slightly malicious satisfaction.

Arabella was thinking along much the same lines as Kitty, though her thoughts were more in the form of questions. Why had Ned not called on her recently? Why had he been so elusive after having been so attentive? He had not even stood up with her for a country dance at the Rutland House ball, much less waltzed with her. Knowing herself to be all that a man could desire and confident that infatuation with her charms couldn't possibly lessen, Arabella cast about for some other reason for this incomprehensible coldness on Ned's part.

She revisited every social scene of the past week—the park, the ball—and the more she thought about it, the more she began to suspect that this change in attitude had something to do with that odious Cassie Cresswell. That sly thing with her cozening ways, Arabella fumed inwardly. Why, I'll make such a May game of her she won't dare set her cap at anyone, much less Ned Mainwaring.

Thus resolved, she began plotting her campaign, the first move of which was to set her maid Susan to find out what she could about the state of affairs at Mainwaring House.

It was some time before Susan could discover anything, but when she did, it was discouraging. With her rival buried in the country, it was somewhat difficult for Arabella to compete with her by showing her up. The more she considered it, though, the odder it seemed that Cassie should interrupt her first Season all because of a nephew's illness. Arabella knew Cassie to be less than devoted to the life of the *ton,* but even someone as cavalier in her attitude toward the fashionable world as Cassie was not so blind to its importance as to leave it in the middle of her come-out.

As she thought about it, she arrived at the same conclusion as Ned, that it must be Cassie and not Teddy who had needed to return to Cresswell. A plan slowly began to take shape in her brain. She smiled slyly to herself. We'll see who is the smart one now, Cassie Cresswell, she vowed as she set about laying her strategy.

It was not that Arabella had set her sights on Ned. While he possessed an attractively large fortune, a handsome countenance, and an air of elegance, he did not appear to be committed to making the best use of these attributes to win an important place for himself in the *ton.* Besides, he didn't have an impressive title, and Arabella was not ready settle for anything less than a marquess. No, she didn't really want Ned. He did have an annoying tendency to see right through one or to become serious over the most boring things. But she could not bear the thought of anyone else attracting someone who had been her most devoted admirer, especially if that someone were that impertinent little tomboy Cassie.

Arabella began to weave her plot. As her scheme depended on convincing her parents that exhausted by the rigors of the Season, she needed to return to a place that she had hitherto referred to in terms of deepest loathing, it took some doing. But Arabella had not been the toast of society without developing her dramatic capabilities to a high degree and she began to cultivate a charmingly languid air which threatened an immediate decline if the beauty were not removed to the restorative climate of the countryside.

Despite their wealth, Sir Lucius and Lady Taylor had never been particularly comfortable in the *ton,* conscious as they were that the fortune which had opened all the doors for them had come from trade on Lady Taylor's side. For them, the simple life of country landlords concerned with parish affairs and the pleasures of gardening and farming was far more attractive than the frenetic pace of the London Season. They would have been more than content to spend their lives without setting foot in Town if it had not been for the social aspirations of their beautiful daughter. Unable to deny her anything, they had put up with the dirt, the crowds, and the noise of the capital, taking pleasure in her happiness and pride in her success. Thus they were entirely surprised but delighted at Arabella's sudden whim and, as always, moved quickly to grant her whatever she wished.

Within days, the *ton* had been deprived of two of its brightest stars, but true to its fickle nature, after some initial comment, it forgot all about them and carried on as always, flirting, dancing, and gossiping.

CHAPTER 29

It would have been too much to hope that a return to the country could restore Cassie's former equanimity, but as she rose each day to peace and solitude and descended to the library after her morning chocolate, and as she took long walks in the lanes around Cresswell, smelling the sweet scent of roses in the hedgerows and responding to the "Good to see you back, Miss Cassie," from passersby, she did begin to regain a measure of serenity. Having put the possibility of meeting Ned as well as the scenes of their latest disastrous encounter at a distance, she was able to gain some objectivity.

At first she resumed her studies only for the diversion they offered, hoping that if she occupied her mind enough with these, it would not revisit the uncomfortable thoughts which had recently been torturing it. Initially the distraction she sought evaded her, but she kept at it, and as the days passed, she discovered that her studies not only took her mind off unhappy memories, they offered solace and a chance to recapture the sense of ease with herself that had been so badly upset by her discovery that she was head over heels in love with Ned Mainwaring.

He was still constantly in her thoughts, but she was freed from the powerful emotions aroused by his immediate presence, and was able to reflect more calmly and rationally on the situation. You were friends before you realized you were in love with him, Cassie Cresswell, and you can continue to be friends no matter whom he loves, she told herself. If this seemed a rather bleak future to look forward to after the intensity of the feelings she had experienced in his company recently, it was at least peaceful and one she could bear to live with. True to say, the passion with which she had reacted to his kisses, though it had exhilarated her, had also frightened her in the power it seemed to have over her. Cassie could imagine nothing more wonderful than surrendering herself to it in Ned's arms, but at the same time she was afraid of what would occur if such a situation did befall her and she did happen to give in and allow herself to be swept along by it.

You're probably well out of it, my girl, she congratulated herself. Why, given the chance, you might degenerate into a mindless hedonist devoting yourself entirely to pleasure. Ned had helped her to discover a propensity for this in herself that was nearly as alarming as the revelation that she was in love with someone who, far from wanting to indulge in these propensities with her, was more accustomed to regarding her in the light of a younger sister, a precocious younger sister, but a younger sister, nevertheless.

Sorting out and coming to terms with all these new and disturbing emotions was a slow process and there were times when Cassie despaired of ever regaining her peace of mind, but gradually she began to take pleasure in life again, helping Teddy practice his cricket, playing fetch with Wellington, punting on the pond, and galloping over the countryside in a way she was never able to do in London.

One day, nearly a fortnight after her flight from Town, she was congratulating herself on the commencement of her recovery from all this madness of love and passion when Teddy burst into the library, trailing his cricket bat and followed by his three devoted spectators. "That lady with the mean eyeth ith here, Aunt Cathie, and she'th looking for you," he announced.

"The lady with mean eyes?" Cassie was mystified.

"You know, the one in the park," he elaborated.

Cassie continued to look blank. Sighing heavily, he continued, "You know, when we were there with 'that man' and we lost the boat and Wellington rethcued it and we saw Ned and that lady with the mean eyeth."

Enlightenment dawned. "You mean Arabella? She's here?" Cassie asked incredulously, not able to fathom the idea of Arabella anywhere else but London in the middle of the Season.

Teddy nodded vigorously just as Arabella, elegant in a peach-colored walking dress, followed the footman into the library. His mission accomplished, Teddy departed with as much haste as possible. Wellington, Nelson, and Ethelred, having taken full measure of the lady with mean eyes and come to no very complimentary assessment of her character, were at his heels.

"Cassie, so delightful to see you," Arabella drawled as she stripped off her gloves and draped herself gracefully on a nearby settee. "Are you rusticating because you are as *ennuyée* and exhausted by the incessant social demands as I?" she asked, heaving a sigh and trying to look as fragile as a voluptuous figure would allow.

Cassie, never ordinarily at a loss for words, remained nonplussed while Arabella, oblivious to her surprise, rattled happily on. "Of course, keeping up one's role as an incomparable can be quite the most wearing thing. I was beginning to look positively hagridden, and Ned"—here she paused significantly before continuing—"*dear* Ned, was naturally so concerned."

"Ned," Cassie repeated stupidly.

"Well, yes. Of course he doesn't want me to tire myself out and he does worry so about my happiness, poor boy, though in the circumstances it's only natural."

"Of course," Cassie agreed, totally missing the careful emphasis her visitor had put on the word "circumstances."

Arabella was becoming quite annoyed. Really, for all her reputation as a bluestocking, Cassie was being remarkably obtuse. Her back to the wall, she was forced to dispense with subtle hints and adopt some degree of falsehood. "Certainly it's only natural, isn't it, for a man to want his intended to be in radiant health?" she inquired archly.

"His intended?" Cassie echoed. "I didn't know. I hadn't heard . . ." Her voice trailed off.

Having committed herself to a course of deception, Arabella could do nothing but brazen it out. And it wasn't such a very big lie, after all. With Cassie disposed of, Arabella felt confident of bringing such a situation to pass. She tossed her head and smiled condescendingly. "Of course it's not yet formally announced, but surely you've known this age of our understanding."

Cassie's mind was reeling. All her hard-won peace of mind evaporated in an instant. She felt dizzy and there was the oddest sensation at the pit of her stomach. Raising her hand to her brow, she said faintly, "Excuse me. I'm afraid that I haven't been the hostess I should be. That's delightful news. Now, if you'll excuse me, I have the most dreadful headache." Without a backward glance she rushed from the room.

"And that," Arabella announced with satisfaction to the empty room, "is that." She pulled on her gloves and rang for a footman, smiling at him prettily as he led her to her carriage.

With no clear idea of where she was going, Cassie ran to her room, tore open the cupboard, and pulled out her oldest, most comfortable riding habit. Struggling with the last few buttons, she raced to the stables calling to Jim to saddle Chiron.

"But Miss Cassie," he protested, "the sky's that dark. It's coming on to storm for certain."

"I don't care!" she snapped in an unusual show of temper. "Just saddle him!"

"Yes, miss," he replied, looking aggrieved. John would have his hide, but when a woman looked that upset, he knew better than to argue with her. He threw her into the saddle and she tore out of the stable yard as though the hounds of hell were after her.

Cassie still had no very clear idea of where she was headed. All she knew was that she had to get away—away from everything and everybody that was familiar. She wanted to escape to the anonymity of the open fields, where she could ride until she was too exhausted to think.

CHAPTER 30

Not long after Arabella's triumphant departure another visitor rode up the gravel drive at Cresswell, rang the bell, and requested to see Miss Cassie. It was Ned. Unable to endure another day of uncertainty, he had ridden down from London the night before. He had spent the night at Camberly, where he made the unpleasant discovery that sleeping in his old room and visiting the scenes of his childhood, so much of which had revolved around Cassie and Freddie, only made the longing to see Cassie and to beg her to marry him that much stronger. He had spent a restless night trying to sort out his thoughts and deciding on the best way to convince someone he had just insulted that he wanted nothing so much out of life as to spend the rest of it with her. Finally, giving up all hope of sleep, he had gotten up and began to pace the floor. At the first light he had thrown on his clothes and ordered Brutus to be saddled and brought 'round. Though it was still far too early to think of calling on anyone, Ned hoped that a long morning ride would clear his head, calm him down, and make the time pass more quickly until he could call on Cassie. He had ridden for hours and poor Brutus's flanks were glistening with sweat before he had the courage to present himself.

"She's not here!" he exclaimed in dismay when the footman who had answered the door returned from an unsuccessful search of all the rooms.

"Perhaps she's out in the garden, sir. If you care to take your horse to the stable, you could ask them there," he suggested apologetically.

Ned led out a sigh of exasperation and headed off to the stables.

"Miss Cassie left some time ago, sir," Jim replied when questioned as to his mistress's whereabouts.

"What?" thundered Ned. "You saw the sky and you let her go? Where are your brains, lad?" An ominous rumbling in the distance made him demand more urgently, "How long has she been gone?"

"Not long, sir. I'm that sorry, sir," the stableboy apologized. "You know Miss Cassie. When she gets something fixed in her mind there's just no stopping her." He shook his head.

"Which direction did she go?" Ned was beginning to sound frantic as another crack of thunder and a flash of lightning increased his concern for Cassie's welfare.

Jim pointed to the fields on his right. "She went that way, sir, but there weren't no stopping her," he spoke again in defense of his actions. If he had been apprehensive before about what John Coachman would say when he discovered that he had let Miss Cassie go off in such weather, he was even more worried by the dreadful expression on Ned's face. Master Ned was a gentleman who could handle anything. Why the stories he'd heard about his and Master Freddie's adventures in India would make your hair curl! But he looked proper frantic now. "I'm sorry . . ." he began again, but his words were cut off as Ned leaped on Brutus and clattered out of the yard.

The wind had picked up by now and the first large drops of rain were beginning to fall. Ned rode like a madman in the direction Jim had pointed, trying vainly to distinguish the outline of a horse and rider as the rain, falling in earnest now, streamed down his face. The motion eased his tension somewhat, and as he began to think more clearly he recalled a favorite ride Cassie often took on the ridge the other side of a small wood. He headed straight into the trees, in too much of a hurry to seek out the path he knew was there. Branches slapped in his face and tore at his clothes. He lowered his head on Brutus's neck, grimly urging him on.

The thunder was closer now and the horse whinnied in terror as there was a loud crack directly overhead.

After what seemed an interminable time he burst clear of the trees and saw before him the ridge with a horse and rider barely visible in the distance. "Cassie! Cassie!" he shouted, even though he knew full well she could never hear him above the storm, especially at that distance.

He urged his horse to greater speed, but just as he was sure he was gaining on Cassie and Chiron there was a terrific flash of lightning followed by a truly deafening clap of thunder. Frantic with fear, Chiron reared, throwing his rider, who landed with sickening speed and lay there ominously quiet.

"Cassie!" Ned was desperate now as he dug his heels into his mount.

Minutes later he was on the ground beside her, lifting her tenderly in his arms and wiping the mud off her face with his soaking handkerchief. "Cassie, my love, are you hurt?" he asked frantically.

She shook her head mutely, the rain streaming down her face.

"Cassie, my precious girl, please tell me you are all right," he pleaded anxiously.

"No," she gasped. "I am *not* all right. I don't know how I could have been so stupid to have fallen except that my mind was on something else." She shook her head defiantly, spraying drops of water in every direction.

He smiled at her tenderly stroking away the tendrils of hair sticking to her face. "That's my lovely Cassie, pluck to the backbone. But what were you thinking of?"

She was silent.

Cupping her chin in his hand, Ned tilted her face up to look at him. "What were you thinking of?" he asked again softly.

A blush crept up her neck, staining her cheeks. "Nothing," she whispered.

He thought she had never looked more adorable and he ached to pull her to him and kiss her until she was breathless, but he wasn't sure. He cared so desperately for her and he didn't want to frighten her or ruin anything now. "It can't have been nothing if it caused Lady Cassandra Cresswell to be unseated by a horse," he teased gently. "Cassie?"

Cassie looked down at her hands as she twisted them nervously.

"Cassie, look at me," he commanded.

She threw back her head defiantly, her eyes bright with unshed tears.

"Oh, my love." He caressed her cheek with his hand. "I passed Arabella's carriage on the road to Cresswell. Did she visit you?"

Cassie nodded.

Ned's face darkened. His previous experience with spoiled beauties, and this one in particular, had taught him that when one of them visited another woman, her motives were highly suspect. "What did she tell you, my love?"

Cassie shook her head.

He tilted her chin so he could look into her eyes, his heart wrung by the sadness he saw there. "Cassie, my darling girl, she means nothing to me. She never truly did. At one time I thought she did. I was infatuated with her, but it's you I love. It always has been you my best, my dearest friend."

A sob escaped her and she buried her face in his shoulder as he pulled her into his arms. "I love you so desperately, my love," he whispered against her hair. "Please tell me that I'm not wrong. Please tell me that you do care."

Cassie pulled away and looked up at him, tears clinging to the dark lashes and drowning the dark blue eyes. "I do. I do love you, only I was so scared," she whispered.

"Scared? Of what, my love?" he asked, smiling tenderly at her.

"Oh, I don't know. Of loving you so much, of wanting you so dreadfully, of losing myself. I was overwhelmed with all sorts of emotions and I wasn't sure I liked that. Oh, I can't explain it." She looked at him pleadingly.

His smile disappeared to be replaced by an expression of

great seriousness. "My beautiful love. You'll never lose yourself. We'll be as we've always been. You'll pursue your own interests and share them with me. I shall pursue mine and share them with you, and we shall continue as the best of friends and lovers." He spoke gravely, striving to reassure her as best he could. "Marry me, Cassie?" It was his turn to look pleading now.

"Yes, Ned," she replied solemnly.

His lips came down on hers and he pulled her close to him, caressing her, warming her, molding her body to fit his as the rain poured down around them.